Alex Pine was born and raised on a council estate in South London and left school at sixteen. Before long, he embarked on a career in journalism, which took him all over the world – many of the stories he covered were crime-related. Among his favourite hobbies are hiking and water-based activities, so he and his family have spent lots of holidays in the Lake District. He now lives with his wife on a marina close to the New Forest on the South Coast – providing him with the best of both worlds!

THE
CHRISTMAS
KILLER

ALEX PINE

avon.

Published by AVON
A division of HarperCollins*Publishers* Ltd
1 London Bridge Street
London SE1 9GF

www.harpercollins.co.uk

A Paperback Original 2020
4

First published in Great Britain by HarperCollins*Publishers* 2020

A catalogue copy of this book is available from the British Library.

ISBN: 978-0-00-840264-8

Typeset in Minion Pro by Palimpsest Book Production Ltd, Falkirk, Stirlingshire
Printed and bound in UK by CPI Group (UK) Ltd, Croydon CR0 4YY

MIX
Paper from
responsible sources
FSC
www.fsc.org   FSC™ C007454

This book is produced from independently certified FSC™ paper to ensure responsible forest management.

For more information visit: www.harpercollins.co.uk/green

To the latest additions to the family – Peyton Scott and Luna Raven. Wishing them both a long and happy life.

PROLOGUE

September

It was 6 p.m. when Annie Walker heard her husband's car pull onto the driveway of their terraced house in Tottenham.

Moments later, he closed the front door behind him and called out to let her know that he was home.

She stayed where she was on the sofa, her heart pounding in her chest. She'd been bracing herself for bad news since he'd texted to tell her what was happening. That was three hours ago though, and the long wait had caused her stomach to twist into an anxious knot.

She held her breath now as he opened the door and entered the living room.

'Hi, hon,' he said. 'I'm sorry I couldn't get away any sooner.'

Annie was struck by how rough he looked. His eyes were glassy with exhaustion and his dark hair was greasy and dishevelled.

'Just tell me what happened?' she said.

James crossed the room and sat down beside her on the sofa.

'It's bad news, I'm afraid, Annie,' he said. 'The bastard has been released.'

Annie closed her eyes. It felt like her heart had stopped beating. James put an arm around her and pulled her close. It made her feel better, but only slightly. It was going to take much more than a hug to repel the nagging sense of dread that was growing inside her.

'This is a bloody nightmare,' she said. 'I thought the bastard was tucked safely away for at least ten years.'

James shook his head. 'It's hard to believe he's got away with it. The trouble is, we haven't been able to disprove what the other guy is saying.'

'So that's it then? He's free again and able to do whatever he wants to.'

'That's right,' James said. 'But you have to try not to worry.'

'That's not going to happen and you know it.'

James switched his gaze from his wife to the half-empty bottle of red wine on the coffee table in front of her.

'I need some of that after the day I've had,' he said. 'Let me grab a glass and we can talk this through.'

'Has the news broken yet?' Annie asked him.

He nodded as he stood. 'Of course. I'm sure the media's all over it.'

'Then can you switch the telly on?'

He did as she asked and used the remote to go straight to the BBC news channel. The story was being aired right then, and the newsreader's words sent a chill through Annie's veins.

'Fifty-eight-year-old Andrew Sullivan has served thirteen months of a life sentence for murder. Though he's always denied killing nightclub owner Brendon Fox, he was

convicted by a jury even though Mr Fox's body had still not been found by the time the case went to trial.

'Three days ago, however, Mr Fox's body was found, the location revealed to police by a man who has confessed to the murder. As a result, a judge has ruled that Mr Sullivan, who was described during his trial as the head of an organised crime gang in London, should be released, and earlier this afternoon he walked out of Belmarsh Prison a free man. Scotland Yard has confirmed that another man in his fifties has been formally charged with Mr Fox's murder. His identity has not yet been disclosed.'

Andrew Sullivan was one of the main reasons Annie had been so desperate to move out of London. When he was sent down it was like a huge weight being lifted from her shoulders.

The newsreader moved on to talking about Sullivan's chequered past, his photograph displayed over the reporter's shoulder. He looked every inch the archetypal villain, a bald, hard-faced individual with a long scar down his right cheek.

James first came across Sullivan while working with the National Crime Agency on a secondment. He spent several years trying to disrupt Sullivan's illicit activities, but had failed to bring him down. In the process he made an enemy of the man, and received several death threats as a result. Then, two years ago, James had moved to Scotland Yard as a detective inspector with the Murder Investigation Team, and was eventually assigned to the Brendon Fox case.

Sullivan had fallen out with Fox after the night club owner banned him from entering his establishment. When their paths crossed early one evening at a pub in Wood Green, they ended up having a fist fight, after which Sullivan was overheard threatening to kill Fox.

In the early hours of the following morning Fox disappeared in suspicious circumstances after leaving his club. His car was abandoned at the roadside with the door open.

Soon afterwards, police unearthed traffic camera footage of Sullivan's van driving past the club half an hour before Fox left the premises. Sullivan was arrested and Fox's blood was found on his shirt. His defence was that the blood had got there during the punch up in the pub. And he claimed he was driving home from a night out when the traffic camera picked up his van near the club.

It was James who charged Andrew Sullivan with murder, after convincing the Crown Prosecution Service to make the arrest despite the absence of a corpse. Then, much to the delight of everyone on James's team, the jury rejected Sullivan's not guilty plea.

But five days ago the case was reopened, and Sullivan's guilt put into question, when a prolific violent offender named Raymond Lynch confessed to killing Fox the night he vanished. He claimed he'd tried to rob the club owner as he was getting into his car. When Fox resisted, he stabbed him in the chest. He said he feared that he might have left traces of blood or DNA on his victim, so he put him into his car boot and drove to woods in Kent where he dumped the body.

Lynch had nothing to lose by confessing to a crime that James did not believe he committed. After all, he was already in prison serving a minimum of thirty years for beating to death a teenage girl in the weeks following Fox's murder. And at the age of fifty-five, it was unlikely he would ever be released. So James and his team were convinced that the

Sullivan family had persuaded Lynch to confess to killing Fox, likely in exchange for protection on the inside.

James returned from the kitchen with a glass and filled it with red wine after topping up Annie's. He'd removed his suit jacket and shoes, and when he spoke his voice was stretched thin with tension.

'You shouldn't work yourself up into a frenzy over this, Annie,' he said. 'I honestly don't think Sullivan poses a serious threat to us. He won't want to put at risk his newly won freedom.'

'But you can't be sure of that,' Annie replied. 'We both know the man's a psycho, and he hates your guts. You've said yourself he's probably killed more than a few people over the years, and I don't want you to become one of his victims. But I've told you so many times that it's not just about him. I don't feel safe here any more. The streets are full of knife-wielding nutters. The traffic is unbearable, and so is the noise. I'm stressed out most of the time, which could be why I haven't conceived. And if we do eventually get lucky, this is not where I want to raise a child.'

James let out a breath. He'd heard it all before, and the issue had put a strain on their relationship. Annie's mother had died eighteen months ago, leaving her the four-bedroomed family home in Cumbria, and since then Annie had been trying to talk James into moving out of London.

Of course, he had given it serious consideration, even to the point of discussing with her the possibility of joining the Cumbrian force and basing himself in Kendal, which was only about twenty-five miles from the cottage in the village of Kirkby Abbey. But James enjoyed working for the Met and, at thirty-nine, was still climbing the career ladder. It didn't help that his extended family – with whom he was close – all lived in North London.

Annie didn't have any strong ties to the capital. Both her parents were dead and she had no siblings, her only relative an uncle who lived in Penrith. And as a supply teacher she could work anywhere – including the small primary school in Kirkby Abbey.

As the evening wore on, James tried to steer the conversation in a different direction, but Annie was having none of it. She continued to express her fears as they got through another bottle of wine and a couple of ready meals heated up in the microwave.

It was 10 p.m. when she finally decided to call it a day. Tired and frustrated, she stood and announced that she was going to bed.

James hauled himself to his feet and started to help her clear the coffee table. But they didn't get to finish the job because at that moment a large object came crashing through the living room window.

Annie screamed as they were both showered with shards of glass.

The object – a brick – smashed into the side of the TV before landing with a thud on the carpet.

James instinctively stepped between Annie and the broken window as they both stared out into their small front garden.

'Who's out there?' Annie yelled. 'Can you see anyone?'

'It's too dark,' James shouted back. 'Stay here while I go and check.'

Fear spiralled through Annie as James rushed out of the room. Her eyes were immediately drawn to the brick on the floor and she noticed that there was a sheet of paper attached to it by elastic bands. Her hands shook violently as she reached down to pick it up and read the note.

I don't forgive and forget. This is just a taste of what's to come.

James returned a few minutes later to say that whoever had thrown the brick had disappeared, which came as no surprise to Annie.

She handed him the note and watched the panic seize his features as he read it.

'I'm willing to bet it's a message from Sullivan,' she said tearfully. 'And if that doesn't convince you that we should move away from here, then I don't know what will.'

CHAPTER ONE

Friday December 16th

According to the Met Office, it was going to be a white, blustery Christmas. The forecast was for severe blizzards across much of the UK, and those people living in northern counties were being warned to brace themselves for the worst of the weather. It was even likely that some towns and villages would find themselves cut off.

The prospect of being snowed in filled James Walker with dread. He wasn't used to dealing with impassable roads and momentous drifts that brought life to a standstill.

In London, things carried on virtually as normal however bad the weather. But now he was living in Cumbria and this would be his first Christmas away from the capital. He was pretty sure it was going to be very different.

He and Annie had made the move seven weeks ago and he was still struggling to adjust. The pace of life was so much slower and he wasn't sure he would ever get used to it.

Barely a month had passed since he'd started his new job as a detective inspector with the Cumbria Constabulary, based in the market town of Kendal, and he was already bored. He was missing the buzz of the Met, the big cases, the rush of adrenaline that he felt speeding to the scene of another major crime.

The cases that had come his way since the transfer included two burglaries, a domestic violence incident on a remote farm and an act of vandalism against a village pub. A far cry from the murder and mayhem that had kept him busy during almost twenty years working in the capital.

He wasn't blaming Annie, though. Remaining in London had simply become too risky after the brick was thrown through their living room window. His wife was lucky not to have been injured, and it had forced him to concede that the threat was one he couldn't ignore. He had to think of Annie and his family – his parents, brother, two sisters, and a bunch of nephews and nieces.

He still couldn't be sure who was behind the attack. There had been no forensic evidence on the brick or the note that was attached to it. Naturally, Andrew Sullivan had denied responsibility when questioned, and he had a cast-iron alibi. But he could have got one of his gang members to do it for him, as revenge against James for the thirteen months Sullivan had spent behind bars before his unexpected release.

James looked across the open plan office from behind the desk that had been allocated to him. It was almost five o'clock on Friday December 16th, and most of the team had already departed for the weekend. No doubt some would be Christmas shopping, while others busied themselves with preparations for the big day.

He left all that stuff to Annie, as she'd always enjoyed buying presents and organising things. This year she had made it extra hard for herself. As well as all the effort she was putting into renovating the house, she'd invited James's entire family to stay with them from Christmas Eve until after Boxing Day.

James had breathed a sigh of relief when he'd learned that only nine of them, including three children, were coming. It meant they could be put up in the three spare bedrooms, while Annie's uncle, Bill Cardwell, used the fold-down camp bed in the study.

Annie hadn't seen Bill since her mother's funeral, when they'd had a bitter row over the fact that the house that he and his sister had grown up in had been left to Annie. He'd stormed out of the wake, claiming it wasn't fair and demanding that she sell the property and give him half the proceeds. But Annie had refused because her mother had stipulated in her will that Annie should keep it so that she could pass it on to her own children when, God willing, she eventually had them.

Annie was now determined to get back on speaking terms with her uncle, hoping her return to Cumbria would be a new beginning for both of them.

'I'm surprised you're still here, guv. There's fuck all going on.'

It was the grating voice of DS Phil Stevens that interrupted James's thoughts. The overweight detective was the only member of the team who had made him feel unwelcome. This was apparently because Stevens's promotion to detective inspector had been put on hold as a result of James's arrival.

He was also clearly jealous of the new DI's years of experience with the Met and NCA, rolling his eyes whenever James mentioned London.

'I was just about to wrap things up and go,' James said. 'What about you?'

Stevens shrugged. 'I'm here till late and that suits me just fine. The in-laws are coming over for a pre-Christmas visit and they're not my favourite people.'

With perfect timing, James's mobile phone rang, providing him with an excuse not to continue the conversation.

He picked it up from his desk, glanced at the caller ID, then smiled at Stevens.

'It's the wife,' he said. 'I'd better take it.'

James answered the phone as he watched his colleague turn and walk across the room towards his own desk.

'Hi, hon,' James said. 'I'll be heading home soon if that's what you're ringing to find out.'

'It's not, actually,' Annie said. 'I forgot to mention that the school nativity play is taking place this evening and I'm here now helping out. It means I most likely won't be in when you get home.'

'No problem. How has your day been?'

'Good. I managed to clear all the junk from the bedrooms before I popped over to Janet Dyer's house for lunch and a catch up.'

'Isn't she the one you used to be friends with at school?'

'That's right. She's a great source of information for me because she knows the whats and wheres that I've missed since I've been away. She does have a tendency to get caught up in the village drama, though, and some people think she's too loud and opinionated, but she's helped me through some tough times in the past, and she's a softie at heart.'

'She sounds interesting,' James said.

'She is. Actually, I'm thinking about inviting her over tomorrow for a cuppa. I want to show her what we're doing to the house and also give her some distraction. She's a single mum and her ex-husband is picking her two boys up in the morning and taking them to spend Christmas with him and his new partner in Carlisle.'

'Then I look forward to meeting her.'

'I'm sure you'll like her,' Annie said. 'Meanwhile, you drive carefully coming home. I've made a cottage pie for you and it's ready to be put straight in the oven.'

'Terrific. Love you lots and see you later.'

'You too, sweetheart.'

One thing James didn't miss about London was the traffic. Driving in the capital was a nightmare, and many streets seemed to be in a permanent state of gridlock.

By comparison, getting from Kendal to Kirkby Abbey was a breeze. He headed east along the A684, crossed over the M6, and then north up the A683.

The roads took him through some of the UK's most beautiful countryside, lying between the Lake District and Yorkshire Dales National Parks. Of course, at this time of night he couldn't see much, as the darkness stretched into the distance on both sides.

It was just after six when he arrived at the village, one of the smallest in the area with a population of just over seven hundred.

He drove past the small Catholic church and The White Hart pub, and turned left at the village store. He then skirted the small square where they held the monthly Saturday farmers' market, and passed through the residential area that was crammed with quaint, stone-built houses.

Their detached home was a short walk from the tiny primary school where Annie worked and had a driveway and a paved front garden. There were other detached houses either side, and across the road was a gated entrance to a field that offered stunning views of the distant peaks.

James parked up and saw that Annie had left the lights on in their two-storey house. As he climbed out of his Audi, he was once again struck by how quiet the place was. It was another aspect of life here in Cumbria that he still hadn't yet got used to.

He was approaching the front door when he noticed that a parcel had been left on the step. It was about the size of a shoebox and wrapped in Christmas paper.

His first thought as he picked it up was that it had been put there by one of the neighbours. But as he let himself inside, it struck him as odd that on the label that was stuck to it there were just three words written with a black marker:

FOR DETECTIVE WALKER

He took the parcel through to the kitchen and placed it on the table. Curiosity compelled him to open it before doing anything else.

He tore off the wrapping and lifted the lid of the cardboard box. What was inside gave him such a shock that an involuntary gasp erupted from his mouth and he jumped back in horror. In the process, his hand struck the edge of the box and knocked it onto the floor.

A wave of revulsion swept through him as he stared down at the object that rolled out. It was a large, blood-soaked bird that was clearly dead.

James tried to swallow but couldn't, and for several moments he just stood there while a pulse thundered in his temples.

He noticed that the bottom of the box was lined with clingfilm, presumably to hold in the blood.

'Why the fuck would someone do this?' he said aloud to himself.

After the shock wore off, he took a deep breath and knelt down to see if there was anything else in the upended box. But there wasn't. However, when he stood again he spotted something attached by Sellotape to the underside of the lid. It was a Christmas card wrapped in clingfilm, and on the front of it were images from the carol *The Twelve Days of Christmas*.

James always carried a pair of latex gloves in his jacket pocket, so he put them on before reaching for the card, aware that he should have done so before opening the box in the first place.

He used the tips of his fingers to peel away the Sellotape and flick the card open. There was no seasonal greeting printed inside. Instead, someone had scrawled a message that caused the air to lock in James's chest.

Here's a Christmas gift for you, detective Walker. It's a little early, I know, but I just couldn't wait. My very own take on the twelve days of Christmas, complete with a dead partridge. Twelve days. Twelve murders. Twelve victims. And they all deserve what's coming to them.

CHAPTER TWO

Annie was struggling to hold back the tears, and her insides were churning with mixed emotions. But she wasn't at all surprised. It was how she usually reacted when she watched a primary school nativity play.

She loved seeing Mary drop baby Jesus, the narrator stumble over his or her words, and the angels giggle amongst themselves because they had no real understanding of what was going on. It was all so touching and hilarious.

But along with the joy there was always a sense of despondency and regret because none of the children on the little stage belonged to her.

The audience began to applaud as the cast rounded off their performance with a stilted rendition of *Silent Night*. Annie felt a jolt of jealousy when the parents started to cheer and wave, their faces glowing with obvious pride. One day, she told herself. One day I'll be sitting amongst them instead of here on the side lines with the other teachers.

'Are you all right, Annie? You look as though you might be about to cry.'

Annie turned to the woman sitting to her right and forced a smile.

'I was just thinking back to when I played the part of Mary on this very stage,' she fibbed. 'I can't believe it was thirty odd years ago.'

Lorna Manning smiled back. 'I wish I'd been here then. It must have been a lot different with at least twice as many pupils and parents.'

Like many other small rural schools across the country, Kirkby Abbey Primary School was under threat because of falling pupil numbers and budget cuts. With only twenty-two children now enrolled, the council was considering closing the school, but Lorna – headmistress for the past ten years – was campaigning hard to keep it open.

If and when it did close, parents would have to transport their kids to the nearest other school, which was some fifteen miles away. It was one of the very few negatives that came with the move back to Cumbria but, as far as Annie was concerned, they were far outweighed by the positives.

She hung around as Lorna stepped up onto the stage to praise the children and thank all those who had come to see the show, especially the villagers who'd turned up to offer their support even though they weren't parents. After that, everyone gathered in the reception area while the hall was cleared and the children got changed.

Annie hadn't expected to get involved with school activities so soon after arriving in the village. But a staff shortage had prompted Lorna to offer her some part-time work as soon as she expressed an interest. And that suited Annie perfectly, because it meant she could divide her time between shifts at the school and renovating the house.

This was the first time since the move that she had been in the company of so many people. Some she recognised from before she left the village and moved to London thirteen years ago, others she'd met during the visits to her mother following her father's death. But a good many of those around her she'd never seen before and she was keen to make their acquaintance.

A table had been laid with free soft drinks, mulled wine and mince pies. Annie positioned herself next to it so that she could explain to people what was on offer and introduce herself to those she didn't know. But the first person to approach the table was Janet Dyer – her twin sons had played shepherds in the play.

'A cracking show as always,' Janet said, helping herself to a wine. 'Just the right mix of chaos and confusion. I loved every minute.'

Annie laughed. 'The twins were adorable, Janet. You must be so proud of them.'

Janet nodded. 'I am. And I intend to do everything I can to make sure they don't turn out to be like their shitty excuse for a father.'

It was three years since Janet's husband Edward had left her for another woman. Annie had seen her a couple of times since then and had talked to her frequently on the phone. In the beginning, Janet had found it hard to cope and had confessed to being lonely. But eventually she had started to embrace being single again.

She was a short, thin woman, with a placid face and neat, shoulder-length, fair hair, who worked as a carer for elderly people living in Kirkby Abbey and the surrounding villages.

17

Annie was about to ask her what time Edward was picking the twins up in the morning, but Janet spoke first.

'Oh, bloody hell,' she said. 'Here comes trouble.'

She was staring at a man and woman who were walking towards them after exiting the hall. Annie recognised them immediately and felt a stab of apprehension.

Charlie and Sonia Jenkins ran The White Hart pub and they were by far the most striking couple in the village. She was slim and in her late thirties, but looked much younger. Her husband, who Annie herself had actually had a crush on in school, was a dead ringer for Michael Bublé. The pair had been together since Sonia fell pregnant with their daughter, Maddie, at the age of seventeen.

Sonia reached them first, and she had a face like thunder.

'I want to ask you a question,' she said, spitting her words at Janet and filling the air between them with the smell of alcohol.

Charlie quickly came up behind his wife and placed his hands on her shoulders.

'I thought we agreed that you wouldn't make a scene here,' he said.

'That was before I saw her looking at you in the hall,' Sonia replied. 'I could tell what she was thinking.'

'Really?' Janet said, her voice dripping with sarcasm. 'Are you able to read minds when you're drunk then?'

Sonia clenched her jaw. 'How dare you say that? I'm not drunk.'

Janet tutted loudly. 'You could have fooled me, Sonia.'

Annie could barely believe what was happening. The Christmas spirit that had prevailed only moments ago was shattered as the two women glared at one another.

Charlie put an arm around his wife and tried to move her away, but she refused to budge.

'I'm not going anywhere until I've heard what she's got to say for herself,' Sonia said.

Janet responded by rolling her eyes. 'Then get to the point, for pity's sake. What is it you want to ask me?'

Annie was tempted to intervene, but didn't dare for fear of inflaming the situation. Most of the other people in the room were still oblivious to what was going on and she didn't want that to change.

Sonia lifted her chin, squared her shoulders, and said, 'I want to know if it's true that you've been having an affair with my husband.'

Janet pulled a face. 'No, it bloody well isn't. Where the hell did you get that idea?'

'You told one of the elderly folks you visit in the village,' Sonia said. 'He told someone who mentioned it to someone else and this morning it was passed on to me.'

'Well it's total rubbish,' Janet insisted. 'I don't sleep with married men. Surely he's told you it didn't happen.'

'Until I was blue in the face,' Charlie said, clearly embarrassed. Then to his wife: 'Look, Sonia, it's either a malicious rumour or a huge misunderstanding. But whatever you think, this is not the place to talk about it.'

Sonia's face changed in an instant, as though she was coming out of a trance. She sucked in a shaky breath and started to speak, but the words tumbled out as wet sobs.

'Let me get you home,' Charlie said, and this time when he ushered her towards the door, she didn't resist.

After watching them go, Janet turned to Annie and said, 'I can't believe that just happened.'

Annie shook her head. 'Me neither. Are you all right?'

'I will be once I've calmed down.'

Annie noticed that she was shaking and her face had paled.

'Is there any truth in what Sonia claimed?' Annie asked.

'Of course not,' Janet replied. 'You heard what I told her. I reckon someone is out to make mischief.'

She reached for another glass of wine and downed it in one go.

'I'd better go and find the twins,' she said. 'I'll call you tomorrow, if that's okay.'

'That'll be great. You take care.'

Annie was relieved that the altercation hadn't spiralled out of control. But it had unsettled her.

She kept her feelings to herself as she bid a fond farewell to the children and their families, then helped Lorna and the other teachers to clean up.

It was eight o'clock when she left the school and headed home. She forced herself not to think about what had happened, but she was in no doubt that it would be one of the topics of conversation when Janet came to the house tomorrow.

It was a beautiful Cumbrian night, the sky crammed with an array of bright stars. Annie's hooded parka kept the cold at bay as she walked along the narrow streets, safe in the knowledge that she wasn't about to be mugged, stabbed or confronted by Andrew Sullivan.

She found comfort in the fact that it was very rare for something really bad to happen in a place like Kirkby Abbey.

CHAPTER THREE

Almost two hours had passed since James had unwrapped the parcel with the dead partridge inside. The repulsive 'gift' and the card that had come with it were still causing his mind to race in all directions.

He just wasn't sure what to make of it. Was it a genuine threat or someone's idea of a sick joke?

It was troubling to think that so much thought and effort must have gone into it. The sender had either killed a bird or found a dead one, then stuffed it into the box with the card, before leaving it on the doorstep. It was strange, reckless, shocking and sinister. It couldn't be ignored.

James had already called it in and had taken photos of the partridge and the handwritten message, which he'd sent to his superior. A patrol car was due to arrive at any minute to pick the bagged parcel up and take it to the forensic lab so it could be analysed for prints, DNA and any other trace evidence that might offer a clue as to who was responsible.

The house to the left was empty, as usual, because the

owners lived in Manchester and stayed there only occasionally. The property to the right was occupied by retired couple Roy and Jennifer Gray. James had just returned from asking them if they'd seen any cars parked out front this evening or noticed anyone carrying a parcel. But they hadn't because they'd been too busy watching television.

If this had been London or any other major city there'd be a good chance that CCTV cameras could be used to help solve the mystery. But there weren't any in Kirkby Abbey, which was not at all unusual for such a small village.

The questions were piling up inside James's head as he sat at the breakfast bar with his hands wrapped round a mug of steaming coffee.

How long had the parcel been lying on the doorstep? Was it put there soon after Annie left the house to go and help out with the school nativity play? If so, was it possible that she'd seen the person who'd left it?

He checked his watch again and wondered when his wife would arrive home. The play must surely have finished by now, but he supposed it was possible she was still helping to clean up or that she had gone for a drink with some of the other school staff at one of the pubs in the village.

He reached for his phone and brought up the photo of the message in the card.

Here's a Christmas gift for you, detective Walker. It's a little early, I know, but I just couldn't wait. My very own take on the twelve days of Christmas, complete with a dead partridge. Twelve days. Twelve murders. Twelve victims. And they all deserve what's coming to them.

His boss, Detective Chief Inspector Jeff Tanner, had asked James if he could think of anyone who might have embarked on a cruel mission to ruin his Christmas.

'It would have to be someone with a twisted fucking mind and a serious grudge against you,' Tanner had said.

There was one person who fit that description, of course. Andrew Sullivan.

Annie arrived home just as the patrol officer was placing the bin bag containing the parcel in the boot of his marked BMW.

James watched her approach and cursed under his breath because he wished he didn't have to tell her what was going on. But he had no choice for two reasons. Firstly, he wasn't prepared to tell an outright lie when she asked him. And secondly, he needed to know if she had any idea who might have done it.

'Is everything all right?' Annie asked when she reached him, her breath steaming in the cold evening air.

James flicked his head towards the house.

'Let's go inside and I'll tell you, hon,' he said. 'It's freezing out here.' He gave the officer the thumbs-up before he and Annie hurried along the short garden path and into the house. He had already cleaned up the kitchen so that she wouldn't be confronted by the bloody mess on the floor.

He helped her off with her coat and scarf and went to make her a hot chocolate while she removed her shoes.

Then he told her what had happened while they sat facing each other across the kitchen table. He showed her the photos on his phone of the dead partridge and the message on the card. The colour drained from her face as she took it all in. When she looked up her eyes were dull with shock.

23

'Please tell me that you don't think this is anything other than a vile prank,' she said.

He dragged in a loud breath and shook his head.

'I can't imagine it being anything other than that. But we have to be sure. I'm hoping that whoever did it left a fingerprint or something for the lab technicians to find.'

Annie stared at him, furrows texturing her brow.

'My God,' she said. 'What if some crazed serial killer has decided to target the people of Kirkby Abbey? And us.'

'Please don't freak out, Annie,' James said as he reached across the table to place his hand on hers.

But she drew it back sharply and snapped at him. 'I'm not freaking out, and I'm not stupid either. You've more or less admitted that it might not be a tasteless joke. Therefore, shouldn't you raise the alarm and warn everyone that they could be in danger? And at the same time flood the village with police officers?'

James fully appreciated where she was coming from, but he knew that the contents of the parcel wouldn't be enough in themselves to trigger a full-blown investigation. It wasn't uncommon for death threats to be sent via letter, parcel and email.

'For all we know that's exactly what the sender wants to happen,' he said. 'If it is just a stupid joke then the more people who get worked up about it the more successful it'll be deemed to be. And we also need to bear in mind that if it's not a hoax then there's no way of knowing if the victims referred to live in this village.'

James could tell from the look on her face that she wasn't convinced, but she decided not to pursue the subject. Instead, she remained silent, holding his gaze while gnawing at the edge of her bottom lip.

'We'll soon get to the bottom of it,' he said, and tried to sound reassuring. 'I promise you that.'

Her expression changed suddenly, as though a thought had crashed into her head.

'Jesus Christ, James,' she yelled. 'What if it's from him? What if the bastard has found us?'

CHAPTER FOUR

Annie's reaction came as no surprise to James. Only three months had passed since the day Andrew Sullivan was released from prison and the brick was thrown through their living room window.

The move to Cumbria had made his wife feel safer, but the threat Sullivan posed still hung over their heads like a dark cloud.

James's transfer to Kendal had been processed quickly and efficiently by the Met, and only a handful of senior officers had been made privy to why he'd requested it, to reduce the possibility that Sullivan would find out where he'd gone and pursue him.

James had hoped and prayed that the man would get on with his life and forget about seeking revenge for the time he'd spent behind bars. But if he was still determined to punish James, then he could probably use his crooked contacts in the Met to find out about their new home in Kirkby Abbey.

'Don't tell me it hasn't already occurred to you that this

could be down to Sullivan,' Annie said. 'It's an easy way to wreck our Christmas and put the fear of God into us.'

'Of course, it's occurred to me,' James said. 'But there's a risk of jumping to the wrong conclusion because of what's happened in the past. I find it hard to believe that Sullivan would bother to put together something so weirdly elaborate when he doesn't need to. It's just not his MO, unlike the note that was attached to the brick and the threats he made to me before we collared him. It doesn't ring true that he would talk about the twelve days of Christmas and tell me he's about to embark on a killing spree just to seize my attention. And then there's the partridge, which strikes me as the kind of theatrical gesture that wouldn't occur to an oaf like Sullivan.'

Annie pushed her chair back and abruptly stood.

'I need something stronger than hot chocolate,' she said.

James watched her cross to the fridge and take out a bottle of white wine. Then it was to the cupboard for the glasses.

It gutted him to think that she had been hurled back onto the emotional rollercoaster. She'd had such a tough time over the past few years, starting with her inability to conceive, building with the threats from Sullivan and culminating with the brick through their window.

Since leaving London she'd been more like her old self – bubbly, confident and full of life. Physically, it was as though she'd had a makeover. She was still as gorgeous as she had always been, with those bright blue eyes, soft facial features and thick black hair that tumbled to her shoulders. But there was a glow about her now, and she appeared fitter and healthier after putting on the weight she'd lost through months of worrying. She was still slim and shapely, though, and she looked terrific in the tight brown sweater and denim jeans that clung to her frame.

The last thing James wanted was for her to be struck by another bout of despair in the run up to Christmas.

'Let's assume for now that it's got nothing to do with Sullivan,' James said. 'Can you think of anyone living here in the village who might be of a mind to dream up something as crazy as this? Perhaps someone who isn't happy about us moving here?'

Annie placed the wine and the glasses on the table and sat down.

'Absolutely not,' she said. 'We've been given a warm welcome. And as far as I know we haven't made any enemies.'

James sat back in the chair and grappled with a new batch of questions that were spinning around in his head.

What would be the next step if no forensic evidence turned up on the parcel and its contents? Would DCI Tanner expect him to pursue it by making discreet enquiries in the village? And if so, who would he approach and what would he ask them?

It was a tricky one, for sure, and he could feel his insides clenching at the thought of how it was going to play out over the days ahead.

Annie poured the wine and pushed James's glass across the table towards him. He thanked her, then asked what time she'd left the house earlier to go to the nativity play.

'It was around half four,' she answered. 'I popped home to grab a bite to eat and change. It was dark by then so I left the lights on for you.'

'I got here just after six so the parcel was placed on the doorstep between those times,' James said. 'The street outside was empty when I arrived, but I suppose somebody could have been watching from the shadows.'

'I don't remember seeing anyone outside either,' Annie said.

'What about when you walked to the school? Did you pass any other people or cars heading this way?'

Annie scrunched up her brow and cast her mind back. It took her mere seconds to shake her head.

'I only saw one other person,' she said. 'It was Keith Patel, who I've seen around the village from time to time. We passed each other on the pavement this side of the square. I said hello to him but he either didn't hear me or chose not to respond.'

'Didn't you think that was odd? Or at least rude?'

'Not really. The man has a reputation for being anti-social. Apparently, he's been like that since his ageing mother died a year ago. Janet told me that the woman fell down her stairs but her body wasn't discovered for a week because nobody called at the house. Patel is now living there but keeps to himself because he believes that she might have been saved if her friends and neighbours in the village had bothered to drop in on her.'

James leaned forward across the table. 'Can you remember if the guy was carrying a box or a bag?'

'He wasn't carrying anything,' Annie said. 'I can remember that clearly. But he *was* pulling a shopping trolley – the kind used by elderly people. He's not exactly old, though, probably in his fifties. I also noticed he was limping.'

'So while you were walking away from our house, he was walking towards it? Is that right?'

Annie nodded. 'But then, he does live down the hill opposite the stables. I'm guessing he was just going home.'

James mulled this over for a few moments, and said, 'As a matter of interest, do you happen to know when exactly his mum died?'

Annie shrugged. 'According to Janet, people think it was last Christmas Eve. But they can't be absolutely sure because her body wasn't found until New Year's Day.'

James felt a sudden twist in his gut as he wondered if Keith Patel should become their first suspect.

CHAPTER FIVE

James spent the rest of the evening in work mode. He found it impossible to concentrate on anything other than the parcel.

He asked Annie lots of questions about the people she knew in Kirkby Abbey, and was particularly interested in the ones she'd had contact with since moving here.

Some of those she mentioned James had already been introduced to, including Lorna Manning, the school headmistress.

'I'm confident that none of them would do such a thing,' Annie said. 'Lorna is my friend as well as my boss. You said yourself how nice she is. The same goes for Father Silver, who has a lot on his plate at the moment, what with his illness and the impending closure of his church. They both have their ears to the ground, so I'm sure they would have told me if someone in the village had it in for us.'

Among the other villagers James had met were Charlie and Sonia Jenkins, landlords of The White Hart pub, and Giles Keegan, a former member of the Cumbria Constabulary who used to work in the same office where James was now based.

31

'They've all been really welcoming,' Annie said. 'But you ought to ask Giles what he thinks. I'm sure that not much happens in Kirkby Abbey that he isn't aware of.'

Among those James hadn't met was Keith Patel and it was Patel's name that James scrawled in his notebook, along with the fact that Annie had seen him walking towards their house pulling a shopping trolley shortly before the parcel was left on their doorstep. Was it just a coincidence? Probably. But that did not mean it wasn't a credible line of inquiry, along with Andrew Sullivan's possible involvement.

Obviously, Annie knew only a very small number of the seven hundred or so people who resided in Kirkby Abbey, and many of those she'd known when she'd lived here with her parents had since left the village. The shrinking population was the main reason that things had changed and were continuing to change. The only church was due to close for good early in the new year because of a dramatic fall in the number of worshippers, and it was thought unlikely that the campaign to save the primary school would succeed.

These were issues that James had raised with Annie in recent months – though they hadn't dampened her enthusiasm for the move – and he had got her to agree not to sell the house in Tottenham or rent it out for at least six months, until they had a better idea of what would happen in Kirkby Abbey. They also needed the time to find out if life in rural England would suit them both.

As well as talking to Annie about the villagers, James sent an email to one of his colleagues in the Met asking for a status report on Andrew Sullivan. He wanted to know where he was and what he'd been up to.

He then went online and pulled up photos of partridges.

It didn't take him long to establish that the poor thing in the box was a grey partridge that was pretty common in Cumbria. It was easily recognisable from its orange face and the dark horseshoe-shaped patch on its chest.

Of course, partridges were immortalized in the carol *The Twelve Days of Christmas*, but James reminded himself of the fact that the real 'twelve days of Christmas' is a period in Christian theology that marks the span between the birth of Christ and the coming of the three wise men. It begins on Christmas Day and runs to January 6th.

So why had the person or persons who delivered the parcel alluded to it in the message? Was it part of a prank aimed at seizing his attention in the most dramatic fashion? Or was it a genuine warning that a killing spree would take place in Kirkby Abbey over the Christmas period?

Both James and Annie had a restless night, unable to sleep properly with so much on their minds. It didn't help that a blustery wind caused the bedroom window to rattle noisily for much of the time.

James awoke at seven on Saturday morning and saw that a layer of snow had settled over the village. Chimneys sprouted through marshmallow rooftops and the street out front was devoid of tyre tracks and footprints. Their two cars, and those belonging to the neighbours, were little more than strange white shapes that looked bulky and out of place in the tranquil setting.

When he switched on the TV in the kitchen, the weather forecaster was saying that there was much worse to come. She used words such as *blizzards* and *disruption* to describe what to expect.

'My advice is to be prepared and don't get caught out,' she said.

James had been looking forward to spending the first day of the weekend relaxing with Annie. The plan had been to see what was on offer at the farmers' market in the village square and then to have a leisurely lunch at The White Hart.

But the parcel had created an unwanted distraction and was bound to occupy their thoughts throughout the day.

He made Annie a cup of tea and took it to her in the bedroom. She asked him what he was going to do about the parcel and he told her that he wasn't sure.

'I'll give it another hour or so and call the lab,' he said. 'They promised to prioritise the tests. Then I'll check with the boss to see what he thinks the next step should be.'

The hour passed quickly enough. By eight thirty, they were both showered and dressed and having a cereal breakfast at the kitchen table. Outside, a light snow had begun to fall, but it seemed like the wind had dropped.

In the end, James didn't have to put in a call to the lab because one of the technicians phoned him. But the news was disappointing. The only prints found on the box, the wrapping paper, clingfilm and card belonged to him. And the initial examination indicated that there was no DNA trace evidence on any of the objects.

'As for the partridge, I can confirm that it was a hen,' the technician said. 'And it had been stabbed it the stomach. We estimate that it was killed at some point in the past twenty-four to thirty-six hours.'

After hanging up with the lab, James phoned DCI Tanner at home to tell him the results.

'I can't say I'm surprised,' Tanner said. 'Whoever did it would have made sure to cover their tracks.'

James told him how Annie had spotted one of the villagers heading towards their house around the time the parcel was dumped on the doorstep.

'It's a tenuous link at best,' Tanner said. 'I'm sure there would have been other people she didn't see. But I suppose it's worth having a chat with him. And you could try to find out if the type of wrapping paper and card that was used can be purchased locally.'

'Leave it with me, guv,' James said. 'Meanwhile, I'm not ruling out Andrew Sullivan. I've asked a former colleague in the Met to check what he's up to for me.'

Tanner was one of the few officers in the Cumbria Constabulary who knew about the brick incident and the threats James had received from Sullivan in the past.

'At this stage let's keep everything low key,' the DCI said. 'My money is on it being a reckless hoax and if I'm right I don't want us to assign people to it who would be more usefully deployed elsewhere. Severe weather is now being predicted for the week ahead and that could mean massive pressure on our resources.'

James came off the phone and told Annie what Tanner had said. She was about to respond when her own phone rang. Annie answered it and smiled when she heard the caller's voice. But it was quickly replaced by a frown. She mumbled a couple of times to whoever was on the line, then looked across the table at James.

'He's with me now,' she said into the phone. 'Of course. Bear with me and I'll put him on.'

As Annie handed her phone to her husband, she said, 'It's

Father Silver at St John's. He's called me because I gave him my number a few weeks ago. But it's you he wants to speak to. He says he thinks it's a police matter.'

James took the phone from Annie. He didn't know the priest as well as she did, but he'd met him several times.

'Hi there, Father,' he said. 'What can I do for you?'

'I'm really sorry to bother you at the weekend, Detective Walker,' the priest said. 'But I'm concerned about an odd message I've received from someone who hasn't provided a name but suggests I talk to you.'

'Really? What kind of message?'

'Well, it's written inside a card depicting The Twelve Days of Christmas.'

James felt a shudder ripple through him.

'Exactly what does it say, Father?' he asked.

The priest cleared his throat and read out the message, which caused the heat to rise in James's chest.

'I'll be right there, Father,' he said. 'And can I ask you to please not show it to anyone else?'

CHAPTER SIX

St John's Church was a distinctive building set back from the road and close to the centre of the village. It was surrounded by dozens of weathered gravestones and a few impressive yew trees, and had an attractive bell tower.

James thought it a great shame that it was being forced to close, but it was the same story in villages, towns and cities across the country as people sought answers outside religion. He'd read somewhere that since the sixties, church attendance in Cumbria had more than halved as society was becoming more secular and religion more diverse.

The snow had stopped falling by the time he arrived at St John's, but the sky remained heavy and grey, and the air felt raw. James wondered if this was the calm before the storm.

Father Thomas Silver was placing bibles on the pews when he entered the church, but as soon as he saw James, he stopped what he was doing and hurried over.

The priest was a tall man in his mid-sixties, thin and wiry, with a few strands of grey hair, a heavily lined pale face, and a large nose.

James had first met him at Annie's mum's funeral, but back then he'd been quite large. The loss of weight had followed a diagnosis of prostate cancer six months ago. He'd made no secret of the fact that it was terminal and that this would in all likelihood be his last Christmas.

Today he was wearing a black suit and clerical shirt with a tunic collar.

'Thank you for coming so quickly, Detective Walker,' he said, shaking James's hand. 'I'm not afraid to admit that the message in the card concerns as well as baffles me. I'm hoping you can shed some light on it.'

James shook his head. 'I wish I could. But I'm as confused as you are, Father. All I can tell you is that I received a similar card yesterday. These things usually turn out to be silly pranks, though.'

'Then let us hope that is the case here.'

'Where is the card now?'

'In the office.'

'Then please lead the way. Has anyone else touched it?'

'No, they haven't. Are you going to have it checked for fingerprints?'

'Yes.'

He followed Father Silver into his office, which was quite compact, with a single window that looked out on some of the headstones at the back of the church. There was a cluttered desk, a small leather sofa, and the walls were adorned with framed prints of scenes from the bible.

The card had been placed on top of a grey metal filing cabinet along with the envelope it had come in. James saw straight away that it matched exactly the one that had been delivered to him.

He'd come prepared and took a pair of latex gloves and an evidence bag from his overcoat pocket. He slipped the gloves on before picking up the card.

The message inside was scrawled in black marker and the handwriting appeared to be a match as well.

You need to prepare for a spate of post-Christmas funerals, Father Silver. If you want to know why then ask Detective James Walker.

'How was this delivered to you, Father?' he asked.

'It was left on the bench inside the front porch,' Father Silver said. 'I saw it when I arrived here this morning from my home in the rectory.'

'And where is that?'

'Just across the road.'

'So it could have been placed there during the night or early today.'

He nodded. 'I left here and closed up about five yesterday evening so that I could go along to the nativity play at the school. It wasn't in the porch then.'

'Was there anyone outside at that time?'

'No. The churchyard was empty. I'm sure of it. I don't recall seeing anyone until I got to the school. After the play I went straight back to the rectory and got an early night. I rarely stay up beyond nine o'clock these days as a result of my condition.'

'Yes, Annie mentioned you had spoken to her about it, Father. I was sorry to hear it.'

'Thank you, my son. But it's God's will so I accept it with good grace.'

'Nevertheless, it can't be easy.'

He smiled. 'It isn't, but it would be much harder if I didn't know that I was going to a better place.'

James didn't want to get involved in a theological discussion at this time so he just nodded, then quickly turned his attention to the envelope. On it was written:

To the priest of St John's

'Do you believe that this card and the one that was sent to you are from the same person?' Father Silver asked.

'I don't think there's any doubt about that,' James said.

'Then perhaps they were sent to other people as well.'

James shrugged. 'If so then I suspect we'll know soon enough.'

James sealed the evidence bag and placed it in his pocket. His head was spinning now with more questions and a lead weight had started to form in his chest.

He just couldn't fathom what was going on. What was the aim of the creep who was behind it? Was it to stir up panic in the village before Christmas just to indulge a warped sense of humour? Or had Andrew Sullivan launched a vicious vendetta against him after learning that he was now enjoying a quiet life in the Yorkshire Dales?

James felt sure that in both these scenarios the threat to kill people was an empty one. He was less certain about the worst-case scenario Annie had put forward – that a crazed serial killer might have decided to target people in Kirkby Abbey. It seemed highly unlikely, but James knew that it wasn't unknown for serial killers to taunt the police with letters and phone calls and to issue warnings about crimes they were planning to commit.

It made him think about the first message:

Twelve days. Twelve murders. Twelve victims. And they all deserve what's coming to them.

Could it really be that a group of people in this quiet village had incurred the wrath of a genuine psychopath, someone who was living amongst them? And now he or she was determined to exact revenge?

A piercing cry from outside broke his contemplation, causing the hairs to stir on the back of his neck.

The priest heard it too and reacted by rushing over to the window behind the desk.

'What's happening?' James asked. 'It sounds like someone is angry or upset.'

'I think you're right on both counts, Detective. The poor man appears to be in a terrible state.'

James stepped up behind him and peered through the window. He saw a rough-looking man waving his fists in the air and yelling at the sky. He was wearing a green parka and black woollen hat.

'Do you know him, Father?'

'Indeed, I do. And I also know what has brought on this reaction.'

'Oh?'

The priest gave a slow nod. 'The headstone on his mother's grave has been defaced again. I saw it yesterday afternoon and had planned to do something about it this morning, but it slipped my mind after I opened the card.'

'So it's happened before then?'

'I'm afraid so. Sadly, Mr Patel is considered fair game for the vandals who get their kicks from damaging and destroying things that don't belong to them.'

James snapped his head towards the priest. 'I'm sorry, Father, but what did you say his name was?'

'It's Patel. Keith Patel. His mother Nadia died in tragic circumstances a year ago this very week. And he still hasn't come to terms with losing her.'

CHAPTER SEVEN

James followed the priest as he hurried into the churchyard. By the time they reached Keith Patel he'd stopped wailing and was just standing there, staring down at his mother's grave.

He turned when he heard them approach, and anger and distress were evident in his expression. His eyes were slits, teeth clenched, and his voice cracked with emotion when he said, 'It's the third time the fuckers have done this. Everyone knows who they are but they get away with it because nobody but me gives a toss.'

'That's not true, Keith,' Father Silver said. 'I care and so do most other people. This is the work of mindless vandals. But rest assured, it won't take me long to clear it up just as I've done before.'

'That's not the point and you know it,' Patel spat back. 'The people in this village ignored my mother when she was alive, partly because she was Indian and they felt she didn't fit in. That's why she died sooner than she should have. And now that she's in her grave they still treat her with total disrespect.'

When James saw why the man was so upset, he couldn't help but feel sorry for him. Red paint had been sprayed on the white granite headstone, obliterating the epitaph that was inscribed on it. The paint also stained the marble chippings within the grave's kerb surround, and a memorial vase was on its side. The flowers that had been in it were scattered across the ground and most of them had been damaged.

Patel suddenly seemed to notice James standing behind the priest, and the lines around his watery eyes deepened into a frown.

'I know who you are,' he said. 'You're the copper who married Annie Kellerman. Are you here because of this?'

James shook his head. 'I just happened to be with Father Silver in his office, Mr Patel. But I'll certainly put the wheels in motion so that it can be investigated.'

'A fat lot of good that'll do. The police got involved before, but could never prove who was responsible. Not that they spent much time trying. So, I don't expect it to be any different this time.'

Patel turned his back on them, knelt down and began picking up the flowers.

'You're in no fit state to do that, Keith,' Father Silver said. 'I insist you go home and leave it to me. It's my responsibility. I've got a bottle of white spirit in the office and some fresh flowers to replace those.'

It seemed at first as if Patel was going to ignore the priest, but after a few seconds he heaved himself to his feet, which seemed to require a great deal of effort.

'I'll come back later this afternoon then,' he said, after taking a shivering breath. 'And by then I expect you to have it sorted.'

The priest nodded. 'I will, Keith. I promise. And I'm so sorry. This is simply not acceptable.'

Patel then turned to James. 'I heard on the grapevine that your wife persuaded you to move here from London. She probably told you that this is a quiet place where everyone is pleasant and friendly. Well, that couldn't be further from the truth. It's a shithole, and most of the people are heartless scumbags and racists. But I reckon you'll soon find that out for yourself. Meanwhile, give my regards to Annie. Her mother was one of the very few people who gave my mum the time of day.'

'Annie told me that you bumped into each other early yesterday evening,' James said. 'You were pulling a shopping trolley and heading towards your house.'

Patel frowned. 'I don't remember that.'

'She said hi to you.'

'Did she? I obviously didn't hear. I'd been to stock up at the store and was in a hurry to get home.'

James didn't want to put him on the spot by challenging his rather unconvincing explanation in front of the priest. He'd do it later, when there was no one else around. Instead, he watched as Patel turned and headed towards the church-yard exit.

'Why is he limping?' James asked Father Silver.

'He suffers from a serious case of rheumatoid arthritis in his knee joints,' the priest said. 'It's getting progressively worse with age.'

'Does he work?'

'No. He manages on benefits and a cash sum his mother left him.'

'Annie told me what happened to her and why he holds a

45

grudge against some of the villagers. But where was he when his mother fell down the stairs?'

'At the time he was working as a shop assistant in Manchester and living in a rented flat. By all accounts he was barely managing to pay the bills, but he came to see his mum, Nadia, as often as possible.'

'So do you know much about him, Father?' James asked.

'Well, I know that his father Floyd passed away some years ago. The man followed the Catholic faith and so did Nadia. She joined our congregation soon after she moved here. A delightful, God-fearing woman who died before her time. She left the house to Keith, who has never married, and he settled here. But in my opinion that was a mistake because he's full of resentment for the villagers. He should have sold up and moved elsewhere.'

'Why didn't he?'

The priest gestured at the grave in front of them. 'He told me he wanted to stay close to her. Couldn't bear the thought of leaving her alone.'

Father Silver then offered to make James a cup of tea.

'That's very kind of you, Father. But before you make it I wonder if you could provide me with a fingerprint sample so that we can distinguish it from any others we might find on the card and envelope.'

'Of course, Detective. That's not a problem.'

Back inside the church, the priest stuck his right thumb and fingers against a small, clear handheld mirror that James placed in another evidence bag.

They had a brief conversation then, during which Father Silver was at pains to point out that Patel's negative comments about the village and its residents were far from true.

'They're good people, with a few exceptions,' he said. 'But I have to acknowledge that the community itself has become quite dispirited. Too many young families have moved away, partly because there's so little work. And things are set to get worse with the closure of this church and the school. It's desperately troubling for me that I won't be around to offer hope and counselling during the tough times that lie ahead, especially if the person responsible for those cards is not a prankster, but is intent on bringing death and destruction to Kirkby Abbey.'

'Try not to lose sleep over it, Father,' James said. 'The odds are that it's a hoax.'

The priest compressed his lips tightly together and nodded.

'I will pray that you're right about that, Detective Walker. But if you're not then I just hope you are able to apprehend this person before he harms anyone.'

CHAPTER EIGHT

Annie was waiting for James to call her after his visit to the church. They were hoping to meet up so they could have a drink and some lunch together, and she was eager to hear if Father Silver knew or suspected who had sent him the threatening card.

She was still reeling from the shock of it. James, typically, had tried to play it down, his face remaining firm and stoic as he'd relayed what the priest had told him over the phone.

But Annie could tell from the look in his eyes that it had rattled him. It was the same look that had been there after the brick was hurled through the window of their home in Tottenham.

This wasn't supposed to be happening. They had moved to Cumbria so that they could feel safe and secure. But suddenly a nagging sense of dread had been planted in her stomach, and she found it hard to think about anything other than the dead partridge and those ominous messages.

She did her best to try to take her mind off it by keeping busy. After tidying the kitchen, she finished off putting up the decorations ready for when James's family arrived en masse on Christmas Eve.

But she was already starting to wonder if they should even come now. God only knew what was going to happen during the next seven days.

She found herself looking at the framed photos on the mantlepiece. There was one of her and James on their wedding day, which took place at a fancy hotel in Kent. Dozens of pictures were taken that day, but this one of them standing either side of the cake was her favourite. They were smiling at each other, and it was clear for all to see that they were so happy and very much in love.

James was a fine figure of a man at the best of times, tall and lean with thick brown hair, but on that day he'd looked really scrumptious in his black Moss Bros. morning suit and waistcoat.

The photo next to it was the last one taken of her parents together. It was at the start of a charity hike on Wild Boar Fell which raised £3,000 for Save The Children. Two months later her dad collapsed and died of a heart attack and her mum never went hiking again.

Guilt always reared its ugly head whenever Annie thought about her father. At the time of his death when she was a teenager, she hadn't been on good terms with him because he had wrecked her relationship with the man she had fallen in love with.

His name was Daniel Curtis and he was a tour guide who lived with his parents in Kirkby Abbey. She'd met him on an organised day trip to the Lake District with some of her friends. He was good-looking and charming, and she was made up when he'd asked for her phone number.

After that they'd met at least twice a week for over three months, but always in secret. There was a good reason for that. At the time Annie had just turned sixteen and he was fourteen years older. Her dad found out about it after someone saw her going into Daniel's house while his parents were away.

Her father, a devout Catholic, hit the roof. He confronted Daniel and accused him of being a paedophile even though Annie had just reached the age of consent.

Daniel agreed not to see her again, and to make it easier on himself he moved from Kirkby Abbey to Keswick. Annie went into a massive teenage sulk for weeks. On the day her father died, she had been staying at Janet Dyer's house, bemoaning the fact that he had ruined her life.

Of course, it wasn't long before she realised that he'd been right to step in and save her from herself. It turned out that Daniel had had a number of girls on the go at the time, and three years later he was convicted of having sex with a minor and jailed for two years. On his release, he'd moved back to Keswick but he did return occasionally to visit his widowed father in Kirkby Abbey. Daniel had never married and at almost fifty he was still single.

Annie knew all this because his father Ron was one of the elderly people who Janet visited on a regular basis as a carer. And, of course, there was no way she could resist passing on what she knew to her long-time friend.

Annie still thought about Daniel from time to time but had long ago come to the conclusion that he hadn't loved her, even though he'd made her believe that he had. She would never forget what her father said to her when he entered her room and found her crying after the break-up: *You need to pull yourself together and grow up, Annie. It's time you faced up to the fact that you were being groomed by that pervert. To him, you were no more than a sex object.'*

Annie had told James as much as she'd dared about that phase of her life, leaving out only one important detail that she didn't want him to know, something she hoped she would never have to reveal it to him. A secret she'd kept for almost twenty years.

James had never come face to face with Daniel Curtis, and she was thankful that the man was now living a hundred or so miles away.

Annie managed to get quite a few chores done before James called.

'I'm just leaving the church,' he said. 'I'll tell you about it when we meet up. Let's say, in an hour, at The White Hart. I've got a few things I need to do first.'

'So you're going to keep me in suspense until then?' Annie replied.

'It's not long for you to wait, and it means I can crack on.'

'Right you are then. I'll see you in the pub.'

Annie sloped off to the kitchen to make herself a cup of tea. She was waiting for the kettle to boil when the doorbell rang.

She wasn't expecting anyone, and she hoped that Royal Mail wasn't about to deliver another unwelcome gift that was too big to slip through the letterbox.

It wasn't, thank God. But she got quite a surprise nonetheless.

'Hello there, Annie,' her visitor said. 'It's good to see you after all this time. It's been eighteen months, by my reckoning.'

Her jaw dropped, and there was a moment's hesitation before she was able to conjure up a smile.

'Uncle Bill! What are you doing here? I didn't expect you until the twenty-second.'

'I decided to come early because I feared that if I left it any later the bad weather would make it impossible for me to get here.'

He was standing on the doormat with a scarf around his neck and his hands buried in the pockets of a thick overcoat. Annie looked over his shoulder at the road.

'So where's your car? And why haven't you got an overnight bag or case?'

'Look, can we please save the questions until I'm inside? I'm so cold my teeth are chattering.'

She stood back to let him in, and the first thing he did when the door was closed was to encase her in a hug. He reeked of sweat and tobacco, but she didn't mind because the gesture was welcome and it caused an ache to swell in her chest.

They hadn't spoken since the bust-up at her mother's wake – it wasn't for want of trying, at least on Annie's part – because every time she'd phoned him, he'd told her that he didn't want to talk to her. She eventually gave up and accepted that he was set in his stubborn ways and a reconciliation was out of the question. Which was why she was so surprised when he accepted with alacrity her invitation to join her and James's family for Christmas in Kirkby Abbey.

'It's good to see you, Annie,' he said, pulling back from the embrace. 'I'm here because I believe it's time we put the past behind us and got reacquainted. I'm sorry I waited so long.'

She felt tears well up as they stared at one another. She thought he looked much older than his sixty-eight years. The lines in his face were deep and unforgiving, and he had pale, bloodshot eyes that were rheumy under dropping lids. Patches of slate-grey hair clung to his shiny scalp, and his skin had a yellow tinge.

He broke eye contact with her and thrust his chin towards the kitchen.

'I wouldn't say no to a brew, my dear,' he said. 'And you can tell me why you decided to move back to the sticks.'

Annie made the teas and they settled in the kitchen to drink them. She started off the conversation by saying that she was meeting James in an hour and invited Bill to join them at the pub.

'I'd love to but I've made other arrangements,' he said. 'I'm having an early lunch with an old pal. But after that I'm free for the rest of the day.'

Annie was taken aback as well as disappointed. Her uncle had come all this way to see her and was already going off by himself.

She chose not to make an issue of it and asked him how he'd been and what life was like in Penrith. In turn, he asked her about James and what had prompted the move from London. She didn't mention Sullivan, and said simply that they'd both decided that they were fed up with the capital.

The conversation was congenial enough, but the more they talked, the more Annie felt that Bill was trying to be careful what he said. Evasive, almost. And several times he appeared to lose his train of thought, which suggested to Annie that he had something else on his mind.

She got the impression from what he said, and from his body language, that he felt more awkward than she did. He was clearly uncomfortable, and seemed far removed from the brash, imperious man she used to know.

She started to wonder if there was something troubling him, and when he responded to her repeated question about where his car was, her curiosity was aroused even further.

'It's in the car park of The King's Head,' he said. 'That's where I'm staying. I arrived early yesterday evening and have booked a room for twelve nights. It's really cheap.'

'But why? I said you could stay here. I've made a bed up for you.'

He shrugged. 'I thought it best for everyone if I didn't stay here. I know James and his brood aren't keen on me after what happened at the funeral, so I made up my mind to have somewhere to go if things became difficult and I felt I wasn't welcome.'

'But that's ridiculous,' Annie said, her voice rising an octave. 'This is going to be a family Christmas in our new home. And you're part of the family.'

'I know, and I'm grateful, but this way I won't feel under so much pressure.'

Annie was sure that there was more to it than that, but she didn't think it likely that he would open up to her just yet.

'I did pop over here to see you soon after I arrived around five,' Bill said. 'But there was no answer even though the lights were on inside.'

'As a matter of interest was there a parcel on the doorstep addressed to James?'

He shook his head. 'Not that I recall. I'm sure I would have seen it if there had been.'

'So what did you do then?'

'I went for a walk through the village and delivered some Christmas cards to a few former acquaintances. After that I headed back to The King's Head for a drink in the bar before going to bed.'

Annie was still trying to get her mind around what he'd just said when he went and dropped another bombshell.

'I did get a bit of a shock when I was walking past the primary school,' he said. 'There was a bloke standing across the road under a tree and he caught my eye when he lit up a fag. I got a good look at his face, and saw that it was your old flame, Daniel Curtis. He has a lot less hair now, but I'd recognise that pervy bastard anywhere. Did you know he was back, Annie?'

She started to reply, but the words got stuck in her throat.

CHAPTER NINE

After phoning Annie, James called headquarters and filed a brief report on the vandalised grave. He sent across pictures he'd taken on his phone with his notes, though he knew full well that not much would come of it. Theft and vandalism at churches across the country were a growing problem and the culprits were rarely apprehended.

He also made arrangements for a patrol car to pick up the card and the mirror containing Father Silver's prints. He did consider driving them over to the lab himself, but decided his time would be better spent making some enquiries in the village.

Before leaving St John's, he'd obtained an assurance from the priest that he'd keep quiet about what he knew.

It had been an interesting meeting, but James came away from it none the wiser as to what was going on. Keith Patel had struck him as a troubled individual, but not someone who would get his own back by murdering – or threatening to murder – those people he believed should have visited his mother before she died of her injuries. All the same, James did intend to speak to him later and perhaps even seek a warrant to search his home. But he knew that once the process became official the word would spread and it could trigger unnecessary panic among the villagers.

He decided that before meeting Annie at the pub, he'd visit the general store to check whether it sold those Twelve Days of Christmas cards. On the way, he took out his phone and called DCI Tanner to update him.

The boss was none too pleased to hear that another card had turned up. He admitted that he hadn't expected it, and was concerned that it'd get picked up by the media.

'If that happens it'll be blown out of all proportion and whatever we do won't be enough,' he said. 'So try to keep a lid on it at least until we can be sure what we're dealing with.'

'It would help if I'd been living here longer,' James said. 'As it is, I'm still not that familiar with the village or those who live here.'

'Well, DS Stevens used to reside over that way before moving to Burneside. You can pick his brain. Or, better still, look up Giles Keegan. He had my job here until five years ago when he retired. It's my understanding he still lives in Kirkby Abbey.'

'He does, guv. I've already met him, and that's actually a good call.'

'Do you need his phone number?'

'He gave it to me. I was planning to ring him so that we can arrange to have a drink together.'

'I'm sure he'll know everything there is to know about the village and you can get him to dish the dirt on his friends and neighbours. Hopefully he'll know of anyone who has form or a screw loose in the head.'

* * *

Kirkby Abbey was much busier than usual because of the monthly farmers' market. About twenty small covered stalls were crammed into the village square, everything on sale locally grown, produced or caught, including meats, cheeses, breads, vegetables, beers, eggs, fish and cakes.

Villagers were mixing with visitors, and it appeared to James as though everyone was immersed in the season of goodwill. In the centre of the square stood a large Christmas tree adorned with bright coloured lights and surrounded by a fence about two feet high.

Above the village, the wind-blown clouds had taken on weight and mass, and it had become shockingly cold. People were wrapped up in heavy coats and scarves, and breath formed in front of their faces.

The general store was just off the square and was part of a traditional limestone terrace. It stocked most of what the village needed to be self-sufficient, and also doubled up as the post office.

A wheelchair ramp was attached to the front and was used mainly by the woman who ran the store with her husband.

Maeve King had been paralysed following a stroke three years ago but continued to work behind the counter as often as she could. Peter King put in most of the hours these days, with the help of a part-time assistant.

He was the one who was working today, but before approaching him, James headed for the display of Christmas-related products at the opposite end of the store. It contained wrapping paper, decorations, festive ornaments, plus a wide range of cards. James found what he was looking for as soon as he started sifting through them.

The same Twelve Days of Christmas cards that had been delivered to his home and the church were here in packs of ten and there were two packs left. He picked one up and took it to the counter.

King was a florid-faced man in his sixties with fleshy pink lips and hair the colour of sea foam. He recognised James and beamed a smile at him.

'How are you today, Detective Walker?' he asked.

'I'm fine, thank you,' James said, placing the cards on the counter. 'Is your wife not with you today?'

King shook his head. 'She doesn't like to venture out if it's too cold. But a friend's spending the day with her so she's making the most of it.' He picked up the cards to check the price. 'You've made a good choice with these. It's such an eye-catching design, and they've proved very popular.'

'Have you sold many of them?'

'Indeed we have. They were in a mixed batch of over a hundred packs we got in eight weeks ago. I'm not sure how many of that particular design have gone out, but I believe there are only a few left.'

'So I reckon a lot of villagers will be sending each other the exact same card.' James said.

King laughed. 'Happens every year, but it's to be expected since we're the only retailer in Kirkby Abbey selling cards.'

'Tell me, Mr King, is it possible to keep track of who buys which packs?'

King wrinkled his brow. 'That's a strange question, Detective. Why do you want to know?'

'I'm just curious. That's all.'

King shrugged. 'Most people pay in cash and only the batch number shows on the till receipt anyway. And, of course, we stocked the same brands last Christmas, so I expect some people still had them in a cupboard or drawer at home.'

As James paid for the cards – with cash – he nodded towards the CCTV camera on the wall to the right of the counter.

'It's great to see that you take security seriously. I've been told that some shops in the area don't even have cameras installed.'

King followed his gaze. 'Between us, it's not been working for weeks. I need to get it repaired or replaced.'

James left the shop disappointed. It was obvious that it would be impossible to identify who had purchased the cards that had been sent to him and the priest.

But at least it now seemed certain that they'd been bought in the village store by a local, which narrowed the list of potential suspects down to . . . hundreds of people.

CHAPTER TEN

The White Hart was the oldest of the two pubs in the village. Unlike The King's Head, it didn't have rooms for rent, and it was in a better position overlooking the square.

There was a gabled entrance and bay windows on the outside. Inside it was a typical cosy Cumbrian pub, with timber floors, open fires, worn leather sofas and a low oak-beamed ceiling.

Country oddments and pictures of the Dales lined the walls, and an archway led from the bar into a restaurant with about fifteen tables.

There were plenty of Christmas decorations, and as James entered, he heard the Mariah Carey classic *All I Want For Christmas Is You* playing in the background.

He was there before his wife and ordered a bottle of her favourite Chardonnay from the landlady, Sonia Jenkins.

James felt sure that there weren't many women in the village as attractive as Sonia. She had a pretty face, stunning figure, and a smile that lit up the room.

But she wasn't smiling now, for whatever reason. After taking his order, she said, 'Will your wife be joining you, Mr Walker?'

'Any minute now,' he said. 'So I'll need two glasses with that and a lunch menu please.'

'Make yourself comfortable and I'll bring them over.' Then she hesitated a moment before continuing. 'I'm sure Annie mentioned what happened at the school yesterday evening after the nativity play. So when she arrives I'd like to take the opportunity to apologise to her. Would that be okay with you?'

James arched his brow. 'Actually, the only thing she told me was that the play was a roaring success.'

Sonia blew out an audible breath. 'Oh, well, perhaps I didn't make as much of a fool of myself as I thought I did.'

'I'm sure that's true,' James said. 'So what did happen?'

She was about to explain when her attention was suddenly drawn to a point beyond him.

'I think I'll leave it to your wife to provide you with the gory details,' she said. 'She's just arrived.'

James turned to see Annie walking towards them while unzipping her parka.

'Right on cue,' he said to her. 'I've ordered wine and if you're hungry we can get some lunch. But first Sonia wants a quick word with you.'

Annie acknowledged Sonia with a pleasant smile as she stepped up to the bar.

'I just want to say that I'm sorry for my little outburst at the school yesterday,' Sonia said. 'It's true I'd had a couple of gin and tonics after I was told about Janet and my husband. So I found it hard to control myself. But I shouldn't have caused a scene in front of you and everyone else. I feel really stupid.'

Annie held onto her smile as she shook her head and told Sonia not to worry.

'It was over in a flash,' she said. 'So you shouldn't let it bother you. We all allow our emotions to get the better of us from time to time.'

'Thanks for being so understanding, Annie,' Sonia said. 'As a token of my appreciation the wine is on the house. Now, go and find somewhere to perch yourselves before the place starts to fill up, which it will soon enough.'

They chose a table in an alcove, and after Sonia brought the wine and menus, Annie told James about the altercation at the school between the two women.

'I forgot to mention it because we both got so wound up talking about the parcel,' she said. 'But it was pretty unpleasant, and the funny thing is I wasn't quite sure who to feel sorry for.'

'What do you mean?' James asked.

Annie shrugged. 'I'm not altogether convinced that Janet was being honest when she denied having a fling with him.'

They didn't dwell on the subject for long because there was so much else to talk about.

Having decided what to eat, James went to the bar and ordered pea soups and crusty bread before filling Annie in on what had happened at the church. She was appalled when she saw the photos of the defaced headstone and expressed sympathy for Keith Patel.

'He claims he was on his way back from the store with shopping when you passed him,' James said. 'But he doesn't recall seeing you or hearing you speak to him.'

'That might well be the case, I suppose. I'm not sure you'll ever be able to prove otherwise.'

'He also sent his regards to you. He said your mum and his mum were friends.'

'I didn't know that,' Annie said. 'But there's a lot I don't know about Mum's life after I left here.'

James showed Annie the cards he'd got at the store and explained why it'd be impossible to find out who else had bought them.

'But I think it's safe to say that the person who delivered the cards to me and Father Silver got them here in Kirkby Abbey,' he said. 'So it's possible that it's someone we know.'

They were interrupted by the arrival of the soups, after which Annie imparted some surprising news about her Uncle Bill.

'I really don't know what's going on with him,' she said. 'He's acting really strangely. First of all he decided to check in to The King's Head instead of staying with us. Then he claims he went off on a walk through the village delivering Christmas cards to Christ knows who. I've invited him for dinner at the house tonight. Six o'clock. Hopefully I'll get more out of him then.'

James had never been a fan of Bill Cardwell. He'd always found him bad-tempered and loud-mouthed. And when he'd shouted at his niece at her mother's funeral, it had taken a lot of will power not to punch him in the face.

'I did ask Bill if he saw the parcel on the doorstep when he came to the house,' Annie said. 'He assured me he didn't, but he claims he did see a man standing across the road from the school smoking a cigarette. And he swears blind that it was Daniel Curtis.'

James could tell that his wife found it uncomfortable even to mention the name. Early on in their relationship she told him about the short, ill-fated affair she'd had with the much older man and how it caused a rift between her and her father. James knew about Curtis's subsequent conviction for having sex with a minor, and he wasn't sure how he'd react if he ever met the guy.

'I thought it was made clear to Curtis that he wasn't welcome here after he got out of prison,' he said.

'It was, and that hasn't changed, but according to Janet he comes here occasionally to see his elderly dad and tries to stay under the radar.'

As James thought about this an uneasy knot formed in his stomach.

After a beat, he said, 'So, for different reasons, Daniel Curtis and Keith Patel have an uncomfortable relationship with the villagers. Curtis has been ostracised and Patel blames them for what happened to his mother. It might make them feel like they have a score to settle. In which case, perhaps it wasn't just a coincidence that they were both out and about yesterday evening when the parcel and cards were being delivered.'

They'd just finished their soups when James's phone rang. It was the patrol officer to say he had arrived in Kirkby Abbey to pick up the card and the priest's fingerprints. James told him to come to The White Hart where he'd be waiting outside.

There were now quite a few more people in the bar and restaurant, and as he walked outside he passed more coming in. The patrol car turned up within minutes and he handed over the two evidence bags.

He was about to go back inside when loud voices suddenly

65

caught his attention. They were coming from the alley just to the right of where he stood, which ran between the pub and the building next door.

James paused to listen, and when he heard a woman yell, 'Just fuck off and leave me alone,' he knew he had to investigate.

A second later, he was standing in the mouth of the alley watching Sonia and Charlie Jenkins having a heated argument.

'The bitch just phoned to tell me that you went to see her this morning,' Sonia screamed at her husband. 'So how do you expect me to react after she changed her story and told me you have been sleeping with her for months? You promised me it would never happen again.'

Charlie was a good six inches taller than his wife and his face was tense, jaw locked, as he gave her a hard, uncompromising stare.

'It's not true,' he told her. 'I went there to tell her to stay away from us and never to set foot in our pub again. She's just out to stir things up.'

'Oh, come off it, Charlie. You're taking me for a mug. Things haven't been right with us for some time and it even occurred to me that you might be seeing someone else, but I didn't want to believe it.'

'She's lying, though.'

'And why would she do that?'

'Because she came on to me and I rejected her. I told her I'd never be unfaithful again.'

Sonia snapped then and slapped him hard around the face.

'You bastard. I wish you were bloody dead. You've destroyed our marriage and let me down a second time.'

Charlie responded by grabbing her wrists, prompting James to rush into the alley to intervene.

'That's enough, you two,' he shouted. 'If it gets physical it gets dangerous.'

They both turned to him, their expressions frozen.

As James approached, Charlie let go of his wife's wrists.

'This has got nothing to do with you,' he said. 'How long have you been standing there?'

'Just long enough to see that it was getting out of hand,' James replied. 'I heard shouting and thought that someone might be in trouble.'

'He *is* in trouble,' Sonia said, poking a finger at her husband. 'But he doesn't think he should be. He's a liar and a cheat and I hate to think what he would have done to me if you hadn't showed up.'

'Oh, come off it,' Charlie said. 'It was you who slapped me.'

'And you're lucky that's all I did.'

With that, Sonia turned sharply on her heels and stormed back into the pub through the side entrance.

Charlie started shaking his head.

'I'm sorry you had to see that,' he said to James. 'We're going through a tough time and the missus is finding it hard to control her temper.'

'It's got nothing to do with me, Mr Jenkins,' James said. 'The only advice I would offer is to argue in the privacy of your own home next time. And to keep your hands off one another.'

Charlie heaved his shoulders. 'I was having a fag break after an hour slaving away in a hot kitchen. She followed me out and it kicked off. She's had a few drinks.'

James didn't want to be drawn into a domestic dispute, so he looked at his watch and told Charlie that he had to return to the restaurant. Charlie then turned and headed back down the alley as James went inside.

He was surprised to see that Sonia was already back behind the bar alongside a young woman named Beth who appeared to be a regular member of the bar staff. Sonia caught his eye and mouthed a silent 'sorry' at him, which prompted him to smile at her. Annie noticed the exchange and gave him a questioning look.

'I heard what I thought might be an assault taking place in the alley,' he said. 'But when I went to look, I saw Sonia and Charlie having a row.'

He told Annie what he'd overheard.

'I'm expecting to see Janet at some point today so I'll ask her about it,' Annie said. 'But I really think that Sonia needs to call time on that relationship if Charlie did cheat on her. I know he's done it at least once before.'

They finished off the bottle of wine and decided to make a move. James paid the bill and was glad that Beth handled the transaction while Sonia served someone else at the other end of the bar.

Outside, the sky continued to be grey and oppressive, but it wasn't stopping people from making the most of the market and all it had to offer.

Annie wanted to check out the stalls before heading home, to get some things for dinner. James was happy to join her in the hope that it would make him feel more relaxed.

But just then his phone pinged with an incoming text. It was a message from the former colleague in the Met. The news did nothing to lift his mood.

Made some calls and chatted to the usual suspects. Sullivan hasn't been seen for days but one usually reliable snout reckons he's gone away on a Christmas break somewhere in the UK. Nobody seems to know where, though.

CHAPTER ELEVEN

The snow-covered market square was teeming with life and the festive spirit was almost palpable. Christmas songs were playing, children were squealing excitedly and the traders were doing brisk business.

James was glad to see that the bustle was providing Annie with a distraction. She was going from stall to stall, sniffing out bargains and loading up a carrier bag with ingredients for tonight's dinner.

But James wasn't able to shake off the unease that was building inside him. The text regarding Andrew Sullivan had raised more disturbing questions.

Why hadn't the guy been seen around for days? It was unusual because he was such a high-profile character at the clubs and boozers in his north London neighbourhood. And if he really was on a Christmas break away from the city, had he by any chance decided to spend it in Cumbria?

James had lied to Annie about the contents of the text so as not to alarm her. Thankfully she had believed him when he'd told her that it was from DCI Tanner requesting an update.

But the text wasn't the only thing playing on his mind. There were at least two other suspects in the frame now – Keith Patel and Daniel Curtis – even if there was no real evidence linking them to the anonymous threats yet. That they both just happened to have been on the streets near James and Annie's home around the time the parcel was placed on their doorstep was reason enough for them to be suspects, in James's opinion.

But who was to say they weren't back in their homes when the card for Father Silver was left in the church porch? According to him, it could have been put there during the night or early this morning.

Then, of course, there was the big unknown. Was this all just a bizarre hoax or a credible threat? Gut instinct told James it was the former, partly because of the melodramatic nature of the messages in the cards and the dead partridge. And the boss was right to be wary of upgrading it to something more serious at this early stage.

Anonymous threats, especially those delivered by post or by hand, were notoriously difficult to investigate, especially those without an obvious suspect or motive. In this case the perp teasingly referred to *Twelve days. Twelve murders. Twelve victims. And they all deserve what's coming to them.* But the message lacked specific information, with no names or references to gender. There was no clue as to the motive, either, other than that the victims were going to get what was coming to them.

'James, will you snap out of it?'

He'd been so lost in thought that he hadn't realised Annie

71

was trying to get his attention until he felt her tugging on his sleeve.

'Sorry, hon, I was miles away,' he said.

She was standing in front of him holding her phone.

'Janet Dyer just called me,' she said quietly. 'She's upset and has asked if I can pop over to her place for a chat. I suspect it's about Charlie going there. Would you mind? I can meet you at home. I won't be long and I've got all I need here.'

He nodded. 'Actually, that's fine with me. I feel I should be doing something so it'll give me a chance to go and have a word with Keith Patel now rather than tomorrow when I was planning to. If he does have anything to do with this then I might be able to nip it in the bud before it gets out of hand.'

'Well, since you'll be passing our house, you can drop the shopping off on the way,' she said, handing him the bag.

Father Silver had given James Keith Patel's address. He found it easily enough and it only took him ten minutes to get there after nipping into his own house and plonking the shopping on the kitchen table.

Patel's detached cottage was on a cobbled street and backed onto a stream that ran through the southern section of the village. Opposite the property was a spectacular view of the Cumbrian countryside: a wild, dramatic landscape shrouded in a pristine sheet of white.

James had a ready excuse for why he was paying him a visit, and he launched into it as soon the man opened his front door.

'Hello again, Mr Patel,' he said. 'I've dropped by to inform you that officers will be looking into the damage done to your

72

mother's grave. I've sent a full report and photographs to headquarters in Kendal, but I'd like to ask you a few quick questions if I may.'

After a couple of beats, Patel said, 'You'd better come in then. The priest just called to tell me he's cleaned the headstone. I'll be popping up there later to see for myself.'

Patel left it to James to close the door and then led the way into a small, untidy living room where two large radiators were belting out oppressive heat. There were no Christmas decorations and a strong smell of tobacco hung heavy in the air.

Patel lowered himself onto one of two threadbare armchairs and gestured for James to sit in the other. James removed his coat before doing so and took out his notebook.

There was more to see of Patel now that he had shed his outdoor gear. He had grey hair and a stocky frame that stretched the black polo sweater he was wearing. He looked pretty healthy despite the arthritis that Father Silver had said affected his knee joints and caused his slight limp.

'You mentioned earlier that vandals have struck twice before,' James said. 'Why do you think they pick on your mother's grave?'

'I should have thought that was bloody obvious,' Patel replied sharply. 'I'm a figure of hate in this village because I never miss an opportunity to condemn what happened to my mum. The medics told me she might have been alive for several days after she fell down the stairs, but she couldn't move because she broke so many bones and suffered a serious blow to the head. I dread to think what she went through as she lay there calling for help. But none of the so-called good neighbours bothered to check on her when she didn't appear.

I don't doubt it was because her skin was a different colour to theirs. Mum was always walking to the shop and tending the back garden. So they must have known that something wasn't right. And her carer, that moron Janet Dyer, was away that weekend and forgot to arrange for someone else to visit.'

'It was indeed a tragedy,' James said. 'Now, you mentioned earlier that everyone knows who the vandals are.'

'That's right. Joseph Paxton and Toby Moore. They're a couple of teenage hooligans who've vandalised the church itself and other landmarks in the village. But nothing ever happens to them because their parents and friends always give them an alibi.'

There was pure venom in his voice, and as he spoke his gaze seemed to go in and out of focus.

'Tell me this, Mr Patel,' James said. 'Have you ever been driven to seek retribution against the people you're angry with?'

'What exactly do you mean by that? Are you suggesting I've done something wrong? Has someone made an accusation against me? Because if so, it's a lie!'

'No, you haven't been accused of anything, Mr Patel. But, given what's happened to you, it's a question that needs to be asked.'

'Well, the answer is no – I haven't done anything that would land me in trouble, even though I've been tempted to on more than one occasion.'

Patel looked at his watch then and got abruptly to his feet, a clear signal that he was calling a halt to the conversation. 'Now, I don't think there's anything else I can tell you so if you don't mind, I've got things to do.'

James saw no point in asking more questions since he really didn't have enough grounds to turn it into a full-blown interrogation just yet. He stood and picked up his coat. 'Thank you for your time, Mr Patel. I'll make sure that you're informed of any progress my colleagues make in respect of your mother's grave.'

'I'm not going to build up my hopes, Detective. I know that your lot have got bigger crimes to solve, so this won't be treated as a priority.'

As James turned towards the door, he spotted something that caused his heart to trip. On top of a sideboard there was a pile of those now all-too-familiar Christmas cards. They and their envelopes had been taken out of the packet.

'It's funny you should have these,' James said, picking one up. 'Yesterday I received the exact same card.'

'The store has got a lot of them in and they're cheap,' Patel said.

'Have you sent any yet? It's late in the day if you want to ensure they get there before Christmas.'

'That's what I intend to do when you've gone. I'll put them in the post before the end of the day.'

James looked at him. 'It's worth saying that the one I got wasn't from a friend or relative. It contained an anonymous threat and I'm now in the process of finding out who it was from. Because I can assure you that I will.'

'Well, it wasn't from me,' Patel said indignantly. 'If I want to threaten someone, I'll do it to their face.'

'I'm not suggesting it was from you,' James said. 'But it's interesting to note that it was left on my doorstep early yesterday evening, about the time my wife saw you walking past our house . . .'

'So what? I have to walk past your place to get here. I do it every fucking day.'

'I appreciate that, Mr Patel, but it would be remiss of me not to wonder if there's a connection.'

'That sounds like another fucking accusation, Detective. Is that the real reason you came here – to see if I had anything to do with it?'

James shook his head. 'Not at all. I simply—'

Patel didn't let him finish. 'Get out of my house now. You're just like the rest of the bastards in this place. I'm guessing you've been put up to it by someone who saw a chance to land me in the shit. Well, I'm not having it. If you want to talk to me again then give me notice and I'll make sure I have a lawyer present.'

James knew he'd be wasting his time trying to reason with the man, so he put the card back down and walked along the hall to let himself out. The door was slammed shut behind him.

CHAPTER TWELVE

By the time Annie got home it was already dark. She'd spent longer with Janet Dyer than she'd expected to, as her friend had been angry and distraught, and had wanted a shoulder to cry on.

James was waiting for her and had made himself useful by peeling the potatoes for dinner and preparing the chicken so it was ready to roast.

He poured them each a glass of wine and they agreed that he would go first and tell Annie about his visit to Keith Patel's house.

She narrowed her eyes when he mentioned the Christmas cards on the sideboard.

'He was adamant that he didn't deliver one to me,' he said. 'And it was impossible to tell if he was lying. He came across as angry rather than panicked.'

James then told Annie what Patel had said about Janet Dyer not arranging for another carer to check on his mother in the days following her fall down the stairs.

This was Annie's cue to talk about her visit to Janet's house.

'She was upset because Charlie Jenkins gave her an earful when he went to see her this morning,' she said. 'To get her own back she phoned Sonia and told her she was lying when she denied sleeping with him. She admitted to having an affair with Charlie, and that she'd made the mistake of telling someone. And that someone just happened to be Daniel Curtis's father, Ron. Mr Curtis was indiscreet and told one of his mates who then told someone else. It eventually got back to Sonia.'

The more James learned about the people of Kirkby Abbey, the more he was beginning to wonder if they had made a huge mistake by moving here.

The following hour or so was spent preparing dinner, drinking wine and trying to relax.

Annie knew that James wasn't looking forward to playing host to her uncle, but he promised her he'd be on his best behaviour.

When six o'clock came and Bill still hadn't turned up, she called him on his mobile. It went to voicemail so she left a message. By six-thirty, they were both becoming concerned.

Annie called The King's Head and asked to be put through to his room. The landlady, Martha Grooms, said he had left the pub earlier after telling her he was spending the evening with an old pal in the nearby village of Ravenstonedale. Annie asked her to check if his car was still parked out back and she was told that it wasn't.

By seven o'clock they accepted that he wouldn't be coming and started on the dinner, though with a marked lack of enthusiasm.

'I'm really worried,' Annie said. 'What if something's happened to him? I just don't believe he simply forgot about it.'

James shrugged. 'Maybe he's getting up to no good some-where. You said yourself he was acting weird.'

As the evening wore on, Annie became increasingly concerned. She tried and failed to reach her uncle by phone several more times. Just before she and James went to bed at 11 p.m. she put in another call to The King's Head and spoke to Martha again.

'He still hasn't arrived back,' the woman said. 'But he has a key so he'll just let himself in through the accommodation entrance after we close the bar and restaurant.'

Annie eventually went to bed but struggled to sleep. She kept wondering where her Uncle Bill was and also why so many disturbing things were happening all at once in the village.

CHAPTER THIRTEEN

It's almost midnight and most of the village is sleeping. But not me. I'm doing what I usually do at this time – walking the dog before sloping off to bed.

I'm a creature of habit, which is one of my many faults. But the truth is I enjoy this time alone with my precious Yorkie, Daisy. She doesn't judge me, or find fault with everything I do. She's loyal and loving and she never lets me down. Unlike some of the people in my life.

I take the same route as always, along the narrow pavement to the store that sells hiking and fishing equipment, then left over the little footbridge that crosses the stream.

The snow has been falling all evening and I'm sure the fells will be covered for the festive period. That's good news for those who won't need to get around. But in heavy snow the countryside can be treacherous, the roads impassable, and villages and towns are often completely cut off from the outside world.

I can hear the wind whimpering in the trees on the fellside, but there's not much to see because the landscape has been consumed by the darkness.

I draw on my ciggy and expel a stream of smoke. Then I let Daisy off the lead. She runs around excitedly before crouching down and emptying her bowels.

It's been a bad day but at last I'm feeling relaxed. Behind me silence has closed over the village like a shroud, and lights twinkle in some of the windows.

Suddenly Daisy starts barking at the ancient beech tree up ahead. The tree marks the point where we always turn around and head back towards home.

Daisy doesn't usually react like this so I assume she's spotted a squirrel or a fox. I call her back but she stays where she is, in a state of high excitement.

I drop my cigarette and walk towards her.

'What's up, girl?' I say to her. 'Has something creeped you out?'

When I get to within a few feet of the tree a figure steps out from behind it. A shiver grabs hold of my spine and I let out a sharp cry of alarm. The figure is ghostly and indistinct, and I can't tell if it's a man or a woman.

I start to speak, but my words are cut off as the figure rushes towards me waving what looks like a long-bladed knife.

Before I can react an explosion of pain erupts in my chest and I hear a horrible scream issue from between my lips.

My legs give way and my eyes lose focus. But then I'm stabbed again, this time in the stomach, and I drop onto the snow like a sack of cement.

The last thing I hear before blacking out is a voice that says, 'This is no more than you deserve.'

CHAPTER FOURTEEN

Sunday December 18th

On Sunday morning, Kirkby Abbey was covered in a blanket of snow several inches deep. It had stopped falling in the early hours, so it wasn't causing serious disruption, but tree branches were hanging low with the weight of it and the village looked like an unfinished painting.

The experts were still warning of more to come, saying that Cumbria was among the counties most likely to be battered by severe blizzards over the coming days. Their advice to hikers was not to get caught in isolated parts of the Yorkshire Dales and Lake District.

James and Annie had no firm plans for most of the day ahead, but they had decided to go along to the carol singing that was due to take place in the village square at ten o'clock that morning.

It was seven when James climbed out of bed and started making the tea after another disturbed sleep. Annie had kept him awake for much of the night worrying about her uncle.

James wasn't so concerned about 'Old Bill,' as he often

referred to him. He didn't know him that well – having met him only about a dozen times since marrying Annie – but he was sure the man was capable of looking after himself. After all, he'd been living alone in Penrith since his wife divorced him eighteen years ago.

According to Annie, he had always been a difficult bloke to get on with, and had a reputation for being unreliable. In fact, he failed to turn up for their wedding even though he'd been sent an official invitation weeks before. His excuse was that he hadn't realised it fell on the same day he was flying back from a work-related trip to Ireland.

As soon as she was up, Annie tried again to reach Bill on his mobile. This time, much to her surprise, he answered straight away. Annie put her phone on speaker so that James could hear what Bill had to say for himself.

'I'm so very sorry, Annie, but I really don't recall you inviting me over,' he said. 'I'd already told Sid Myers that I'd visit him in Ravenstonedale. We used to work together but hadn't seen each other in years. It wasn't a great evening, as it turned out, because I couldn't drink and had forgotten how dull the man can be when you're sober.'

'So what time did you get back?'

'Just after midnight. And it wasn't a pleasant drive in the snow either.'

'I tried ringing you throughout the evening, Bill.'

'I can see that from the list of missed calls on my phone. But I forgot to take it with me and left it on the bed.'

'So will we see you today?'

'Of course. I'll come over whenever you want me to and I promise not to forget this time.'

'Well, if you're interested, James and I are joining in the

carol singing in the village square. It starts at ten, weather permitting.'

'That sounds good. It'll give me time to have a shower and breakfast. They do a tasty fry-up in this place and it comes with the room.'

'So we'll see you there, then.'

'You will indeed.'

Annie hung up and turned to James.

'It still makes no sense to me,' she said. 'I really don't believe he forgot that I invited him. We only had the conversation yesterday morning, for heaven's sake.'

'Maybe he didn't forget,' James said. 'Maybe he just couldn't stand the thought of having dinner with us.'

Annie shook her head. 'That can't be it. He didn't have to join us here for Christmas. He chose to. No, I've got a feeling that it's more complicated. There's something he's not telling me and I'm determined to find out what the bloody hell it is.'

Singing carols in the open with lots of other people had never been James's or Annie's idea of fun but they were joining in this year because Annie was keen to take part in community activities. So, they walked hand in hand through the village, the snow softening their steps.

The air was cold but invigorating, and the views of the stark white landscape in the distance were awe-inspiring. It didn't surprise James that Cumbria was considered one of the UK's most beautiful counties, with its soaring fells, amazing waterfalls and stunning lakes. No wonder it had inspired so many famous stories and poems.

And he had to admit that strolling through Kirkby Abbey was much more pleasant that traversing the grimy streets of

Tottenham. At least here the air wasn't filled with toxic fumes and the constant roar of traffic.

This, to him, was the upside of living in Cumbria. It was quiet, picturesque, and a safe distance from the mess that had become of his beloved London.

It wasn't enough to stop him feeling a little homesick, though. And it wasn't just the job in the Met that he missed. It was the vibrancy of the city, the fact that shops were open 24/7, and that virtually every member of his close-knit family lived only a short drive away.

But he accepted that he was going to have to get used to this new life, if only for a short time. Keeping Annie safe was his main priority and it always would be.

There were between seventy and a hundred people in the square by the time they got there. According to Annie, that was many more than had shown up in previous years. They were gathered on one side of the Christmas tree waiting for Father Silver to get things going.

He had entered the spirit of the occasion by wearing a Santa Claus hat that was in striking contrast to his black overcoat and gloves. James suspected that he was the reason for the high turn-out. The priest was a popular figure in the village and had organised the carol singing for years. But sadly, this was likely going to be the last time due to his illness. There was no doubting he would be missed, along with his church, which had for so long been a focal point for the community.

But as he waved and smiled at the people who had turned up, it was clear that he wasn't going to let his illness cast a shadow over the event.

James and Annie took up position at the back of the crowd

and were handed leaflets with the order of service and lyrics. The first carol was going to be *Joy to the World* followed by *O Come All Ye Faithful*.

As the singing was about to begin there was still no sign of Bill. Annie tried to call him but it seemed his phone was switched off.

'Don't worry about it,' James told her. 'He's probably on his way or somewhere in the crowd.'

On the dot of ten Father Silver began to speak. He welcomed everyone and said that he was delighted to see that so many people had turned up for what promised to be a memorable occasion.

Before he could burst into song, however, someone started screaming. All eyes moved from Father Silver to a woman who was running towards them along the pavement. It was clear from the terrified look on her face that something very bad had happened.

James didn't recognise the woman. She was wearing hiking boots and had a rucksack strapped to her back.

She stopped screaming as she approached the crowd and started to shout hysterically.

'There's a body in the field. And lots of blood. Someone needs to call the police.'

James moved like a greyhound out of the traps. He reached the woman just as she entered the square and was already holding up his warrant card.

'I'm Detective Inspector James Walker,' he said. 'Please calm down and talk to me. Are you by yourself?'

She nodded and took a couple of deep breaths before responding.

'I'm staying at a bed and breakfast here in the village,' she said. 'I was starting out on a short walk when I saw a figure, a person, lying in the snow. When I got up close, I saw the blood.'

'Are you sure this person is dead?'

'I'm positive. I called out and nudged the body with my foot, but there was no movement. And the face is covered with snow, so I don't know if it's a man or woman. You should go see for yourself. It's on the other side of the stream next to the old beech tree. Just across the footbridge. Oh God, it's horrible. I can't believe it.'

'Okay, well—'

'And that's not all,' she continued breathlessly, her voice high and brittle. 'There's a small dog as well. It looks to be frozen stiff.'

James reached out and placed a hand gently on her shoulder, aware at the same time that others had closed in on them, eager to find out what was going on.

'I'll go straight over there and take a look,' he said. 'But before I do, please tell me your name.'

'It's Fiona. Fiona Birch. I'm spending Christmas here with a few hiking friends but they don't arrive until this afternoon.'

'Right, well, you wait here, Fiona, and I'll take a statement from you when I get back.'

He turned to the group that had gathered behind him and saw that they were at least twenty strong, and included Annie and Father Silver.

'Now what this lady has told me needs investigating,' he said out loud. 'While I do that you must all stay here because if a crime has been committed, I don't want to risk anyone destroying or contaminating possible evidence.'

Annie stepped forward and gently grasped Fiona's arm.

'Just go check, James,' she said. 'And I suggest you hurry up.'

From the look she gave him it was obvious they were thinking the same thing – that it wouldn't be long before curiosity drove some people across the footbridge and into the field.

He broke into a run and it took him only minutes to reach the little bridge. He had walked across it himself only a couple of weeks ago, when Annie had taken him to see some of the finest views of the surrounding countryside, so he was familiar with the field in question and the ancient beech tree that Fiona had mentioned.

He saw the body when he was some way off, a dark bump rising like a rock out of the smooth white snow.

There was only one set of footprints leading away from him, which must have been left by Fiona. He walked parallel with them until he reached the body. The size and shape told him it was a man but be couldn't be sure.

Fiona had been right about the blood. There was a lot of it, bright red stains that spread in shapeless patches across the parts of the figure not covered by snow.

James knelt down next to the body and flicked the flakes from the face with a gloved hand.

As the grey, swollen features were revealed, he saw that he was indeed looking down at a male. It was clear that he was dead and that he must have been lying here for hours.

It took James several seconds longer to realise that he recognised the face. It belonged to Charlie Jenkins, landlord of The White Hart pub.

CHAPTER FIFTEEN

James felt his breath stall as he stared down at the body of Charlie Jenkins. At the same time his heart started racing, punching at his chest like a steam hammer.

Before touching the body again, he called it in and told control that backup and a SOCO team, plus a pathologist, needed to be dispatched right away.

He then took great care to brush the snow from the torso. Jenkins was wearing a thick coat that was soaked through. Most of the blood had formed on the chest and stomach, and that was where James spotted the holes in the material.

He had seen enough knife wounds in his career to know that the man had been stabbed at least twice and with brute force. He would leave it to the scene of crime technicians to delve beneath the layers of clothing. The last thing he wanted to do was damage or destroy vital pieces of evidence.

But there was no doubting the fact that Jenkins had been murdered, and it had happened at some time during the night or early hours of this morning.

James stood and started to frantically process the scene, not an easy task given that the whole area was under a layer of snow. He then remembered what the woman who had stumbled upon the body had said about a dog.

It didn't take him long to spot the small mound a few yards away. He stepped over to it and crouched down for a closer look. It wasn't covered by as much snow due to the overhanging branches of the beech tree, so James could tell that it was a small, brown Yorkshire Terrier. There didn't appear to be any blood on or around it so he suspected it must have frozen to death while remaining at its owner's side.

James gritted his teeth and tried to think, and the first thing that popped into his mind was the chilling message written on the card he'd received.

Twelve days. Twelve murders. Twelve victims. And they all deserve what's coming to them.

So was Charlie Jenkins the first victim? Was his murder proof that it wasn't a hoax after all? Or did this have nothing to do with the Twelve Days of Christmas warning? Was it simply a hideous coincidence?

More questions came thick and fast. Where was Charlie's wife, Sonia? If he had been here for most of the night, why hadn't she come looking for him or raised the alarm? Was it conceivable that she was the person who had killed him, perhaps in a jealous rage over his affair with Janet Dyer?

James looked back towards the village, which was about a hundred yards away. A number of buildings, including The White Hart pub, overlooked the field. But it was extremely unlikely that anyone would have witnessed the attack from any of the windows. There was no lighting, and as well as the dark, the falling snow would have reduced visibility.

James hoped it wouldn't take the forensic officers long to reach the village. The crime scene already presented them with a major challenge, and if it started snowing again their task would be even more difficult.

He took photos of the body from various angles and a couple of the dog. Then he called Tanner and broke the news.

'There's no way I can get there today so you're in charge of this case as senior investigating officer,' the DCI said. 'I'll get DS Stevens to assist. He's on call. And I'll warn the press office to be ready for an avalanche of enquiries.'

'Thank you, sir.'

'Meanwhile, we can only hope that it's a one-off and has nothing to do with that message in the card. But if it is, then we've got a big fucking problem on our hands.'

'I agree,' James said. 'So how do we play it, guv? Should we disclose the existence of the message at this stage?'

'No way. I don't want everyone to panic, especially since we still can't be sure that there is a link. We can certainly issue a warning to people in the village to be on their guard, though. For now, concentrate on those who might have harboured a grudge against the victim. And it seems to me that his wife should be at the top of the list after what happened between them yesterday.'

'She'll be my first port of call,' James said. 'But if she doesn't have anything to do with it then I'm about to break the news to her that her husband has been murdered.'

James knew he should have stayed with the body until backup arrived, but he didn't know how long that would be. He

91

decided to head back towards the village to make the crowd aware that the situation was under control. He would also get someone to help him seal off the crime scene.

He knew that once he made it known that there had been a murder the news would spread like wildfire. And he felt sure there would be those who would demonstrate a distinct lack of sympathy because Charlie had betrayed and humiliated his wife.

This thought prompted James to recall another line from the message in the card.

And they all deserve what's coming to them.

He knew well enough that not all killers believe their victims deserve to die. Most resort to murder for selfish reasons, driven, among other things, by hatred, greed, envy and sometimes a warped sense of justice.

In London, fatal stabbings were all too common. James had investigated dozens of them during his time with the Met, and most were carried out by perps who did not know their victims. But Kirkby Abbey was a world away from those inner-city areas where gang wars are rife and muggers lurk around every street corner. For that reason, James believed that Jenkins would have known his killer. Perhaps they were out walking together when the attack took place. Or maybe Jenkins was taken by surprise and the knife was plunged into him before he even realised what was happening.

Back at the square the crowd was waiting with bated breath. James gulped air into his lungs as he tried to work out how best to handle the situation. He needed to persuade them to clear the square, but he sensed that wasn't going to be easy.

A man broke away from the crowd as he approached and hurried towards him. It was Giles Keegan, the retired detective who used to be based at the Kendal office.

'Is it true?' he asked excitedly. 'Is there a body?'

Keegan was a big fella in his mid-sixties who stayed in shape by regularly walking the fells. He was over six feet tall with a barrel chest and a large, square head that rested on wide shoulders.

James found his presence somewhat reassuring, and it gave him an idea.

He stopped in front of the ex-cop, and said, 'I need you to listen in to what I'm about to announce, Giles. And then I'd appreciate your help in keeping things steady here until the troops arrive. They're on their way.'

'Just tell me what you want me to do,' Keegan replied. 'I'm at your disposal.'

James thanked him and got straight on with addressing the crowd. As he spoke, he took in their worried expressions and noted that Fiona the hiker was standing between Annie and Father Silver.

'First let me explain for those who don't know me that I'm Detective Inspector James Walker, serving with the Cumbria force, and I recently moved into the village,' he said. 'I can confirm that there is a man's body in the field on the other side of the stream.'

He paused there and waited for the ripple of nervous chatter to die down before continuing.

'The circumstances of this person's death have yet to be established, and I would ask you all to stay clear of that area until it's been processed by forensic officers. Needless to say, in these circumstances, the carol singing will have to be postponed. It would be helpful if you could leave the square immediately to make way for police vehicles that will be here shortly.

'However, if any of you saw anything last night or early this morning that might in any way be relevant to this, then please make yourselves known to me.'

Inevitably there were questions, and the first came from a man at the front.

'Do you know who he is?' the man said.

'I do, but I'm not at liberty to reveal the identity until relatives have been informed.'

'Was he murdered?' someone else shouted.

James held up his arms.

'Look, I realise what a terrible shock this is to you all, but I'm not in a position to answer questions at this stage. So please be patient and do not venture onto the field. When my colleagues arrive an incident centre will be set up to deal with enquiries.'

He turned away from the crowd and lowered his voice to speak to Giles Keegan.

'You can help by making sure that nobody gets close to the body before backup arrives,' he said. 'The quickest way to the field is across the footbridge so that's the best place to position yourself.'

'Consider it done,' Keegan said. 'I take it we're dealing with a murder?'

James nodded. 'The victim was stabbed at least twice and it seems to have happened while he was walking his dog.'

'Is he a local man?'

'Charlie Jenkins, the pub landlord.'

'Holy shit.'

James shifted his gaze from Keegan to The White Horse pub, which was thirty or so yards away to his right.

It appeared to be still closed, but there was a figure standing at one of the upstairs windows. James was pretty sure it was Sonia Jenkins, and she was looking down on the square.

CHAPTER SIXTEEN

The crowd showed no sign of dispersing even as the marked police cars started arriving in the square.

James was there to direct them along the road to the scene of the crime.

Both Annie and Father Silver tried to grab his attention, but he asked them to bear with him as he instructed the uniformed officers to encourage people to return to their homes.

DS Stevens arrived in a pool car behind the forensics van. James filled them all in without referring to the threat in the Christmas card. But Stevens let it be known that the DCI had told him about it over the phone.

'Keep it to yourself for now along with the victim's name,' James said. 'I don't want his identity known until I've talked to the wife.'

'Is she a suspect?' Stevens asked.

'Right now everyone in this village is,' James said.

'So what do you want me to do?'

'Go and see what turns up when the techies start on the

corpse,' James said. 'And get someone to coordinate a search of the area around it. I don't expect much to come of it because of the snow, but we have to try.'

James then pointed out Fiona Birch to one of the uniforms.

'She's the woman who came across the body,' he said. 'Take down her details and a statement. Then escort her back to whichever B&B she's staying in.'

He then took Annie to one side and told her about Charlie Jenkins. Her eyes stretched wide and she clamped her top lip between her teeth.

'Oh Jesus,' she said. 'That's terrible. Does Sonia know?'

'That's what I'm about to find out,' James said. 'After I've spoken to her I intend to talk to Janet Dyer, so can you text me her address and phone number?'

'You don't seriously think that either of them had anything to do with it, do you?'

He shrugged. 'Who knows? I've got to start somewhere, and since they both had a bust-up with Charlie yesterday, they have to be in the frame.'

'But that's crazy. What about whoever is behind those messages? Isn't it more likely that Charlie is the first of the victims and you were wrong to assume it was a prank?'

'Look, I don't want you to mention the cards to anyone, Annie,' he said. 'We need to keep it to ourselves for now. Charlie's murder will be enough to put the fear of God into people. Telling them he could be the first of many won't make them any safer, but it will result in mass hysteria and that'll hinder the investigation.'

'But don't you think that the villagers should know what we know?'

'All we actually know is that someone scrawled an anonymous

threat inside a Christmas card,' James said. 'As of this moment we have no idea if it's connected to what has happened to Charlie. The most likely scenario is that his murder is simply a coincidence.'

'But what if it isn't. What if—'

'Annie, just drop it for now. Please. I need to get this investigation started and then take it one step at a time. It could be that by the end of the day we're able to identify Charlie's killer and rule out any connection with the cards.'

Annie drew a tremulous breath and nodded.

'Okay, fair enough. I'm sorry. I appreciate you're better equipped to handle this than I am. It's all so scary.'

'I know, hon. But I suggest you go home and find something to occupy your mind. I'm going to be tied up all day now.'

'Very well,' she said. 'First I'll see if I can find Bill. He still hasn't made an appearance.'

'Ah, good luck with that. And don't forget to text me Janet's details.'

James kissed Annie on the cheek and then headed towards The White Hart. He noticed that Sonia Jenkins was no longer peering out of the upstairs window. She was now standing in front of the entrance and waving at him.

CHAPTER SEVENTEEN

As James walked towards Sonia, he saw that she was wearing a dark blue dressing gown. Her hair hadn't been brushed and it exploded from her head in thick brown tangles. It made him wonder if she had only just got out of bed.

'What's all the commotion?' she asked as he approached her. 'I was expecting carol singing this morning, not a chorus of police sirens.'

'I'll tell you about it inside,' James said. 'Are you by yourself?'

'I am at the moment. Beth and Josh, our chef, are due any minute, and I'm guessing my husband is out walking the dog. I just went to the spare room to wake him up, but he wasn't there and the dog's gone, too.'

'So you sleep in separate rooms.'

'Only when we fall out, which up until now hasn't been very often. But I can't imagine sharing a bed with him any time soon.'

They stepped inside, and James pushed the door closed

behind them. Sonia walked over to the bar and rested her elbow on it, turning to face him.

'I appreciate you taking the time to come over and tell me what's going on,' she said. 'I couldn't get anyone else's attention.'

James slipped out of his coat and draped it over the nearest chair. Sonia watched him, a frown forming on her face.

'So has something really bad happened?' she said. 'Or is it another case of a hiker getting lost on the fells? That's usually why cop cars turn up here.'

James looked at her and couldn't tell whether she was putting on an act or if she really didn't know.

'I'm afraid I have some bad news about your husband, Mrs Jenkins,' he said.

'Charlie! What's he done now?'

James gestured towards one of the sofas.

'I think we should sit down. What I'm about to—'

'Just spit it out, Detective. Has my husband been involved in an accident or has he upset Janet Dyer again?'

An image of Charlie's body lying in the snow resurfaced in James's mind. He felt his insides clench up.

'Your husband is dead, Mrs Jenkins,' he said. 'His body was found a short time ago in the field behind these buildings.'

At first she just stared at him, mouth open, forehead creased above raised eyebrows. Then she started shaking her head.

'No, that can't be right,' she said, her voice cracking. 'Please tell me it isn't true.'

'I wish I could, Mrs Jenkins, but I've seen your husband's body myself and there's no mistake.'

She seemed suddenly unsteady on her feet, so James held onto her arm and guided her to a chair. He sat down next to her and studied her expression. It didn't appear that she was faking it. The shock seemed genuine.

'I don't understand,' she said. 'When did it happen? And how?'

'The exact time of death has yet to be established,' James said. 'But it seems certain that he was killed late last night. When was the last time you saw him?'

Tears were clouding her eyes now and the words rasped in her throat as she spoke

'After we closed up. It was almost midnight. We weren't talking and I'd had a lot to drink so I went to bed. I heard Charlie say he was taking Daisy for a walk, which he does every night.'

'And you didn't hear him return?'

'I crashed out as soon as my head hit the pillow. So no, I didn't.'

'I see. Well, we—'

'What about Daisy?' she cut in. 'Our dog. Where is she?'

'I was about to tell you, Mrs Jenkins,' James said. 'A Yorkshire Terrier was found close to Charlie's body. I'm sorry to say she's also dead, probably from the cold.'

A great sob escaped her, and suddenly her face was red and distorted.

'I c-can't believe this,' she stammered. 'It feels like I'm dreaming. That none of this is real.'

'Is there someone I can contact who can come and be with you?' James asked.

Sonia ignored the question and shot to her feet. 'Take me to him,' she blurted. 'I need to see for myself. I can't just take your word for it. What if it's a mistake and he's still alive?'

James stood to join her and rested a hand on her shoulder.

'That won't be possible, Mrs Jenkins. The field is now a crime scene and forensic officers are working there. But I can assure you it's not a mistake. You will be asked to formally identify your husband, but not yet.'

She sat back down and started crying, sobs wracking her body. She produced a tissue from her dressing gown pocket and started to dab at her eyes.

'You still haven't told me what happened,' she said, her voice laced with despair. 'How did Charlie die?'

There was no easy way to tell her, so James just came right out with it.

'It appears he was attacked while walking across the field and stabbed at least twice,' he said. 'I suspect he died from his wounds almost immediately.'

More tears came then and this time she buried her face in her hands.

James's heart went out to her, but at the same time he knew he had to keep an open mind. He had interviewed people in the past who had convinced him at first that they were innocent through performances worthy of an Oscar.

So, despite the tears, Sonia Jenkins had to be their prime suspect for now. Just hours before her husband was killed, they'd had a serious row over Janet Dyer, during which James had witnessed Sonia telling Charlie that she wished he was dead.

Was it possible that she had followed him when he left the pub last night? Had she gone armed with a knife, intending to get revenge?

She stopped crying abruptly and stared at him, as though reading his mind.

'Do you have any idea who did it?' she asked.

'Not yet, we don't,' James replied.

'Please don't tell me you think it was me, because it wasn't,' she said. 'Of course, I was angry with him and deeply hurt. He had an affair three years ago and it almost split us up. He swore to me it wouldn't happen again. But I would never kill him. In fact, I know I would have forgiven him again in time.'

'You must appreciate that I have to treat everyone as a suspect until they can be ruled out, and that includes you, Mrs Jenkins,' James said.

'I've told you exactly what happened last night, and you have to believe me. I could never hurt anyone, especially not Charlie. And Daisy meant the world to me. Do you really think I would leave her out there to freeze to death?'

'I hear what you're saying, and I can assure you I'm not jumping to any conclusions, Mrs Jenkins. But let me ask you this: Have you any idea who might have wanted to kill your husband?'

'Well, you can start with that cow Janet Dyer,' she said. 'She was really pissed off with him for going to her house yesterday. And if he had ended their relationship she probably wanted to get her own back.'

Just then the door to the pub opened and a man and a woman entered. James recognised Beth the barmaid and assumed the guy was Josh the chef.

'Sorry we're late,' Beth said when she spotted Sonia. 'But all hell has broken out and . . .'

She trailed off mid-sentence when she realised that the atmosphere in the room was charged and that her boss was clearly distressed.

'What is it, Sonia?' she said. 'What on earth is wrong?'

It was up to James to put the pair of them in the picture. They were already aware that a body had been found and that was why the police had descended on Kirkby Abbey. But they were shocked to learn that the dead man was Charlie Jenkins.

James told them the pub would have to remain closed and asked them if they would sit with Sonia for a while. He learned from Sonia that her parents were still alive and living in Leeds, and her twenty-two-year-old daughter, Maddie, was living and working as a nanny in Dubai. Charlie had a mother in York and a brother in Sheffield.

He asked Beth to write down their contact details and told Sonia that he would make sure they were all told what had happened.

'I want to break the news to Maddie myself,' Sonia said. 'I'll call her.'

'Are you sure?'

She nodded. 'I can't let a stranger do it.'

James fully understood where she was coming from. He knew that in her position he would feel the same way.

'I have to go and see what's going on, Mrs Jenkins,' he said. 'But I'll arrange for an officer to come and stay with you. He or she will answer any questions you have and keep you informed of progress with the investigation. I'll come back and see you in a little while.'

She looked up at him, her eyes pleading. 'You have to find out who did this to Charlie. He was far from perfect, but he didn't deserve to be murdered like that.'

James nodded. 'I promise I will do everything I can to find whoever did this. In the meantime, I'd like your permission for us to go through your husband's belongings. It's possible we'll find something that will provide us with vital information.'

'Do whatever you have to,' Sonia said, before breaking down in tears again.

CHAPTER EIGHTEEN

There were still dozens of people in the square when James exited The White Hart. They were mostly huddled together in groups or being spoken to by uniformed officers.

It was much gloomier now, thanks to a threatening mass of dark cloud that hung over the village, looking ready to unleash another pile of snow.

He picked out one of the uniforms he'd never met before, and asked her to go and stay with Sonia Jenkins.

'Don't let her out of your sight,' he said. 'And call me if there's a problem. I'll be back shortly.'

As he started walking in the direction of the field he heard someone call out his name. He turned to see Father Silver striding towards him after breaking away from a group that included the school's headmistress, Lorna Manning, and Peter King from the grocery store.

'I've been hoping to catch you, Detective Walker,' the priest said. 'I think we need to talk.'

James guessed what was on the priest's mind. He'd want

to know if there was a link between the body and the card delivered to the church.

Before engaging him in conversation, though, James made sure there was no one else close enough to hear them.

Father Silver's face was pinched and solemn. He was no longer wearing the Santa Claus hat and his scalp was shiny beneath what little hair he had.

'How much do you know, Father?' James asked him without preamble.

'I know that a body has been found in the field on the other side of the footbridge,' the priest replied. 'According to rumours that are already circulating, it's a man and he was murdered. I heard what the woman who came across him said about the blood. Now I want you to tell me if you think it's got anything to do with the cards we received.'

'It's too early to know for sure, but I very much doubt it,' James said. 'You haven't told anyone about the messages, have you?'

'Of course not. You asked me not to and I completely understand why. But I would like to know who the victim is. You were seen going into The White Hart just now, so it's got people wondering if it's Mr Jenkins.'

'It is,' James said. 'I've just informed his wife and she's naturally very distraught. He was out walking his dog when it happened.'

The priest made the sign of the cross on his chest.

'If it's all right with you I'll go and do my best to help comfort her,' he said.

'By all means. But be aware that she's a suspect. If she says anything that makes you in the least bit suspicious, you must let me know.'

'Of course, but I have to tell you, Detective Walker, that I'm not as confident as you are that this has nothing to do with the messages in the cards. It seems like too much of a coincidence.'

'But coincidences do happen, Father,' James said. 'So why don't you pray that what we're dealing with here is exactly that.'

James carried on towards the footbridge and on the way he met Giles Keegan, who was heading back to the square.

'There's a uniform on the bridge now so I'm no longer needed,' Keegan said. 'But it was a good thing you asked me to go there when you did. I managed to stop two people venturing onto the field to have a look.'

'Thanks for your help, Giles,' James said.

'You're welcome. I had a brief chat with DS Stevens who, as you might know, I worked with for a time. I told him to call on me if he feels there's anything more I can do to help. I hope that was okay.'

James experienced a jolt of irritation. He wanted to tell Keegan that he should have spoken to him first as he was the most senior officer, rather than the DS. But he held back and said, 'Of course, Giles. You might be retired but you're still one of us. Did you know Charlie well?'

'Quite well, I suppose. I've been a regular at The White Hart for years. He was an affable guy and we sometimes played cards together. But it's worth you knowing that he hasn't always been faithful to his wife. Not so long ago he got caught out having an affair, but she forgave him.'

'Do you think she could have done it?'

The question took Keegan by surprise and he gave it some thought before responding.

'I suppose it's possible,' he said. 'We both know from experience that everyone has it in them to react violently if they're pushed hard enough. And it could be that in Sonia's case she was emboldened by booze. You might not be aware that she has a bit of a drink problem.'

'How do you know?'

'Well, it's been obvious for ages to anyone who visits The White Hart on a regular basis. I lost count of the number of times Charlie told her to go and sleep it off and to stop drinking the profits. It could be quite embarrassing at times.'

James checked his watch. 'Look, I'd like to have a longer chat with you, Giles, but not right now. Can we get together later so I can pick your brain? DCI Tanner told me that you know everything there is to know about this village and the people who live here.'

He grinned. 'Just call me. You have my number. I live by myself so anytime will be fine. As far as I know this is the first murder ever committed in Kirkby Abbey so I'd like nothing more than to help solve it, even though I'm retired.'

At the crime scene, a lot had been achieved in a short space of time and SOCOs in pale blue protective overalls were going about their business with grim determination.

All the snow had been removed from Charlie's body and the forensic pathologist, Dr Pam Flint, was carrying out a close examination of the wounds.

Daisy the dog had been lifted out of the snow and placed on a blanket.

About a dozen uniformed officers were carrying out a search of the immediate area and a few villagers could be seen watching from a distance.

James noticed that the ancient beech tree stood between

where the body lay and the rear of The White Hart. He was glad because it meant that Sonia wouldn't be able to see her husband.

DS Stevens was watching the pathologist working on the body, and as James approached him, he said, 'Any joy with the wife, guv?'

'She claims that the last time she saw him was when he took the dog out for a walk just before midnight,' James said. 'They've been sleeping in separate rooms and when she got up this morning she saw that he wasn't in his bed and assumed he'd gone out for another walk.'

James relayed what else Sonia had said and told Stevens about the couple's marriage problems.

'It got quite nasty over the past couple of days,' James said. 'I bore witness to it myself only yesterday, when I saw them having a spat.'

He described what he'd seen in the alley next to the pub and what Annie said had happened after the school nativity play.

'So what does your gut tell you?' Stevens asked.

James shrugged. 'That Sonia Jenkins might or might not have murdered her husband. She had motive and opportunity, but she seemed genuinely shocked and upset when I told her that he was dead.'

'So is she the only suspect we have?'

James told him about Janet Dyer and said they needed to find out if Charlie had any enemies.

'I think we should bring in more help,' Stevens said.

'I agree. Meanwhile, I've asked uniforms to carry out a door-to-door along the road leading to the square, to find out if anyone saw or heard anything late last night.'

James shifted his attention to the pathologist, Pam, who was still crouching next to the body.

This was the first time their paths had crossed because none of the cases he had so far dealt with in his new role had involved a corpse. But she had a solid reputation and was highly regarded by his colleagues in Kendal.

He was about to introduce himself when she stood, lowered her face mask, and turned towards him.

'You must be Detective Walker,' she said. 'DS Stevens here told me you're SIO on this case.'

'That's correct. It's good to meet you.'

'Likewise. But we'll save the handshake until later so that I don't cover you in blood.'

She had a stern face and deep voice, and James took an instant liking to her.

'So what can you tell us about our victim?' he said.

'As you're probably already aware, there are stab wounds to the chest and stomach that were inflicted by a long-bladed knife,' she said. 'Either one of them could have proved fatal. There are no obvious defence wounds so I'm guessing he was taken by surprise. It could be that his killer jumped out from behind that tree over there and attacked him. As for time of death, I would say around midnight.

'But these are very much initial observations. I'll be able to tell you more once I get him back to the mortuary. I've asked for the body to be picked up as soon as possible, before the bad weather closes in.'

'What about his dog?' James said.

'I've carried out a cursory examination and can tell you that there are no surface wounds of any kind. The poor thing almost certainly froze to death. I gather the temperature

110

dropped to minus twelve last night and that's seriously low for a dog that size. I suspect she didn't want to leave her owner.'

As Pam crouched down again next to the body, Stevens told James that he had been through the victim's pockets and all he'd been carrying was a set of keys and a mobile phone. Both items had been bagged and were in the forensic van.

'I tried to check the phone,' Stevens said. 'But it's password-protected so we'll need to get the techies to have a look.'

The DS then raised the subject of the message in the Christmas card.

'So what's our position on it, guv?' he said. 'Are we taking the view that this could be the first of a series of murders or do we treat it as a one-off that's unconnected to the threat?'

'That's an issue I'm grappling with,' James said. 'And I realise that it's going to seriously affect how we move forward with the investigation.'

'You're not wrong there, guv. In fact, I'm already struggling to get my brain around it. Take Sonia Jenkins, for instance. I accept it's quite possible she killed her husband in a fit of rage, but I can't imagine her sending you that card or the dead partridge. Or threatening to kill a bunch of other people because she believes they deserve to die.'

James nodded. 'That's exactly the problem we're faced with. So I can only suggest that at this stage we simply follow the evidence. That includes finding out who had a grudge against Charlie Jenkins, and if that person also has a serious problem with other people in this village.'

'That's sensible, I suppose, but it'll make things much harder.'

'I realise that,' James said. 'But the fact is, the only way we'll know for certain whether or not we're dealing with a serial killer is if he or she claims another victim.'

CHAPTER NINETEEN

When Annie returned home her mind was spinning in circles and she was struggling to suppress an ugly fear that was making her stomach churn.

The news about Charlie Jenkins had hit her hard. He was someone she had known, the first boy she had ever kissed when they were at school together. She'd seen him just two days ago and had spoken to his wife only yesterday.

It just didn't seem possible that he was dead.

Brutally stabbed.

Murdered.

Annie could not banish the thought that he might still be alive if James hadn't played down the significance of the message in the Christmas card.

Was it a failure on her husband's part that he hadn't taken it more seriously? Should he and his colleagues in the police have acted immediately to ensure that everyone in Kirkby Abbey was made aware of the threat? Maybe then Charlie would have stayed indoors instead of taking his dog for a walk in the middle of the night.

The parcel with the dead partridge and Christmas card had been left on their doorstep on Friday evening, and around thirty hours later, on Saturday night, Charlie was slain.

Twelve days. Twelve murders. Twelve victims. And they all deserve what's coming to them.

Those words from the message in the card were on repeat inside Annie's head. It was enough to convince her that Charlie's death was not a coincidence. And she did not believe for a single second that Sonia was responsible. James was obviously hoping that she was, because then it would prove to be an open and shut case, yet to Annie it was anything but.

All her instincts were telling her that this was the start of something profoundly wicked. Something that had been planned with the aim of causing a great deal of pain and suffering. A lot of thought had gone into packaging the dead bird and preparing the cards that were sent to James and Father Silver.

Of course, there were lots of unanswered questions. Why were James and the priest singled out? Why the reference to *The Twelve Days of Christmas*? Why now? Why here?

Then there were the two men who had already aroused suspicion. Daniel Curtis and Keith Patel. They were both seen close to the house around the time the parcel was placed on the doorstep. It seemed odd to Annie that Curtis had been lurking outside the school. And wasn't it strange that Patel had in his home a pack of those distinctive Christmas cards?

These were all avenues of inquiry that she hoped James would pursue. And she was sure he would. In fact, she experienced a twinge of guilt for assuming he was taking the wrong approach. After all, he was a top rate copper and had investigated dozens of murders while working in London. He knew what he was doing, and who was she to suggest otherwise?

Thinking about it was making her chest feel tight so she poured herself a glass of water and sat at the kitchen table.

There was just too much to process, too much pressure to handle all at once.

One consequence of these ghastly events was that she was no longer looking forward to Christmas. She decided that when James got home she would tell him that they should cancel his family's visit. It wouldn't be fair on them. They should do the sensible thing and tell them to stay safe in London.

The dark irony of the situation wasn't lost on her, either. It was beginning to look as though they had moved from one hell to another.

It seemed inconceivable that within weeks of setting up home in this quiet Cumbrian village a murder would be committed. They had come here to feel safer, and to distance themselves from the likes of Andrew Sullivan and the rest of the scum who made London so dangerous and unpleasant. But it seemed that trouble had followed them, and it looked set to ruin their first Christmas here.

Annie was still sitting at the kitchen table ten minutes later, wondering what to do with herself during the rest of the day, when her phone rang. She expected it to be James and was surprised when she saw that it was her Uncle Bill who was calling. She had tried to ring him several times after he failed to show up in the square, but he hadn't answered, so she was in no mood now to listen to any more bullshit excuses.

'Are you deliberately trying to wind me up, Bill?' she said before he could get a word in. 'I thought you came here to spend time with me, but you keep disappearing.'

'I know, Annie, and I'm sorry,' he said, his voice barely above a whisper.

'So where are you now?'

'Well, that's the thing. I've done something really stupid and I've got nobody to blame but myself.'

'What are you talking about?'

'I'll tell you when I see you. But right now you have to come and get me. Please, Annie. I've fucked up and I need your help.'

CHAPTER TWENTY

James spent some time at the crime scene taking notes and snapping photos on his phone.

He watched Charlie Jenkins being manoeuvred into a body bag while, at the same time, his dog was wrapped in a blanket. They were both carried away from the field to a waiting vehicle.

It was all done in a hurry in order to beat the bad weather that was predicted to hit the area soon.

The search of the field was proving fruitless. The snow had filled in any footprints that might have been left by the killer, and if the murder weapon was lying nearby it was going to take a huge stroke of luck to find it. What's more, there were only a few hours of daylight left and there would be no point carrying on after dark.

James looked out beyond the field to a landscape festooned with low drystone walls. Thick clouds circled the peaks in the distance and the wind was blowing them towards Kirkby Abbey.

'We need to wrap up here soon, guv,' Stevens said, his voice tight. 'I've lived in these parts long enough to know that we're in for a bastard of a blizzard. Maybe not today or tomorrow, but it's on the way.'

James took a deep breath and held it for a moment before speaking.

'How bad is it likely to get?' he asked.

Stevens released a thin whistle from between his lips.

'Put it this way,' he said, in what James sensed was a patronising tone. 'In London, a fierce snowstorm would almost certainly have zero impact on a murder investigation. The roads would stay open, there'd be no problem reaching suspects to interview them, and you'd have a plentiful supply of officers to call on for support. But here, everything can grind to a halt. Roads get blocked by snowdrifts, phone lines can be disabled and trying to get to remote villages such as this one can be a frigging nightmare.'

It felt to James as though his DS had just taken great pleasure in talking to him like he was a clueless outsider, which was how Stevens had viewed him since he'd arrived at Kendal HQ and got in the way of the guy's promotion. James just hoped that he didn't persist with the attitude since this was the first time they'd worked together on a major case.

But what he'd said had given James something to think about. Since he had moved to Cumbria the weather had been cold but stable. And he had never experienced severe storms during previous visits. But he'd heard how bad it could get and Annie had told him how the village had often been cut off when she was a child.

'We'll just have to keep a close eye on the weather, then, if the investigation drags on,' he said. 'If necessary, we can arrange for some officers to bed down at the B&Bs in the village.'

'That's not a bad idea,' Stevens said. 'I'll call control and let them know it's a possibility so they can prepare for it.'

'Well, hopefully it won't come to it. Meanwhile, let's go back over the bridge and have a team talk. I want to know if the uniforms have come up with anything and we can work out where to go from there.'

The uniforms had been hard at work. As well as cracking on with door-to-door enquiries, they had also managed to gain access to the small village hall so that it could be used as a base.

It was just behind the square and a short walk from the crime scene. A group of pensioners who had been taking part in a social gathering there had been asked to leave and they'd been only too willing to oblige. Like everyone else in the village they were in a state of shock and struggling to come to terms with what had happened.

The inspector in charge was waiting in the hall with four other uniformed officers. His name was Dave Boyd, a portly northerner with a pencil moustache. He was clearly on top of things and was in constant touch with those members of his team who were searching the field and talking to people in the village.

'We've managed to bring in twenty officers,' he told the two detectives. 'That's more than I expected, given the pressure on resources.'

James briefed the officers on what he'd learned from Sonia Jenkins and the pathologist. He also mentioned the threatening message and the dead partridge, but stressed that at this stage there was no evidence to indicate a connection.

'Obviously we're hoping there won't be,' he said. 'But that doesn't mean it's not a serious line of inquiry. I want you to pass the information onto the team, but impress on them that it's not to be made public.'

The update from Inspector Boyd was not encouraging. So far nobody who'd been questioned had seen or heard anything during the night.

'It seems that very few people ever venture out that late, so the streets are almost always empty,' he said. 'But some have spotted Charlie Jenkins walking his dog in the past around the square and across the footbridge into the field.'

'So he'd established a routine that his killer was probably aware of,' James said. 'He or she would have known where the best place was to strike. And it wouldn't surprise me if the pathologist is right and the perp was waiting behind the tree. The dog might well have led Charlie right into the trap.'

'It's also possible he'd arranged to meet someone in the field,' Stevens said. 'Maybe the woman he'd been seeing. They argued and things turned nasty.'

There were numerous scenarios to consider, but James was convinced that the initial focus should be on the wife.

'We'll go and have another chat with Sonia Jenkins,' he said. 'And this time, we'll also sift through Charlie's belongings and get a sample of Sonia's handwriting to compare with the message in the Christmas cards.'

He told the inspector to call him immediately if his officers turned up anything interesting.

The detectives then walked out of the village hall to find a young man waiting for them.

Stevens reacted by reeling off a bunch of expletives under his breath.

Then he said, 'I might have known that you'd be the first of the vultures to turn up.'

A tight smile twisted on the man's lips.

'And it's good to see you too, DS Stevens.' Turning to James, the man went on: 'And you must be Detective Inspector Walker. I understand you're in charge.'

'I am,' James said. 'Who are you?'

'The name's Gordon Carver. I'm a reporter with the *Cumbria Gazette*, based in Kendal, but I live here in Kirkby Abbey. I also freelance for the nationals and they're all eager for information on the murder.'

Carver looked to be in his late twenties. He was of medium height with sharp features and reddish hair cropped close to his scalp. He was wearing a knee-length overcoat and clutching a notebook and pen.

'You need to contact the press office,' James said. 'I'm sure they're about to release a statement.'

'All they're saying is that you're investigating a suspicious death,' Carver said. 'I already know much more than that.'

'Exactly what do you know?' Stevens asked him.

Carver read from his notes. 'The victim is pub landlord Charlie Jenkins, who I knew reasonably well. He was found dead with stab wounds in the field on the other side of the stream. It's believed it happened during the night while he was walking his dog, Daisy, who was also found dead.'

'Where did you get that information?' James said, without trying to conceal his irritation.

'It's all over the village already,' Carver said. 'This is the sort of place where news spreads quickly, Detective Inspector. I just need you to confirm it all and tell me if you've got any idea who did it.'

'Look, Mr Carver, you really need to bear with us on this,' James said. 'The body was discovered less than three hours ago, and I'm surprised you know as much as you do. We're still trying to pull the facts together ourselves and it's taking time. But you can quote me as saying that an investigation has indeed been launched and we'd like to hear from anyone who might have information pertaining to what I'd describe as a brutal crime.'

Carver started making notes as James continued.

'I would ask you not to approach Mrs Jenkins at this time for obvious reasons,' he said. 'The news came as a terrible shock to her and she's naturally very distressed. And for the record we have no suspects at this early stage.'

'Can you tell me how many times Mr Jenkins was stabbed?' Carver asked.

James shook his head. 'We'll release that information after the pathologist has carried out a detailed examination of the body. But for now I'd like you to leave it at that. I've said more than I would normally say because I suspect that during this case we can be helpful to one another. You live in the village so I'm sure you'll be picking up information that will be useful to us. If you're happy to share it before writing it up, then you'll be given preferential treatment when it comes to releasing updates to the media.'

'That sounds fair to me,' Carver said, without hesitation. 'Can I suggest we exchange cards and shake on it?'

After that was done, they set off in different directions.

'I'm not sure that was sensible, guv,' Stevens said as he and James headed towards The White Hart. 'He's one of the least popular journos on the patch, and he's written more negative stories about the force than anyone else.'

'Don't worry,' James said. 'I've had a ton of experience dealing with the press in London. I know what I'm doing.'

'With respect, guv, this isn't London. Up here we tend not to trust hacks.'

James chose not to give Stevens the satisfaction of responding to the remark. That would be a sure way of creating further tension between them and they could do without that this early in the investigation.

But if the DS continued with his petulant gibes, he would put him in his place and send him back to Kendal with a flea in his ear.

CHAPTER TWENTY-ONE

Annie's heart was beating high up in her chest as she drove towards where Bill was waiting. At the same time the blood pulsed and hammered inside her head.

She still wasn't sure what to make of his alarming SOS call. He'd refused to provide her with details over the phone other than to say that he was stranded about two miles outside the village.

'Just get here as quickly as you can,' he'd said.

It had taken her three goes to get her own car started because she hadn't used it in over a week. She'd thought about calling James, but decided it wouldn't be fair as he already had enough on his plate with Charlie's murder.

The roads were slippery and there were lots of icy patches which forced her to take it slowly.

The location Bill had given her was just off the A683, between Kirkby Abbey and Sedbergh. She had no idea what he was doing there or what kind of mess he had got himself into. And, because of that, she wasn't able to rein in her imagination.

Why had he been acting so strangely? she kept asking herself. And was it merely a coincidence that soon after he arrived the parcel with the partridge inside was left on their doorstep? Plus, he claimed he'd delivered Christmas cards to 'old acquaintances' in the village. Did that include Father Silver?

And then the weird behaviour continued when he failed to turn up for dinner, saying that he didn't remember Annie inviting him. Surely that was either a daft excuse or an outright lie. But why had he felt the need to do that? It made no sense.

At any other time, Annie would have shrugged it off and put it down to his age. But because of what was happening her mind was all over the place. She couldn't help wondering if her uncle had done something stupid or bad and was now seriously regretting it.

Traffic was light on the A683 as it meandered through an artwork of a landscape. Snow-covered hills reached towards a sky that was filled with low, bloated clouds.

Suddenly she found herself approaching the old stone bridge that crosses the River Rawthey. Just beyond this was a layby, and that was where Bill said he'd be waiting. Only, when Annie reached it, she couldn't see him.

She pulled onto the layby and stopped the car. At this point the narrow river that hugged the road was out of sight at the bottom of an overgrown embankment.

Annie got out of the car and looked around, but Bill was nowhere to be seen so she called his name.

'I'm down here,' he shouted back.

She walked to the edge of the layby and looked down towards the frozen river. And there was her uncle, sitting on a rock a few yards to the right of his bright red Ford Escort. The vehicle was resting precariously on the embankment and would have slid down into the water if the front hadn't been crushed up against a tree. It was immediately obvious to Annie what had happened. Bill had for some reason careered off the road and plunged down the embankment. But it looked as though the damage was restricted to the front bumper and bonnet.

Annie stumbled down the steep incline towards him and was immensely relieved when he stood and turned towards her. He looked to be in one piece, thankfully.

'My God, are you all right?' she said as she reached him.

He nodded. 'I'm fine. Just a bit shaken. And ruddy freezing.'

'So you're not hurt?'

'I was lucky,' he said. 'The tree saved me.'

His face was ghostly pale and he was trembling beneath his heavy coat.

'Maybe I should take you straight to a hospital,' Annie said. 'Just to be sure.'

'There's no need for that, my dear. Just get me back to the village so I can arrange for the garage to come and drag the old girl out of here. And then I'll have a stiff drink or two.'

'Are you sure?'

'Absolutely.'

'But what the hell happened?'

He shrugged. 'As I said on the phone, I did something stupid. When I realised I was going too fast I braked hard and lost control on the icy road. Ended up going over the edge and hitting the tree.'

'I suppose it could have been much worse.'

'I know that, Annie,' he said. 'It's my own fault for coming here. I should have passed up on your invitation to spend Christmas in Kirkby Abbey. I made a stupid mistake that has almost cost me my life.'

Annie felt her stomach pitch. 'You're doing it again, Bill. You're not making any sense. What is wrong with you? You've been acting odd since you arrived. I just don't get it and, if I'm honest, it's quite upsetting.'

Bill heaved a sigh and reached out to take her hand.

'You really don't need to worry, Annie,' he said. 'There's nothing wrong with me. I'm just getting old.'

Annie wasn't convinced. Instinct told her that he was not being entirely honest, but she had no idea why.

CHAPTER TWENTY-TWO

Back at The White Hart James was having another conversation with Sonia Jenkins. While he'd been gone, she'd changed out of her dressing gown and into jeans and a jumper.

She was still an emotional wreck, though, and struggling to hold it together. He noted that she had also been drinking. A bottle of vodka and a half-filled glass was on the table in front of her.

Beth and Josh had stayed to help console her, and Father Silver was still there. All three were talking amongst themselves on the other side of the bar area while DS Stevens and a couple of uniforms were searching the upstairs flat and going through Charlie's belongings.

James was sitting facing Sonia at a table in the restaurant as he gently asked her questions about her husband's movements in the hours before he went out with the dog.

'After the argument at lunchtime, which you saw, we hardly spoke to each other,' she said. 'But there was no need to, anyway, because we were really busy. Charlie spent most of the time in the kitchen and serving at the tables while I stayed behind the bar. Being market day, we remained open and we were at it non-stop. After closing up, I went straight to bed and he took Daisy for her walk.'

But there was no one to confirm that she did go to bed and stay there until the morning. He was being asked to take her word for it. She did sound convincing, though, and he found it hard not to believe that she was telling the truth.

So far, she had cooperated fully. She'd provided them with the password to the laptop the couple had shared and had given her permission for the place to be searched.

'Have you spoken to Janet yet?' she asked him. 'Like I told you earlier, she was furious with Charlie for going to her house yesterday morning.'

'I intend to talk to her shortly, Mrs Jenkins. But can you tell me exactly what she said to you? When I heard you and Charlie arguing in the alley, he claimed he went there to tell her not to set foot in this place again.'

She nodded. 'That's right. But she said he also tore her off a strip for letting on to Ron Curtis that they'd been having an affair. She said Charlie threatened her and said he'd make sure she'd regret it if she ever talked about him again to anyone.'

'And what did you say to her?'

'Nothing at all. Before I could respond she slammed the phone down on me. And that was when I went outside and confronted Charlie in the alley. And for your information, I didn't really mean it when I told him I wished he was dead. I was just so wound up.'

'So you believed what Janet told you?'

She nodded. 'Of course. The woman had no reason to lie. What Charlie did was stupid. And wrong. It really got to me because he'd promised he'd never do it again.'

She closed her eyes and dragged in a long breath. James left it a moment and then told her that officers had, in the last few minutes, broken the news to Charlie's mother in York and brother in Sheffield. They'd also contacted Sonia's parents in Leeds.

She opened her eyes and choked back more tears.

'I've tried calling my daughter in Dubai,' she said. 'But I can't get through so I expect her phone is switched off. She's going to be devastated. They were very close.'

'We'll keep trying to get in touch. Meanwhile, is there anything you need?'

'Only to be left alone for a while,' she sobbed. 'I appreciate that Beth, Josh and the priest are trying to be helpful, but I'd rather just go and lie on my bed.'

'I quite understand,' James said. 'I'll see if they're finished upstairs. And just so you know, a family liaison officer is on her way. She'll make sure you're not pestered by anyone during the night, and will be the point of contact between you and us, keeping you informed of how the investigation is progressing.'

'We're just about done here,' DS Stevens said when James went upstairs to tell him that Sonia wanted to retreat to her bedroom. 'We haven't found anything that gives rise to suspicion, but I've got a few things for the techs to have a look at in the lab.'

He held up a carrier bag and explained that it contained the couple's laptop and three long-bladed knives from the kitchen in the flat, plus two from the restaurant downstairs.

Then he dipped a hand into the bag and took out a Christmas card with an image of Santa Claus on the front.

'This was on the mantlepiece in their living room,' he said. 'It's from Mrs Jenkins to her husband. As you can see, the writing is smaller and much neater than the message that was scrawled on the card that you received. It doesn't look to me as though they were written by the same person.'

James took the card and read it.

To Charlie

Merry Christmas from me. Love you lots and always will.

Sonia x

James agreed that the writing was very different, and it served to reinforce the conclusion he was coming to that Sonia Jenkins was not responsible for the Twelve Days of Christmas threats.

'To do a proper sweep of the flat and the bar, we'll need to bring in SOCOs,' he said. 'But it's my guess they'll be hard-pressed to come up with anything that's hugely significant.'

Back downstairs, James told Sonia that they were taking some objects away for analysis. She didn't even bother to ask what they were and this suggested to him that either she had nothing to hide or she knew they wouldn't find anything incriminating.

As she went up to the bedroom, James instructed one of the uniforms to hang around until the family liaison officer arrived. He then thanked Beth, Josh and Father Silver for staying with Sonia. Beth and Josh left immediately, but the priest held back, eager to have a quiet word with James.

'That poor woman had nothing to do with her husband's death,' he said. 'I am absolutely certain of it. Her grief is real and she simply doesn't have it in her to commit murder. Surely you can see that.'

'You might well be right, Father,' James said. 'But we have to go through the motions. The fact is, she had a good reason to be angry with Charlie, which gave her a motive. And there's no one to verify her story that she was in bed asleep when it happened.'

The priest shook his head. 'My mind keeps leaping back to the card that was left for me at the church, Detective Walker. I'm convinced that the message inside it was from someone other than Sonia Jenkins. Surely that's obvious.'

'I'm inclined to believe you, but we haven't established a link between the cards and Charlie's murder, so we can't just assume that there is one – we need proof. In the meantime, we have to handle this investigation like any other, which entails identifying and interviewing potential suspects.'

'Does that mean you're still not prepared to make public the existence of those cards and messages?' the priest said.

'It does, Father. And for the same reason I gave you before. It would serve only to scare people and cause panic.'

The priest tilted his head to one side for a few moments and sucked on his bottom lip in concentration.

Then he said, 'Well, I just hope that you know what you're doing, Detective. I would hate for someone to die because the police decided not to warn people that their lives are in danger.'

CHAPTER TWENTY-THREE

The priest's words continued to play on James's mind as he and DS Stevens left The White Hart. But he was forced to accept that there was no simple answer to the problem that confronted them.

In London, which had a population of almost nine million, it wouldn't have mattered so much if the anonymous threat was made public. But Kirkby Abbey was a community of only seven hundred residents and so the impact on the villagers, if they got wind of it, would be far greater.

He could just imagine how some would react, especially elderly people living by themselves and those with children. It just wouldn't be fair to instil fear in them if the threat did indeed turn out to be a hoax.

'Where to now, guv?' Stevens said, breaking into James's thoughts.

James looked at his watch. It was almost three o'clock and he couldn't believe how quickly the time had passed.

'I'd like you to go back to the hall,' he said. 'See what

information you can drum up on Charlie Jenkins and his wife, and run their two members of staff through the system. They worked for the guy so we need to check them out.'

'And what about you?'

'I'll go and talk to Janet Dyer. She told Sonia that Charlie threatened her, so she has to be a person of interest to us.'

Annie had texted him Janet's address. It was quite close to the square, and he could easily have walked there, but the uniformed officer he chose to go with him had a patrol car to hand so they went in that.

The village was far less busy now, the carollers having dispersed. The place was still ablaze with Christmas lights, but James could tell that the atmosphere had changed. It was now sombre and subdued, and the yuletide jollity had vanished.

Janet Dyer lived in a small detached house just off the main road that passed through the village.

As they walked up to the front door after parking the patrol car at the kerb, James reminded himself what Annie had told him about her childhood friend.

She was divorced and lived here with her twin sons, who had gone to Carlisle to spend Christmas with her ex-husband. They'd been married for ten years before he'd left her and the kids and moved in with a woman he'd met at work.

Janet worked for an agency that provided homecare to old folk in the village and surrounding area and, according to Annie, she was a well-meaning woman who far too often allowed her mouth to run away with her.

From the way Annie had described Janet, he expected her to be a larger than life character with a domineering personality. So he got quite a surprise when she opened the door to them.

She was only just over five feet tall and had a pleasant face with delicate features. Her large brown eyes were swollen and traces of mascara were running down her cheeks. She was wearing jeans and a V-neck sweater that showed a hint of cleavage, and on her feet were a pair of fluffy indoor slippers.

She was clearly shocked to see them and caught her breath as she looked from James to the uniformed officer who was standing behind him.

'I take it you're Miss Janet Dyer,' James said, holding up his ID.

She took a deep breath through her nose, causing her nostrils to flare.

'Yes, I am,' she said. 'Is this about Charlie? I've had two people call me to say that his body was found in one of the fields. It's awful. Like something out of a nightmare.'

'It is about him, Miss Dyer. I'd like to talk to you because I know you had contact with him yesterday morning. My name is Walker. Detective Inspector James Walker.'

'You're Annie's husband.'

'That's correct. May we come in?'

'I suppose so, but all I know is what I've been told. I haven't been out of the house all day.'

'As well as investigating the circumstances of his death, we also need to build up a picture of the man himself,' James said. 'I'm hoping you can help us in that respect.'

The house was modest and quite messy inside. As Janet led them through to the living room, she explained that she was in the midst of giving the place a clean.

'I've got my sister coming for Christmas, and I want it to look tidy. I don't get a chance to do it when the boys are here,' she said. 'It's their dad's turn to have them for the holidays so they're staying with him in Carlisle until the New Year.'

An artificial Christmas tree stood in front of the patio doors in the living room and decorations hung from the ceiling. There were framed photos of her twins on a sideboard and a bunch of toys were piled up in a corner. Janet had to move stuff from the sofa so that James and the officer could sit down. She sat on the chair facing them and wrapped her arms around herself.

'I assume you know that Charlie came here yesterday morning to have a go at me,' she said. 'I told Annie about it. He was out of order and I told him so.'

'I gather you also told his wife.'

She nodded, a shadow crossing her face. 'It was my way of getting my own back. He was horrible to me and I was really upset.'

'You told Sonia Jenkins that he threatened you.'

'That's because he did. He said I'd regret it if I spoke to anyone else about what happened between us.'

'Did it get physical?'

'What do you mean by that?'

'Did he hit you?'

She shook her head. 'Of course not. Charlie wasn't a violent man. Just self-centred and thoughtless. His bark was worse than his bite. That's why I'm gutted that he's dead. I loved him, you see – we had a connection.'

'So how long did the affair with him last?' James asked.

'Almost four months. He came on to me one night in The White Hart when Sonia was away. I was flattered and it went from there. I knew it was wrong because he was married, but I didn't care because I'd been single for so long and it excited me.'

'So when did it end and why?'

'I called a halt to it a month ago because he finally admitted to me that he would never leave his wife,' she said. 'He'd led me to believe that he would and we'd even talked about moving to Carlisle together so it would be easy for my boys to spend time with their dad. I took him at his word but should have known better. I wasn't the first woman he'd had an affair with.'

'How did it ending make you feel?'

'Really bad. He meant the world to me and I wanted to spend the rest of my life with him.'

She inhaled a long, ragged breath and exhaled slowly. James paused for a few seconds to allow her to compose herself before continuing.

'So Mr Jenkins was furious with you because you were indiscreet about the affair and mentioned it to one of the elderly gentlemen you visit in your role as a carer? A man named Ron Curtis.'

'It was a huge mistake and I regret it,' she said. 'But I visited Ron the day after I ended it with Charlie. I was in a proper state, and when he asked me what was wrong I broke down and poured my heart out to him. He had no idea about the affair and I told him not to tell anyone. But I should have known that he would. And that it would eventually get back to Sonia.'

James was about to ask another question, but she interrupted him.

'Are you aware that Charlie went to see Ron yesterday, after he left here?' she said.

'No, I didn't know that.'

'Well, he did. Ron phoned me afterwards to have a moan.

He was really cross because Charlie barged into his house when he opened the door and yelled at him. He told Ron not to spread gossip about him again and called him a mischievous old bastard. '

'I'll need to go and talk to Ron Curtis. Do you have his address?'

She gave him the address and he wrote it down in his notebook.

'Is it true that Charlie was stabbed repeatedly by whoever attacked him in the field?' Janet asked. 'Nobody seems to know exactly what happened. All kinds of rumours are circulating.'

James decided not to reveal details about the murder and concluded the interview by asking her where she was last night around the time Charlie Jenkins was murdered.

'I had an early night,' she said. 'I went to bed after taking a sleeping pill and woke up about ten this morning. I didn't hear what had happened to Charlie until earlier this afternoon.'

CHAPTER TWENTY-FOUR

It seemed curious to James that the Curtis name had come up twice during the past couple of days.

First Annie's uncle said that he saw Daniel Curtis hanging around outside the school on Friday evening. Then it emerged that Janet had told Daniel's father Ron about her affair with Charlie Jenkins, which had sparked an almighty row after Ron passed it on to someone else.

James was now wondering whether it was significant that Charlie was murdered only a matter of hours after he angrily confronted Ron Curtis in his home.

Had the old man sought retribution or got someone else to seek it for him? It didn't seem likely, but James had to acknowledge that it wasn't inconceivable.

Ron Curtis's bungalow was on the outskirts of the village between a doctor's surgery and a small garden centre. James told the uniformed officer to wait in the patrol car and headed towards the front door. There were no cars on the driveway and he wondered if that meant Ron's son Daniel wasn't in.

He felt uncomfortable at the thought of coming face to face with the man who had been Annie's first love all those years ago. What made it worse was the fact that the guy had turned out to be a child molester, and had spent a couple of years inside.

It therefore came as a relief when the front door was opened by a man who was probably in his eighties. His thin, drawn face had been ravaged by age and there were only a few strands of grey hair lying flat across his scalp. He was wearing a dark brown cardigan and baggy jeans, and he did not look strong enough or fit enough to walk very far by himself, let alone stalk and then murder someone half his age.

James showed his warrant card. 'Good afternoon, sir. I'm Detective Inspector James Walker with the Cumbria police. Are you Mr Ron Curtis?'

'I was the last time I checked,' came the response. 'What do you want?'

'I'd like to talk to you about Charlie Jenkins. I know he came here to see you yesterday.'

'He did indeed, and I told him in no uncertain terms to fuck off after he had a pop at me. He wouldn't have been so lippy if I was younger or if my son had been here.'

'Out of curiosity, where was your son at the time and where is he now?' James asked.

'He had to go back to his place in Keswick to attend to some business,' Ron said. 'He stayed there last night and is coming back later on this evening to spend Christmas with me.'

James nodded. 'I see. So would it be all right if I came in, sir? I won't keep you long.'

The old man shrugged. 'Don't see why not, especially if

what I've got to say will get that bastard Jenkins into trouble. Never did like him when I used to go drinking in his pub. Too cocky by half.'

A surprised look crossed James's face as he entered the bungalow. It appeared that Ron Curtis did not know that Charlie Jenkins was dead.

The interior was cramped, gloomy and in need of a make-over, with damp stains on the walls and worn patches on the carpets. And there was a noticeable absence of Christmas decorations. Not a single bauble, card or flurry of tinsel.

Ron walked slowly with an awkward gait. By the time he got to the living room, where he dropped into an armchair, he was out of breath.

'I'd offer to make you a cup of tea, but I've already had one,' he said. 'And I was just about to have my afternoon nap. So I suggest you ask your questions before I doze off, which I'm prone to do even in the middle of a conversation these days.'

James sat and launched into his questions. The first thing he wanted was confirmation of what Janet had told him

'Let me start by asking you why Mr Jenkins came here yesterday,' he said.

Ron shrugged his shoulders. 'To bollock me. He was fucked off because I told my pal Tommy Shepherd about his fling with Janet Dyer. Tommy then told someone else and it eventually reached the ears of Charlie's wife. But it served him right for playing the field and I told him so.'

'And did he threaten you?'

'He tried to, but I just laughed in his face and he didn't like that. He called me an old gossip and a mischievous bastard, but when I picked up the phone to call the police he stormed out.'

'Did you have any contact with him after that?'

'No.'

'And did you speak to anyone about what happened?'

'Only my lad, Daniel, and of course Janet, bless her. She was upset too because he had already been around to her place. I told her that she needed to stay well clear of him.'

'And what did your son say?'

'He was spitting blood. He wants to go to The White Hart when he gets back later to give that knobhead a roasting. But I'm not sure it's a good idea. I don't want Daniel getting pinched.'

James made a mental note to check up on Daniel's movements. He wanted to know if he had really gone to Keswick yesterday and spent the night there.

'So what is this is all about?' Ron said. 'Are you going to nick Jenkins for harassing Janet and me? Is that it?'

James leaned forward, rested his elbows on his knees, and said, 'You're obviously unaware of events that have taken place in the village overnight and this morning, Mr Curtis.'

'That's because I haven't been outside or spoken to anyone. So what have I missed?'

'Mr Jenkins is dead. His body was found in a field this morning, and it appears he was murdered during the night while out walking his dog.'

The old man's eyes became thin slits as he stared at James. Then after a couple of beats his mouth curved into a smile.

'All I can say is that it couldn't have happened to a nicer guy, Inspector,' he said. 'Rats like him don't deserve to live.'

It wasn't the reaction that James had expected and it must have shown on his face.

'You don't have to look so surprised,' Ron said. 'I'm at an

age where I can tell it how it is without having to worry what people think. No way am I prepared to express fake sympathy for that prick. But I will say that whoever did it deserves a fucking medal. He wasn't a nice man.'

'I appreciate your honesty,' James said. 'But I gather most people in the village liked him.'

'So they'd have you believe now that he's dead. But a lot of folks thought he was flash and full of himself. In truth, he was nasty and, as I said, I had many problems with him, not least of which being the fact he said a lot of horrible things about my boy.'

'Are you referring to your son's predilection for young girls?'

'You know I am, Inspector. I might be old but I'm not senile. As soon as you gave me your name at the door it clicked. Janet told me weeks ago that Annie Kellerman had moved back here with her policeman husband and that her name is now Annie Walker. I assumed she told you all about her relationship with Daniel, which, by the way, came as much of a shock to me as it did to her parents. Her dad and me fell out over it and we never did get back on speaking terms before he died. And that was a shame because I liked him. The whole thing fucked up Daniel's life and he was forced to relocate, which was when he got himself into even more trouble.'

'So why does he come back here to Kirkby Abbey when he knows he's not wanted?' James asked.

'Because I'm his father, his only living relative, and I want to see him. I know most people will never forgive him for what he did, but I have. He's not like that any more and I want to spend as much time with him as I can before it's my turn to part from this world.'

143

James could see that the old man was getting worked up and he didn't want to be the one to bring on a heart attack. So he stood and thanked him for his time. But before leaving he got Ron to give him Daniel's phone number and address in Keswick, which he did with a clear degree of reluctance.

Back in the patrol car, James turned the conversation over in his mind. The bit that stood out was Ron saying, *'Rats like him don't deserve to live.'*

It reminded James of the sentence in the Twelve Days of Christmas card he'd received:

And they all deserve what's coming to them.

CHAPTER TWENTY-FIVE

The debrief got under way in the village hall at five-thirty. By then it was dark outside and the temperature had begun to plummet. But the blizzards that were forecast still hadn't arrived and that was something that James and the team were thankful for.

Inspector Boyd began by saying that his officers had drawn a blank on the house-to-house. Nobody they spoke to had spotted Charlie Jenkins walking his dog on Saturday night. The last time he was seen by anyone other than his wife had been in The White Hart just before closing time.

The news from the crime scene was just as disappointing. An exhaustive search of the field where the body was found had yielded sod all.

James then gave an account of his interviews with Sonia Jenkins, Janet Dyer and Ron Curtis.

'All three of them had serious issues with the victim,' he said. 'And all three claim they were in bed when he was attacked. At the moment, the wife is saying all the right things and she sounds convincing, but it could be a front. It's possible her husband's infidelity caused her to snap and she followed him into that field. But if she did, would she really have left their dog out all night to freeze to death? I'm not so sure.'

James moved on to Janet Dyer and referred to the salient points that arose during their conversation, including her claim that Charlie had told her she would regret it if she spoke to anyone else about their affair.

'Despite his threat, she insists that she loved the guy,' James said. 'She's clearly upset that he's dead. But not so Ron Curtis. It was apparently news to the old man that there had been a murder and he said the killer ought to be given a medal. He also said that rats like Charlie don't deserve to live, which echoes the sentiment of one of the lines from the Christmas card I received.' James pulled up the picture of the message to remind the team.

'Now, I don't believe that Ron Curtis is physically able to have committed the murder,' he said. 'He's in no fit state to do something like that – he struggles even to move around in his bungalow – but I do think it raises questions in respect of his son, Daniel, who was angry with Charlie because he had a go at his dad. Ron said Daniel spent yesterday and last night in Keswick, where he lives, and that he is due back here later this evening. He gave me his son's number and I've tried to ring it but the phone is switched off. We need to talk to him and find out if he was in Keswick, or if it was a story that father and son concocted so that Daniel could go and top Charlie.'

This prompted questions and a brief discussion that ended with agreement that it was a credible scenario and needed to be followed up.

'I think it's fair to say that the investigation hasn't got off to a very promising start,' James said. 'We'll have to wait until tomorrow to find out if the forensic technicians come up with anything on Charlie's laptop and phone, plus the kitchen knives we took away. I'll also talk again to Sonia and hopefully track down Daniel Curtis. There's no point everyone staying in the village overnight, but I'd like at least one officer to hold the fort here in the hall in case anything happens.'

Before ending the meeting, James called DCI Tanner and gave him a full update.

'The story's out there,' Tanner said. 'I just watched it on the news. We've issued a holding statement which will suffice for now. I suggest we all get together at HQ tomorrow at nine and decide how to proceed.'

He then asked James if he was confident that Charlie's murder was unconnected to the threat in the Christmas card.

'I wish I could tell you what you want to hear, guv,' he said. 'But, based on what we know so far, I really can't be sure.'

'That's what I was afraid you were going to say,' Tanner said.

CHAPTER TWENTY-SIX

DS Stevens offered to drive his boss home in the pool car, but James decided to walk.

He felt leaden and frustrated, and he hoped that the cold, fresh air would help to clear his head. It had started snowing again, fat white flakes drifting lazily down. James wiped them from his face and shook them out of his hair.

At any other time he would have found this weather to be exhilarating, even exciting. But right now he was too preoccupied to embrace it.

This was the most challenging case that had come his way since the move to Cumbria. Half the problem was not knowing if the murder was linked to the anonymous threats in the Christmas cards. And it didn't help that it was all so very personal.

The card and the dead partridge had been delivered to James. He had also spoken to Charlie Jenkins only hours before he was stabbed to death. And one of the suspects was a man who his own wife had once been infatuated with.

As if that wasn't enough to have playing on his mind, there was also the spectre of Andrew Sullivan waiting in the background. It wouldn't have been so bad if he knew where the bastard was, but he had apparently buggered off on a Christmas break.

James didn't like to admit, even to himself, that he was feeling overwhelmed by what seemed like a sudden avalanche of problems and issues. It was a perfect storm and he was smack bang in the middle of it with no idea how rough it was going to get.

He experienced a sudden yearning to be back in The Smoke where he had never felt out of his depth or out of his comfort zone. Here in Cumbria it was like living and working in a fishbowl, with his every move being scrutinised and judged.

He knew that if he fucked up this case there would be consequences for both himself and for Annie.

As soon as James arrived home, he knew that something was wrong. Annie opened the front door just as he was about to slip his key into the lock, her eyes puffy from crying and her complexion a sickly hue.

'I was about to call to see what time you'd be back,' she said. 'I gather from the news that you still don't know who did it.'

James closed the door behind him, pulled off his coat, gloves and scarf, then kissed her on the forehead.

'I'll update you over a glass of wine,' he said. 'And you can tell me what's up with you. I can't believe you've been shedding tears over Charlie Jenkins.'

'This is not about him,' she said, as she moved into the kitchen. 'It's Bill. I had to go and pick him up after he crashed his bloody car.'

'Blimey, Annie. Is he okay?'

'He wasn't hurt, luckily, but he could have been. The car skidded on ice and went over an embankment. If it hadn't struck a tree it would have landed in a river.'

'Where is he now?'

'Back at The King's Head, I suppose. But who knows? His behaviour is really puzzling me. One minute he's nice and friendly and the next he's distant and evasive. Something is going on with him and I don't know what it could be.'

'But he was always a bit of a strange character,' James said, as he took a bottle of wine from the fridge. 'And as I remember he had a pretty short temper as well.'

'He wasn't always like that,' Annie said. 'When I was young, he was such a jolly soul. And very protective of me. He started to change after his wife left him. He withdrew into himself and became more argumentative. I remember some of the rows he had with Mum. They were quite ugly and one time my dad pushed him out of the house.'

James poured the wine and sat down next to Annie at the table.

'You shouldn't let him get to you like this,' he said. 'Don't forget you invited him here for Christmas so that you could rekindle your relationship with him.'

She clenched her eyes shut and tears trickled from under the lids.

'It's not just that,' she said. 'It's everything else that's happened as well. Charlie's murder, that gruesome parcel, the fact that we don't know if any more people are going to be killed. This is not how it was meant to be. We came here to get away from all the bad stuff.'

'I know and I feel the same, hon. It's hard to take it all in.'

Annie opened her eyes and looked at him.

'I don't think your family should come here right now, James. You have to call them so that they've got plenty of time to make other arrangements.'

He knew she was right and he was surprised that it hadn't already occurred to him.

'I'll phone my brother later,' he said. 'He can let the others know and sort out what they'll do instead.'

James was disappointed, of course, but he was sure it was the right thing to do. Kirkby Abbey was not a safe place to be, it turned out, and it was unlikely that the villagers were going to be in the mood to celebrate Christmas as the big day approached.

The TV was tuned to BBC News and the mention of Cumbria seized their attention. The murder of Charlie Jenkins was being treated as a major story. There was aerial footage of the village and the field where his body had been found, along with shots of uniformed police shown talking to residents.

Gordon Carver, the reporter with the *Cumbria Gazette*, appeared on the screen, saying, 'I understand that Mr Jenkins was stabbed several times. His body was discovered about ten o'clock this morning by a hiker. The body of his pet dog was found nearby. It's believed the animal froze to death. The officer leading the investigation, Detective Inspector James Walker, is himself a resident in Kirkby Abbey. He told me that there are no suspects at the moment, but he's confident that his team will find the killer.'

There were shots of The White Hart, and a photo of Charlie with his wife, then several residents gave sound bites in which they expressed shock and revulsion.

Among them was Father Silver, who was interviewed in front of his church. He described Charlie as a well-liked member of the community who would be greatly missed.

'Our prayers are with his wife and the rest of his family who are obviously devastated,' he said. 'Nothing like this has ever happened in our village and tomorrow I intend to hold a special service here to honour Charlie's memory.'

It came as a huge relief to James that the priest didn't mention the card he'd received with the message about the post-Christmas funerals.

'Let's open another bottle of wine,' Annie said when the report ended. 'I'm not ready to go upstairs yet and a few more glasses might help me to drop off.'

'Sounds good to me,' James replied. 'But I'll just have the one because I'm sure that tomorrow is going to be another hellish day and I'll need to have a clear head.'

CHAPTER TWENTY-SEVEN

I'm in bed but I'm not asleep. I'm lying in the dark listening to the noises the house is making as it's battered by the harsh wind.

But it wasn't the bumps and creaks and rattling of the windows that woke me up about half an hour ago. It was the dream. The one that takes me back to the night I killed someone. It happened a long time ago but the memory continues to blight my life.

Only one person knows what I did and I'm sure that my secret is safe with him. When we see each other in the village he never alludes to it or looks at me in a way that reminds me what a terrible person I am.

He probably thinks that the guilt that weighs me down is punishment enough for what I did. But, of course, it isn't. I ended a young woman's life and got away with it. Her family was denied justice. All because I was a coward and feared going to prison.

I sometimes contemplate turning myself into the police in the hope that it will bring closure to the family and end my own suffering. But I don't do it because I fear I won't survive if I'm sent to jail.

The sound of breaking glass makes me jump.

It came from downstairs and my first thought is that an object whipped up by the wind has smashed through a window. That's because it happened once before, not so long ago, and I went down to find a large tree branch on the living room floor and glass everywhere.

But that doesn't mean I'm not apprehensive as I climb out of bed and slip on my dressing gown. I can't help wondering if it might not be an accident. What if someone has deliberately broken a window in order to scare me or gain access to my house? What if it's the person who murdered Charlie Jenkins last night? Or someone who knows about the blood on my own hands and has come to seek revenge?

I hesitate at the top of the stairs. I could lock myself in the bedroom and call the police but it would take them ages to get here, and I would most likely be wasting their time.

Oh how I wish I didn't live alone. Being single means there's no one to help or advise me. No one to tell me I'm being over cautious. No one to give me strength.

I decide after a few moments that I have no choice but to go down, so I turn on the landing light and take one careful step at a time.

I reach the hall and see that the front door and the windows either side of it are intact. That means the damage is in either the living room or the kitchen.

The living room is the nearest so I push open the door and switch on the light. But to my relief the windows aren't broken.

When I enter the kitchen a couple of seconds later it's a different story. A glass panel in the door that leads out onto the patio has been smashed. But what alarms me even more is the fact that the door itself is open and the wind is whistling through it.

As I step forward to close it two things happen.

First, the light I just turned on is suddenly switched off and the room is plunged into darkness.

Second, I hear a voice behind me saying, 'Now it's your turn to die.'

CHAPTER TWENTY-EIGHT

Monday December 19th

Monday morning arrived with rain showers over Cumbria, which caused much of the snow that had settled in and around Kirkby Abbey to turn to slush.

James watched with dismay from their bedroom window. It was only half five and still dark, but he could see the mess it was making of the street in front of the house.

It never ceased to amaze him how extreme and changeable the weather could be in this part of the country. It sometimes went from snow to rain to blazing sunshine over the course of a day. It was one of the reasons he hadn't been keen to move here. It could be so disruptive, so annoying, so bloody unpredictable.

'Are you coming back to bed?' Annie asked him.

They had both been awake for ages, but he'd got fed up with lying there stressing over what needed to be done today.

'No point, hon,' he said. 'I can't sleep and I don't think either of us is in the mood for morning sex. So I might as well crack on. Shall I make you a cup of tea?'

'Yes please. I think I'll get up as well.'

'What have you got on today?'

'I thought I'd go and spend some time with Bill and then attend the church service that Father Silver is holding for Charlie,' she said. 'After that I'm going to the school. It's closed now for Christmas, but Lorna asked me to go in for a couple of hours to help with the end of term tidy up.'

'Well, it'll be good if you can keep busy. I'm going to the office this morning for a case conference, but I won't be there for long.'

'Do you think you're getting close to finding out who did it?'

James shrugged. 'It's impossible to say. We've got no evidence that directly implicates any of the people we've spoken to in Charlie's murder. I've a feeling this investigation will be a slog.'

'What are the chances that the killer is someone outside the village?'

'Pretty slim, I reckon,' James said. 'I'm convinced that whoever did it was familiar with Charlie's routine of walking his dog across that particular field at that time of night. He or she probably got there first and waited behind the tree for him to show up, then struck.'

James thought Annie was going to ask another question, but instead she said, 'You can bring me that cuppa in bed. I'll stay here while you get showered and dressed.'

Forty minutes later, James slipped his suit jacket on over a shirt and tie and stepped into the kitchen. He put the kettle on to make fresh coffee and then sat at the table to check his phone for messages. He only had one and it was from his dad, saying how gutted he and the rest of the family were that they wouldn't be coming up for Christmas. But they understood why.

James had spoken to his brother Ed last night and explained the situation. Ed had said that James and Annie should come to London, but James had explained that it wasn't possible because of the investigation and the fact that Annie's uncle had arrived early.

After pouring himself a cup of coffee he set about making a list of the things he had to do, including seeking out and interviewing Daniel Curtis, talking again to Sonia Jenkins and checking in with the forensic lab. He would also put in a call to his pal in the Met to see if he had an update on Andrew Sullivan's whereabouts.

But first there was the conference at HQ where he was hoping to get an idea of how many people and resources would be assigned to the case. His plan was to set out at seven-thirty, which would allow him plenty of time to get there.

Annie came down after her shower and offered to make them both some breakfast.

'Just toast for me, thanks,' James said. 'I don't have much of an appetite.'

'Mind if I turn the telly on?' she asked.

'Not at all. I was about to do that myself.'

It was a small TV that they'd recently had installed on the wall behind the breakfast bar.

As soon as it was on, Annie switched to Sky News and within minutes there was coverage of Charlie's murder. But not much was new apart from an interview with a member of the media-liaison team who said there would be a press conference later in the morning.

James knew he'd be expected to attend as the senior

investigating officer and it wasn't something he was looking forward to.

A lot was also made of the weather forecast. The Met Office had issued what it described as a more accurate prediction of the storm that was approaching the country from the east. It was apparently going to bring heavy snowfall and potentially major disruption to large parts of the North of England and Scotland.

'We expect this storm to bring severe blizzards and drifting snow,' the forecaster said. 'There's a strong possibility it will cause road closures, power cuts and some damage to buildings.'

It wasn't what James wanted to hear as he knew it would tie up police resources and slow things down.

'We can only hope that we solve the case before everything grinds to a standstill,' he said to Annie as she gave him his toast and topped up his coffee.

But that hope was dashed within minutes when he received a call on his mobile from DCI Tanner.

'I've cancelled this morning's briefing and press conference and you need to stay where you are,' he told James. 'A few minutes ago someone in Kirkby Abbey made a three nines call and I want you to respond right away.'

'What's happened, sir?'

'According to the caller another body has just turned up in the village, and it sounds very much like we've got a second murder on our hands.'

CHAPTER TWENTY-NINE

It was the postman who made the 999 call. He was delivering mail to a property in Willow Road when he discovered the body.

He told the emergency call handler that he was convinced it was a case of murder because of the amount of blood. He was also able to provide the name of the victim.

James had shared the information with Annie before leaving the house and it had shaken her to the core. He would have stayed with her if he'd had a choice, but he had to get to the scene as quickly as possible.

'Oh, please don't let it be her,' Annie had said. 'Call or text me when you know for sure that the postman hasn't made a mistake.'

As James walked at a hurried pace through the village, his heart was hammering in his chest.

He was hoping to God that the postman had indeed made a mistake, but not just about the identity of the deceased. With any luck, he had also jumped to the wrong conclusion about it being a murder. After all, copious amounts of blood were not uncommon in certain accidental deaths and suicides. If a second premeditated killing had taken place the spotlight would fall on the warning in the Twelve Days of Christmas card.

Twelve days. Twelve murders. Twelve victims. And they all deserve what's coming to them.

It took James only eight minutes to reach his destination. Falling temperatures had turned the rain to sleet, but the slush on the pavements made him wish he had worn boots instead of shoes. His socks and trouser bottoms were soaked, and his feet felt like blocks of ice.

Willow Road had detached properties on one side and open fields on the other. James saw the post office van parked outside a house halfway along. The postman, wearing a high-vis jacket, was standing next to it smoking a cigarette.

James was both surprised and relieved to see that the guy was alone. He'd expected at least a few nosey neighbours to have gathered by now.

The postman was in his forties with a beard and a pasty white face. James flashed his card and explained that he was responding to the 999 call because he happened to live only a couple of streets away.

The postman gave his name as Paul Mason and pointed to the house.

'As you can see the front door is open,' he said in a trembling voice. 'It was half-open when I arrived to deliver a letter. It struck me as odd because it was so cold and wet and there was nobody outside. So I called out but got no response. I've met the woman who lives here a few times so I took the liberty of pushing the door all the way open and calling out her name. But that was when I saw the body. You see, the hallway is short and leads up to the kitchen. That door was open too and she was lying on the floor.'

'So what did you do?' James asked him.

'I ran straight in thinking she had fainted or something. But then I saw the blood and what had been done to her throat. I came straight out again and threw up my guts in the road before phoning 999.'

'Did you touch her or anything else in the room?'

'No way. I saw she was dead and couldn't get out of there quick enough.'

'And is there anyone else in the house?'

'I didn't see anyone, but I can't be sure. I do know the lady lives alone, though. She's not married.'

'Do any of the neighbours know what's going on?'

'I don't think so. Nobody has come out, but then it's not unusual for my van to be parked here.'

James looked at his watch. Seven-fifteen.

'More officers will be here soon,' he said. 'Just stay put while I go inside. And make sure no one goes through the gate.'

The postman gave a sharp nod. 'Gotcha.'

James felt the tension in his limbs as he walked up to the house. He'd brought with him latex gloves and paper shoe covers, which he slipped on before stepping over the threshold.

Inside it was just as the postman had described and there was enough light to see the body on the floor. But before moving towards it, James asked out loud if there was anyone in the house. There was no response so he proceeded along the hallway.

The woman was lying on her back and wearing only a dressing gown that hung open to reveal her left breast and panties.

And the blood that covered much of her flesh.

It was strikingly obvious from the gashes in her throat and abdomen that she had been murdered. The blood had pooled beneath her and spread across the lino floor. There were also splash marks on several of the kitchen units and the front of the dishwasher.

James dragged his eyes away from the body and the blood and looked around the room. Nothing appeared to be out of place until he noticed that a glass panel in the back door was broken. It was the one closest to the key that was sticking out of the lock.

James wondered if the killer had gained access to the house by smashing the glass and reaching a hand in to turn the key. He would look closer in a bit but, for now, he returned his attention to the victim and focused on her face. He'd met her a couple of times but needed to be sure who she was before he let Annie know whether or not the postman had made a mistake.

He hadn't.

The woman lying on the floor was Lorna Manning, the headmistress of the village primary school.

CHAPTER THIRTY

Within an hour of James arriving at Lorna Manning's house the scene in and around it had been transformed. Forensic officers were starting to sweep the rooms and gardens for evidence, and a small crowd had gathered in Willow Road.

While waiting for the team to arrive, James had carried out his own checks. He'd searched the house and confirmed that there was no one else in it, noting that it hadn't been ransacked.

The place was comfortable and well kept, with smart, modern furniture and a few framed photos of a couple with a small child. An artificial Christmas tree was set up in the living room and there were some unobtrusive decorations.

James had also noted that Lorna's bed had been slept in and the light was on. It led him to believe that she had probably been woken up by the sound of an intruder breaking the door panel in the kitchen. She'd then gone downstairs to investigate and was stabbed to death.

James called Annie at the first opportunity, and not just to tell her what she didn't want to hear. He needed to extract some information from her about the woman who had been her boss.

His wife could barely speak, though, and he had to wait for her to get a handle on her emotions.

'Lorna was a lovely woman,' she said. 'I can't think why anyone would want to do this to her.'

Between sobs she told him that Lorna Manning had been single and aged fifty-eight. She had one son from a marriage that ended in divorce fifteen years ago. He was living in Southend, Essex, with his wife and daughter.

'She moved around quite a bit and came here ten years ago when she was offered the head's job at the school,' Annie said. 'She put her heart and soul into it and everyone liked and respected her. But the truth is she never seemed happy or settled. I put it down to the fact that the school has been threatened with closure, but others believe it went deeper than that and was rooted in something that happened to her in the past. But she rarely talked about her personal life, even on social occasions. As I understand it, she hadn't been in a relationship for years. Her whole focus was always on the school and the kids.'

'We'll be visiting the school,' James said. 'And we'll have to search Lorna's office and interview some of the staff.'

'Will that include me?'

'It'll have to.'

Annie shook her head. 'I'm just finding it so hard to believe what's happened.'

'I just wish I could be there with you, hon. But I can't.'

'I know, but look, this *must* mean that the threat in the Christmas card you got wasn't a hoax,' she said. 'There's a fucking serial killer in this village, so surely it's time people were told.'

She lost it then and began to cry.

'Look, I'll call you later,' James said, and was gutted that he couldn't go straight home to comfort her.

'I'll be all right,' she replied. 'Just do what you can to find the creature who did this.'

James kept thinking about what Annie had said as he kick-started this new murder investigation.

A serial killer stalking the streets of Kirkby Abbey was no longer such a far-fetched notion. Two people had been slain within twenty-four hours of one another. They'd both been stabbed and no effort had been made to conceal the bodies. In fact, the opposite was true – the killer had clearly wanted them to be easily found.

Charlie Jenkins was left in a field where the killer would have known that someone would soon come across his body. And the front door to Lorna's house was left open, presumably so that her body would not remain undiscovered for long.

James spelled this out to DS Stevens and two other detectives from Kendal HQ when he briefed them outside the house.

'We need to find out if the pair were connected in any way,' he said. 'Apart from living in the same village is it possible they were in a relationship or had a shared interest? Hopefully the neighbours and her colleagues at the school will help provide some answers.'

He told them what Annie had said about Lorna and explained that she had been due at the school this morning for an end of term tidy up.

'I'd like one of you to contact her son as soon as possible,' he said. 'Break the news and see what he can tell us about his mum and whether she had any enemies.'

They were still deep in conversation when Gordon Carver turned up. The *Cumbria Gazette* reporter made his presence known by calling out to James from beyond the crime scene tape that had been set up.

'I'd better have a word with him,' James said. He told the detectives to organise a house-to-house in Willow Road and arrange for officers to visit the school. He then signalled for the uniforms keeping the growing crowd at bay to let Carver through.

The reporter's first question to James was, 'Is it true that Lorna Manning has been murdered?'

'I'm not at liberty to—'

'Don't bother feeding me that line, Inspector,' Carver said. 'I've already spoken to the postman who found the body. So I know she's the victim and I know about the blood. I've already filed a story.'

James sighed. 'In that case, you might as well know that I believe she was murdered by an intruder. When you update your story I'd like you to include an appeal for witnesses. It happened at some time during the night and we'd like to hear from anyone who saw someone acting suspiciously in or around Willow Road.'

'So how was she killed?'

'As soon as I've had cause of death confirmed, I'll let you know,' James said. 'The pathologist is in there as we speak.'

'Oh, come on, Inspector. You've been in there yourself so you must have a pretty good idea. Was she stabbed, and if so, do you believe the killer is the same person who murdered Charlie Jenkins?'

'It's impossible to know at this early stage if there's a link between the two deaths,' James answered. 'But, of course, it's something that warrants consideration, and we'll be looking for similarities and connections.'

'So what message do you want to send to the people of Kirkby Abbey?' Carver said. 'Should they be worried that a maniac is on the prowl and that nobody is safe?'

James shook his head. 'That'd be irresponsible and you know it.'

'Okay, then what advice have you got for those who will be understandably concerned after they hear that there has been another murder?'

'The main thing is that there's no need to panic,' James said. 'But at the same time, it makes sense for people to be extra vigilant until the person responsible is in custody.'

Carver was eager to ask more questions, but a uniformed officer approached them and whispered to James that the pathologist needed an urgent word with him inside the house.

James told Carver he would speak to him again later and went looking for Dr Flint. He found her in the kitchen looking down on Lorna Manning's body.

Removing her face mask, she said, 'First, I can confirm that the victim's throat was slashed and she was stabbed in the stomach. There are no other wounds. The murder weapon could well be the same knife that was used to kill Charlie Jenkins. I'll need to do more work to be sure.'

Dr Flint reached behind her and picked up an envelope from the worktop.

'This was in her dressing gown pocket,' she said. 'I thought you should see it before anyone else.'

James put his latex gloves back on before taking the envelope from her. An ugly fear spread through him when he saw that his own name had been scrawled on the front with a black marker.

The envelope wasn't stuck shut so he opened it and pulled out another of the Twelve Days of Christmas cards.

There was a short message inside, and it caused the blood to thunder through his veins.

Two down, ten to go.

Merry Christmas to the people of Kirkby Abbey.

CHAPTER THIRTY-ONE

Annie was in a state of absolute despair. Her face was awash with tears for the second day in a row and there was a grinding ache in her chest.

She was trying hard to concentrate on the television news, but her thoughts kept drifting to poor Lorna. What had happened to the woman was so wrong and tragic and despicable. She had been a good person, a kind person, a person who always put others before herself. It made no sense to Annie that someone had felt compelled to take her life in such a brutal fashion.

Unless, of course, she was picked at random by a killer who was so deranged that he or she thought it would be fun to flag up their evil intentions in a Christmas card that was placed in a parcel alongside a dead bird.

It was like being trapped in a never-ending nightmare that began three months ago when Andrew Sullivan was released from prison. Then came the gruesome murder of Charlie Jenkins, the man who she'd had a crush on in their youth.

After that, the cancellation of family Christmas. And now this. Annie's boss stabbed to death in her own home.

A memory came to her suddenly, of when she'd first met Lorna. She went to the school to let them know that she was a supply teacher and had moved to Kirkby Abbey. Lorna invited her into her office where they chatted for a good hour before the woman offered her regular shifts. They hit it off immediately and Annie was struck by how committed Lorna was to the campaign for keeping the school open. She knew for sure that the staff and the children were going to be devastated by Lorna's death.

An image on the TV screen snapped her back to the present. It was mobile phone footage of the scene outside Lorna's house in Willow Road. The newsreader was explaining that it had been sent to them by their correspondent, Gordon Carver, who lived in Kirkby Abbey.

'Police have yet to confirm the identity of the victim or the manner of her death, but have told us that a murder investigation has been launched,' the newsreader said. 'Locals say the house is owned by a Miss Lorna Manning, headmistress of the village primary school. This is the second murder in Kirkby Abbey in just twenty-four hours. On Saturday night pub landlord Charlie Jenkins was stabbed to death while walking his dog in a field less than a quarter of a mile from Lorna Manning's house in Willow Road. Police insist that at this point there is no obvious link between the two killings.'

There was no mention of the threat contained in the Christmas card and Annie was anxious to know what would finally convince James and his colleagues to make it public.

Would it be a third murder?

*   *   *

171

Annie stayed at home for another half an hour, by which time it felt like the walls were closing in on her. The pounding in her head filled her ears and her heart was in overdrive.

She had to get out of the house and talk to someone. The news about Lorna had made her forget what she'd been planning to do this morning. But now it came back to her that she was going to visit Uncle Bill before attending the church service for Charlie. The service wasn't due to start until two but she supposed there was a good chance it would now be cancelled.

She decided to stick roughly to the plan and pop along to The King's Head to check on Bill. She'd tried calling his mobile, but as per usual he hadn't answered. She'd stay with him for only a short time because she intended to drop in at the school before going to the church, even though James had advised her not to. She expected most of the staff to turn up there and she wanted to show her face as well.

On the way to the pub she was stopped three times by people she knew who asked her if she had heard about Lorna. The shock was evident in their expressions, and one woman who had a son at the school began to cry.

When Annie reached The King's Head the landlady, Martha, was outside sweeping the snow away from the entrance. She acknowledged Annie with a curt nod instead of her usual warm smile.

'I'm sure you would have been one of the first to hear about Lorna,' she said. 'It's so terrible, Annie. I still can't believe it.'

'You and me both,' Annie said.

'Do you know how she was killed? Was she stabbed like Charlie?'

'I've not been told,' Annie lied.

'But I heard that your husband is in charge.'

Annie nodded. 'He is, but when it comes to police protocol, he treats me like any other member of the public.'

They talked about it for a couple of minutes and Martha told Annie that she last saw Lorna on Wednesday evening.

'She came here and had dinner with Giles Keegan,' Martha said. 'I'd never seen them together before and they seemed to really enjoy each other's company. She was telling him about life as a headmistress, and he was regaling her with stories about his years with the police before he retired.'

Annie expressed her surprise. 'Were they an item? If so, then it wasn't common knowledge.'

Martha shrugged. 'I have no idea. But I thought it was nice to see her out with a man. Usually she came here by herself or with other women.'

Annie would have been happy to carry on talking for a while, but time was pressing so she asked if her Uncle Bill was still in his room.

'I know for a fact that he isn't because I just made it up,' Martha said. 'He left here about eleven after having breakfast and he didn't say where he was going. He's in and out of here more often than any guest we've ever had. And he told me about his car accident. That really shook him up.'

'I just hope he managed to get a good night's sleep,' Annie said.

'I'm not sure he did. He went out just before we closed up and I didn't see or hear him come back in later.'

'He's always been a restless soul. I think he's finding it harder to relax the older he gets.'

'I know the feeling,' Martha said with a laugh that sounded forced. Understandable, given all that had happened.

Knowing now she wouldn't find her uncle, Annie took her leave.

'I'd better be getting on, Martha, thanks for your help.'

Waving goodbye, Annie turned and was heading for the school when a horrid thought occurred her. What if Bill couldn't account for his movements last night? Would he become a suspect in Lorna's murder?

CHAPTER THIRTY-TWO

Ninety minutes had passed since the pathologist had handed James the card that was found on Lorna Manning's body. But the words inside it were still causing his heart to beat at a rapid rate.

Two down, ten to go.

Merry Christmas to the people of Kirkby Abbey.

He'd shown the card to DS Stevens before it was sealed in a bag and handed to a forensic officer. So far, only the pair of them, plus Dr Flint, knew about it. James hadn't yet told Tanner because the DCI was on his way to Kirkby Abbey and would be put in the picture when he arrived.

The two detectives had finally found time to sit in one of the patrol cars so that they could talk about it.

'Surely this is positive proof that Lorna Manning was killed by the same person who murdered Charlie Jenkins,' the DS said. 'The same psycho who delivered the dead partridge to your house.'

James nodded. He couldn't really disagree.

James checked the photo on his phone of the first message he had received.

Here's a Christmas gift for you, detective Walker. It's a little early, I know, but I just couldn't wait. My very own take on the twelve days of Christmas, complete with a dead partridge. Twelve days. Twelve murders. Twelve victims. And they all deserve what's coming to them.

He showed it to Stevens and said, 'That final sentence suggests that Charlie and Lorna were not randomly picked. The perp, for whatever reason, believes they both deserved to die. Or that's just an excuse his warped mind has come up with to justify a killing spree.'

'You shouldn't assume the killer is male,' Stevens said, his tone sharp.

James blew out an exasperated breath. 'I'm not. But we both know it probably is a bloke since more than 90 per cent of homicides are committed by men.'

'But there's no clear evidence that this one was.'

'I accept that, but we'll refer to the perp as a "he" for now, just to keep things simple. Have you got a problem with that?'

Stevens shook his head and wisely chose not to argue the point. 'Of course not, guv.'

'Good. Now back to the case. We have to accept that it's possible the killer thought Charlie deserved to die because he'd committed adultery at least twice, although we can't know for sure if he would have known about the fling with Janet.'

'But what about Lorna?' Stevens said. 'There's been no suggestion that she's done anything that could be perceived as seriously wrong.'

'We need to look into that,' James said. 'Her son might have some thoughts on it.'

Through the windscreen James could see that the crowd of onlookers had grown. So, too, had the number of uniformed officers who were managing the site and the SOCOs moving in and out of Lorna Manning's house. Some were taking photos while others were on their knees in the front garden searching for clues.

After discussing a few more issues, the detectives got out of the car and went back into the house.

Dr Flint told them she had done all she could do on site and had arranged for the body to be removed. She also promised not to mouth a word about the card found in the victim's pocket.

'I just hope you catch the bastard because I don't want my visits to this village to become a daily event,' she said with a mirthless grin.

The chief forensic officer explained that his team still had a lot more work to do, but they hadn't so far come across a murder weapon or evidence to suggest that any of Lorna's belongings had been stolen. He agreed with James's theory that the perp had broken into the house through the back door and Lorna had got out of bed and come downstairs to investigate.

James intended to have another look around the house himself, but his phone rang and the call was from a number he didn't recognise.

'DI Walker,' he said.

'It's Father Silver here, Detective Walker. Are you able to talk?'

'Not right now, Father.'

'It's just that something else has turned up here, in the churchyard. It relates to Miss Manning's death and I really think you should come and see it without delay,' the priest said.

James and DS Stevens were driven to the church in a patrol car. Neither of them knew what to expect, but James was anticipating another bizarre development.

The last couple of days had been like none he had ever experienced. Two brutal murders and a threat to kill that was off the scale in terms of its creepy originality.

He was satisfied now that it was all related and therefore three investigations had merged into one. On that basis, it would hopefully be easy to persuade Tanner and those above him to assign enough people to it.

His mind kept taking him back to the crime scenes and each time he felt his skin go cold.

The blood on the snow and the kitchen floor. The terrible wounds inflicted on each of the victims. The heartless way the two lives had been cut short.

He had attended hundreds of crime scenes while working for the Met in London. He'd seen murder victims who had been stabbed, shot, strangled and battered. But this was different, because it was happening in the small village where he and Annie had just set up home.

Both murders had been committed a short walk from their front door. And they had a connection with the victims. Plus, there was no way they could distance themselves from any of it – because either of them could become the killer's next victim if he got it into his head that they, too, deserved to die.

Father Silver was waiting for them just inside the churchyard gate. He was rubbing his hands together and stamping his feet against the cold.

'We got here as quickly as we could, Father,' James said. 'What's turned up? Is it another Christmas card?'

The ashen-faced priest shook his head. 'It's worse than that, Inspector. To say I'm shocked would be a gross understatement. Whoever is behind what is going on is one sick individual.'

Gravel crunched under their shoes as they followed the priest along a path that led to the rear of the church.

'I happened upon what you're about to see during a walk around the churchyard,' he said. 'I needed some space to think because I learned about what had happened to Miss Manning while I was preparing for the service for Mr Jenkins. I found it hard to take in.'

'I can well understand that, Father,' James said. 'This has come as a shock to all of us.'

He took them to a spot that James was familiar with. It was the grave of Nadia Patel.

On Saturday morning her son Keith had kicked up a stink because the white headstone had been sprayed with paint by vandals. Well, now the paint was gone, but resting up against the headstone was a colour photo of Lorna Manning. It was about eight inches square and in a thin silver frame. There were several spots of what looked like dried blood on the glass. And a message in black marker ink that read:

Lorna Manning deserved to die. The woman in this grave did not.

Father Silver had known Lorna Manning reasonably well. She had practised Catholicism and had occasionally attended Sunday Mass. They'd also worked together helping to organise various events in the village.

'I've been to Lorna's home several times,' he told James, pointing to the framed photo that was lying against the headstone. 'I'm certain that picture was on the display unit in the living room alongside photos of her son and granddaughter.'

While DS Stevens went back to the patrol car to get a bag to put the photo in, James asked Father Silver if anyone had been in the churchyard this morning or last night.

'I left here at seven o'clock last evening and arrived back at nine this morning,' the priest answered. 'If someone was here between those times, I wouldn't have seen them.'

'Is the gate locked at night?'

'If it was, it wouldn't keep people out. As you can see, the surrounding wall is only a few feet high.'

'Annie said that Lorna appeared to be unsettled and not very happy. Do you know what might have been the cause?' James asked.

'Sometimes she struck me as quite depressed. I tried a number of times to get her to open up, but she wouldn't. She was a very private person, but immensely likeable. She'll be greatly missed.'

'Do you know if she was in a relationship?'

'I don't think so. Whenever I saw her out in the village she was by herself and never mentioned a partner. But she was married at one time.'

'And do you know if there was any ill-feeling between her and Keith Patel? Was she one of the people he blamed for not calling on his mother while the woman was lying on the floor after her accident?'

'You will have to ask him about that, Inspector. I wouldn't know. But they weren't neighbours. Mr Patel lives on the opposite side of the village to Willow Road.'

The priest paused before changing the subject abruptly. 'I haven't been able to stop thinking about the card I received. And now that we've had two murders in the village, I'm inclined to believe it was a statement of fact and not some baseless threat.'

James saw no reason not to be honest with the man. After all, they were both on the murderer's Christmas card list.

'I accept that the evidence is now overwhelming, Father,' he said. 'It's a frightening thought, I know, and for that reason we have to think carefully about how much information we release to the public. Myself and other senior officers will be discussing all the options at a meeting this afternoon. The safety of the villagers is paramount, but we have to balance that against the likelihood that if people know about the threat it could trigger serious panic.'

'You're faced with an agonising dilemma, Inspector,' the priest replied. 'And I know that you'll do everything you can to protect the people of Kirkby Abbey. But surely they have a right to know what the situation is. Those who feel threatened can then take extra precautions to keep themselves safe, which may well entail going to stay with friends or relatives until the killer is caught.'

DS Stevens arrived back with a plastic bag for the photograph just then and James thanked the priest for calling him.

'Could you please keep this development to yourself, just as you have the card containing the funeral message, Father?' he said.

'Of course,' Father Silver said. 'Will you be going to speak to Keith Patel?'

'His house is our next stop after leaving here,' James told him.

CHAPTER THIRTY-THREE

Keith Patel was none too pleased to see them. He complained that he was in the middle of his lunch and asked them to come back later.

'That won't be possible, Mr Patel,' James said. 'Either you allow us to come in so we can ask you some questions or we'll be forced to take you for a ride, all the way to the station in Kendal.'

'Are you kidding? What do you want to talk to me about?'

'It's in relation to the death of Lorna Manning and the photograph of her that was placed on your mother's grave at some point during the night.'

His demeanour shifted. 'Are you talking about the school-teacher woman? I didn't know she was dead. And what the fuck else has happened to Mum's grave?'

James refused to go into the details on the doorstep so Patel allowed them in. They followed him to the living room where the television was on.

Patel dropped into an armchair and released a loud breath.

In front of him on the coffee table rested a bowl of brown soup and a glass of orange juice.

The two detectives remained standing, and James nodded at the television.

'Have you seen or heard the news this morning, Mr Patel?' he asked.

Patel shook his head. 'I try to avoid it. Too full of crap. Now what's this about Lorna Manning and Mum's grave?'

He appeared genuinely surprised when James told him about the latest murder. But surprise turned to confusion when James showed him a picture he'd taken on his phone of the framed photo against the headstone.

Patel couldn't see the words written on it so James read them out to him.

'That's some weird shit,' Patel said. 'But whoever wrote it was right about my mum. She didn't deserve to die.'

'Have you seen that photo of Miss Manning before, Mr Patel?' James asked him.

'Of course I haven't. I know who she is and we've said hello to each other in passing, but that's about it. Do you seriously think I put it there?'

James shrugged. 'It seems odd that of all the graves in the churchyard it should end up on your mother's.'

'Well, it's got sod all to do with me.'

'So can you tell us if you were anywhere near Miss Manning's house in Willow Road last night?' This from Stevens.

'I haven't been out of the house since yesterday. My knees have been playing up so I thought I'd rest them. And besides, it's been years since I walked over to that part of the village. No reason to.'

'Did your mother know Miss Manning?' James said.

'I don't think so. She was never mentioned and Mum rarely got out of here.'

'So Miss Manning wasn't one of the villagers who you believe should have checked up on your mother after her fall.'

'No, she wasn't.'

'And what about Charlie Jenkins, Mr Patel? Did you have a problem with him?'

The question seemed to trigger a warning bell in his head. He bared his teeth and gave James a hard look.

'I don't fucking believe this,' he shouted. 'The last time you came here you more or less accused me of sending you a threatening message in a Christmas card. Now you're trying to pin two murders on me. Well, I'll say what I said before, and that is I won't be answering any more of your questions unless I've got a lawyer with me. So piss off and find some other poor sod to harass.'

After leaving Keith Patel's house, the two detectives headed straight for the village hall in the patrol car. But they didn't have time to discuss what the guy had told them because as soon as they set off, James's phone rang. It was Annie, and she sounded anxious.

'I need to talk to you, James,' she said. 'Is now a good time?'

'I've got a few minutes; fire away.'

He thought she was going to ask him to update her on the investigation. Instead she wanted to tell him that her Uncle Bill had gone AWOL again.

'He's not answering his phone and I haven't got a clue where he is,' she said.

'Well, he won't be going far without his car so I don't think you need to worry.'

'But I can't help it. His behaviour concerns me.'

James felt sorry for Annie, but he couldn't allow himself to be distracted by her uncle.

'Look, I'll keep an eye out for him,' he said. 'If I spot him, I'll call you. But have you checked to see if he's at The King's Head?'

'Of course I have. I left there a little while ago. I spoke to Martha Grooms and she said he went out about eleven.'

'He's probably wondering around the village then.'

'But she also told me that he went out last night after the pub closed.'

'So what? He obviously got back safely.'

'Yes, but Martha didn't know what time that was. He could have been out all night. And who the hell knows what he got up to.'

It was a change in the tone of her voice that made James twig what she was getting at.

'Jesus, Annie, do you seriously think that he might have something to do with what happened to Lorna Manning?'

'I don't know what to think,' she said, her voice faltering. 'But he also went missing on Saturday night, and that was when Charlie Jenkins was killed.'

James knew that Annie would have struggled with her conscience over whether or not to mention this to him, but he was glad she had.

'You shouldn't work yourself into a panic over this,' he said. 'There's absolutely no reason to suspect that Bill had anything to do with either murder. You know he wouldn't be capable of doing something like that.'

'But you're forgetting that I don't really know him any more,' Annie said. 'The last time I saw him before this weekend

186

was eighteen months ago when he was vile to me at Mum's funeral. Now he's like a stranger to me. And there's another thing to consider. He arrived in the village on Friday, about the time that parcel was put on our doorstep. That in itself strikes me as odd.'

'Then to put your mind at rest I'll make some enquiries and ask my officers to look out for him,' James said. 'But in the meantime, you need to stay calm. If you see him or he turns up then call me right away. Okay?'

'Okay.'

'Are you going back home now?'

'No. I've decided to pop along to the school and then to the church for Charlie's service.'

James decided not to tell her that he'd just left the church. She would only freak out even more if she knew about Lorna Manning's photograph being left on the grave.

'Try not to overthink this, Annie. I reckon it's more likely that the murders were carried out by an alien than your doddery old Uncle Bill,' he said, trying to lighten the mood.

They said their goodbyes and when James came off the phone he said to Stevens, 'We've another suspect, but would you believe he's my wife's own fucking uncle?'

Annie called James again just as the patrol car dropped them outside the village hall. He told DS Stevens to go in ahead of him while he answered it.

'What's up now, Annie?' he said. 'Has Bill shown up?'

'Not in the last few minutes, he hasn't,' she said. 'But that's not why I'm ringing. There was something I forgot to tell you before. It's about Lorna.'

'I'm listening,' he said.

'Martha Grooms told me that she last saw Lorna on Wednesday evening at The King's Head. She was having dinner there.'

'What's so unusual about that? I'm sure she could afford to eat out occasionally.'

'Yes, I know, but she was with Giles Keegan and Martha made it sound like they were on a date.'

'I thought you said she wasn't in a relationship.'

'That's the thing. I didn't think she was, and it might well have been a first date or just two friends getting together. But in view of what's happened I thought I should tell you.'

'And you were right to do so, Annie. It's really helpful. We need to find out as much as we can about Lorna and the people she spent time with.'

'So, will you be speaking to Giles?'

'You bet we will. And we'll do it before the day is out.'

CHAPTER THIRTY-FOUR

The village hall had been turned into a makeshift incident room. Several tables were being used as desks and the wall-mounted display panel was now an evidence board.

James was surprised and impressed that so much had been put in place so quickly. But it made perfect sense to set up an operational base as early as possible.

There were twelve officers present – four detectives, a SOCO, and seven uniforms, including Inspector Boyd. DCI Tanner had arrived and was deep in conversation with DS Stevens.

It was a fairly small hall and so it already looked pretty crowded. Meanwhile, more officers were still up at the crime scene in Willow Road as well as at the nearby primary school.

James went straight over to Tanner who, as usual, was well-groomed and sharply dressed in a dark grey suit, pale blue shirt and striking red tie.

He was a thick-set middle-aged man with cropped greying hair and a goatee that didn't suit his plump face.

James still didn't have the full measure of the man, but had already given him seven out of ten as a DCI. His big weakness was his habit of delegating as much as he could to more junior detectives, and his reluctance to get out of the office to attend crime scenes. But he was here now, which was a clear indication of how concerned he was about what was happening in Kirkby Abbey.

'Are you up to speed on everything, sir?' James asked him.

Tanner nodded, grim-faced. 'DS Stevens has just told me about the card found in Miss Manning's dressing gown pocket and he's shown me a photo of the picture that was left on the grave in the churchyard. This is a real shit fest, James. In all my time as a police officer I've not known anything like it.'

'Me neither, sir. I was hoping the message I received on Friday was a prank, but I'm certain now that it isn't.'

'I'm afraid I have to agree. I've spoken to the Chief Constable and she wants me to update her as soon as possible so I suggest we steam ahead with the briefing. We've got some important decisions to make and I'm under pressure to stage a press conference back at headquarters later in the day.'

Tanner called everyone together and launched into a short introduction. He explained that evidence had come to light that established a clear link between the murders of Charlie Jenkins and Lorna Manning.

'We also have reason to believe that this could be the start of a killing spree targeting other people in this village,' he said. 'So this is now the Constabulary's biggest and most high-profile case. It's already attracting the attention of the media and that means the pressure will be on us to resolve it quickly.

'We can count ourselves lucky in one respect – the senior investigating officer, DI Walker, actually lives here. He's therefore perfectly placed to carry on heading up the investigation from this end. It'll be my job to coordinate things back at headquarters and to liaise with the media and those upstairs. But we need to prepare ourselves for a tough time ahead because it seems like we're dealing with a ruthless killer who has embarked on a mission that's probably been a long time in the planning.'

After delivering his ominous warning, Tanner handed over to James, who began by referring to the timeline.

'It started on Friday when I arrived home to find the parcel with the dead partridge and Christmas card on my doorstep,' he said. 'Then the following morning I got a call from Father Silver. Another card, with the same Twelve Days of Christmas design, had also been left in the church porch on Friday night.'

He read out both messages for the benefit of those officers who hadn't been made privy to them. He then explained that he'd spoken to Keith Patel because Annie had spotted him on Friday evening close to their home.

'I wondered at first if he was responsible because of his deep-rooted grudge against the villagers,' James said. 'He's gone so far as to accuse them of being racist, but when I spoke to him about the cards he claimed not to know anything about them, even though I saw several cards with the same design in his home. Unfortunately, the only fingerprints on the card and parcel sent to me were my own. I'm still waiting to hear about potential prints on the card left at the church, but I suspect they will only belong to the priest.'

James said he had checked in at the village shop and discovered that those same cards were in stock and quite a few packages had already been sold.

'Back to the timeline,' he continued. 'On Saturday night,

Charlie Jenkins was murdered and his body was found in the field on Sunday morning. Suspicion fell initially on his wife Sonia, and the carer Janet Dyer. Charlie had an affair with Janet and she recently told one of the elderly gentlemen in her care, Ron Curtis. He then told someone else and it got back to Sonia who went apeshit, partly because it wasn't Charlie's first affair.'

James told the team how Charlie then confronted both Janet and Ron.

'So that was where we were up to when the postman found Lorna Manning's body this morning,' he said. 'The victim received two knife wounds just as Charlie Jenkins did and the pathologist suspects the same knife was used. But on Lorna's body the killer left another card. The message inside was short and to the point. It read: *Two down, ten to go. Merry Christmas to the people of Kirkby Abbey.*'

James paused for a few moments to let this sink in and several of the officers let out audible gasps.

'This is why we're now taking the threat deadly seriously and treating it as a single investigation,' he added.

James held up the framed photo of Lorna Manning and explained how it was taken from her home and placed on Nadia Patel's grave. He said they had questioned Keith Patel a second time and he claimed to have no knowledge of the photo or how it got there.

'So there are a whole bunch of questions that need answering,' he went on. 'And one of them is how much of what we've just talked about do we make public.'

At this point, DCI Tanner spoke up, saying that the briefing needed to be paused for a short time so that he could respond to a text he'd just received from the Chief Constable.

James was happy with that for two reasons. Firstly, it gave him the opportunity to find out if any useful information had resulted from the house-to-house in Willow Road.

Secondly, it allowed him time to work out exactly how he was going to point the finger of suspicion at one of his own relatives.

CHAPTER THIRTY-FIVE

Annie was finding it hard to get through the day. It felt like she was caught up in an emotional whirlwind. Fear, grief and guilt were raising goose bumps on her flesh and causing her stomach to knot like a ball of twine.

She was terrified that more murders were going to be committed. Her heart was in pieces over what had happened to Charlie and Lorna. And she was feeling bad for allowing the irrational part of her brain to latch onto the possibility that her uncle might have been responsible.

She had spent an hour at the school with some of her shell-shocked colleagues. Flowers, tributes and cards had already started arriving. Tears flowed and fears were expressed. Everyone was in an awful state.

The police had been there too, searching Lorna's office for clues and talking to her deputy, Francine Moore, and the school secretary, Tabitha Reynolds.

Annie had sobbed along with the others and it took every ounce of her willpower not to tell them about the threat contained in the Twelve Days of Christmas card.

Now she had arrived at the church and the scene was just as distressing. There were several uniformed police officers outside, along with two television news camera crews. A number of villagers were giving interviews, while others were wandering in and out of the churchyard as though in a semi-trance.

Inside, the service for Charlie Jenkins was about to begin, and forty or so people had turned up. Charlie's widow, Sonia, was among them and was sitting in the front pew between two women Annie didn't recognise. Others she did recognise included Maeve King, who was in her wheelchair, and next to her was her husband, Peter. Janet had stayed away and Annie considered that a wise move on her friend's part.

The whispering among those present ceased abruptly when a fully robed Father Silver took up position in front of the altar. Even from a distance, Annie could see the strain etched into his features and she couldn't help but feel sorry for the man. His beloved God had treated him cruelly after his years of devotion to the faith. There was the diagnosis of terminal cancer, the imminent closure of his church, and now these shocking murders in his own parish. It was a dreadful burden to carry during the final chapter of his life.

He held his head high and paused for about five seconds before speaking.

'As you all know, I decided to hold this special service in order to bring people together following the tragic death of Charlie Jenkins,' he said. 'I wanted to give you all the opportunity to pay tribute to the man and to pray for his soul. But sadly, Charlie has now been joined in the hereafter by Lorna Manning, another much-loved member of our community.

'I am therefore devoting this service to both of them. Their sudden, unexpected passing is a blow to us all and will test the strength of our faith in God. The devil himself has descended on our small village, but we must not let his dark shadow extinguish all the light in our hearts. We have to remain strong and resilient in the face of this despicable evil.'

Father Silver spoke about Charlie first and said he had left behind a wife and daughter who had loved him very much.

'Sonia is here today and she knows that our thoughts are with her as she grieves for the husband she has lost,' he said. 'And I believe I speak for us all when I tell her that we will do what we can to help her through this difficult time.'

Annie looked over at Sonia and saw that she was leaning forward and weeping silently into her hands, while the woman to her right had an arm around her shoulders.

Father Silver talked for several more minutes about Charlie and how he and his wife had made such a success of The White Hart pub. Then he moved on to Lorna Manning and described her as a kind and committed teacher who had dedicated herself to helping the children of Kirkby Abbey.

By now, most of the women sitting in the pews were sobbing, including Annie, and so were some of the men. Several prayers were then read out, followed by a few minutes of silent reflection.

Annie was pleased that she'd made the effort to be here, and she felt that what the priest had said had been both moving and relevant. But it pained her to think that this was just the start of the grieving process. There were the two funeral services to come – or perhaps more, if James and his team failed to find the killer soon.

* * *

It took a while for everyone to leave the church. Annie was among those who held back in order to offer her condolences to Sonia.

'Thank you so much, Annie,' Sonia responded tearfully. 'I'm grateful that you and so many other people came along.'

Back outside, Annie noticed that the wind had picked up and was blowing dark, threatening clouds over the village. She could feel the cold sting of it on her face as she walked through the churchyard. She made a point of stopping by the graves of her parents. They were next to each other, close to the path. The granite headstones were both black, and the graves themselves were covered in glass and stone chippings.

Annie closed her eyes and silently told her mum and dad how much she missed them and how sorry she was that she had stayed away for so long.

There was so much more she felt like telling them. She wanted her father to know how sorry she still was that she didn't reconcile with him before he died. And how grateful she was, in hindsight, that he had stepped in to stop her from ruining her life.

And she wanted her mother to know that she was sorry that she hadn't given her a grandchild while she was alive. It was something she deeply regretted, even though it wasn't her fault.

But she knew that if she hung around she would start crying again and she didn't want that to happen, so she moved swiftly on.

When she reached the street, she joined a group of mothers who were discussing how to tell their children that their headmistress would not be returning to the school because something bad had happened to her.

They thought that Annie, being a supply teacher, could offer some advice. She told them it was probably best to be open and honest but not to go into too much detail.

'The one thing to remember about children is that they move on very quickly,' she said. 'Unlike us, most of them won't have many sleepless nights.'

As she spoke, she wondered how the mothers would react if she came clean about the threat in the Christmas card. Would they panic and flee the village with their children? Would they demand to know why they had been kept in the dark for so long? Would they condemn Annie for toeing the police line despite her own reservations?

These questions were still causing her pulse to race as she headed home a few minutes later. And she only stopped thinking about them when something caught her eye as she was approaching the village square.

It was a shiny white Range Rover that had slowed down to allow an elderly woman to cross the road.

Annie spotted her Uncle Bill in the front passenger seat. Her first instinct was to rush forward and wave, to seize his attention.

But she stopped herself when she saw the face of the driver. Even after all this time, and even if he'd lost most of his dark, wavy hair, she couldn't fail to recognise the man she had once been in love with – convicted child abuser Daniel Curtis.

As the old woman reached the other side of the road, the Range Rover picked up speed and drove off.

Annie was left staring after it, her heart banging against her ribcage.

CHAPTER THIRTY-SIX

The briefing session in the village hall resumed shortly after DCI Tanner finished his phone conversation with the Chief Constable.

'She told me that a press conference has been scheduled for seven o'clock,' he announced to the team. 'It'll be at the constabulary headquarters in Penrith and she wants me to front it. So let's get this done.'

James went back over some of the ground he had already covered and then provided an update from the crime scene in Willow Road.

'Lorna Manning's body has been removed and a thorough search of the property has taken place,' he said. 'No weapon has been found and forensics are confident that the only thing taken was the photo of Lorna from the living room. Meanwhile, all the neighbours have now been spoken to. None of them saw anything last night, but the woman who lives directly next door to Lorna's house did hear what she thought was breaking glass.'

James consulted his notebook before continuing. 'Her name is Doreen Sinclair and she told officers that she was lying in bed awake when she heard it at just after midnight. She's sure it came from the rear of Lorna's house but assumed it was an outside light or an ornamental feature that was blown over by the strong wind. She heard nothing more after that so didn't bother to get up. We've checked the rear patio and garden, and the only thing that's broken is the glass panel in the kitchen door. So it's safe to assume that the intruder broke in and killed Lorna shortly after midnight.'

James went on to point out that the rear garden backed onto a narrow lane with only a few detached houses on it.

'It would have been easy for the killer to approach the house along the lane and climb over the low garden fence,' he said. 'As ever, the lack of CCTV cameras means we don't have the luxury of viewing video footage that might have captured the perp.'

James explained that checks were being carried out on Lorna's phone, laptop and social media history. Officers had also been searching her office at the school and speaking to colleagues there, but nothing of interest had so far emerged.

'We haven't yet established a meaningful link between our two victims other than that they both lived in Kirkby Abbey,' he said. 'But the killer seems to believe that they did have one thing in common – they both deserved to die. And if this is indeed the motive, then we need to find out as much as we can about Lorna Manning and Charlie Jenkins.

'One thing that does seem to be in doubt is whether Lorna was in a relationship. Most of her friends and colleagues don't believe she was, but it turns out that on Wednesday evening she had a meal at The King's Head with Giles Keegan, who you all know was one of us before he retired. Now, it could be they were just acquaintances, but either way, I intend to talk to Giles about it. I'm also planning to interview Daniel Curtis. It was his father who spread the gossip about Charlie's affair with Janet Dyer. But Daniel was also seen loitering outside the school on Friday evening and I want to know if it had anything to do with Lorna. For people who aren't familiar with Daniel Curtis, he served a prison sentence for having sex with a minor and was ostracised by the people of this village.'

James decided not to mention his wife's involvement with the man, but he couldn't help wondering if any of them already knew about it.

'Do we know anything about Lorna Manning's movements over the weekend?' one of the uniformed officers asked.

'Good question,' James said. 'Right now, all we know for certain is that she went to the square on Sunday for the carol singing and was there when Charlie's body was found. I saw her myself. And I'm told that a couple of her neighbours saw her coming and going on both days, but no one noticed if she had any visitors. So we need to look into it some more.'

James invited Stevens to update the team on enquiries relating to Charlie Jenkins. The DS had just spoken to someone back at the office in Kendal who had been collating information.

'The headline point is that forensics haven't come up with anything that moves the investigation forward,' he said. 'They found no unusual or suspicious activity on his phone and computer. And the kitchen knives taken from the pub and the flat above it contained no blood traces. I've also talked to the FLO who is with his wife, Sonia. She says the woman has given her no reason to suspect that she killed him. Sonia didn't leave the flat last night at all and only emerged this morning to attend the church service for her husband. So she's most definitely not a suspect in Lorna Manning's murder.'

The discussion then moved swiftly onto the messages in the Christmas cards and the implied threat that ten more people were going to be murdered.

'I've been giving this a great deal of thought,' DCI Tanner said. 'Now that there's been a second killing, we can't remain completely silent on the matter. It's best we say something because there's bound to be a leak at some point. What I propose we do is make it known that we suspect that the same person could be responsible for both murders and that there's a possibility he or she will strike again. That way we cover ourselves if it gets out. I touched on this with the Chief Constable and she's happy to go ahead with it for now. She agrees with me that if we go public with everything, we might well encourage a few nutters to start sending out their own bogus threats in Christmas cards. We will, or course, reassure people that we're looking out for them by having officers patrolling the village day and night on foot and in cars.'

Nobody questioned this approach or raised objections to it and James thought it made perfect sense. If they said absolutely nothing about the threat then they ran the risk of a major backlash once it got out.

Tanner wound up the meeting and said he was leaving it to James and Inspector Boyd to organise the patrols and the next steps in the investigation.

'Finally, we all need to bear in mind that, apart from everything else, we're going to have to cope with what we're being led to believe will be one of the worst storms to hit this part of the country in years. And we all know how the chaos caused by really bad weather can create huge problems for us. So just make sure we're as prepared as we can be.'

There was just one more issue that James wanted to talk to Tanner about but he waited until they were alone outside before doing so.

'Sir, my wife's uncle has come to stay with us for Christmas,' James said. 'He's been behaving strangely and Annie is now wondering if he's got anything to do with what's been happening. But if I broach the subject with him it creates a conflict of interest.'

James told Tanner what Annie had said and made it clear that he thought she was worrying unnecessarily.

'It doesn't sound like he's our killer,' Tanner said. 'But you're right to mention it. I suggest you suss him out yourself, but if you feel that it should move to the next level then get DS Stevens to interview him formally.'

'Thank you, sir. I'll do that.'

'And one last thing, James,' Tanner said. 'I want you to know that I'm glad we've got someone with your vast experience on this case. You have my full support and I'm confident that if anyone can find the bastard responsible for this, it's you.'

CHAPTER THIRTY-SEVEN

Annie was desperate to know what her Uncle Bill had been doing in Daniel Curtis's Range Rover. Her mind raced through various dark scenarios as she walked in the direction they had been heading when she saw them.

It was a small village, so it didn't take her long to spot the Range Rover again, pulling away from the kerb in front of The King's Head. Daniel was now alone at the wheel so Annie assumed he had dropped Bill off.

She quickly stepped behind a tree so that he wouldn't see her as he drove past.

When he was gone, she hurried across the road towards the pub. It was then she remembered that her uncle had said he saw Daniel loitering outside the school on Friday evening. She could even recall his exact words: *I'd recognise that pervy bastard anywhere. Did you know he was back, Annie?*

Bill had sided with her parents when her relationship with the much older Daniel was exposed. And on the one and only occasion when Daniel came to the house to speak to her father, Bill called him a paedo and told him to fuck off. Her uncle had hated the man with a vengeance back then. So why the hell was he riding around in Daniel's Range Rover only days after returning to Kirkby Abbey?

Annie was determined to get an answer to that and other questions as she strode into the pub. There were only a handful of people in the bar so she spotted Bill easily enough. He was sitting alone at one of the tables with a pint in front of him. As she approached, he stood and smiled.

'Order a drink at the bar,' he said. 'Tell them I'll pay for it when I get another round in.'

Annie was thrown by the fact that he seemed so pleased to see her. It caused her to pause for a second before deciding to take him up on his offer.

Martha's husband Luke was behind the bar and she got him to pour her a large glass of Pinot. She carried it over to Bill's table and sat down facing him after taking her coat off.

'Cheers, Annie,' he said, holding up his glass. 'This is a nice surprise.'

'I came here looking for you earlier,' Annie said. 'But you'd already gone out.'

'Well, I'm sorry about that. I went to the garage. They'd let me know that they'd recovered my car and I wanted to see how much damage there was and how much it was likely to cost to repair.'

Annie took a sip of wine and wondered whether he was telling the truth.

'But you'll never guess who I met when I left there,' Bill said. 'In fact, he gave me a lift back here and only dropped me off a few minutes ago.'

Annie put her glass down on the table and lifted her brow.

'So who was it?'

'Your old flame. That filthy scumbag, Daniel Curtis. I couldn't believe it when he pulled up in his fancy fucking car and asked me if I wanted a lift. He didn't realise it was me at first, because my face was half-covered with the hat and scarf, so I had to tell him who I was, and then I said I'd rather walk. But he insisted and so I swallowed my pride because I was bleeding lost.'

'I don't understand,' Annie said. 'The garage is only a few hundred yards from here.'

'I know, but while I was there the guys were all talking about another murder in the village and police cars were driving by with their lights flashing. It put the shits up me and when I left there I was confused and disorientated. I started walking away from the village and pretty soon didn't know where I was. I'd gone about half a mile, I think, before Curtis stopped.'

Annie felt another frisson of unease. It seemed like such an implausible explanation.

'I tried to call you,' she said. 'But I'm guessing you're going to tell me you left your phone in the room, again.'

'That I did, Annie. I'm not used to carrying the pesky thing around with me.'

'I heard you went out late last night,' Annie said as casually as she could. 'Where'd you go?'

'For a walk,' he replied. 'I got bored in the room and they don't allow smoking. So I wandered around for a bit, had a couple of ciggies, and then went back. I had a good sleep after that.'

'Did you see anyone else?'

He shook his head. 'The village was dead and that suited me. I was in no mood for conversation.'

'So what kind of conversation did you have in the car with Daniel Curtis?'

Bill drank some of his beer and licked the froth from his top lip before answering.

'He asked me if I'd moved back to the village and I told him I was staying just for Christmas. He said he was spending the holiday with his dad.'

'And did he mention me?'

Bill nodded. 'He said he'd heard you were living here again with your husband but that he hadn't seen you around.'

'And that was all?'

Bill's brow twitched and he seemed uncomfortable suddenly.

'Don't hold anything back, Bill,' Annie said. 'I've a right to know.'

'Well, he did ask me if something that Janet Dyer had told his old man was true,' he said.

Annie felt the blood fill her cheeks. 'And what was that?'

Bill gave her a sympathetic look. 'Surely you can guess, love. It was the secret that years ago we all agreed to keep in the family. It seems you were the one who let it out by confiding in your old school friend.'

CHAPTER THIRTY-EIGHT

It was coming up to five o'clock and James and DS Stevens were about to leave the village hall. Outside, darkness had descended on Kirkby Abbey. It had also started to snow, and though it wasn't yet heavy enough to cause problems, it was making members of the team a little anxious. Some were keen to call it a day so they could get home before the weather deteriorated further.

'You can't blame them,' DS Stevens said to James. 'Most have been here all day and they don't want to be stuck here all night as well.'

James had some sympathy, which was why he'd already agreed to let the majority head off at seven. Most of the initial legwork had already been carried out, including the house-to-house, and the forensic sweep of Lorna Manning's home would soon be wrapping up. A lot of what else had to be done could wait until tomorrow and would be determined by what leads needed to be followed up.

Half a dozen officers whose shifts had started late would

remain in the village overnight. They would take turns patrolling on foot and in a marked car and remaining in the village hall. Hopefully that was going to make the people of Kirkby Abbey feel safer and stop them from panicking.

These days it wasn't possible anywhere in the country to have large teams of officers working around the clock. There just weren't the numbers, and even hardy coppers needed to sleep and rest.

The Cumbria Constabulary covered an area of some 2,613 square miles, including 200 miles of coastline, and the county had seen a significant increase in crime in recent years. And yet there were only just under 1,500 officers.

James had been given an assurance that he would get all the people he needed, but he knew that would depend on how long the investigation lasted and whether there were other major crimes or incidents that would need to be resourced. That was why the predicted storms were of such concern. You just didn't know how many serious problems they'd throw up.

Unfortunately, this wasn't going to be one of those cases where everything quickly falls into place and it doesn't take long to narrow down the list of suspects. Two murders meant double the amount of work and things would get tougher and vastly more complicated if more bodies turned up.

James had worked on two serial killer investigations during his police career. But the victims in both cases had been picked at random by psychopaths who murdered for the sheer pleasure of it, and the killings had taken place at various locations around London. This was so very different.

In this case, the first two victims were known to each other and had lived in the same small, rural community. It seemed likely that they had also known their executioner. The perp appeared to have a warped but organised agenda and he wanted to draw attention to his mission through weird messages in pretty Christmas cards.

James was frustrated because there were so many questions that they still couldn't answer. For instance, why were the killings linked to the Twelve Days of Christmas? Would the killer really try to claim that many victims? What could have triggered such a murderous spree? And what made the perp think he could carry on killing with impunity in a village with a population of barely seven hundred people?

'Shall we make a move, guv?' DS Stevens said, breaking into James's thoughts.

James nodded as he threw on his coat and wrapped a scarf around his neck.

A patrol car was waiting outside for them with its engine running. Their first stop was going to be Ron Curtis's house as his son Daniel had finally turned up there and they had arranged to interview him.

James wasn't looking forward to meeting the man who had seduced Annie when she was a teenager, but he had to admit he was curious to know what Daniel Curtis was like.

Ron Curtis had claimed that his son was no longer interested in young girls but James doubted that was true. He was probably just finding it harder to seduce and groom them now that he was in his fifties.

On the way to the Curtis house, James and DS Stevens went over the reasons why Daniel was a person of interest.

'He'd been ostracised by the villagers after his stint in jail, and it was made clear to him that he wasn't welcome in Kirkby Abbey,' James said. 'So he might well have decided to get revenge. He also is said to have reacted angrily after Charlie Jenkins confronted and threatened his old man.'

Stevens nodded. 'Ron told us that Daniel was back at his own home in Keswick when Charlie was murdered on Saturday night but this can't be confirmed. Is it possible Ron was lying or had Daniel lied to him? And then there's the fact that Daniel was spotted lurking outside the school on Friday evening. Was he there hoping to catch a glimpse of Lorna Manning, or perhaps planning to follow her home from there?'

Just before the patrol car arrived at Ron's house, James said to Stevens, 'There's something else you need to know about Daniel Curtis. Three years before he was done for having sex with a minor, he had a brief fling with my wife Annie, who was sixteen at the time. When her father found out he put a stop to it. Before then her dad and Ron Curtis were mates, but after that they didn't talk to each other. I should have mentioned it when the guy's name first cropped up, but I didn't think it would come to this and we'd have to talk to him.'

'Don't sweat it, guv,' Stevens said. 'That was nearly twenty years ago by my reckoning and Annie wasn't a minor. So I don't think we're into conflict of interest territory. It'll be a different matter with her uncle if things stack up against him, though.'

James shook his head. 'I really don't think they will. I'm sure it's a case of Annie overreacting.'

Stevens cocked an eyebrow. 'For both your sakes, I hope you're right about that, guv.'

* * *

This time there was a white Range Rover on the driveway of Ron Curtis's bungalow. It was only a couple of years old and looked as though it had recently been cleaned.

The bungalow's front door was opened before James and DS Stevens reached it. A tall man greeted them with a nod and a smile. He was wearing a grey jumper and tight black jeans.

'I'm Daniel Curtis,' he said. 'I'm sorry you weren't able to reach me before today. My phone packed up on me after I dropped it so I had to get a new one.'

It irked James that the guy did not look a day over forty-five. He'd lost most of his hair but not his looks, and it was obvious that he kept himself in shape. He had a square jawline that was covered in designer stubble, and deep-set brown eyes.

The two detectives went through the formality of showing their warrant cards before Daniel waved them inside.

'My dad's in the living room so go straight through,' he said. 'Is there anything I can get you? Tea or coffee, or perhaps something stronger? We have beer and wine.'

He had a soft voice and a pleasant, polite manner, and he struck James as the kind of bloke who would find it easy to charm the ladies, especially those who were young and vulnerable.

'Thank you, but we'll pass,' James said. 'This is not a social call, and I'm hoping we won't take up much of your time.'

James felt his neck grow hot under his collar as he walked along the hallway. He had to remind himself to treat Daniel Curtis like any other interviewee. But he knew that was going to be difficult as an image of a young Annie making love to the guy rose unbidden in his mind.

He wished now that she had never told him about that

phase of her life. But she had, and so he needed to resist the urge to bring it up and tell Daniel Curtis what he thought of him.

Ron was in the same armchair he'd sat in during James's last visit. Stevens introduced himself and the old man grunted a response and flicked a hand towards the sofa.

They both sat down and James opened up his notebook. Daniel lowered himself onto the other armchair and said, 'Before you start asking your questions, you should know that I've been in touch with my solicitor who has advised me not to talk to you without him being present. But I agreed to because this is a nasty business and I want to be as helpful as I can. You need to be honest with me from the outset, though. Do you guys actually suspect me of killing Charlie Jenkins?'

'Everyone in this village is a suspect right now, Mr Curtis,' James said. 'We're going through the process of eliminating a number of individuals from our enquiries. You're one of those people because only a matter of hours before Mr Jenkins was killed, he came here and threatened your father for spreading gossip about an extra-marital affair he had with Janet Dyer. You were naturally very angry and told your father that you would go to The White Hart to confront Mr Jenkins.'

'And I had every intention of doing so,' Daniel said. 'But when Dad phoned me, I was in Keswick and didn't get back until Sunday evening, by which time Charlie was dead.'

'That's how we understand it,' James said. 'But obviously we need confirmation of that. So I would like you to provide a detailed account of your movements on Saturday and Sunday. Where did you go and who did you come into contact with? You'll have to be specific in respect of times, locations and names.'

Daniel responded with a wide, smug grin that took James by surprise.

'I don't have a problem with any of that, Detective Inspector,' he said. 'You see, as soon as my dad told me you'd been here and had asked about me, I knew I'd be next on your list. I even anticipated the questions you were going to ask me. So I decided to have the answers ready.'

He reached into his pocket and produced a folded sheet of paper, which he handed to James.

'It's all written down there,' he said. 'I live in Keswick, as you know, and that's where I run my own business selling tyres. I had to go back unexpectedly on Saturday because one of my three staff members had an unfortunate accident when a car drove over his foot. I needed to sort things out and I was there until seven in the evening so I decided to stay overnight at my flat. On Sunday morning, I went back to the factory to check things over and stayed for most of the day. While I was there, I dropped and damaged my phone, which is why you were unable to reach me. This morning I drove into Kendal and got a replacement. I've written down my address, the address of my business, and the names and contact details of my employees.'

James forced a smile onto his face. 'That's most helpful, Mr Curtis. But did you meet anyone else while you were in Keswick?'

'No, I did not.'

'When you left your business premises at seven on Saturday, where did you go?'

'I went straight back to the flat and was in bed by nine.'

'And were you alone?'

Daniel's jaw tensed. 'Yes, I was. And for your information

there are security cameras covering the entrance to the block and the car park. So you won't have trouble verifying that.'

There was a long pause before James spoke again.

'How well did you know Mr Jenkins?' he asked.

Daniel shrugged. 'Not well at all. Before I left the village, I saw him from time to time in the pub and we had short but unmemorable conversations. I haven't seen him in ages. When I come back to see my father, I usually go to The King's Head, though not when it's busy, for obvious reasons.'

'You mean because you know you're not welcome here in Kirkby Abbey,' James said.

Daniel rolled his eyes. 'That's exactly right, Detective Inspector. People here hate me and Jenkins was among those who were verbally abusive to me. If it wasn't for my father, I would never set foot in this place again.'

'Do you think they're being unfair given your history?'

Daniel rubbed a hand across his face. 'Look, that stuff is all behind me. I'm a different person now and very much regret what I did. But I do understand why people here can't forgive and forget. To them, I'll always be a pariah.'

'That must make you very angry.'

'Only when I see how some of them look at me or when someone has a go at my dad as though it was all his fault.'

'Angry enough to make you want to hit back at them?' DS Stevens said.

Daniel looked at him, his eyes suddenly bright and alert.

'I can see where this is going and the answer to that question is an emphatic no,' he said. 'I don't hold a grudge and I'm not a bloody murderer.'

There was a sheen of sweat on his forehead now and spittle had gathered at the corners of his mouth.

James decided it was time to shift the focus onto the second murder.

'Now, can you tell us where you were last night, Mr Curtis?' he said.

A frown gathered on Daniel's face and his eyes narrowed. 'Why do you want to know that?' he said, his voice rising. 'Is it because of Lorna Manning? Do you honestly suspect that I did her in as well?'

'We'll be asking everyone we speak to the same question,' James said. 'So we'd appreciate an answer.'

'Well, the answer is I was here all night with my dad,' he said. 'We both sat up watching the box until almost midnight. Then we turned in and I didn't get up until ten this morning.'

James turned to Ron Curtis, who had a dark crease of worry above his eyes.

'And did you have a good night's sleep, Mr Curtis?' he asked.

'I always do, thanks to the pills I take.'

'And these pills knock you out, do they? Enough that you wouldn't necessarily have known if your son got up and left the house?'

The old man opened his mouth to speak but Daniel beat him to it.

'Oh for fuck's sake. This is getting silly,' he snapped. 'I did not go out and kill Lorna Manning. I've never spoken to the woman and I had no reason to want to hurt her.'

'So why were you hanging around outside her school on Friday evening?' James said. 'Were you waiting for her to come out?'

Daniel looked surprised. 'Did Giles Keegan tell you he saw me there? Is that why you're asking?'

'As a matter of fact, it was someone else who spotted you watching the school from across the road while smoking a cigarette,' James said. 'But tell me about Giles Keegan.'

'There's not much to tell. He was walking past on the other side of the road when he saw me. He crossed over and demanded to know what I was doing there. I told him he wasn't a detective any more so to bugger off and mind his own business. But he started shouting at me, so after a minute or so I walked away so as not to attract attention.'

'Why was Mr Keegan so angry?' James asked.

'We knew each other years ago, when I lived here. He was one of the coppers who testified against me and got me sent down. And he doesn't like it when I come back to the village, even though I don't usually stay for longer than a few days at a time.'

James made some notes, and while he was doing so Stevens asked Daniel to explain why he was waiting outside the school on Friday.

Daniel took a long time to answer, and when he did, he switched his gaze to James.

'I went there because I wanted to see your wife, Annie,' he said. 'I knew she was at the nativity play and I wanted to ask her a question that's been bugging me for weeks. I didn't dare go to your house because I couldn't be sure you wouldn't be there.'

James felt a dull thud in his chest. 'What are you talking about?'

Daniel's face coloured slightly. 'I know you're aware that she and I were in a relationship a long time ago, but I was hoping it wouldn't come up during this interview. I certainly wouldn't have mentioned it if you hadn't forced me to.'

'Just get to the point,' James said. 'What is it you want to ask her?'

'I want to know if something that Janet Dyer told my father is true. I put the question to Annie's uncle when I saw him today and he said it wasn't, but I didn't believe him.'

James felt the grip of anxiety in his stomach as he struggled to grasp what he was hearing.

'Tell me what it is you want to know,' he said through gritted teeth.

Daniel took a deep breath and said, 'Janet Dyer claimed that Annie had an abortion soon after we split up. I want to know if it's true that your wife killed my baby.'

CHAPTER THIRTY-NINE

Before Annie left her uncle at The King's Head, she downed two large glasses of wine. Bill polished off three pints of beer and worked his way through a plate of cod and chips but Annie had lost her appetite the moment he told her about his encounter with Daniel Curtis. She was still finding it hard to believe that Janet had broken her promise never to tell anyone about the abortion.

It was Annie's father who had insisted on keeping it secret back then. He said he didn't want Daniel to know and he didn't want to bring shame on the family.

Annie had confided in Janet because she had needed to talk to someone, other than her mum and dad, and she had mistakenly believed that her friend could be trusted. Over the years the subject was never raised by either of them, but she was now wondering who else Janet had told.

Knowing that Daniel had found out was like a fist clenching Annie's heart. Bill said he had told him it wasn't true, but he probably didn't believe that.

So . . . what next? she wondered. Would Daniel want to ask her himself? And if he did, what would she tell him?

Of more concern was whether James would find out. She'd never mentioned it to him because she hadn't wanted him to know that she'd got pregnant with the man she'd foolishly fallen in love with at sixteen.

And, despite the doctors she'd consulted telling her that in most cases an abortion does not affect fertility or future pregnancies, it was always at the back of her mind that the choice she'd had to make at sixteen was the reason she wasn't able to conceive now.

She felt a shiver as a memory surfaced. It was of the moment she broke the news to her parents after the pregnancy test proved positive. Her mother had started to cry and her father looked at her as though she were scum.

'You'll have to get rid of it,' he said. 'No way am I letting you have that bastard's child.'

'It's not up to you, Dad,' she told him. 'It's my body and my baby. If I want to go through with it then you can't stop me.'

'You're so young and you have no idea what it will do to your life,' he said. 'Please listen to me, Annie, and be sensible about this. I'm only thinking about what's best for you.'

They'd argued about it for days and during that time it was always at the back of Annie's mind that having the baby could bring her and Daniel back together.

Eventually, though, she succumbed to the pressure from her mum and dad, as well as her uncle.

The only people who knew about the procedure were her parents and Bill.

Until she went and told Janet.

Annie had a sudden urge to confront the woman for

revealing her secret. *She needs to know how pissed off I am,* she told herself.

Without giving it any more thought, she headed towards Janet's house, the wine buzzing in her ears. She was probably a little drunk, which was why she was acting on impulse for a change. Normally she shied away from confrontation, especially with people she knew. But this was an issue she wasn't prepared to bottle up.

When Janet opened her front door, it was immediately obvious to Annie that there was something wrong. Her normally immaculate fair hair was a mess, and it looked as though tears had washed away most of her make-up. Her eyes were wide and bloodshot, and there were dark circles beneath them.

The sight of her shocked Annie and stopped her from launching into the blistering tirade that had been building in her head. Instead, she felt a sobering flush of concern for the woman and instinctively reached out and placed a hand on her shoulder.

'My God, are you all right?' she said. 'You look sick.'

Janet shook her head. 'I'm not ill, Annie. It's just that I've had the day from hell and I can't stop crying.'

'Well, I've had a bad day too so let me come in and we can compare notes,' Annie said.

Janet gave a wearing sigh. 'Okay, but you'll have to forgive the mess I've made. I lost my temper and let rip.'

Annie got another shock as she stepped into the living room. It was indeed a mess. The artificial Christmas tree was on the floor along with various decorations. And there was a large wet stain on one wall just above an area of carpet speckled with shards of glass.

'It won't take me long to clear it up,' Janet said from behind Annie. 'That wall could do with a fresh coat of paint anyway.'

'So what happened?' Annie asked her.

'You know what I'm like,' Janet said. 'I have a short fuse at times and lash out. Today everything got on top of me. The last straw was when my sister called to say she wouldn't be coming for Christmas because of the murders. And I was so looking forward to seeing her. I threw my favourite gin glass at the wall and knocked over the tree. I know it was stupid but it did make me feel a bit better for a short time.'

'Come through to the kitchen. I can make you a hot drink or you can share a bottle of wine with me.

Annie opted for the wine and they sat at the table beneath the kitchen window. On top of it was a pile of about ten envelopes with names on.

'One of those is a Christmas card for you,' Janet said. 'I was planning to deliver them today but I never got around to it.'

Janet took a bottle of white wine from the fridge and filled two glasses. It made Annie realise that she'd drunk twice as much alcohol in the last couple of days as she usually did.

'It's nice to see you,' Janet said, placing a glass in front of Annie. 'Did you drop by for any particular reason?'

Annie shrugged, features impassive. 'There is something I want to chat to you about, but first tell me why your day has been so horrid.'

Janet swallowed some wine and pursed her lips. 'It got off to a bad start when I heard the terrible news about Lorna. I was still trying to digest it when Sonia Jenkins turned up here to tell me that I wouldn't be welcome at the church service for Charlie. I had intended to go, but she was very aggressive and warned me that she would make a scene if I did. Then, an hour later, my ex rang to say he won't allow the twins to come back home until the police have caught whoever killed Charlie and Lorna. We had words and he hung up on me before I could speak to the boys. Soon after that my sis phoned and I felt like slitting my wrists.'

'Were you not meant to be working today?' Annie asked her.

'I've scaled back on visits over Christmas. There are a few people in the village I'll be seeing, but my usual rounds outside are being covered by someone else.'

'Will Ron Curtis be among those you'll be seeing?' Annie asked her.

The question surprised Janet and her body visibly stiffened.

'I'm due to call in at his house on Christmas Eve,' she said. 'Why do you ask?'

'Because I was wondering if you knew that Daniel is staying with him.'

'As a matter of fact, I did know.'

'So have you spoken to him? Daniel, I mean.'

'Only briefly. He turned up when I was last there and—'

That was when she twigged and the breath caught in her throat. 'Is that why you came here, Annie? To ask me about Daniel? Has he been round to your place?'

'He wouldn't dare,' Annie said. 'But he gave my Uncle Bill a lift in his car earlier today and he took the opportunity to ask him if it was true that he made me pregnant and I had an abortion after we split up. He said Ron told him that after you told Ron.'

Tears sparkled in Janet's eyes and she started to slowly shake her head.

223

'Oh God, I am so sorry, Annie. But Ron put me in an awkward position by asking me outright when he heard you were moving back here. He said he had always suspected it because of something your father told him at the time.'

'So why didn't you tell him that it wasn't true?'

Janet shook her head. 'I don't know. It just came out and as soon as it did I knew I'd boobed. I swore the old man to secrecy. But he let me down just as he did after I told him about me and Charlie. I've got a big mouth, I know, but I beg you to forgive me.'

'Did you tell anyone else?'

'No, I didn't. I swear.'

'And what about Daniel?'

'When he asked me about it, I told him it was nonsense and said his dad was mistaken. I thought he believed me and that would be the end of the matter.'

'Well, it wasn't and I expect that sooner or later the bastard will approach me.'

'Then all you have to say is that it didn't happen. It's ancient history, anyway, so I can't imagine he'll make a fuss about it.'

When Janet stopped speaking her face folded and she began to cry. It was enough to convince Annie that there was no point in bawling her out. Janet knew she had been wrong to betray Annie's confidence and her contrition seemed genuine. And besides, she'd had enough pressure piled on her for one day.

'Look, don't worry about it,' Annie said. 'I accept your apology and with all that's been going on it doesn't seem like such a big deal. Let's have another drink and then I'd better be off. James will probably be home soon.'

After some more tears were shed, Janet wiped her eyes and

topped up their glasses. Then she rifled through the envelopes on the table and picked one up, passing it to Annie.

'Don't forget to take this with you,' she said. 'It's to you and James.'

CHAPTER FORTY

James resisted the urge to phone Annie when he and Stevens moved on from the Curtis house. He wanted to know if it was true that she'd had an abortion, and if so, why she hadn't told him.

It wouldn't upset him if she had. After all, it was some twenty years ago – long before she'd ever met him – and, given the circumstances, it was probably the sensible thing to do.

But the way it had come out was a source of embarrassment for him, especially when he wasn't able to answer the question, and could only warn Daniel not to approach Annie about it.

'Two decades have passed since you and she were together,' he'd said. 'So take my advice and let it rest.'

Before going back to the patrol car, James asked DS Stevens if he'd mind keeping what had been said in the Curtis home to himself.

'Of course, guv,' he replied. 'My lips are sealed. It's a private matter and nothing to do with me.'

He didn't know if he could trust Stevens – after all, they hadn't been the best of mates since the move to Cumbria – but there wasn't much he could do other than take him at his word. He had too much on his mind to worry about it.

But he was annoyed. It was as though his position as senior investigating officer was being compromised at every turn. First Annie's Uncle Bill gets thrown into the mix, and now this link between his wife and another suspect.

As they headed towards the home of former detective Giles Keegan, James hoped that he wasn't about to be hit for six by yet another unwelcome surprise.

Of all the houses James had visited during the past couple of days, Giles Keegan's was by far the most impressive.

It was a detached converted barn, with stone walls and striking views of the dales from the back windows. James had driven past it many times without realising that it was where the ex-cop was enjoying his retirement from the force.

When the patrol car pulled up outside it was still snowing and the wind had strengthened, but before them was a picture postcard setting, with lights from the downstairs windows glowing in the dark and flakes of snow swirling and dancing all around them.

Keegan hadn't been told they were coming so he was surprised to see them. And James was surprised that he appeared to be ready for bed even though it was not yet six o'clock. He was wearing a thick dressing gown and clutching a paperback book.

'I was about to have a bath to try to take my mind off what's happening,' he said, a little flustered. 'You should have let me know you were going to drop by.'

'It wasn't planned,' James said. 'But as you're aware we're now investigating a second murder and we're hoping you can provide us with some information about the latest victim.'

'You mean Lorna?'

James nodded. 'You were seen socialising with her last week and it raises the question of whether or not you were in a relationship.'

His eyes widened. 'Oh, I see. Well, that's an easy one to answer. No, we were not in a relationship, but I wanted us to be. You'd better come in and let me explain.'

DS Stevens had already told James a few things about Keegan. He was a widower, his wife having died of cancer five years ago, and he had a son who was living in London. He had spent his entire career with the Cumbria Constabulary, working his way up from a PC to DCI.

He'd lived in Kirkby Abbey for thirty years and had married his wife in the village church. He had a commendable record, according to Stevens, and had been highly rated as a detective.

His home was warm and spacious, the décor tasteful and modern. He took them through to a large kitchen-cum-dining room and invited them to be seated at a glass-topped table. They declined his offer of a drink and James got straight down to business.

'So tell us about Lorna Manning, Giles,' he said.

Keegan sat down himself, placing his book on the table.

'First, you should know that I went over to the crime scene earlier hoping to speak to you, but you weren't around and none of the other officers would talk to me,' Keegan said. 'I didn't like to bother you after that as I knew how busy you'd be so I came back here and climbed into bed because her death has hit me hard. I feel like I can't function.'

'So what, if anything, was going on between you and Lorna?' James asked.

Keegan leaned forward, resting his elbows on the table, and James could see the grief clouding his features. The pain in his eyes was palpable, and his voice cracked when he spoke.

'We'd known each other for six or seven years,' he said. 'My wife and Lorna were friends and when Christine died she was one of the people who helped me get through the worst of it. More recently we tended only to see each other at events in the village organised by the church and the school.

'But then just over a week ago I was out on one of my regular walks across the fields when I spotted her sitting by herself next to the stream. I noticed she was crying so I went over to see if she was all right. She said she was, apart from being terribly embarrassed. She wouldn't tell me what was wrong and she asked me not to keep asking. So I didn't. But I did persuade her to come back into the village and I walked her home.

'She invited me in for a cup of tea and we talked for a while. I realised then that she was just as lonely as me, and I thought we got on really well, so I invited her out for a meal on Wednesday evening at The King's Head, which I'm guessing is where we were seen together. It was really great and we agreed to do it again before Christmas. I was hoping it might lead to something more serious.'

His eyes were glazed now and James could tell he was on the verge of losing it.

'When was the last time you saw her, Giles?' he asked.

'That would be yesterday. We'd agreed to meet at the carol singing, but got split up after Charlie's body was found. I popped round to her house later in the afternoon to see if she was okay.'

'And was she?'

'Not really. Like everyone else, she was shocked and upset.'

'So how long did you stay there?'

'A couple of hours, I think. I left about five because she said she had some school work to do.'

'And how was she when you left?'

'Much the same. She was struggling to understand what's going on in the village and she kept saying how worried she was for the children.'

'Do you know if she intended to meet up with anyone else later in the evening?'

'She told me she was going to bed early. I asked her if she was planning to go to the church service for Charlie and she said she was.' There were tears in his eyes now and phlegm rattled noisily in his throat. 'I assume you're linking the two murders. But please tell me you're making some headway. The villagers are rightly terrified.'

'Well, as you more than others can appreciate, it's early days still,' James said. 'But we do suspect the same person is responsible.'

'So we've got a serial killer in Kirkby Abbey.'

James shrugged in a noncommittal way. 'I don't suppose you have any idea who it might be?'

Keegan took offence at that, shaking his head and fixing James with a belligerent stare.

'Don't you think I would tell you if I knew?' he said. 'I've been racking my brain but getting nowhere. None of it makes sense. This is a small village in Cumbria, for Christ's sake. It isn't crime-ridden London.'

Keegan fell silent for a few seconds, his wet eyes distant, his lips trembling.

'Sorry about that,' he said eventually. 'But this is all so close to home. I had feelings for Lorna and I can't believe what's happened to her.'

Stevens asked him if he had managed to find out why Lorna had been crying that day by the stream. The DS also pointed out that several people, including Father Silver, had mentioned that she had often appeared depressed.

He nodded. 'I'm sure there was something bubbling beneath the surface, but she wouldn't tell me what it was, and I wasn't inclined to push it. I wish now that I had. Do you think it had something to do with why she was killed?'

'We don't know,' Stevens said. 'It's possible.'

'We've just come from interviewing Daniel Curtis. He told us you had an encounter with him on Friday evening,' James said. 'Can you explain what that was all about?'

Anger flashed across Keegan's features. 'Sure, I can. That pervert was standing outside the school. I saw him when I left the nativity play. He must have been waiting to ogle the girls.'

'So what did you do?'

'Told him to shove off. The guy's a nonce, and I should know because I was part of the team that helped get him convicted.'

'And did he resist?'

'He started to but then thought better of it and left. I hate it when he comes back here to see his old man because I don't trust him.'

James had no intention of telling him that Daniel claimed he had been waiting outside the school to speak to Annie. The fewer people who knew about that the better.

He was about to wrap up the interview when Keegan's expression changed.

'Hold on a minute,' he said. 'Something has just occurred to me. What if the git was waiting for Lorna? She was in the school and would have left there soon after me.'

'There's no reason to believe he was, unless you know something we don't,' James said. 'Did Lorna have reason to even know the man?'

He thought about it while shaking his head. 'I'm certain that she didn't. But it could be that she got on his bad side. Maybe she'd seen him before outside the school and warned him to stay away and he didn't like it.'

'It's hardly a motive for murder,' James said.

'That man has an evil streak running through him, and to my mind he's capable of anything. You need to look into it and find out if he's had any issues recently with Charlie Jenkins. If it was me leading this fucking investigation I would—'

'Stop there, Giles,' James interrupted him, his voice stern. 'You are not in charge, and I don't appreciate you telling me how to do my job. We'll be following up every lead, you can be sure of that. In the meantime, I'll expect you not to get involved. And that means staying away from Daniel Curtis.'

CHAPTER FORTY-ONE

The two detectives came away from Giles Keegan's house feeling more than a little disappointed.

The ex-police officer had shed some light on Lorna Manning's private life, but he hadn't helped them move any closer to solving the murders.

James had no reason to doubt what Giles had told them and he couldn't help but pity the guy. His hopes of a more fulfilling future with Lorna had been dashed and the full impact of it was hitting him hard.

'It's a shame she didn't confide in him,' DS Stevens said in the patrol car. 'Something had obviously been troubling the poor woman for a long time. I would love to know what it was. It could be key to this.'

'In my mind I keep coming back to the Christmas cards,' James said. 'If the perp is planning on killing twelve people then what links them? Were they involved in something together at some point in the past? Something nefarious, perhaps, and it's backfired on them all? Maybe there's no connection and they've been picked at random?'

'And why is the killer being so brazen about it?' Stevens said. 'It's as though he wants to draw attention to his actions and cause a shit storm.'

James's unease was growing by the minute, causing his temples to throb and ache. He was frustrated by the lack of progress and shocked at the pace at which things were moving. Two murders on two consecutive nights. Did it mean the killer would strike again tonight and another body would be discovered in the morning?

The more James thought about it, the harder it was to ignore the panic that was churning in his stomach.

James decided to make two stops before calling it a day. The first would be the crime scene at Lorna Manning's house to see what progress the SOCOs had made. He'd then call in at the village hall to check that it was proving effective as a remote hub of operations.

He told Stevens to go home so as to avoid being stranded by the weather. It was agreed that he'd head straight to Kendal HQ on Tuesday morning where he would look into Daniel's alibi for Saturday night, stage a briefing for the team, and arrange for somebody to attend the victim post-mortems.

'We'll play the rest of it by ear,' James said. 'What we do tomorrow very much depends on what happens overnight. But for now, assume I'm staying here, and you might need to come back as well.'

When they arrived in Willow Road, Stevens headed to his car and James didn't envy him the twenty-mile journey to his home in Burnside. The snow was still coming down and it was bound to make it hard going on the roads.

The street was clear of people but there were still police and forensic vehicles outside Lorna's house.

As James entered, his phone rang with a call from Tanner. The DCI wanted to know if there were any updates before he fronted the press conference at seven o'clock.

'I'm afraid not, sir,' James told him. 'You know all there is to know.'

Tanner groaned. 'Unfortunately, that's not enough to quash fears that the killing spree has only just begun.'

James knew his boss was right, but he didn't bother to tell him so. Instead he wished him good luck and said he would try to catch coverage of the presser on TV.

The house had been turned upside down, testimony to the thorough job the SOCOs had done. They were still at it, but there were fewer of them now. Two were searching for clues in the back garden, aided by halogen arch-lamps on stands, and two others were in the kitchen scrubbing at the floor where Lorna's body had been found.

The chief forensic officer told James that they hadn't come across anything significant, but they'd be returning tomorrow.

He pointed to a small, black, wheeled, carry-on suitcase. 'We found this under the victim's bed,' he said. 'It's filled with personal documents and diaries. One of the other detectives was supposed to take it away with him but he must have forgotten.'

'Have you been through it?' James asked.

'No, we haven't. There's a lot of it and I don't reckon it will throw up any forensic evidence pertaining to the murder.'

'But it might provide us with some useful information on the woman herself. Leave it with me and I'll sign it out.'

James took the case with him to the village hall. There was a uniformed officer outside who James didn't know so he had to show his warrant card. A sign had been stuck to the door that read: POLICE NOTICE. TEMPORARILY CLOSED TO THE PUBLIC.

Inside the hall, the desks had been moved around and a bunch of laptops, phones and a couple of TVs were now on top of them. Photos of the crime scene, including the bodies in situ, had been pinned to the board on the wall, along with names of potential suspects and printed copies of the messages in the Twelve Days of Christmas cards.

There were five uniforms present and they all looked busy. James quickly briefed them and was told who would be manning the fort during the night.

He then checked his watch and saw it was almost seven. He sent a text to Annie to say he'd be home soon and settled in a chair to watch live coverage on BBC News of the press conference in Penrith.

He was still waiting for it to start when his mobile rang. He answered it without checking the caller ID.

He recognised the voice immediately and it sent a chill through his body.

'Andrew Sullivan,' he blurted. 'Is that you?'

'It's nice of you to remember my dulcet tones,' came the reply.

'How did you get this number and what the fuck do you want?'

Sullivan laughed. 'I got the number from one of your former colleagues at the Yard. He rang to tell me you were urgently trying to find out where I am and what I'm up to. So, for old times' sake, I thought I'd give you a bell to let you know.'

James was momentarily lost for words and he sat in stunned silence, listening to the vile thug who had driven him and Annie out of London.

CHAPTER FORTY-TWO

Annie was at home when she received James's text. Normally she would have asked him if he wanted her to prepare some dinner, but food was the last thing on her mind.

Instead, she poured herself another glass of wine in the hope that it would dull her senses and help her to get to sleep later.

She felt seriously uptight, and her mind was swamped by negative thoughts. But that was surely to be expected since it had been another harrowing day.

She carried the wine into the living room, switched on the television, and dropped onto the sofa.

She had already made up her mind to tell James about the abortion when he arrived home. If she didn't, he was bound to hear it from someone else now that the cat was out of the bag.

She wasn't sure how he was going to feel about her keeping it from him. They'd told each other years ago that they'd be open about their pasts. But she hadn't, not entirely, and now she felt guilty about that. Was it likely to put further strain on their marriage at a time when they were faced with so many other challenges?

On the TV the newscaster announced that they were going over live to a press conference at Cumbria police headquarters in Penrith. Three people were sitting behind a table and Annie recognised James's boss, DCI Tanner. She'd never met the man, but James had shown her pictures of him and she'd seen him on the local news.

He was the one who kicked off the conference by welcoming members of the press and the broadcast media.

'We've invited you here this evening to answer your questions about the terrible events that have taken place in the Cumbrian village of Kirkby Abbey,' he said. 'As you are aware, a second murder was committed there last night. The victim has been identified as Miss Lorna Manning, the headmistress of the village primary school. This followed the murder on Saturday night of local publican Charlie Jenkins, who was killed while walking his dog.

'You should know that we believe the two murders were committed by the same person or persons. Both victims received fatal stab wounds to the body and there is other circumstantial evidence, which I'm unable to share with you at this time, that indicates a link. I fully understand that people in Kirkby Abbey are very worried, and so we've set up an incident room in the village hall. Officers in cars and on foot will patrol the streets throughout the night. At the same time, a major investigation is under way, led by Detective Inspector James Walker, who is himself a resident in the village.'

There were lots of questions, but it would have been obvious to anyone watching that the police were short on answers.

Annie was glad that they were at least acknowledging that the killings were linked even though they'd elected not to mention the threats in the Christmas cards.

Nothing she heard reassured her that this crisis was going to be short-lived. It was clear they feared there would be more killings.

Annie found herself reflecting on something Father Silver had said during the service earlier in the day.

'The devil himself has descended on our small village, but we must not let his dark shadow extinguish all the light in our hearts.'

That was easier said than done, Annie thought, especially for the majority of people in the village whose faith in God wasn't as resilient as Father Silver's.

On the TV the story changed to dire warnings about the bad weather. Widespread disruption was predicted and councils were being advised to prepare for the worst.

Annie had never known the run up to Christmas to be so horrendously depressing. It was meant to be the season of peace and goodwill to all. But here in Kirkby Abbey it was like hell on earth, and soon the weather would make things even more perilous.

During all her years in London she had never been so scared or disillusioned, not even when James was receiving threats from that degenerate criminal, Andrew Sullivan.

It was getting to the point where she was thinking that she should never have persuaded James to move to Cumbria. What if it proved to be the biggest mistake she had ever made?

She went to drink some wine and realised that her glass was empty.

'Just one more,' she told herself as she got up and headed for the kitchen.

When she got there, she noticed the card from Janet, which she'd left on the table. She put the glass down, picked it up and tore it open.

When she slid the card out of the envelope the sight of it caused her heart to curl in on itself. She only just managed to stifle a scream by clamping a hand over her mouth.

CHAPTER FORTY-THREE

James had decided to walk home from the village hall to give himself time to think. He moved slowly, forcing his limbs into an uneven rhythm, while pulling Lorna Manning's wheeled case.

Snow crunched under his shoes and a fierce wind whipped the flakes against his face and coat. The temperature had dropped dramatically, and had frozen the slush that had piled up earlier on paths and driveways, but he was oblivious to how cold and uncomfortable he was because in his head he kept replaying the strange conversation he'd had with Andrew Sullivan.

'One of my snouts wanted me to know that a couple of his colleagues at the Yard have been making enquiries on your behalf,' he'd said. *'You've apparently got it into your head that I've followed you and your wife to your little hideaway up north so that I can get my own back for what you did to me.'*

James wasn't surprised that a couple of bent coppers had tipped him off, but he was surprised that Sullivan had responded by contacting him directly.

'*Well, I hate to disappoint you, Detective Walker, but I'm nowhere near your place,*' he'd continued. '*I'm taking a break in good old Cornwall, and I'm just leaving the police station in Newquay after telling them exactly what I've been up to this past week. You'll soon be getting a call from a detective sergeant named Ackerman.*'

'*Are you being serious?*' James had replied.

'*You better believe it, man. No way am I being drawn into whatever shit is going down where you are. But while I've got you on the line, I will remind you that you and me do have some unfinished business. So sooner or later we will be meeting up. And it'll be at a time and place of my choosing.*'

The call from Detective Ackerman in Newquay came just minutes later.

The DS identified himself and gave his office number so that James could check it out if he had any doubts about him being who he said he was. He explained that Andrew Sullivan had arrived unexpectedly, told them who he was and demanded to speak to a senior officer.

'He told me he wants to prove to you that he's been here in Cornwall for the past five days,' Ackerman said. 'He's given me the name of the hotel he's staying in and listed all the places he's been to. He says he fears you might try to stitch him up for something he hasn't done.'

James asked him to look into the alibi Sullivan had given and spelled out why he wanted to know about Sullivan's movements.

'If the bastard is telling the truth and isn't involved in what's going on here then it'll be a big weight off my shoulders,' James said.

'Then I'll make it my business to get back to you as soon as possible,' Ackerman replied.

It was seven-forty-five when James let himself into the house. He had time to hang up his coat and kick off his shoes before Annie appeared in the hallway.

'I'm so glad you're back,' she said. 'I've got some things to tell you.'

Her appearance startled him, but he tried to mask his reaction to it with a smile.

'I've got things to tell you too, hon,' he said. 'But can we pour ourselves a couple of strong drinks before we chat?'

She held up a glass that he hadn't realised she was holding.

'I'm already way ahead of you,' she said.

James knew she'd had a rough day, what with Lorna Manning's murder, the church service, and her Uncle Bill. It was also likely that she'd been told that Daniel Curtis wanted to know if she'd had an abortion. If she had, then maybe she was about to confront the issue head-on by telling him whether or not it was true. He was ready to assure her that it didn't matter to him either way.

Her eyes were dry but raw, and she looked smaller somehow, as though crushed by the weight of grief and worry. His heart went out to her, so he stepped forward and gave her a hug.

'We'll get through this, hon,' he whispered, his lips brushing her cheek. 'We've just got to tough it out like everyone else in the village.'

Annie eased herself away from him and grasped his elbow with her free hand.

'Come into the kitchen,' she said. 'I've already poured you a large whiskey. I've just got to add the ice.'

He sat at the table while she fixed his drink and topped up her own glass with wine. He wondered how many she'd had but thought it best not to ask. He'd never known her to drink so much and he knew the stress was to blame.

He was keen to tell her about his conversation with Andrew Sullivan, though not the part where he'd talked about meeting James to settle some 'unfinished business'. If the guy's alibi checked out then it'd be one less thing for Annie to worry about. But he wouldn't say anything until she got what she needed to get off her chest.

He stayed quiet as she put their drinks on the table. But before sitting down she returned to the worktop and picked up an object that was all too familiar to him.

'I went to see Janet Dyer today and she gave me this,' she said, handing it to him. 'I didn't open it until a short time ago and it gave me a shock.'

It was another card with the Twelve Days of Christmas design. James opened it up and read the message inside, which was scrawled in blue ballpoint.

To Annie and James.
Merry Christmas and a happy New Year to you both.

Janet xxx

'I can see why it gave you a fright, Annie,' he said. 'It's the same as the cards that were placed on Lorna Manning's body and delivered to me and Father Silver. But I don't think it means that Janet is—'

'Hold on a sec,' she broke in. 'What's this about a card on Lorna's body? You haven't told me anything about that.'

He realised his mistake and sighed. 'That's because I haven't seen you since we found it.'

'Did it contain another message?'

He nodded. 'I'm afraid it did.'

'Then are you going to tell me what it was?'

'I really shouldn't.'

'Oh, come on, James. Don't start hiding things from me. I'm caught up in this whether you like it or not. So I've a bloody right to know.'

He conceded the point, and after a swig of whiskey, he brought her up to date. He told her about the card found in Lorna's dressing gown and the message that read: *Two down, ten to go. Merry Christmas to the people of Kirkby Abbey.*

Annie's eyes shot wide as she sucked in a loud breath.

'Oh, my Lord, James. That's shocking.'

'I know, Annie. But the perp's living in La La Land if he really believes he can claim ten more victims.'

He then showed her the picture on his phone of the framed photo of Lorna that was left on Nadia Patel's grave.

Annie listened to him without speaking, a variety of emotions twisting her features out of shape.

It was when he got to the phone call from Andrew Sullivan that she was prompted to ask a question.

'Do you think he was being honest?' she said.

James shrugged. 'His alibi is being checked out, but it's got to the point where I genuinely don't believe he's behind this. The evidence, such as it is, points to someone living here in the village. And by the way, Janet Dyer is not on our list of suspects. She probably bought a bunch of those cards from the village store just like so many other people have.'

'I do hope you're right,' Annie said. 'I would hate to think she's somehow involved.'

'I'm sure she isn't,' James said. 'But I will go and talk to her tomorrow. Now, what about your uncle? Did you manage to track him down?'

She nodded. 'I had a drink with him at The King's Head after I left the church. He said he went for a walk last night but didn't meet up with anyone. This morning he went to the garage to check on his car, which had been recovered.'

'Well, I did mention to the DCI what you said about Bill,' James said. 'It's been agreed that I should have a chat with him, just to be sure I'm right in believing he's not the perp.'

'I don't think he is either,' Annie said. 'It's just that his behaviour has been so odd and all this bad stuff started happening as soon as he arrived here.'

'I'll go and see him tomorrow,' he told her. 'But to be on the safe side I'll get a uniform to put The King's Head under surveillance tonight. If he ventures out, we'll know. Now, have you told me everything you know about his movements last night and today?'

Annie gave it some thought before replying.

'There is one other thing you should know,' she said. 'Bill says he got confused after leaving the garage and started walking away from the village. Daniel Curtis was passing in his car and stopped to offer him a lift. He accepted.'

She paused there and chewed on her bottom lip. James could see she was struggling with how much to reveal to him.

'I already know about that, Annie,' he said. 'Daniel Curtis was the last person I interviewed today and he told me.'

Annie's back straightened and her jaw inched forward.

'Did he also tell you that he pumped Bill for information about me?' she said.

James nodded. 'He's trying to find out if he made you pregnant just before you broke up with him. Janet Dyer told his father that you had an abortion.'

Annie stared at her husband for several seconds, one eye squinting.

Then she said, 'It's true. I got pregnant and had the baby aborted. I'm really sorry I didn't tell you. It isn't something I'm proud of. And I certainly don't want Daniel Curtis to know about it. Janet was the only person who knew outside the family and she should not have told Daniel's dad. I've been to see her and she knows I'm not happy.'

She made a noise in the back of her throat and started sobbing. James stood and walked around the table to comfort her.

'Don't let it upset you, hon,' he said. 'It really doesn't bother me that you had an abortion back then or that you didn't tell me. It was none of my business. All that concerns me is your wellbeing. Whatever you did or didn't do in the past won't change how much I love you.'

CHAPTER FORTY-FOUR

Annie had been in bed for the best part of an hour, but James was still wide awake and struggling to get his thoughts into some kind of order.

He'd stayed up because he knew he wouldn't be able to sleep with so much on his mind. He was trying to pull together a plan for tomorrow while reflecting on the long, emotional conversation he'd had with Annie.

It was now 11 p.m. and he was on his fourth whiskey. It'd be the last though, because he didn't want to wake up in the morning with a stinking hangover.

When they had talked about the abortion his wife's eyes had teared up. It was clear that the secret coming to light had resurrected so many bad memories and made her question once again her decision to go through with it. She had even confessed to James that she was fearful that it might be the reason she hadn't become pregnant, despite their trying. James very much doubted that was the case and had tried his best to console and reassure her. He told her that he had warned

Daniel Curtis to stay away from her. But he didn't go so far as to make her aware of the other man's loathsome remark – *I want to know if it's true that your wife killed my baby.*

The guy was so obviously a shitbag, and it concerned James that he appeared so worked up over something that happened twenty years ago. Was it because he was now in his fifties and without children of his own? Or did he resent the fact that Annie had taken action without consulting him and he wanted to make her pay for that?

James knew that Daniel wouldn't believe Annie, even if she told him that she'd never had an abortion, and he didn't think she should have to lie. She was only sixteen at the time and they had split up – it was the right choice for her given the situation. There was no reason for her not to tell the truth.

James switched off the television. He had seen and heard enough of the news, which had been dominated by the weather and 'The Christmas Killer' who was terrorising a Cumbrian village.

But he wasn't ready for bed so he turned his attention to Lorna Manning's suitcase. He'd already emptied the contents onto the coffee table, but hadn't yet sifted through it all. There were small personal diaries going back some ten years, plus a bunch of cardboard folders and large brown envelopes.

He didn't plan to wade through them all tonight, and would send them over to Kendal tomorrow, but he was curious to know if any of the files and documents offered a useful insight into their second victim.

The first three envelopes he opened contained the sort of things that are often stored away in drawers, filing cabinets and cases. There were Lorna's divorce papers, her son's birth certificate, life and home insurance policies, and documents relating to her career as a teacher.

It was when he picked up the fourth envelope in the pile that he realised he hadn't been wasting his time. On the front was written a single sentence: *Open in the event of my death.*

Inside was a sheet of A4 paper with a number of printed paragraphs on one side, along with two newspaper cuttings dated ten years ago.

Once James had read through them, he had the answer as to why the headmistress had been such a troubled soul.

CHAPTER FORTY-FIVE

Tuesday December 20th

James snapped awake to the blare of the alarm clock on Tuesday morning, five days before Christmas. He turned on his side, stretched out an arm, and flicked it off.

It was 7 a.m. and it took him a moment to realise that he was alone in the bed. He hadn't heard Annie get up, which was unusual, and he put it down to the whiskey in his system.

He felt limp with fatigue as he climbed out of bed, but at least he didn't have a hangover. He pulled on tracksuit bottoms and a T-shirt, and opened the curtains.

Snow as white as a new page hugged the village like a blanket, and though it had stopped falling, James knew it was just a brief respite. An opaque, grey sky offered the promise that more was on the way.

Annie was sitting at the table in the kitchen. She looked exhausted, her eyes squinting with tiredness.

'There's coffee in the perc,' she said. 'And I've already put milk in your mug.'

'Thank you, hon. How long have you been up?'

'An hour or so. But I was awake for ages. My head's a total mess with all that's going on. And it doesn't help that I don't know what to do with myself. I no longer have to prepare for the family get-together, the school's in virtual shut-down, and the thought of doing any renovating really didn't appeal. To top it all, mistakes I made in the past have come back to haunt me.' She blinked and puffed out her cheeks. 'But enough about me. Did you manage to get much sleep?'

'About five hours, I reckon.'

'I didn't hear you come to bed.'

'That's because it was after midnight and you were out cold.'

'Why did you stay up so late?'

'I found something of interest in Lorna Manning's suitcase,' he said. 'I think it solves the mystery of why she seemed depressed much of the time. But whether it helps lead us to her killer is another matter.'

He placed his mug on the table and went into the living room, where he'd left the envelope with the words *Open in the event of my death* on the front, and grabbed it off the coffee table.

Back in the kitchen, he showed it to Annie and slid out the two newspaper cuttings and the sheet of A4 paper.

'The stories appeared in *The Sun* and *The Mail* ten years ago, when Lorna was living in Hampshire,' James said. 'As you can see, they're both reports of a hit-and-run on a country lane in the New Forest. An eighteen-year-old girl was knocked down and killed, and left by the side of the road. I did a Google search last night and it seems the police never found out who the driver was.'

'So, what has this got to do with Lorna?' Annie asked.

'Well, it turns out that Lorna Manning was the driver. That typewritten note is a confession and it's her signature on the bottom. She says she was returning home from an impromptu party in Christchurch when her car struck the girl, who was walking along the side of the road after her own vehicle broke down. Lorna says she got out to check and found the girl was dead. But she drove off in a panic because she'd been drinking and was way over the limit.'

Annie was now shaking her head in disbelief, her eyes out on stalks.

'She admits she's a coward and ashamed of herself because she couldn't face going to prison,' James continued. 'She asks whoever opens the envelope to contact the girl's parents so they can have closure. She tells them how sorry she is for accidentally killing their daughter and for not going to the police.'

As Annie read the notes and the reports, James thought about what Lorna had done and how it had blighted her life afterwards. She joined the long list of drunk drivers who had taken similar action after colliding with a pedestrian, only to regret it afterwards.

In the note, Lorna said that she hadn't told anyone about what happened on that night in the forest. But James wondered if she was lying, or if someone had found out and decided to make her pay. It was stretching it to think that her victim's parents had tracked her down to Kirkby Abbey. But if they had, then it would mean that someone else had murdered Charlie Jenkins, and James was convinced that wasn't the case.

'I'll send copies of these to Hampshire police,' he said. 'They can show them to the girl's parents. They'll also have to check that they have an alibi for Sunday night.'

Annie looked up sharply from the cuttings. 'You don't honestly believe that the girl's father or mother would have come here to kill her, do you?'

James shook his head. 'No, I don't, but they had motive so will have to be ruled out. I'm sure it won't take long.'

James saw Annie's jaw clench, her eyes tighten.

'I'm really not sure how I feel about Lorna now,' she said. 'The person I knew was kind and caring, and great with the children. And I'm sure it's true that what happened ten years ago was a terrible accident. But she should never have been driving whilst drunk, and leaving the poor girl there was reprehensible. What if she was unconscious and not dead? Maybe paramedics could have saved her if they'd got there quickly enough.'

An hour later, James was suited and booted, and ready to crack on with the investigation.

He was relieved that no one had called to tell him that another body had turned up. But that didn't mean the killer hadn't struck for a third time during the night, of course. It could simply be that the victim hadn't yet been discovered.

He retreated to his study while Annie got herself ready for the day. She had asked him to find out if her uncle had left The King's Head overnight, so that was the first thing he did when he was behind his desk.

The uniformed officer who was tasked with watching the pub admitted he hadn't been able to provide continuous surveillance.

'I needed toilet breaks, sir,' he said. 'And at one point I was instructed to check out a report of an intruder in someone's garden. It turned out to be a fox, though. That was between one and two this morning.'

James was a little annoyed, but not surprised given how few officers had been on duty in the village.

'Were there any other incidents?' he asked. 'Or suspicious activity of any kind?'

'Nothing at all, sir. It was eerily quiet. A couple of people were stopped just before midnight, and they had a good excuse to be out. But after that the lads didn't come across anyone. For most of the night the only movement we saw was the snow coming down.'

Next, James called the office and got put through to DS Stevens, who said he had been in since 6 a.m.

'I can't see the point in coming to Kendal this morning,' James said. 'I suggest you front a meeting to update everyone. If I can participate via video link I will. If not, you can tell them that as far as we know there hasn't been another murder. But put the team on standby in case it turns out there has been and we just don't know it yet.'

He told Stevens about Lorna Manning's written confession and said he would arrange for one of the patrols to take it to Kendal.

'Get someone to liaise with Hampshire police on this,' he added. 'They need to run a check on the parents of the girl she killed in the hit-and-run. They're going to be very upset but I want to know if they can account for their movements on Sunday night. And let me know as soon as you've looked into Daniel Curtis's story of where he was and what he did on Saturday night.'

'Do you want me to come to Kirkby Abbey?' Stevens asked.

'Let's talk about that in a couple of hours,' James said. 'If no more bodies appear then I think you'll be more useful staying in the office. But I do want a fresh batch of uniforms here.'

'That's in hand, guv. DC Abbott left here a while ago with half a dozen uniforms.'

'Good. I intend to talk to Janet Dyer and Annie's Uncle Bill this morning. At best, they're low-level suspects,' he said. 'What we desperately need are some new leads. That's why I'm hoping forensics might offer up something concrete today.'

'I wouldn't count on it, guv. Our perp seems to have mastered the art of killing without leaving behind a single piece of evidence.'

James then rang Tanner and repeated what he'd told Stevens. The DCI said he had agreed to stage another press conference later in the day.

'If you get even a sniff of something then let me know,' Tanner said. 'The pressure from both the powers-that-be and the media is fucking unbearable. If there's been another killing then I hate to think what the reaction will be.'

After ending the call, James checked online for stories about the murders and found there were scores of them. It was splashed across the front pages of several national newspapers.

Second brutal murder in tiny Cumbrian village

The Christmas Killer claims another victim

Village in shock following two murders

Back in the kitchen, James poured himself another coffee and put some bread in the toaster. When Annie joined him, he said he'd be heading out as soon as he'd eaten. He also told her that it appeared Bill had remained in his room at The King's Head all night.

'I have to point out that the pub wasn't under surveillance continuously and we've had no word of another body being found.'

'Will you let me know when you've spoken to him?' Annie said. 'I want to meet up with him myself today.'

'Of course, hon. That won't be a problem.'

James ate his toast while watching the news. They were running footage of the snow storm lashing parts of Scotland. Disruption to transport services was severe, and in some rural areas visibility was reduced to just a few yards. A map was then put up showing another fast-moving storm bearing down on England from the East. There were fears that it would dump up to nine inches of snow and bring with it winds of 70 mph or more.

James felt a stab of panic when he saw that Kirkby Abbey was among the villages and towns lying directly in its path.

CHAPTER FORTY-SIX

A group of about twenty people were gathered outside the village hall when James got there. They were facing two uniformed officers and a woman who, at first, James didn't recognise because she was bundled up in a heavy coat, scarf and woollen hat.

As he got closer, he saw that she was Detective Constable Jessica Abbott, who was part of the team in Kendal. She was doing her best to mollify the group, who were demanding to know what the police were doing to protect them.

James didn't need to be told that they were worried villagers, and as he approached, he heard one of them say, 'Why are there so few coppers here? There's a killer roaming these streets and we're all shit scared.'

DC Abbott responded, her voice loud and confident. 'Our officers have been patrolling the village throughout the night and as we investigate these appalling crimes, we're doing everything we can to ensure that you're all safe.'

She spotted James and her expression changed, prompting

most of the group to turn towards him. He was recognised instantly, and suddenly became the focus of their attention.

'You're the detective we came here to see,' one of the women called out. 'So, tell us what's going on and how worried we should be.'

Before James could reply, another question was thrown at him by a young man wearing a Puffa jacket. 'On the news they're saying that the person who committed the murders almost certainly lives in the village. If that's true then I don't intend to hang around. I've got a wife and two kids to watch out for.'

More questions were fired at James, but he didn't say anything until he was standing next to DC Abbott.

'What my colleague has just told you is the truth,' he said. 'We are working around the clock to solve these murders and to keep you all safe. I'm afraid we don't know for sure if the person responsible lives here in Kirkby Abbey, or why Mr Jenkins and Miss Manning were targeted. But, obviously, everyone in the village needs to be vigilant and cautious.' He pointed at the man in the Puffa jacket. 'And if moving away temporarily will make you and your family feel more secure then you should do it, sir.'

James stood his ground and answered more questions. He had to explain why the police weren't raiding every house in the village in their search for the killer, and why the inside of the village hall was out of bounds to the public. He was also asked how close they were to finding the perpetrator.

For James, it was like facing a bunch of tough, clued-up reporters at a press conference. But he answered every question as clearly and honestly as possible.

The villagers were far from satisfied, though, and when he

said he had to go there were mumblings about the need for a proper public meeting.

Inside the single-storey building, James thanked DC Abbott for the way she had handled the situation.

'It wasn't a problem, guv,' she said. 'They got here just before I did and so I walked right into it. But it's not as if they were a rowdy bunch.'

Jessica Abbott was of Irish and East African descent and had been based in Kendal since being promoted to detective constable a year ago. She was an enthusiastic officer with angelic features that masked a fierce and determined personality. Colleagues and criminals alike too often underestimated her and came to regret it.

'I've been instructed to tell you that two more detectives are on their way here,' she said as they took off their coats. 'They're coming directly from their homes and should be arriving within the hour.'

'Then we need to work out what tasks to assign them,' James said.

He was pleased to see that things were happening in the hall. He counted seven uniformed officers, including Inspector Boyd, all busy speaking into phones, tapping at computer keyboards and making notes.

James crossed the room and stood in front of the makeshift evidence board before clapping his hands twice to get their attention.

'Okay everyone, listen up,' he said. 'We've got another busy and unpredictable day ahead of us. While we pursue enquiries here, the rest of the team will get on with things back at base. The pressure on the force is gathering pace and it won't ease off until we get a result. I've drawn up a list of tasks and I'll go through them shortly. But first the good news is that no more bodies have turned up so far this morning. If, God forbid, the killing isn't over then we will respond accordingly. There's also plenty of bad news, though, I'm afraid. We're not making sufficient progress, the villagers are starting to panic, and this area will soon be battered by a disruptive storm. Just how bad that will be remains to be seen.

'Today I'd like us to speak to as many people as we can in the village to find out more about the two victims. We know quite a bit already, but I'm sure there's a lot we're missing.'

He held up Lorna Manning's confession envelope and explained what was inside. He then handed it to Inspector Boyd and asked him to arrange for it to be taken to Kendal.

As the briefing continued, James purposely omitted mention of Andrew Sullivan and Annie's Uncle Bill. He wanted to limit the number of people who knew why they were in the frame.

Finally, he shared that he planned another visit to Lorna Manning's house in Willow Road and would talk again to Janet Dyer and Sonia Jenkins.

'Sonia's had time to get over the initial shock of losing her husband,' he said. 'I therefore want to see if she can recall things about him that she hasn't already mentioned to us. For instance, I'd like to know if he was involved in any way with Lorna Manning.'

There followed a short discussion about who would do what, and James told DC Abbott that she would spend the morning with him. The other two detectives would be assigned jobs when they arrived.

He took out his phone to call DS Stevens, as he wanted to know when the team briefing in Kendal would get under way, but just then a uniformed officer with a worried look on his face approached him.

'There's a reporter outside from the *Cumbria Gazette* and he says it's imperative that he talks to you, sir,' he said. 'His name is Gordon Carver and he reckons you know him.'

'I do, but was he more specific?' James asked.

The officer nodded. 'He said he's received some information that has a bearing on the case.'

'Then go get him,' James said. 'We'll use the office along the corridor.'

Gordon Carver walked into the cramped office clutching a small leather briefcase under his arm.

James was sitting behind the desk that was usually occupied by the hall caretaker.

'Hello again, Mr Carver,' he said. 'Take a pew and tell me what information you have that you're so keen for me to see.'

Carver sat opposite James and placed his briefcase on the desk.

'I believe I've had a communication from the killer,' Carver said. 'If so, then it raises some questions that I would like you to answer, Detective Walker.'

The reporter reached into the briefcase and brought out an envelope. As soon as James saw it, he felt a shiver of apprehension.

'It's a Christmas card,' Carver said. 'It was pushed through my letterbox during the night and I found it this morning just as I was leaving the house.'

He dropped it onto the desk and James saw that the reporter's name was scrawled on it in black marker.

'Has anyone touched this apart from you, Mr Carver?' he asked.

'Only whoever wrote it,' Carver replied.

James quickly pulled on the gloves he was now carrying with him everywhere and used the tips of his fingers to pull the card out of the envelope.

His pulse spiked when he saw the now familiar Twelve Days of Christmas image. Then when he read the message inside, he felt a cold numbness envelop him.

Mr Reporter

I've decided to tell you what I've told the police.

Charlie Jenkins and Lorna Manning both deserved to die. The same applies to the other ten people whose lives I intend to end. They have all done bad things.

I suggest you ask Detective Walker about the Christmas card I left on Lorna's body.

CHAPTER FORTY-SEVEN

Once again, Annie struggled with being by herself at home. Soon after James left the house anxiety started gnawing at her gut.

She wasn't used to having nothing to do and no one to talk to. She didn't want to keep cleaning the house, and the renovations had been put on hold. She just couldn't think about what colours to paint the walls, what floors to carpet and whether or not to convert the attic into a bedroom. In order to do the kind of job that would make her mum proud she needed a clear head.

It meant there was nothing to distract her from the nightmare that was engulfing her and everyone else in the village. She kept thinking about Lorna and Charlie, and the message in the card found on Lorna's body. It confirmed her worst fear that it was the work of a heartless serial killer, and the possibility that she might actually know this person was making her flesh crawl.

She decided to go for a walk and pop into the store for some groceries. Hopefully, James would let her know soon that he'd spoken to her uncle and had satisfied himself that her suspicions about him were totally unfounded. Then she would try to catch up with Bill.

She put on her coat, scarf and gloves, and checked herself in the hallway mirror. She didn't much like what she saw. Her face was pale and gaunt, and the make-up she'd put on failed to conceal the darkness beneath her eyes.

As soon as she stepped outside, she filled her lungs with draughts of cold air. And she was struck once again by how beautiful the village was when gift-wrapped in snow. It was like an image from a winter holiday brochure. But she doubted that Kirkby Abbey would be a popular destination for tourists for some time to come. It would more than likely become a hotspot for ghouls attracted by its reputation as the location of the infamous Christmas killings.

Annie's heart raced along with her breath as she trudged through the village. A light snow was falling and the wind was pulling and pushing the upper branches of the trees. It brought back memories of her childhood when the Arctic weather had been something to look forward to. She remembered her parents taking her onto the fells so that she could sled down them. She used to hold onto her father's hand when they ventured onto frozen lakes and streams. And there was the time her Uncle Bill turned up at the house with a Christmas tree that was so big it had to be trimmed before it would fit through the front door.

Back then, everyone in the village seemed so happy and content and safe. It was the perfect environment in which to raise a family and enjoy life to the full. But Annie had come to realise that things were very different now. So much had changed and not for the better. It was such a crying shame.

Today the streets were quiet, but she saw a few people, including a uniformed police officer and a television news camera crew.

After about five minutes she started to look back over her shoulder because she had the strangest feeling that she was being watched. This continued as she walked past the church and into the square. But she didn't spot anyone following her.

In the store, she bought a jar of decaf coffee, a newspaper and some washing up liquid.

Peter King drew her into a conversation for a few minutes and asked her if James was close to catching the killer.

'I can only hope he is,' she told him. 'But he's not allowed to share details of the investigation, even with me.'

'Well, it's all anyone is talking about,' King said. 'Some of our customers are even stocking up with provisions so that they don't have to leave their homes. They're so scared.'

'I can understand that,' Annie said.

'Do you think there will be any more murders?'

'I don't know, but I hope not.'

When she left the store, she decided to walk across the village to the garage to see how far they'd got with repairs on her uncle's car.

She was halfway there, walking along a cobbled street between two rows of houses, when she heard someone call out her name. She stopped and turned, and saw a man hurrying towards her.

When she realised who it was her heart leapt in her chest.

'I saw you crossing the road,' Daniel said when he got to her. 'I thought I'd catch up so we can have a chat.'

Annie's breath suddenly roared in her ears. 'Have you been following me?' she said accusingly.

He shook his head. 'I just happened to spot you from a distance. I was on my way to my dad's place.'

She didn't believe him and was tempted to walk away, but she couldn't bring herself to do it.

'Please just spare me a minute of your time, Annie,' he said. 'I realise I'm the last person you want to talk to and I understand why. But there's something I need to know.'

Annie didn't flinch from his gaze. It was strange for her to see him again after all this time and it occurred to her that he hadn't aged as much as he probably should have. Yet, where once she had felt a warm glow when they were this close, now she felt nothing but revulsion and contempt.

'I know what you want to ask me because you've already put the question to my husband and my uncle,' she said. 'And the answer is no. You did not make me pregnant, thank God. What Janet told your father wasn't true. It was probably a misunderstanding on her part because I told her once back then that I was worried that you might make me pregnant. But believe me, it never happened. She made a mistake. Now I would ask you not to go around talking about it, and also to stay the fuck away from me.'

She started to turn her back on him but he reached out and put a hand on her arm to stop her.

She flinched and jumped back.

'How dare you touch me,' she said.

'Oh, don't be a bloody drama queen,' he said. 'You can't say what you just did and expect that to be the end of it.'

'I've answered your question. What more do you want?'

'I want to talk about it because I think you're lying.'

'I don't care what you think, Daniel. And even if it were true, I wouldn't be obliged to tell you. We haven't spoken for almost twenty years and in all that time not a day has passed when I haven't thought what a lucky escape I had.'

'I didn't want us to break up, Annie, but I was given no choice. Everyone turned against me when they found out we were seeing each other and I never got a chance to explain myself.'

'And what would you have told me? That I wasn't the only girl you were shagging at the time, and that one of the others was even younger than me?'

His face contorted into a grimace, ugly and threatening, and it made Annie suddenly fear for her safety.

'Just tell me the truth,' he shouted at her. 'Did you kill our child?'

Annie was determined not to let him see how shaken she was. With her breath thumping in her ears, she said, 'I've got nothing more to say to you, Daniel. If you try to stop me walking away again I'll call the police and have you arrested for assault.'

He began to speak, but by then she'd turned away and was striding across the cobbles, hoping he wouldn't be reckless enough to come after her.

She carried on walking and did not look back until she reached the end of the street. To her relief Daniel was nowhere to be seen.

The encounter had shaken her, though, and her thoughts were now swimming in feverish circles. There was a tightness in her chest and her hands were trembling. But at least she had confronted the issue and hopefully that would be the end of it.

During the rest of the walk she had to force herself not to

dwell on what had happened, but his face and his voice kept forcing themselves into her mind, causing an intense pressure to build behind her eyes.

When she got to the garage, the mechanic recognised her from when she'd dropped in with Bill to arrange for his car to be picked up. She was told it was still being fixed and wouldn't be ready until tomorrow at the earliest.

James still hadn't phoned or sent her a message, but it was only ten-thirty. She decided to drop the groceries off at home before making up her mind what to do next.

But on the way home she saw Daniel again. This time he was about fifty yards ahead of her in the middle of the village square. And he was engaged in what looked like a fierce argument with Giles Keegan.

The former policeman was jabbing a finger at Daniel and Annie could just about hear his raised, angry voice but couldn't make out the words.

The pair of them were the only ones in the square. Annie stepped up behind a tree so that if they looked her way, they wouldn't see her. But she could see them and for about a minute she watched them shout at each other.

The altercation ended when Daniel threw his arms up in the air, then turned sharply on his heels and stomped off.

Keegan treated him to a two-fingered salute and then moved away in the other direction.

Annie waited until they were both out of sight before she resumed her journey home.

She was curious to know what they had been arguing about and made a mental note to tell James what she'd seen.

CHAPTER FORTY-EIGHT

James had been forced to take Gordon Carver into his confidence. He saw it as the only way to stop the reporter from rushing into print with the scoop that had been handed to him on a plate by the killer.

The Twelve Days of Christmas card delivered to the guy's home had understandably got his journalistic juices flowing.

'I don't want you to fob me off by saying this is a hoax if you know it isn't,' he'd said. 'And if you're going to ask me to sit on the story then you'll have to give me a bloody good reason why.'

It was a familiar situation faced by detectives – a reporter comes into possession of information that, if released, would be detrimental to the investigation. More often than not the hacks – and their publications – will drop or delay a story if they can be persuaded that it's not in the public interest to run it.

And that was what Carver agreed to do after James decided to be completely open with him. He told the reporter about the first card that had arrived on his own doorstep along with the dead partridge, and then about the one that was dropped off at the church for Father Silver. Finally, he'd mentioned the card found inside Lorna Manning's dressing gown pocket.

James had explained that he was withholding the information to avoid causing panic in the village. But he had felt it necessary to inform the public that the police believed the murders were committed by the same person. Carver had accepted that it was a sensible strategy, and said that, as a resident himself, he could imagine how alarmed people would be if they knew about the cards.

He'd promised not to pitch the story to the nationals for at least twenty-four hours. His own weekly paper wasn't due out until Saturday, but there was an online edition, so he would also hold off on alerting his own editor.

'In return I'll expect you to keep me well ahead of the curve as the story develops,' he'd said, and James had agreed.

Carver had left the hall ten minutes ago and James had immediately arranged for the latest Christmas card to be taken to the lab.

He was now on a conference call with DCI Tanner and DS Stevens and they'd been put in the picture.

'It makes you wonder if going to the press was part of the perp's grand plan from the outset,' Tanner said. 'Or is he just frustrated because we've kept a lid on the cards? He probably wants everyone to know about them. I mean, why else would he make use of them?'

'What gets me is how audacious this person is,' Stevens said. 'He would have known that we had patrols out last night and that the streets were virtually empty. And yet he still went and posted the card through the reporter's letter box.'

'According to Carver, it would have happened after eleven because he didn't go to bed until then and he made sure the front door was locked before going upstairs,' James said.

'Our man obviously knows the village like the back of his hand,' Tanner said. 'Which of course he would, if he lives there.'

'We can't patrol every street and alleyway,' James said. 'Kirkby Abbey is pretty small, but that actually makes it easy for someone familiar with the place to move around in the dark without being seen.'

'It intrigues me that the perp is so obsessed with getting the message out there that his victims deserve what's happening to them,' Stevens said. 'It certainly gives rise to the possibility that he knows about Lorna Manning's hit-and-run secret.'

'And as we already know, Charlie Jenkins is no angel.'

They could have discussed the case for much longer, but there were things to do, so James took the initiative and called time on the conversation. He said he wouldn't be joining the team briefing by video link and suggested the three of them have another catch up later.

He then rang Annie, but she didn't answer so he left a voice message.

'Hi, hon. I've been wondering about the chat I need to have with your uncle and I think that for his sake it should be as informal as possible. So, can you get him to come to the house later? Maybe for dinner? If there's a problem then let me know.'

When he hung up, DC Abbott had a message for him.

'We've just taken a call from one of the villagers,' she said. 'A Miss Edith Palmer. I think we should go and see her.'

'Why is that?'

'She claims she saw a man on the pavement outside her home in Peabody Street around midnight last night. He apparently ducked into a doorway when our patrol car drove past. It struck her as suspicious.'

'I'm not surprised. Did she recognise him?'

'It appears so. His name is Peter King and he runs the village grocery store.'

'That's interesting,' James said. 'I spoke to Mr King on Saturday when I visited the store. He's the one selling those Twelve Days of Christmas cards.'

'Then we need to find out what he's been up to,' Abbott said. 'I'll get his address.'

'You do that, but I expect he'll be at the store.'

In the patrol car on the way to Edith Palmer's house James told DC Abbott what he knew about Peter King, which wasn't much.

'He runs the store with his wife, Maeve,' he said. 'But she's confined to a wheelchair following a stroke so isn't as involved as she used to be.'

'It can't be easy for him,' Abbott said. 'My eldest sister lost the use of both her legs in a car accident. Her husband has really struggled to take care of her.'

'That's tough. Do you see them often?'

'Not as much as I used to. They live in Norwich and having this job and a boyfriend who works all hours as a paramedic doesn't leave me with a lot of free time.'

'Have you been together long?'

'Two years. We've talked about getting married, but we're just not ready to start a family yet. What about you, guv? Do you have children?'

It was the question that James hated being asked.

'We don't, unfortunately, but it's not through want of trying. We'd both like a child, or more than one, if possible.'

'Well, if it's any consolation, I have a friend who tried for years to conceive with her husband and when she finally did, she had triplets.'

James couldn't help but smile. It made him realise how glad he was that DC Abbott had been assigned to the case. She was a breath of fresh air after DS Stevens, who seemed unable to shake off the chip on his shoulder.

'Anyway, from babies back to the job in hand,' James said. 'Do we know anything else about this Edith Palmer apart from her name and address?'

'Only that she lives alone and got put through to us after contacting the office in Kendal,' DC Abbott said. 'The officer who took the call didn't ask many questions, but told her we'd be coming to see her.'

Just as she finished talking the patrol car pulled up outside Edith Palmer's terraced house in Peabody Street. James noted that facing it across the road was an estate agent with a recessed entrance.

'I wonder if that's the doorway that Miss Palmer is referring to,' he said as they climbed out of the car.

'We're about to find out,' DC Abbott said.

The woman was small and plump and somewhere in her late sixties or early seventies. She had grey hair and wrinkled features and greeted them with a warm smile, inviting them into her kitchen, where they both declined her offer of tea.

'I'm afraid we haven't got time, Miss Palmer,' James said. 'Can you please just tell us what you saw last night?'

'Of course, but I don't want you to get the idea that I'm

275

someone who spies on people. I just happened to look out of my bedroom window because I couldn't sleep and wanted to see if it was snowing.'

'And what did you see?' James asked her.

'Like I told the officer I spoke to on the phone, I watched a police car coming along the street. At the same time, I happened to spot a man across the road walking towards it. As it got closer, he darted into the estate agent opposite and flattened himself against the window. Once the police car drove past he stepped out again and carried on walking. And that's when I recognised him as Peter King, who owns the general store in the village.'

'And you're sure it was him?'

'Oh, absolutely. I've known him for years, but he doesn't live in this part of the village and what he did struck me as odd, suspicious even. I couldn't make up my mind whether to tell you so I slept on it and when I watched the news again this morning, I realised that I ought to.'

'I'm glad that you did, Miss Palmer,' James said. 'We'll go and have a word with Mr King. I'm sure there's an innocent explanation for his behaviour. And in the meantime, can I ask you to keep this to yourself?'

'You have my word, Detective,' she said. 'But I do hope you're right. Peter and his wife are such nice people. I can't imagine why he found it necessary to hide from the police.'

CHAPTER FORTY-NINE

Peter King was alone in his store when the two detectives got there. He was reading a newspaper that was spread out on the counter.

'I'm guessing it's been a quiet day so far,' James said when they approached him.

King looked up and nodded. 'Indeed it has, Detective Walker. I've served only six customers. You would never guess it's Christmas.'

James introduced DC Abbott and explained that she was part of the team investigating the murders.

'It's such a terrible business,' King said. 'Lorna Manning came in here most mornings on her way to the school. I can't believe I won't see her and Charlie again.'

'Did you know them well?'

'Reasonably so. I'd chat with Lorna when she popped in and I've always been a regular at The White Hart.'

'Can you think of a reason why anyone would want to kill them?'

'Definitely not. That's what's so weird about it. And why everyone in the village is so nervous. Most are afraid to go out, especially after dark.'

James nodded. 'That strikes me as sensible. It's actually the reason we've come here to speak to you, Mr King.'

'Really? Why?'

'Well, we've discovered that you were one of several people who were walking around in the village late last night. And as part of our investigation we need you to account for your movements.'

The blood retreated from King's face and he ran a tongue over his lips before responding.

'What makes you believe that I was out last night?' he said.

'Are you going to tell us that you weren't?' James asked him.

King swallowed a lump. 'Not at all. I, er, went for a walk, because I felt I needed some exercise before going to bed.'

'And where did you go?'

'Nowhere. Just strolled for a while but not far from my house.'

'But you were spotted on Peabody Street around midnight. That's on the other side of the village from your house.'

He looked nervously from James to Abbott and then back to James. 'I don't understand why you're making a big deal of this. I'm allowed to walk around my own village whenever I want to.'

'And just walking wouldn't normally arouse suspicion,' Abbott said. 'But you were seen ducking into a doorway so that a police patrol wouldn't spot you. And before you deny it, you should know that a witness has come forward to say she saw you from her window and she recognised you straight away.'

King started to speak, but James interrupted him.

'I wouldn't advise you to drag this out, Mr King. You need to convince us that you haven't been up to no good. The killer we're looking for claimed both his victims around midnight on Saturday and Sunday. We don't yet know for certain if he struck again last night, but we do know he delivered something through the letterbox of a house in Grange Road, which is not far from Peabody Street. So please wise up and be honest with us. You went out last night and took steps to make sure the police wouldn't see you. Why was that? Are you our killer, Mr King? Or can you offer up an innocent explanation?'

King just stood there in stunned silence for several seconds, his mouth agape, panic flashing across his features.

James could see that he'd been right to go in hard, rather than take a soft approach. It was obvious to him that the man was trying to conceal something.

Eventually King spoke, his voice low and quivering.

'I really don't want to tell you where I went last night but I can see I don't have a choice,' he said. 'I beg you not to tell my wife, though. It would just add to her suffering.'

'I can't promise you that, Mr King,' James said. 'Not until I'm in possession of the facts. So I suggest you get it off your chest. If you've done nothing wrong we won't have to waste any more of your time or ours.'

Before King told them what they wanted to know he locked the door to the store and put a closed sign in the window.

'I haven't killed anyone,' he said, after taking them through to the office-cum-kitchen where he stood shame-faced with his back against the desk. 'But the truth is I didn't just go for a walk last night. I went to see a woman named Felicity Bower.

She lives on the other side of the village and I was coming back from there when I saw the police car.'

'So why did you rush into a doorway?'

'I feared that if the officers spotted me they would ask me to explain where I'd been and where I was going.'

'And why would that have been a problem?'

'Because I visit Felicity in order to have sex with her,' he said bluntly. 'It's an arrangement we've had for the past year and we didn't want anyone to know about it. And before you judge either of us you should take into account that Felicity is a widow and doesn't have a partner. And although I love my wife dearly she can no longer satisfy my needs because of her condition. What Felicity and I do makes life more bearable for the both of us.'

'How have you managed to get away with it for so long?' Abbott asked. 'Doesn't your wife suspect anything when you disappear in the evening?'

'Maeve can't sleep without pills and after she takes them a nuclear explosion wouldn't wake her up. And I take the view that what she doesn't know won't hurt her.'

CHAPTER FIFTY

What began as a promising lead had quickly fizzled out.

James left DC Abbott with Peter King in the store and went to see if Felicity Bower would corroborate his story. She did, and she also confirmed that he was with her from 9 p.m. until just before midnight.

'That's usually how long he stays when he comes over,' she said. 'We have a chat, a few drinks and then spend some time in bed. But it's not an affair, as such. It's an arrangement. And it's helped us both get through a difficult time in our lives.'

She was in her fifties with short brown hair, a slim figure and an attractive face.

When she'd opened the door to James and the officer, she had been understandably alarmed. And when he'd asked her to verify King's alibi her face had turned white. But she'd relaxed as soon as he explained that they needed to know because King was seen walking through the village late at night.

'I can assure you that Peter is not the maniac who killed

Charlie and Lorna,' she said now. 'He's a good man. A gentle man. And everyone who knows him will tell you that.'

She then told James something else that would, if confirmed, rule King out as a suspect.

'On Saturday night, when Charlie was murdered, Peter and Maeve were at a party at Craig and Barbara Wilson's house,' she said. 'I was there too, along with ten other people, and none of us left until about two in the morning. Peter then had to push Maeve home in her wheelchair.'

'So you and Peter's wife are acquainted,' James said, surprised.

She nodded. 'I've known her since before she had her stroke. And Peter too. That's why it's so important that we keep our arrangement secret.'

Back at the store, where DC Abbott had been joined by two more officers, James told King what Felicity Bower had said.

'She also told me that you were at a Christmas party on Saturday night,' he said. 'Is that true?'

'Yes it is,' King replied. 'You can check with Craig Wilson. He invited Maeve and I.'

Abbott then told James that the officers had carried out a quick search of the house and nothing suspicious had turned up.

She pointed to a small pile of cards on the counter, all with the Twelve Days of Christmas design.

'Those were on display,' she said. 'And there are a few more out back.'

King was clearly puzzled. 'I remember you asked about those when you came here on Saturday,' he said to James. 'What's so special about them?'

'Those same cards have been delivered anonymously to several homes in the village,' James said. 'And they contained malicious messages.'

'That's not my doing. I just sell them, and as I told you before, I don't keep details of exactly who bought them.'

James said that they might need to talk to him again, but added, 'I'm satisfied that what you've told us is the truth, Mr King. We will be asking Mr and Mrs Wilson to confirm that you were at their party on Saturday, but that's just a formality. And rest assured that I see no reason to mention any of this to your wife. Your secret is safe for now.'

After leaving the store, James asked one of the uniforms to go and speak to the Wilsons.

'Ask about the party and get a list of who else was there,' he said. 'Tell them it's just a routine enquiry and don't mention Peter King by name.'

James and DC Abbott then climbed into the patrol car and he told the driver to take them to Lorna Manning's house in Willow Road.

'I want to see if the SOCOs have found anything more of interest,' he said.

On the way there Abbott lamented the fact that over two hours had been wasted.

'Not entirely,' James said. 'I've learned that this village has more than its share of sordid little secrets. It exudes charm on the outside, but scratch the surface and smelly pus seeps out.'

Abbott laughed. 'Are you wishing that you had never moved here, guv?'

He looked at her and managed a flat smile. 'I think the jury is still out on that one, Detective.'

'Well, for what it's worth, me and the rest of the team are hoping you'll stick with it. And that includes DS Stevens, even though he doesn't make it obvious. We value your experience and like your approach. And we're glad that you're here to help us with this.'

James was touched as well as surprised.

'All I can say is that I hope I don't let you down,' he said.

CHAPTER FIFTY-ONE

Lorna Manning's house was still taped off and a police officer in a high-vis jacket manned the front gate. He approached James as soon as he climbed out of the patrol car.

'You might like to know, sir, that the victim's son arrived here just a few minutes ago,' he said. 'I explained that he couldn't enter the house until the forensics team had finished up.'

The officer was holding a business card which he handed over to James.

'He gave this to me and asked if someone could call him when he's allowed access to his mother's house. I suggested he drop by the village hall to leave his details and have a word with someone. He said he would, but first he intended to visit the church to talk to the priest about funeral arrangements.'

James looked at the card: *CHRIS DRAKE, FINANCIAL ADVISER.*

James remembered reading somewhere in Lorna's documents that her married name had been Drake.

He thanked the officer, pocketed the card and told DC Abbott that they would have a word with the son next.

Inside, the SOCOs had almost completed their work. Every inch of the house had been checked over, especially the kitchen where the smell of various chemicals assaulted the nostrils.

Items had been taken away for analysis and most surfaces had been dusted for fingerprints and swabbed for DNA traces. But it was clear to James that the killer had been scrupulously careful, just as he'd been in the field where Charlie Jenkins was stabbed to death.

The senior forensic officer told James that he would produce a report by the end of the day and make testing of all the samples a priority.

As the two detectives left the house, James took out Chris Drake's business card and called the mobile number printed on it. The man answered on the second ring and James identified himself and asked if they could meet up. Drake said he was in Father Silver's office at the church so James told him to wait there.

After hanging up, he turned to DC Abbott and said, 'We can kill two birds with one stone. I was planning to update the priest on where we are. And I need to tell him that Gordon Carver now knows about the cards and the photo left in the church graveyard.'

Chris Drake was a slightly overweight man in his thirties with a round face and a full head of short black hair. He was sitting on the leather sofa in Father Silver's office at the church when the two detectives walked in.

James could see that he was consumed by grief, his eyes bright with pain.

Father Silver had positioned two chairs so they were facing the sofa, and he invited James and DC Abbott to sit on them. Before doing so, James performed the introductions and offered his condolences to Lorna's son.

The priest then sat next to Drake on the sofa and said they had been discussing his mother's funeral.

'I've explained to Mr Drake that in view of the circumstances it might not take place for some weeks,' he said.

James was struck by how tired and strung out the priest looked. He assumed it was due to a combination of stress and the cancer that was destined to shorten his life.

James started by asking Drake how much he knew about his mother's death.

'The officers who came to see me at my home in Southend told me only that she'd been murdered by an intruder,' he said as he tried to control the emotion in his voice. 'I've learned more from the news, and when I contacted your office in Kendal, they said they would provide me with more information when I came to formally identify my mother's body.'

James told him what they knew, including the fact that they believed his mother was killed by the same person who murdered Charlie Jenkins.

Drake just stared at James, his eyes glistening, as his mind struggled to process what he was hearing.

Then he said, 'So that means her death could have been avoided if you had made it known that you were hunting a serial killer. Mum would surely have been more careful.'

'But we didn't know, Mr Drake,' James said. 'We thought and hoped that the first murder was a one-off.'

'So what makes you so sure that Mum was the victim of the same killer?'

'There are various reasons, Mr Drake, including the fact that in both cases the murder weapon was a knife. I'll disclose more information to you about the circumstances of your mother's death when I am able. In the meantime, I'm afraid we can't let you enter the house just yet. I can tell you that some of your mother's personal possessions have been taken away to be analysed. Among them is a small suitcase containing various files and documents. I'll get it to you as soon as we've finished with it.'

Drake nodded. 'I know about the case, Inspector. Mum told my wife and I that when she died, we should look through it because it held all her personal stuff, including her will.'

'And did she also mention a sealed envelope that contained a secret she'd kept for the past ten years?' James asked delicately.

Drake knotted his brow. 'I don't know what you're talking about.'

James drew in a chest full of air and told him about his mother's confession.

Drake's eyes went saucer-wide and his mouth sagged open in disbelief.

'She never told me about any hit-and-run,' he said after a beat. 'Are you sure that she wrote it? Mum would never have done something like that. And she was always telling me not to drink and drive.'

'We're one hundred per cent sure that your mother wrote it,' James said. 'It was a clear confession and she signed it. On the envelope were instructions to open it in the event of her death.'

Unable to speak, Drake raked both hands through his hair and squeezed his eyes shut.

'That has to be why Lorna had such a hard time enjoying life,' Father Silver said. 'She must have been struggling to cope with the guilt for all those years. It ate away at her.'

'So you didn't know about it either, Father,' James said.

The priest shook his head. 'I wish I had. I would have tried to help her. I told you before that I thought she was probably troubled by something that happened in the past. But she would never talk about it.'

Drake opened his eyes and said, 'I remember now how Mum started to withdraw into herself. It was just before she moved here and that was ten years ago. She began having mood swings and we thought it was because she wasn't happy about being single. I tried to get her to open up but she kept saying it was probably the menopause. After she moved I didn't see as much of her. When we did get together, she seemed okay. But I could always tell she was making a big effort for our benefit.'

'When was the last time you saw her?' DC Abbott asked.

'That was back in the summer when she came to stay with us for a few days during the school holidays. But we talked on the phone at least once a week. In fact, the last time was on Sunday evening, only a few hours before—'

His eyes flared with emotion suddenly and he drew in a sharp breath and held it for several seconds. When he started to speak again, his voice shuddered.

'She called to tell me about the man who was murdered in the field. She said she would have phoned earlier but she had a visitor and had to wait until he'd left.'

'Do you know who the visitor was?' James asked.

Drake nodded. 'A bloke named Giles Keegan. She reckoned he was smitten with her.'

'And was she very fond of him?'

'I think so. They'd known each other for quite a while and she said it was good to go on a date again after so long.'

'I've spoken to Mr Keegan and he told me that he saw your mum on Sunday,' James said. 'They were attending the carol singing together in the square when the man's body was discovered. Keegan went to her house later in the afternoon to see if she was all right. He also told me that he really liked her and was hoping they might have a long-term relationship.'

'I gather she liked him too, but I'm not convinced it would have come to anything serious. On Sunday she said she'd had to tell him to go because he was getting on her nerves. She pretended she had some school work to do.'

'Did she say what he was saying or doing that was grating on her?' James asked.

'Well, as you probably know, he's a retired detective. According to Mum all he ever talked about was how nobody is safe any more, even in places like this. He complained about the breakdown of law and order and said he was sick of seeing so many criminals escape justice. He even told her that there were some people in this village who should be behind bars. And he's right, isn't he? It was probably one of the bastards who murdered my mum.'

He started to cry then, great wracking sobs that shook his entire body.

Father Silver put an arm around Drake's shoulders and DC Abbott got up, took a tissue from her pocket, and handed it to him.

But James remained seated, his mind whirring from what Drake had said about Giles Keegan.

Had the man really told Lorna Manning that there were

people in the village who should be locked up and that he was sick of seeing criminals escape justice?

In themselves the remarks didn't amount to much and could not be taken as evidence that Giles Keegan was a murdering psycho. But in the context of what was going on in Kirkby Abbey, they did suggest to James that he needed to have another word with the ex-police officer.

CHAPTER FIFTY-TWO

It turned out that Chris Drake had driven the three hundred miles to Kirkby Abbey from his home in Southend. He planned to stay over and had reserved a room at The King's Head.

'I didn't know how long I would have to be here,' he said, after he'd stopped crying and had regained his composure. 'So, I'm booked in for two nights to start.'

'Okay, Would you mind going along to the village hall to make a statement about the last conversation you had with your mother?' James asked.

'Of course,' Drake said.

'Great. The team will sort out the arrangements for you to formally identify her body and update you on the situation regarding her house and belongings,' he said.

It was agreed that Drake would come back and talk to Father Silver tomorrow about funeral arrangements. James then asked DC Abbott to take him to the hall in the patrol car.

'And stay there until you hear from me,' he told her. 'I

need to have a few words with Father Silver before I leave here. Then I'll either walk to the hall or ask you to meet me somewhere.'

As soon as Abbott and Drake had left the office, Father Silver closed the door behind them and said, 'I wasn't aware that Lorna and Giles Keegan had been seeing each other. How long had it been going on?'

'Days rather than weeks,' James said. 'He seemed genuinely upset when I spoke to him.'

'Does he know about Lorna's confession?'

'I don't believe so. But he was aware that she appeared to suffer from bouts of depression.' He went on to describe how Keegan had spotted Lorna sitting next to the stream while crying.

Father Silver shook his head. 'It's just one shock after another. I still can't imagine that Lorna would drive away from the scene of a terrible accident and not report it.'

'People do such things all the time, Father.'

'I know that, Detective Walker. Nevertheless, I'm hoping that you won't have to make public what she did back then, for the sake of her son and those in the village who looked up to her.'

'I'll do my best to keep a lid on it,' James said.

He then warned the priest that he might soon be approached by Gordon Carver.

'He's been made aware of the Christmas card that was left here at the church and the photo of Lorna that was placed on Nadia Patel's grave,' he said.

Father Silver was clearly puzzled. 'I'm surprised you told a reporter about the cards.'

James shrugged. 'I didn't have a choice. The same Twelve

Days of Christmas card we received was posted through his door last night. Inside was a message claiming that the police were withholding information. He was all set to publish it, but I persuaded him to hold off by giving him the full story and stressing how dangerous and disruptive it would be if it got out.'

Father Silver frowned. 'But do you really believe he'll keep it to himself?'

'He assured me that he would, at least for the time being. We've agreed to have another conversation tomorrow.'

The priest mulled it over for a few seconds, then said, 'Well, I suggest you treat whatever he tells you with extreme caution, Detective. I've known Mr Carver for some years, and I most certainly would not consider him the most trustworthy of individuals.'

After James left the church, he stopped on the pavement to check his to-do list. Thankfully, the snow had eased off and so had the wind. But fat feathery flakes were still dancing in the air like white-winged butterflies looking for somewhere to land.

His intention for today had been to re-interview three people – Sonia Jenkins, Janet Dyer and Bill Cardwell. But now he took out his pen and added Giles Keegan to the list. He would drop in on the retired copper at some point and tell him what Lorna's son had said. His response would determine whether there was a need to take it further and interview him under caution.

Though James wanted DC Abbott with him when he spoke to Janet about the card she gave to Annie, he was quite happy to go and see Sonia Jenkins by himself. As the walk back to the village hall would take him past The White Hart he'd see if she was in.

As he set off, he sent a text to Annie asking her if she'd listened to the voice message he'd left about getting Bill to come over to the house. She replied immediately:

Just spoken to him. He'll be here at six for dinner.
And this time he's promised not to forget.

James tapped out a reply:

That's great, hon. It'll give me plenty of time to talk to
him xx

As James walked through the village, the silence pressed against his ears. The place was dead, like a ghost town, and despite its obvious charm, which was enhanced by the Christmas decorations, he could sense a dark malevolence lurking beneath the surface. It was surreal, like being on the set of a creepy movie where nothing is as it seems.

It was obvious that many of the villagers were now afraid to leave their homes. And he could hardly blame them. There was a killer in their midst and in all likelihood he would strike again.

It made James feel guilty. He needed to up his game, start making more progress. Almost fifty hours had passed since Charlie Jenkins was found dead in the field on Sunday morning. And Lorna's Manning's body was discovered on her kitchen floor around twenty-six hours ago. Yet James felt they were still flailing about in the dark. They had no firm leads, no highly credible suspects, and they faced the grim prospect of soon having to deal with another murder.

The killer was taunting them with his Christmas cards

and messages, while moving around the village like the invisible man.

James suspected it was time to ask for more resources so they could cast the net wider. They could get officers to visit every home in the village and search all those where the owner or occupant aroused suspicion. There was only one road in and out of the village, so perhaps they should also get officers to check all cars entering and leaving. They could even impose a curfew prohibiting anyone from taking to the streets after dark.

These were extreme measures, and he wasn't sure that Tanner and the people above him would support them, but right now, James was prepared to do whatever it took to catch the killer and stop the body count from rising still further.

It came as no surprise to James that The White Hart was still closed. He doubted that it would open in the foreseeable future.

He rang the front doorbell and had to wait for a full minute before Sonia Jenkins appeared. A grim smile flitted across her face when she saw him.

'Have you come to tell me that you've arrested Charlie's killer?' she said.

'I'm afraid I haven't, Mrs Jenkins,' he replied. 'I've dropped by to see how you are and to ask you a couple more questions. May I come in?'

'Of course.'

She was wearing a baggy green tracksuit, and her hair was swept away from her face into a ponytail.

He followed her through the bar and up the stairs to the flat.

When they reached the kitchen, he accepted her offer of a coffee and said, 'Are you here by yourself?'

She nodded, flicking on the kettle. 'I have been since yesterday when I told your family liaison officer that she didn't need to stay any longer. My daughter Maddie is due to arrive at Heathrow from Dubai this afternoon. She'll be coming straight here.'

'How are you coping?'

'It's not easy, and it got harder after I heard about Lorna Manning. I gather you believe that whoever killed Charlie also killed her.'

James removed his coat and sat at the table.

'It certainly looks that way,' he said. 'In fact, one of the questions I was going to ask you concerns Miss Manning.'

She turned to face him, resting her back against the worktop.

'I suppose you'd like to know if she and Charlie were involved with each other in any way.'

'Well, were they?'

'I'm convinced they weren't. And whenever Lorna came here to the pub to eat or drink, which wasn't often, he didn't seem particularly interested in her. I'm sure I would have noticed if he had.'

'So did he ever talk about her to you?'

'Not that I recall. And I can't actually think of a single thing they had in common.'

Sonia poured the coffees and put both mugs on the table. She sat opposite James and he felt a rush of compassion for her. Charlie obviously hadn't been the perfect husband, and had let her down, but it was clear that she had loved him, and now missed him.

'Is there anything you need?' he asked her. 'We can help in any way, and if you'd like to speak to the liaison officer again you only have to give her a call.'

'I'm fine,' she said. 'My bar staff have been really good and they're here for most of the time. I'm hoping to open up again before Christmas. That's what Charlie would have wanted.'

'Have you spoken to many of your customers?'

'A few have popped in and those who haven't have sent me flowers and cards. I'm surprised at how many people have told me that Charlie was a great guy and that everyone will miss him. Their comments have helped. In fact, I've only received one nasty note in a Christmas card.'

'Who was it from?'

'No idea. It was put through the door some time yesterday. There was no name on it, but it's obviously someone who didn't like him.'

James felt his chest tighten. 'What did you do with the card, Mrs Jenkins?'

'I threw it away. Why?'

'I would like to have seen it.'

'Well, it's still in the bin,' she said.

'Can you fish it out for me please?'

'Don't see why not. It's downstairs.'

James went down with her and watched as she rummaged in the bin behind the bar. He wasn't surprised when she pulled out a Twelve Days of Christmas card. Inside, in black marker, was a message:

Your husband was a cheat, Mrs Jenkins.

He deserved to die and you're better off without him.

Merry Christmas.

CHAPTER FIFTY-THREE

The village hall was still buzzing when James arrived back.

DC Abbott was deep in conversation with the two other detectives who had just arrived, and Lorna Manning's son, Chris, was in the caretaker's office with a uniformed officer who was taking down his statement.

James got everyone together for a brief update. He began by showing them the card that had been delivered to The White Hart for Charlie Jenkins's grieving widow.

After reading out the message inside, James said, 'No question, it's from the killer. And once again the bastard makes the point that as far as he's concerned, Charlie deserved to die. Five of these same cards have now turned up in the village and they've all been delivered by the killer himself.

'We'll send this to the forensic lab like the others but I doubt it will contain any prints or DNA. The problem we have is that these cards have been on sale in the village store and quite a few people have bought them,' he said. 'I saw a bunch of them in Keith Patel's house. He's the guy whose mother died a year ago after falling down the stairs in her home. The killer put Lorna's photo on her grave. When I asked Patel about the cards, he told me he planned to send them out to friends and denied sending one to me. But he was seen close to my house when the parcel was left on my doorstep.

'The same Christmas card was also handed to my wife yesterday by Janet Dyer, the woman who had an affair with Charlie Jenkins. The message in it wasn't sinister and it hadn't been written with a black marker. However, I still intend to go and ask her about it.'

He then pointed to one of the newly arrived detectives, DC Colin Patterson.

'I'd like you to take some uniforms and go house-to-house again in Willow Road. When we first spoke to Lorna's neighbours, they were all in a state of shock. Their heads will be clearer now so maybe they'll recall something they forgot to mention on Sunday about Lorna herself.'

James was then told that Craig and Barbara Wilson had been spoken to and had confirmed that Peter King and his wife had attended their Christmas party on Saturday night.

They carried on discussing the case for another thirty minutes, during which a number of tasks were assigned, including obtaining a warrant to access the phone records and digital footprints of Giles Keegan and Keith Patel. Someone back in Kendal would also be instructed to go through the electoral roll for Kirkby Abbey and check to see if any of the residents on it sparked a red flag, perhaps because they had a criminal record.

Three of the patrol officers were told to take to the streets and to make themselves highly visible.

'Engage with anyone who approaches you,' James said. 'And be suspicious of those who come on strong and ask a lot of detailed questions about what progress we're making. It's not uncommon for murderers, and especially serial killers, to try to solicit information about a case or even embed themselves in the investigation if they can.'

James then received a call from DS Stevens in Kendal off the back of the team briefing there.

'I've got a few updates for you, guv,' he said. 'Detective Ackerman in Cornwall just got back to us. He's confirmed that Andrew Sullivan was telling the truth about being down there for the past week. They've checked his accommodation and CCTV clips which show him at various locations in Newquay between Friday and Monday. Daniel Curtis's alibi also checks out. He was definitely in Kendal on Saturday night when Charlie Jenkins was murdered.'

'So those two come off the list of suspects,' James said. 'It doesn't leave us with much.'

'The news from the forensic lab won't cheer you up either,' Stevens said. 'Nothing has shown up on any of the cards or items taken from the victims' homes. And I've spoken to the pathologist who has now carried out both post-mortems. She confirms that there is no evidence to suggest that Charlie and Lorna struggled with their assailant. The stab wounds on both of them have the same characteristics. Penetration up to eight inches, which indicates an exceptionally long non-serrated blade. The blade is also wider and thicker than most kitchen knives. So it's possible that some kind of fixed-blade fighting or hunting knife, such as a Bowie knife, was used.'

'There are plenty of those around,' James said. 'These days every young villain seems to have one.'

He took down notes, and when the call ended, he passed on the information to the rest of the team. He then checked his watch and saw it was already 1 p.m.

He decided that it was time to go and ask Janet Dyer a few more questions. But just as he and DC Abbott were about to leave, one of the uniforms arrived with two carrier bags filled with sandwiches and other bits from the village store.

It put a smile on James's face, and he told Abbott to get stuck in.

'It might be the only chance we get to fill our bellies before dinner,' he said.

CHAPTER FIFTY-FOUR

James hadn't seen Janet Dyer since Sunday and her appearance had changed considerably. She wasn't wearing make-up and looked at least five years older.

Her eyes were heavy and red from crying, and the skin of her face was greyer than he remembered.

When she opened the door to them, she was holding a glass in one hand that was half-filled with red wine.

'Is this about Annie and Daniel Curtis?' she asked. 'Because if it is, I've already told her that I'm sorry for what happened. I made a mistake.'

'It has nothing to do with that,' James said, noting the frown on DC Abbott's face. 'But we do need to talk to you.'

'You'd better come in then,' Janet said.

She turned, and as they followed her through the house it seemed pretty obvious to James that she'd had a fair amount to drink.

In the kitchen the first thing she did was top up her glass with more wine.

'I would ask you to join me,' she said. 'But since you're on duty I'm guessing you'd just say no.'

'And you're absolutely right, Miss Dyer,' James said. 'May we sit down?'

'Please do. And if you're wondering why I'm on the booze so early it's because it's helping me to get through another fucking horrendous day. I've rowed with my ex again over the kids and, like everyone else in the village, I'm shit scared that I'm about to be murdered.'

She swallowed some more wine, the drink staining her lips. Then she dropped onto the chair facing the two detectives.

'I suppose you want to ask me more questions about my relationship with Charlie,' she said, slurring her words slightly. 'I can't tell you any more than I already have. I honestly haven't held anything back. If his wife – or rather, his widow – is saying anything different, then she's bloody well lying.'

'This has nothing to do with what you and Charlie got up to,' James said. 'We're here to ask you about the Christmas card you gave to Annie.'

She squinted at him through one eye. 'What on earth for? It's a lovely card.'

'Indeed, it is, Miss Dyer. But cards with exactly the same design have been delivered to homes in the village. And they've contained vile and threatening messages.'

Her eyes grew wide. 'What has that got to do with me? You can't possibly think that I was responsible.'

'That's something we need to establish,' James said. 'So my first question is: did you purchase that card at the village store?'

She pushed out her bottom lip. 'Of course I did. Where else would I have got it? They had loads in.'

'And how many did you buy?'

'Only one pack. That was enough for me. I still haven't posted the rest.'

'And do you know of anyone else who bought those same cards?'

'Well, I know that old Ron did because he gave one to me when I was last over at his house.'

'Do you mean Daniel's dad?'

She nodded. 'I'm one of his carers, as you know.'

James felt a flutter in his stomach. 'So where is this card?'

Janet shrugged. 'In the lounge. Go and see for yourself. It's on the sideboard with the others.'

Seconds later James was holding the card in his hands. It was indeed the same design as the others, but the writing inside was very different from the killer's scrawl. And just as with the card that Janet gave to Annie, the message inside was benign.

Merry Christmas Jan

Thanks for looking after me and for sharing all the gossip. It keeps me going

Ron x

James saw no point in wasting any more time on Janet Dyer.

'You need to pull your finger out, Detective Walker,' DCI Tanner said. 'This is not good enough. I'm getting grief from all sides now. The Chief Constable, the local MP, the media. And I'll soon be going into another press conference where I'll have to admit we've made hardly any progress.'

It was the first bollocking James had received from a superior officer since coming to Cumbria. It was tame in comparison to some he'd had in the Met, but it still jarred.

Tanner was responding to what James had told him about how they were going with the investigation. The DCI had called him soon after he returned from Janet Dyer's house.

'With Daniel Curtis and Andrew Sullivan no longer in the frame we're desperately short of suspects,' Tanner said, stating the obvious. 'And I'm nervous about hounding Giles Keegan. I know the guy well and it's inconceivable that he'd do something like this. Plus, he still has plenty of friends in the constabulary.'

'I'm not hounding him, sir,' James said. 'He was trying to start a relationship with our second victim and he may well have been the last person to have seen her alive. He's also—'

'I don't believe that should count against him,' Tanner interrupted. 'And neither should the fact that he allegedly had a moan about perps escaping justice and claimed that some people living in the village should be banged up. Isn't that the kind of thing most of us coppers say when we're frustrated, angry and upset?'

'I accept that, sir, but I still intend to have another conversation with him. I've got this feeling that he's not being entirely up front with us.'

'That's your call and I won't stop you. But tread softly. Keegan knows the rules of play better than anyone and I don't want this blowing up in our faces.'

'I assure you it won't, sir,' James said.

After a pause, Tanner said, 'So where do we go from here?'

'We need to think about mounting a door-to-door across the entire village,' James said. 'Canvas as many people as we can. I find it hard to believe that the killer has been moving around unseen or that no one has noticed something out of kilter. And to make it harder for him to strike again we could have more overnight patrols and perhaps even put a curfew in place.'

'Steady on, Detective. You need to appreciate that, unlike in London, we don't have unlimited people and resources to draw on. And even for a high-priority case like this I'm not sure it would be right to impose a curfew. It'll have to be managed, and even in a village the size of Kirkby Abbey that would be hugely problematic. And let's not forget that we're preparing for the blizzards that are about to smash into this part of the country. You may not realise it because you haven't been with us long, but they put a huge strain on manpower.'

'But what if there's another murder, sir?' James said.

'Well, that's why you're there, Detective – to make sure there isn't. Find our killer and stop him running rings around us. In the meantime, I'll reassess the staff situation, and if I can beef up numbers on the team I will. That's a promise.'

James came away from the conversation only slightly reassured. But he wasn't going to let that distract him from what had to be done. After all, Tanner's reaction hadn't come as a great surprise. The longer the case went on, the more the pressure on him would grow.

And James did appreciate the points he had raised. The number of officers and amount of resources to commit to an investigation always become an issue at some point in the process for every force in the country. Tanner had been right to point out that imposing a controversial measure such as a curfew could create all kinds of problems. One would be the question of how long to leave it in place. Another would be what penalty to impose on those who flouted it.

The day was slipping away at a rate of knots so James decided to hold another briefing. This time he got someone to set up a video link with the team in Kendal.

There was a lot to discuss and he began by asking DS Stevens what progress they had made at their end.

'I can tell you that we've heard back from the handwriting expert who was asked to analyse the messages in the Christmas cards,' he said. 'He's adamant that they were all written by the same person. We already assumed that, but at least this provides confirmation.

'We've also been in contact with our colleagues in Hampshire. They've spoken to the parents of the young woman who Lorna Manning knocked down and killed. They were shown a copy of her confession and were naturally shocked and livid. They insist they knew nothing about it and had never heard of the woman. The couple also have a cast-iron alibi for Sunday night.'

James then passed on feedback from the officers who were talking again to Lorna's neighbours in Willow Road – so far they'd drawn a blank and no one had given them any new information – and mentioned that Lorna's son had checked into a room at one of the village pubs, having been in to the command centre to make a statement about the last conversation he had with his mother.

'As a result of what he told us I will be speaking to Giles Keegan again.' James pointed to Inspector Boyd and added, ' Let me know once we've been granted access to his phone records and those of Keith Patel, who remains a person of interest.'

The briefing then turned into a brainstorming session that lasted a further hour. James noted down all the points and suggestions, and these helped him to decide what to do the following day. One of the tasks would be to draw up a list of all the parents with children at the school. They would check to see if any of them had fallen out with the headmistress or had links with Charlie Jenkins.

Following the briefing, the three detectives who had come to Kirkby Abbey were told to return in the morning, and to allow themselves plenty of time to get here in case the weather made travelling difficult.

DC Abbott surprised James by saying she had come prepared and had made a reservation at one of the three bed and breakfast establishments in the village.

'I cleared it first with DS Stevens,' she said. 'I live in Staveley and I don't want to risk being stuck there if it turns really bad.'

'Good thinking,' James said. He then turned to Inspector Boyd and asked how many uniforms would be on duty in the village overnight.

'Five late shifters are due to arrive in the next hour, replacing those who've been here all day,' the inspector answered. 'We'll also have two patrol cars.'

It was 5 p.m. by the time they were through and it coincided with the start of the latest press conference being held in Penrith.

DCI Tanner was fronting it once again and was given a pretty hard time by the hacks. He pointed out that they were only three days into the investigation and everything possible was being done to find the murderer.

'A team of officers will once again be located in Kirkby

Abbey throughout the night,' he said. 'They are there to offer protection to the villagers and to ensure that the enquiries continue twenty-four-seven.'

BBC News then cut to their reporter in the village, who said that most residents were staying in their homes because they were too afraid to venture out. He did a piece to camera in front of the village hall.

'The police team, led by Detective Inspector James Walker, have taken over this hall and turned it into a mini incident room,' he said. 'This morning a number of villagers came here demanding to know more about what is going on. There's huge concern that more murders will be committed and they say the police have been unable to allay their fears.'

When the report ended, James took part in another conference call with Tanner and Stevens, but nothing new came out of it. Following that, he and DC Abbott set off for Giles Keegan's house in a patrol car, only to find that the guy wasn't in. James rang his mobile but there was no answer.

'We'll try again tomorrow,' he said to Abbott. 'I have to go home now anyway so you may as well check into your B&B and try to get a good night's sleep. Shall we drop you off there?'

'I have to pick my own car up from outside the hall,' she said. 'My overnight bag is in the boot.'

James told the driver to drop him off at home first and on the way there, Abbott said, 'There's something I've been meaning to ask you, guv. When we arrived at Janet Dyer's house, she thought we were going to talk to her about something that happened between Daniel Curtis and your wife, Annie. Is it something that I need to be across?'

James caught the eye of the driver in the rear-view mirror

and decided it wouldn't be fair on Annie to say anything in front of him.

'It's nothing important,' he said, shaking his head. 'Trust me, it has no relevance whatsoever to the case.'

CHAPTER FIFTY-FIVE

The smell of something cooking greeted James as he entered the house.

Annie called out to say that she was in the kitchen preparing dinner. It was almost six so he half expected to see her uncle with her. But she was alone, stirring what smelled like his favourite chicken stew in a saucepan.

'How are you, hon?' he said.

She let go of the wooden spoon, turned and walked straight into his arms.

'I'm glad you're home at last,' she said as he pulled her close. 'It's been a long day. I was tempted to ring you a couple of times just for a chat, but I didn't because I knew you'd be busy.'

'It wouldn't have been a problem,' he said. 'I'll always find time to talk to you.'

She squeezed him back. 'Bill is on his way over, in case you're wondering. I rang him half an hour ago and he said he hadn't forgotten and was getting ready.'

He let go of her and stepped back. 'Has he said or done anything else that's given you cause for concern?'

'No, but then I haven't seen him. He told me he'd been for a walk, had lunch at The King's Head, and then watched television in his room for most of the afternoon.'

'I hope he doesn't realise that we've asked him here so that I can give him a grilling.'

'I'm sure he won't, so long as you don't make it obvious.'

'I'll do my best.'

She turned back to the oven and continued to stir the stew.

'I just watched the news,' she said. 'They made it sound like you're not getting anywhere with the investigation. Is that really the case or are you holding stuff back from the media?'

'It's true, I'm afraid, hon. Progress is slow. But that doesn't mean I haven't been busy. I spoke to Lorna Manning's son today as well as Janet Dyer and Sonia Jenkins. Let me pour us each a glass of wine and I'll bring you up to date before your uncle gets here.'

Wine poured, they sat down together.

'You'll be glad to hear that Janet Dyer is no longer a suspect. The card she gave you was in a batch she bought in the store,' he said. 'She even received one of those same cards herself from Ron Curtis. The problem is the store has sold quite a few of them so they're all over the village. In fact, Sonia Jenkins also had one put through her door, but the message inside claimed her husband was a bad man and deserved to die.'

Annie snapped her head towards him. 'Oh God, does that mean it was from the killer?'

He nodded. 'Almost certainly. I've sent it to be analysed.'

'But I don't get it. Why keep sending out those same stupid cards? What's the point?'

'That's the million-dollar question,' James said. 'It could be any one of a number of reasons. He likes playing games, he wants to generate as much fear and confusion as he can, or he just wants to draw attention to what he's doing. It could also be that The Twelve Days of Christmas carol holds a special significance for him. Maybe that's why he's intending to target twelve people.'

'If his aim is to get inside our heads he's certainly succeeding,' Annie said, her voice shrill. 'He's ramping up the fear factor by the hour. And that's before the rest of the villagers get to know about the cards and the threats.'

'That might not be long in coming,' James said, before going on to tell her about the card that was sent to Gordon Carver.

'I've persuaded him not to rush into print with it, but he won't hold off for long and we can't make him. Once it's out there it'll be a game changer for me and for the villagers.'

James watched the blood drain from her cheeks. It was one of the reasons he didn't like to tell her too much. She became increasingly anxious with every piece of information he shared.

In a bid to strike a positive note he told her that Andrew Sullivan's alibi checked out and that Daniel Curtis was in Kendal when Charlie Jenkins was murdered.

She took a moment to respond and did so after taking a deep breath.

'I need to tell you something about Daniel,' she said. 'He approached me in the street today while I was walking to the garage.'

James felt his hackles rise. 'I told the bastard to stay away from you.'

'Well, he didn't. He denied that he had been following me, but I'm convinced he was lying.'

'So, what did he say?'

'He asked me if it was true that I'd aborted his baby. I said it wasn't and told him to fuck off.'

'And did he?'

Annie nodded. 'Not straight away. He wanted to talk but I wouldn't be drawn.'

James was furious. 'I'll go and see him. I should have known he wouldn't let it rest until he'd spoken to you.'

'I'd rather you didn't, love. Leave it now. Please. Hopefully he'll shut up about it.'

James wasn't happy but he knew she was probably right.

'Okay, but are you sure he didn't follow you after that encounter?'

'I'm positive. But I did actually see him again. He was in the village square having what looked like a stand-up row with Giles Keegan.'

'But I told Keegan to steer clear of Daniel. That obviously fell on deaf ears.'

'Do you have any idea what it would have been about?'

James nodded. 'Keegan thinks Daniel could have been stalking Lorna, and that he might even have killed her.'

'But why would he think that?'

'As you know, Daniel was hanging around outside the school on Friday evening. When Giles saw him there, he confronted him because he suspected he was waiting to eye up the kids as they came out. But while he was being questioned by me about Lorna it suddenly occurred to him that

Daniel might have been waiting there for her to appear. I didn't tell him that Daniel told me he was actually waiting to see you.'

Annie's lips started to form a question just as the doorbell rang.

'That'll be your uncle,' James said. 'We'll talk again later.'

Eighteen months had passed since James last saw Bill Cardwell. In that time the man had aged considerably. His face was heavily lined, the eyes dull and ringed with fatigue.

'Hi there, Bill,' he said, shaking his hand.

Bill tipped his head forward. 'Hello, James. It's been too long, mate, and that's all down to me. I got myself in a right state after Sis's funeral and I couldn't drag myself out of it. I hope you don't bear a grudge.'

'Of course not.'

'Good. And meanwhile I'm glad to see you're looking so well.'

'You look good too, Bill.'

Bill laughed. 'It's kind of you to say so, James, but I know it's not true. I look like shit and that's exactly how I feel. But I'm sure Annie's stew will cheer me up.'

The stew was, as usual, cooked to perfection, and Annie's uncle seemed to appreciate it as much as James did.

'That was delicious, Annie,' Bill said. 'You take after your mum when it comes to cooking. She made stews to die for.'

The three of them sat at the table for the best part of an hour, and it was much less awkward than James had feared it would be. Bill seemed completely relaxed and showed no hesitation in answering all the questions that were put to him.

James did his best to make it seem like a conversation

316

rather than an interrogation. Bill's responses to the questions were short and sharp. No, he had never met Lorna Manning. Yes, he had known Charlie Jenkins, but not very well. No, he didn't have a clue who might have murdered them. Yes, he often went out walking at night because it helped him to sleep when his head eventually hit the pillow. And so on . . .

James even showed Bill the Twelve Days of Christmas card from Janet to see how he'd react. But all he did was smile and tell them he thought it was a nice picture.

James had been hoping that by the end of the meal he'd have convinced himself that Bill wasn't the killer. But unfortunately, that turned out not to be the case. A nagging doubt remained, primarily because it seemed that Bill was keeping something from them. It was a vibe he got from the man's demeanour and the way he struggled to articulate his thoughts.

He said as much to Annie when they were alone in the kitchen and the surprise was evident on her face.

'But I don't understand,' she said. 'It sounded like he was being honest to me.'

'It could be that I've read him wrong, hon. I'll keep an open mind but I'll also need to make sure I know where he is at all times.'

They tried to persuade Bill to stay the night but he declined the offer, saying he would have to return to The King's Head anyway to get his things. He wouldn't let James walk with him either, insisting he was 'old enough and ugly enough' to find his own way there, even in the dark.

After he'd gone, Annie said she was too tired and distraught to sit up and needed to go to bed. James said he wasn't ready to call it a night so he offered to clear up the dinner things.

'I'll be up in a little while,' he said. 'I just need to sort out a couple of things ready for tomorrow.'

After tidying the dining room, he went to his study and typed up a short report about what had happened during the day. Then he wrote down a list of action points for tomorrow.

The files, envelopes and diaries from Lorna Manning's suitcase were still piled up on his desk. He'd already decided that he would have to sift through them all before sending them to the station. After all, the confession had provided one clue so maybe there were more to be found.

He skimmed through the contents of all the envelopes and files first and then turned his attention to the diaries. They went back ten years; it appeared she'd started keeping them after moving to her new life in Kirkby Abbey.

James read through the first couple and found no suspicious entries or any mention of the hit-and-run accident that Lorna had been involved in.

By now he was struggling to stay awake and his eyes were sore. He decided to look through the rest of the diaries tomorrow.

He left the study and before going up to bed he turned off all the downstairs lights. And that was when he realised what was happening outside. Through the window he could see snow falling like confetti, smothering everything in the back garden.

He realised it was finally the start of the truly dire weather conditions that had been forecast and it sent a chill flushing through his body.

CHAPTER FIFTY-SIX

I know I've had too much to drink, but I don't give a toss. If the bar had stayed open, I'd still be there, throwing back triple vodkas while watching the news on the big wall-mounted television screen.

It's been good to get out. I needed to try and forget what another shit day I've had. The snow that's coming down doesn't bother me. In fact, I find it curiously comforting because it makes it less likely that anyone else who's out this late will spot me walking unsteadily through the village. And that includes the coppers who are wandering around trying, and failing, to make everyone feel safer.

There's a lot of stuff swirling around inside my head, including the voice of the newsreader as she described in sombre tones what had happened in Kirkby Abbey.

Two murders. Two bodies. Hundreds of people living in fear for their lives. There were interviews with some of them, along with video clips of Lorna Manning's house and the field where Charlie Jenkins was found lying in the snow.

It still doesn't seem to me like it's really happening. It's so scary, so weird, so fucking unbelievable.

And the police are saying the killer probably lives in the village, which makes it even more shocking.

I can't imagine it would be any of the people I know – most of them are vile, judgemental cretins – but I'm pretty sure that none of them would be capable of committing multiple murders.

There are hundreds of people living in Kirkby Abbey who I don't know, though. And I suppose any one of them could be a raving psychopath.

This is what I'm thinking about as I pass the village square. Even through the snow I can see the lights on the giant Christmas tree, and suddenly it seems so out of place at the centre of a community living beneath a cloak of terror.

Everything else is in darkness, including The White Hart pub, the hair salon and the only clothes shop in the village.

I find it hard to imagine that life here will ever be the same again. The place will always be tainted by the blood of the killer's innocent victims.

As I turn off the square, I start to feel dizzy. The vodka is finally hitting the spot, just as I knew it would. But that's okay because I haven't got far to go, and soon I'll be crashed out on the bed. Booze always helps me to sleep, which is partly why I tend to drink more than I should.

I'm heading towards the outskirts of the village now and the relentless snow is beginning to get on my nerves. I keep having to wipe it from my face, and I'm finding it harder to see where I'm going. The cold is also getting to me, and I'm shivering under my heavy coat and thick jumper.

It comes as a relief when I spot the sign for the garden centre up ahead. It means I'm almost there. I decide to have a nightcap before getting into bed; a large, strong drink to warm me up.

As I draw level with the garden centre's low wall, I hear what sounds like someone fighting for breath close behind me.

Acting on instinct, I stop and turn, but there's no time for me to react to what happens next. There's only time to register the familiar face that's barely an arm's length away.

Then comes a sharp pain, and I think I've been punched in the stomach. But when my head drops, I see the knife being wrenched out of me.

I stagger back against the wall, but I'm not able to stop the knife being plunged into me a second time.

The ground suddenly opens up beneath me and I feel myself being dragged down into a dark pit, with the words of my assailant ringing in my ears.

'This is no more than you deserve, and it's been a long time coming.'

CHAPTER FIFTY-SEVEN

Wednesday December 21st

It was snowing heavily when James and Annie woke up on Wednesday morning.

On the TV news there were reports of trees coming down and roads being blocked. As predicted, it was Scotland and the northern counties of England that were the worst hit. Some areas were already without power, and commuters heading for work were facing traffic chaos.

A story broke just as James was about to take a mug of tea up to Annie who was still in bed. There had been a major pile-up on the M6 a few miles south of Penrith. Dozens of vehicles were involved, and it was feared there would be multiple casualties. The motorway was now closed in both directions to enable emergency vehicles to get to the scene, and traffic was backed up for miles.

James knew there was no knowing how many officers would make it to Kirkby Abbey, either because roads were blocked or because they were about to be reassigned.

He told Annie how bad it was out there and she reminded him that the village could be cut off.

'A big problem for us is that there's only one road in and out,' she said. 'And it doesn't take much to make it impassable.'

It was the last thing James wanted to hear as he turned his thoughts to the day ahead. The case was already proving to be a tough one to crack, and now they would have to persevere in Arctic conditions and most likely with fewer people.

He showered and dressed before making any calls. It was 7.30 a.m. when he rang DS Stevens, only to discover that he was still at his home in Burneside, digging his car out of the driveway.

'I didn't realise how much came down last night,' he told James. 'I couldn't believe it when I got up this morning. My house is in a dip so the snow piles up. But it shouldn't take me much longer to get going.'

Stevens was aware of the M6 pile-up and had heard that so far three people were known to have been killed.

'It's a serious one, for sure,' he said. 'And I expect there'll be many more accidents by the end of the day. Resources will be stretched.'

James then phoned the office in Kendal. Thankfully, most of the team had already turned up and others were on their way in, including DCI Tanner. James was told that the officers in Kirkby Abbey had called in with nothing to report. It had been a quiet night and they hadn't had to respond to any incidents.

Next James called DC Abbott on her mobile. She was having breakfast in her B&B and said she would pick him up in her car if he wanted her to.

'You can see now why I decided to stay overnight here, guv,' she said. 'I know what it's like in these parts when the snows come.'

'It was a good call,' James said. 'How hard do you think it will be for others to reach the village?'

'That depends how bad the roads are. I haven't checked yet, but I'll put a call in to control if you like and get the latest from them.'

'Good idea. By the way did you sleep well?'

'Like a log,' she said. 'The bed is twice the size of the one I've got at home and I didn't have to share it with my boyfriend.'

He told her he would call her when he was ready to leave and they would go first to the village hall.

Annie joined him downstairs while she was still in her dressing gown.

'I'm having some toast before I set off,' he said. 'Do you want some?'

She shook her head. 'I'll make myself something when you've gone. Will you let me know how things go?'

'Of course. What have you got planned?'

'Nothing at all, apart from a visit to the store. And I suppose I'll have to touch base with my uncle. It's such a shame that he decided to come here so soon before Christmas. He'd have avoided all that's going on if he'd come on the twenty-second, as agreed.'

'But didn't he come early because he was worried that the weather might stop him from getting here?'

Annie nodded. 'Exactly. How gloriously ironic.'

'Is he intent on staying?'

'I'm not sure. We should have asked him last night when we had the chance. He can't leave anyway until his car's ready.'

324

James had just started to butter his toast when his phone rang. He picked it up from the table, saw that it was Father Silver who was calling, and felt a flicker of trepidation.

'Good morning, Father,' he said. 'Any chance you're not ringing me with more bad news?'

'Sadly no, Detective Walker,' he said. 'You need to come to the rectory right away. I've received another card and you are not going to like what's written inside.'

CHAPTER FIFTY-EIGHT

James arrived at the rectory fifteen minutes later in DC Abbott's Fiat after a quick drive through the snow-covered streets of the village.

Father Silver was waiting for them at the door, a mournful expression on his face. 'I can't believe it's happened again. Why am I being singled out like this?'

'You're not, Father,' James told him. 'You're just one of an unfortunate group of people on the killer's mailing list. Now where is the latest card?'

'Follow me.'

James had never been inside the rectory and was struck by how cluttered it was. There was an over-abundance of furniture and most of it was old and large – from the floor-to-ceiling bookcase in the hallway to the table that was far too big for the modestly sized kitchen.

The card was on the table, the distinctive Twelve Days of Christmas image facing them as they entered.

'I've been careful only to touch it at the edges,' Father Silver said. 'And I've also kept the envelope.'

James put on latex gloves before he picked it up. DC Abbott peered over his shoulder as he read the message inside, which once again had been scrawled in black marker.

I want you to know that I've taken the life of another sinner, Father. Someone else who did the work of the devil. Someone who brought shame on our tiny community and therefore deserved to die.

Merry Christmas once again.

James and Abbott exchanged a look and it was the DC who put into words what they were both thinking.

'This must mean there was another murder last night,' she said, with a tremor in her voice. 'We just haven't heard about it yet.'

James felt his heart sink into his boots. 'That's probably because it's still early and not many people have ventured out.'

'Then we need to mount a search, guv. The snow won't make things easy for us, though.'

James took an evidence bag from his pocket and put the card and envelope into it.

Then he turned to the priest. 'You told me it was put through your letter box. Have you any idea when that would have been?'

'I went to bed at ten o'clock last night,' Father Silver said. 'I didn't know it was there until I came downstairs this morning to have breakfast before going to the church.'

'And you didn't hear or see anyone outside during the night?'

He shook his head. 'I'm a heavy sleeper, Detective Walker. It takes a lot to wake me once I'm in bed.'

'And have you given any thought to who might be responsible? I know it sounds like a silly question, but I have to ask it.'

'Well, the answer is yes, I have given it a great deal of thought, but for the life of me I can't think of anyone I know who would commit such heinous crimes. And that makes it all the more disturbing because the clear impression I get from those messages is that the person who wrote them knows me.'

James nodded. 'There's a good chance he does, Father. There's no doubt in our minds that he's local and appears to have his finger on the pulse of the community.'

'Why are you so sure that this isn't the work of a woman? You're always referring to the killer as a man.'

'We're basing that on experience and on what little evidence we have,' James said. 'But there is an outside chance that we could be wrong, and for that reason our list of potential suspects includes both men and women.'

'That's good to know,' the priest said.

'There's one other thing before we go, Father. As always, please don't mention this to anyone else.'

The priest put a finger to his lips. 'You have my word, Detective Walker. But if there is another victim out there then I would ask you to let me know as soon as possible so that I can pray for his or her soul.'

'It's a deal,' James said.

* * *

328

James got an unwelcome surprise when he arrived at the village hall. Three of the seven uniformed officers who had worked through the night had departed for home several hours ago, their replacements had been diverted to the M6 to help handle the pile-up, and the two detectives who had been part of the team yesterday were having trouble reaching the village.

DC Abbott put in a quick call to control to find out how bad the situation was on the roads and the news added to James's woes.

'The snow is causing havoc,' she said. 'A lot of the minor roads are blocked and there's monumental congestion.'

'Any updates on the motorway accident?'

'The death toll remains at three, but six people have been taken to hospital. And some drivers are waiting to be cut out of wrecked vehicles. It sounds horrendous, guv.'

James called what remained of the team together and broke the news about the latest card. Inspector Boyd informed him that in spite of the snow his officers had carried out patrols throughout the night, but they hadn't come across anyone on the streets.

'If the message in the card is to be believed, there's been a third murder,' he said. 'We've still got one patrol car at our disposal and four officers. So, let's get out there and start looking around. Meanwhile, I'll brief the boss in Kendal. If there is another body then we'll need more help.'

James called DCI Tanner, who had only just arrived at the station. He responded to the news about the latest card with a long, heavy silence.

'So far there's no word of a body turning up,' James said. 'But my gut is telling me that it's only a matter of time.'

'This is all we fucking need,' Tanner said, breaking his silence. 'It never rains but it pours.'

'Always the way, sir. But we're going to need more help here, and fast.'

He told Tanner about the officers who'd been diverted to the M6 and the detectives who were struggling to get in.

'Leave it with me,' Tanner said. 'I'll get to work on it. But I know how difficult things are out there because it's just taken me an hour and a half to get in instead of the usual twenty minutes.'

James said he would keep Tanner informed and hung up. Just as he did so the inspector seized his attention.

'The owner of the garden centre here in the village just phoned 999, sir,' he said. 'He claims he's found a body on the property.'

CHAPTER FIFTY-NINE

The patrol car beat them to the garden centre. DC Abbott pulled up behind it in her Fiat and she and James climbed out.

Fortunately, the wind had eased by this time and so had the snow. It was still falling but less aggressively.

There was a low wall in front of the small, single-storey building, and the uniformed officer from the patrol car was standing on the other side of it.

By peering over the wall James could see victim number three. The scene was similar to the one he had encountered on Sunday morning. But Charlie Jenkins had been lying on his back in the field. This poor soul was face down.

'The owner of the garden centre is a Mr Paul Granger,' the officer said. 'I told him to wait inside. He found the body when he arrived to open up. He brushed off some of the snow just to make sure it wasn't a pile of clothes or something else.'

'It's definitely a fella,' DC Abbott said, and that was obvious to James as well.

The guy was wearing black trainers, denim jeans and a thick green coat. But his face wasn't visible and the back of his head was sprinkled with snowflakes.

'We need to turn him over,' James said. 'See what we've got.'

He did it with the help of the uniformed officer, and once the victim was on his back, they saw the blood that stained the front of his coat and the flattened snow beneath him.

But the sight of the man's face came as a bigger shock to James.

He let out an involuntary gasp when he saw that the killer's latest victim was none other than Daniel Curtis.

It took them a few minutes to establish certain facts.

Daniel Curtis had been stabbed twice in the stomach. He'd bled profusely and had almost certainly died very quickly.

The attack had taken place barely twenty-five yards from his father's bungalow. In his coat pocket they found his mobile phone, which was password-protected, and his wallet. Stuffed loosely in the wallet was a receipt for drinks at The King's Head dated the previous evening.

'My guess is he was walking home from the pub when he was attacked,' James said. 'It would have happened on the pavement and he either fell or was pushed over the wall. Any footprints the killer might have left have been erased by the snow.'

'So, it's possible he was followed from the pub.' Abbott said. 'And this was the perfect place to strike. The garden centre on one side of the road and an open field on the other. And the snow would have helped conceal his actions.'

James nodded in agreement. 'We need to summon forensics and the pathologist right away. But by the time they get here, if they can get here, our victim could be under a foot of snow.'

'Plus, the scene has already been seriously contaminated by the weather and us trampling all over it,' Abbott said.

It was the uniform who was thinking on his feet and came up with a sound suggestion.

'Mr Granger is bound to have some tarpaulin inside, or if not we can get a tent from the outdoor shop off the square.'

'That's a good idea,' James said. 'Tell him he'll need to stay closed today and to keep this to himself for now, and find out who else works here. When you call the inspector, tell him he needs to protect this spot as discreetly as possible.'

James then returned to Abbott's car to phone DCI Tanner, whose reaction was predictable.

'This is the worst possible news,' he said. 'How bad do you think it will look when everyone knows that the killer struck while we were patrolling the village? It happened right under our fucking noses, for Christ's sake.'

'That's not my number one concern at the moment, sir,' James said, not caring if his words weren't well received. 'I just need to know how quickly you can send me backup and SOCOs.'

He heard Tanner take a breath before speaking again.

'You're right, of course,' he said. 'I'll sort it and get back to you. Meanwhile ask DS Abbott to text or email the details over to me. I need to be ready when the media latches onto this.'

James instructed Abbott to forward the information to Tanner, including the victim's identity and a photo of the body. He then pointed to the bungalow along the road.

'After you've done that we'll have to go and tell Ron Curtis that his only son is dead.'

CHAPTER SIXTY

It took a while for Ron to respond to the doorbell. When he did, he was wearing a robe over pyjamas and moaned that they had woken him up.

'What is it you want now?' he said. 'It's only just gone ten, and I was having a lie-in.'

'We have to come in and speak to you, Mr Curtis,' James said. 'It's about your son.'

'If you just want to give him more grief you'll have to come back later. He had a late night at the pub and I reckon he's still spark out upstairs.'

'We really do need to come in, sir,' James insisted. 'You see, Daniel isn't upstairs because he didn't return here last night.'

Ron's face creased up. 'How do you know? Has he been arrested or something?'

James felt the emotion grip his throat. He swallowed hard and said, 'Daniel was the victim of a crime late last night, Mr Curtis. And it saddens me to have to tell you that he's dead.'

The old man's chest heaved suddenly, thirsty for oxygen.

'That's not p-possible,' he stammered. 'My Daniel's in bed. He must be.'

James seized the initiative and stepped forward. He put an arm around Ron and eased him gently back into the hallway.

'Let's go inside and we'll tell you what's happened,' he said, leaving Abbott to close the door behind them.

In the living room, James got Ron to sit down in his armchair before he gave him the details.

It took a minute or so for the man to process what he was being told. When he got there the shock began to vent itself through shoulder-wrenching sobs.

Over the next half an hour they managed to establish that Ron had last seen his son about eight o'clock the previous evening.

'That was when I told him I was going to bed,' Ron said. 'I was dog-tired and bored watching the same old rubbish on the box. Daniel said he was going to pop along to the pub. I heard him go out and that was that.'

'Did he often go to The King's Head?' James asked.

'Not really. When he was here, he usually stayed in with me because he didn't like it when people looked down their noses at him. But these last few days he's been really down and anxious, for obvious reasons. He liked to drink and I don't keep much in the house so he's been out a couple of times to clear his head.'

Ron allowed them to go and look around Daniel's room, but they found nothing of interest. He'd brought little with him for his Christmas stay with his father.

Back downstairs, James asked Ron if there was anyone they could contact who could come and be with him.

'Janet,' he blurted without hesitation. 'Ask Janet to come over.'

When they left him, he was sobbing in the armchair, his face smeared with saliva and mucus from his nose and mouth.

They headed straight to Janet Dyer's place and found that she was up and dressed, but nursing a hangover.

When James told her about Daniel, she blinked a couple of times, completely nonplussed.

'Was he murdered like the others?' she said. 'Is that what happened to him?'

'It's too early to say for sure, Miss Dyer,' James said. 'His body has only just been found. The reason we're here is that his father has naturally taken the news very badly. When I asked him if he would like someone to be with him, he said he wanted you.'

Janet pushed back her shoulders and gave a stiff nod.

'That's not a problem,' she said. 'I'm his carer so I'll go over there right away.'

'That's great, Miss Dyer. Thank you. But first I'd like to check something with you. Daniel spent last evening drinking at The King's Head. Were you also there, by any chance?'

She glared at him and shook her head. 'I was here all by myself all night, Detective. I had only wine and gin for company. And if that's not a convincing enough alibi then tough shit.'

James and DC Abbott made two stops on the way to The King's Head. The first was at the church, where James told Father Silver that a murder had indeed been committed. The priest reacted by dipping his head and giving the sign of the cross.

'I will pray for him, Detective Walker,' he said. 'And I'll pray that you quickly find whoever was responsible.'

James got Abbott to stop outside his own home next.

'You wait here while I go and break the news to my wife,' he said. 'She knew Daniel Curtis and I don't want her to hear it from anyone else.'

Annie was having breakfast in the kitchen when James entered.

'What's happened?' she said. 'I can tell by your face that it's something bad.'

Her eyes bulged when he told her, and her body started to shake.

'Over the years I learned to hate the man,' she said. 'But I would never have wished something like this on him. You have to stop this happening, James. It can't go on.'

He wanted to stay with her but he said he couldn't and she understood.

'You just go out there and find the bastard who's doing this,' she said. 'And don't rest until you've got him.'

The King's Head wasn't yet open for business, but the landlady, Martha, was getting things ready for the lunchtime session, aided by two members of her staff.

She knew James, but was nevertheless obviously surprised to see him. He introduced DC Abbott and asked if they could ask her some questions.

Martha blinked warily, clearly nervous. 'Please don't tell me that something has happened to my husband. He's supposed to be coming back from Manchester this morning and he's not answering his phone. I've heard about the crash on the M6 and—'

'This has nothing to do with your husband, Mrs Grooms,' James said. 'And I'm sure he's fine. His phone is probably switched off or he's driving and can't answer it.'

She blew out a breath. 'That's a relief. Now, you can ask your questions here in the bar or we can go into the lounge area where it's more comfortable.'

James opted for the lounge and seconds later the three of them were seated on sofas.

'So how can I help you?' Martha said.

James already had his notebook out and resting on his knee.

'Firstly, were you working here in the bar last night?' he asked her.

'Yes, I was. And I was on my own because it was so quiet.'

'It's our understanding that Daniel Curtis was among your customers.'

'That's right. I served him myself. He got through about half a bottle of vodka, as I recall.'

'And was he by himself?'

She nodded. 'He sat at the table closest to the TV all evening. No one joined him, but then no one ever does when he comes in here.'

'Is that because of his conviction in the past?'

'Obviously. I know many villagers don't think we should let him drink here, but my husband and I don't believe it would be fair to stop him. It can sometimes cause friction, though. In fact, last night was a good example of how some people get wound up just being in the same room with him.'

'What happened last night?'

She shrugged. 'Well, nothing came of it, and luckily there were only a few people in the bar, but that cantankerous old sod Keith Patel was one of them. He was here when Daniel arrived about half eight. He'd had a fair amount to drink by then, and when Daniel stood next to him at the bar, he asked him in a really loud voice if he'd molested any young girls lately. To his credit, Daniel didn't rise to it. He turned his back on Patel and returned to his seat.'

'So, what happened next?' James asked.

'I could tell that Patel was up for making a nuisance of himself so I told him to go home and sober up,' Martha said. 'I think he realised he'd stepped over the line because he finished his beer and left without saying another word.'

'And what about Daniel?'

'He stayed put until closing time. He left as soon as I rang the bell.'

'And can you recall if anyone followed him out the door?'

'I know for sure that nobody did because there was only one other punter left in the bar and that was your Annie's Uncle Bill. And he went out through the internal door to his room upstairs.'

James felt his heart move up a gear.

'Bill was drinking here too?' he said.

'He came in for a quick pint when he got back from your house. He told me he had a lovely stew there. But after downing one pint he had a couple more.'

'And did he interact with Daniel Curtis at all?'

She shook her head. 'He sat at a table on the other side of the room and they didn't speak to each other. I did see Bill giving Daniel black looks from time to time but he certainly didn't cause any trouble. Now, are you going to tell me what this is all about?'

CHAPTER SIXTY-ONE

If Bill had been in his room James would have gone up to speak to him. But according to the landlady he'd left The King's Head earlier without saying where he was going.

'Is there anything I should know about your wife's uncle, guv?' DC Abbott asked when they were back in the car.

James had been expecting the question and felt obliged to answer it.

'Bill knew Daniel Curtis years ago when they both lived here in Kirkby Abbey,' James said. 'So, like most people in the village, he considered Daniel a pariah. Since Bill came back here on Friday, to spend Christmas with us, his behaviour has been somewhat strange. It's aroused a certain amount of suspicion. I've spoken to DCI Tanner about it and we agreed I'd have a chat with Bill, which I did last night. I'm convinced he's not our perp, but I will have another conversation with him since he was among the last people to see Daniel alive. That doesn't mean I've changed my mind about him. Just that I don't want to leave any stone unturned.'

'That seems fair enough, guv,' Abbott said. 'Do you want to find out where he is so that we can go and see him?'

'Bill can wait,' James said. 'I think we should go back to the village hall to take stock and find out where we are with backup and forensics.'

'And what about suspects, guv? Who gets a visit from us after that?'

James chewed on his tongue as he mulled this over.

'We start with Keith Patel,' he said. 'The guy made it clear to us what he thought about Daniel. And then we move onto Giles Keegan. He clashed with Daniel twice during the past couple of days.'

'So do you actually think that those two might also have killed Charlie Jenkins and Lorna Manning?' Abbott asked.

James pulled a face because the question felt like a heavy weight pressing down on him.

'At this stage in the game I think anything is possible,' he said.

There was some good and some bad news waiting for them at the village hall.

The bad news was that the two detectives who'd been travelling to Kirkby Abbey had been forced to head to Kendal instead because of impassable roads.

The good news was that a police helicopter was to be used to transport a couple of SOCOs to the village. The same chopper would then take Daniel's body to the mortuary.

'It's not an ideal situation, I know,' DCI Tanner said. 'But it's the best we can do at this time. I don't want the body left there longer than is necessary.'

DS Stevens had arrived at the office and was taking part

in the conference call. He revealed that the press had already been tipped off that another body had turned up.

'That doesn't surprise me,' James said. 'Word spreads quickly in this place.'

'But on a case like this we need to control the narrative,' Tanner said. 'So, let's make sure that everything goes through the press office. No off the record briefings. I don't want to give the impression that we're having problems coping.'

But the truth was they were having problems, and James feared that it could still get worse.

After the call ended, he and DC Abbott left the hall intending to visit Keith Patel and Giles Keegan. But first they returned to the crime scene outside the garden centre.

The officers had been forced to close one side of the road and put up a tape cordon because a number of villagers were braving the snow to see what was happening.

Daniel's body had been covered with some heavy-duty green tarpaulin and three uniforms in high-vis jackets were standing guard. They'd been told the police helicopter would arrive in about an hour and had arranged for it to land in the field opposite.

As requested, the garden centre had remained closed and the owner, along with his two members of staff, had provided all their details.

There were several other detached bungalows along this stretch of road, plus a doctor's surgery. Another officer had been going door-to-door trying to find out if Daniel Curtis or anyone else had been seen walking past their homes last night. But all those spoken to so far had said they were in bed and saw nothing.

'Once the body has been taken away, we should try to

retrace Daniel's steps back to The King's Head,' he told the officers. 'If he was stalked through the village then someone might have spotted it. But, of course, it's also possible that the killer was lying in wait for him along this road.'

The more James thought about everything the more difficult it was to stay focused. Three murders had now been committed over four nights. And they were in no position to assure the public that there wouldn't be a fourth, let alone any more beyond that.

The pressure on James to find this particular killer was like nothing he had ever experienced. And it was causing him to question his own abilities, which had never happened before.

It didn't help that the weather had delivered a hammer blow to the investigation just when they needed to accelerate it, restricting what they could do for the time being.

James was sure the killer would eventually make a mistake and they'd have him. But by then he might well have claimed more victims.

So it was imperative they got a result soon. But for that to happen they needed a breakthrough or a big stroke of luck.

He was so lost in thought that Abbott had to nudge him to get his attention.

'Over there, guv,' she said, pointing. 'It's that local reporter. He's waving.'

Gordon Carver was standing behind the tape and the sight of him sent a roll of heat up James's neck

'I'd better go and talk to him,' James said. 'You wait here.'

He signalled for Carver to follow him over to the garden centre entrance where they'd be sheltered from the snow. When they got there, it was the reporter who got the first word in.

'Let me start by telling you what I already know, Detective Walker,' he said. 'It'll save you having to fob me off by telling me to speak to the press office.'

'That is what I've been instructed to do, Mr Carver,' James said.

'Yeah, well there's no point. The man lying dead over there is Daniel Curtis. I was tipped off by a member of the garden centre staff before you placed what amounts to a gagging order on them. Mr Curtis was attacked last night and stabbed to death – just as Charlie Jenkins and Lorna Manning were.'

'I take it you want me to confirm that?' James said.

Carver shook his head. 'There's no need. I know it to be true. What I'd like is a quote about how the Kirkby Abbey killer has been sending out Christmas cards in which he flags up what he'd done and what he intends to do.'

'That will serve only to make things much more difficult for us, Mr Carver, and you know it.'

'I promised you I wouldn't pitch the story about the cards for twenty-four hours and I've kept my word. But I can't hold off any longer. If I don't go with it now then someone else will. The people of this village have a right to know what I know. And they also deserve to know how the killer managed to claim a third victim even as the police were patrolling the streets.'

James spent another ten minutes trying to persuade Carver not to reveal more than the press office were putting out. But he insisted he had to go with it all.

In the end, James felt there was only one thing he could say on the record to the reporter, and that was: 'More information will be forthcoming at the next press conference.'

CHAPTER SIXTY-TWO

On the way to Keith Patel's cottage, James rang DCI Tanner to tell him about his encounter with the reporter.

'You need to alert the press office, sir,' he said. 'They're going to be asked about the Christmas cards and why we chose not to make them public.'

'We'll just tell the truth,' Tanner replied. 'We didn't want to alarm the villagers and cause panic when there was no way of knowing if the threats in them were genuine.'

'Are you holding another press conference today?'

'We'll have to, but there'll be more to talk about than your case. Would you believe we have another murder on our hands?'

'You're kidding.'

'I wish I was. And it's right here in Kendal. So we're being stretched even further now.'

'What do we know?'

'A young man yet to be identified. His body was found just over an hour ago next to the river path off Beezon Fields. He was bludgeoned to death late last night or in the early hours of this morning. Too soon to know the circumstances.'

'That's all we need,' James said.

'My sentiments exactly.'

After hanging up, James told DC Abbott about the body found in Kendal.

'When I came to Cumbria, I thought I'd be in for a quiet life,' he said.

Abbott grinned. 'I'd like a pound for every copper from down south who has said that to me. But what you need to remember is that up here it's all about peaks and troughs. Even crime. And right now we're at the top of an almighty frigging peak.'

It was James's third visit to Keith Patel's house, and before they reached it he told DC Abbott to brace herself for a hostile reception.

'The last time I was here he told me to piss off and said he wouldn't talk to us again unless he had a lawyer with him.'

They arrived at the cottage just as Patel was about to step out. He answered the door wearing a coat, boots and a woollen hat.

'What in God's name do you want with me now?' he said. 'Surely you lot have got more important things to do than harass me.'

'Where are you off to, Mr Patel?' James asked him.

'Not that it's any of your business, but I've run out of fags so I'm going to the store.'

'Well, you'll have to delay your trip because we need to come in and talk to you.'

'What for this time?'

'There's been another murder, Mr Patel. And it turns out that you were one of the last people to see the victim alive.'

Patel's jaw dropped, as if a hinge had come loose.

'Who are you talking about?' he said.

'I'm talking about Daniel Curtis. He was stabbed to death last night while walking home from The King's Head. It would have happened not long after you asked him if he'd molested any young girls lately.'

For a few moments Patel appeared too shocked to speak. As he stared at James, the tendons in his neck became so taut they looked ready to snap.

When he finally spoke, his voice was acidic. 'This is beyond a fucking joke now. When you were here before you tried to pin those first two murders on me. Now you think I killed that pervert Curtis. Well, I didn't.'

'We should discuss this inside,' James said.

'But I made it clear last time that I won't talk to you again without a lawyer.'

'In that case we'll have to take you to the station in Kendal and you can call one from there. Or we can arrange for the duty solicitor to represent you.'

The prospect of a trip to Kendal clearly did not appeal to him. He let out a loud breath through his teeth and gave a resigned nod.

'Bugger that,' he said. 'I've got nothing to hide so come in and let's get this over with.'

He took off his coat and hat and they followed him into the living room.

'This is Detective Constable Abbott,' James said when they were all seated.

Patel didn't even look at her. Instead, he maintained

347

eye-contact with James, and said, 'It's true I had a dig at Daniel Curtis when he stood next to me in the pub. I couldn't resist it. The guy was a nonce and he wasn't welcome in this village. It annoyed us all that he kept on coming back. But when Martha suggested I leave that's what I did. And I came straight home.'

'Did anyone see you?' James said.

'Not likely. It was late and most of my neighbours don't do late.'

'Did you have any run-ins with Daniel in the past?' DC Abbott asked him.

'I threw the occasional insult his way,' he said. 'But it was never more than that.'

'And was Daniel one of the people you hold responsible for your mother's death?'

The muscles around his eyes tightened a little. 'Not at all. He didn't know Mum, but she knew about his antics so she would not have let him anywhere near her house, even if he was her only option.'

The more questions they put to him the more irritable he became. His breath was coming in fast, high-pitched gasps and the tension showed in his features.

When James asked him if they could search the house, he expected Patel to start yelling for a lawyer. But he surprised them by shrugging his shoulders.

It should have been a job for a forensic team but James didn't know how long it would take them to show up. He told Abbott to search upstairs while he checked the kitchen and living room. But it didn't take them long to decide there was either nothing to find, or Patel had got rid of anything that would tie him to one or all three murders.

'We'll probably want to talk to you again, Mr Patel,' James said. 'And we may want to carry out a more thorough search of your property.'

'Well, next time I won't be so accommodating and you'll have to go through a solicitor,' Patel said.

Before leaving the cottage, he agreed to provide them with a DNA swab and gave them a glass covered with his fingerprints.

CHAPTER SIXTY-THREE

Giles Keegan was home when they got to his house this time. He was clearly surprised to see them, but didn't hesitate to invite them in.

'I've heard about Daniel Curtis,' he said. 'I can't believe I actually suspected him of being the perp.'

'How did you find out about it, Giles?' James asked him after introducing DC Abbott.

'Gordon Carver phoned me for a comment. He knows I was part of the team that put Daniel away.'

The three of them sat around the table in Keegan's kitchen-cum-dining room. To James, Keegan looked pale and anxious, and he didn't seem to know what to do with his hands. Was that a sign of guilt, James wondered? Or just nerves?

'So, here's the thing, Giles,' James said. 'We're here to question you as a suspect and I strongly suggest that you cooperate to save a lot of time and aggravation.'

Keegan's eyes lit up with a sudden fury. 'Do your superiors know about this, Detective? Because if not I'm sure—'

'Stop right there,' James interjected. 'You are not above the law just because you're an ex-copper. You're someone who got involved with two of the three people who've been murdered. And only a couple of days ago you also made it clear to me that you hated Daniel Curtis. You said he had an evil streak running through him. And that's enough to make you a person of interest to us.'

'I disagree, Detective. I've explained why I confronted Daniel Curtis outside the school on Friday and I've told you about my relationship with Lorna. And if that's all you've got to go on then you've got sod all.'

'Actually, that's not all we've got, Giles. For instance, we know you had an argument with Daniel in the square yesterday. And Lorna's son has told us that his mum was glad to get shot of you on the night she was killed.'

Keegan was suddenly on the back foot, and it was obvious to James that he knew it. His nostrils flared as he drew the back of his hand across his stubble.

'Let's start with your encounter with Daniel yesterday,' James said. 'A witness described it as a heated argument.'

'Who was the witness?'

'I'm not at liberty to say and you know it. I'm assuming you're not going to deny it?'

Keegan licked his lips and a shadow settled behind his eyes.

'I saw him while I was walking through the village so I confronted him about Lorna,' he said. 'I wanted to know if he'd been waiting for her outside the school.'

'But I warned you not to approach him,' James said.

'I know, but I couldn't hold myself back.'

'What did he say when you confronted him?'

351

'He told me I was crazy and that if I didn't leave him alone, he'd call the police. I tried to get him to say more but he wouldn't. Then he walked away and I went home. That was the last I saw of him.'

'So that must have pissed you off.'

'It did, but not enough to make me go out later and kill him.'

'Then what did you do last night?' This from Abbott.

'I sat here thinking about Lorna and wondering why life is so fucking unfair. What else was there for me to do?'

James took a second to collect his thoughts, then told Keegan that he had spoken to Lorna's son, who had arrived in the village yesterday.

'He had a conversation by phone with his mum after you left her house on Sunday evening,' James said. 'And she made a point of telling him that you'd been getting on her nerves, which was why she asked you to go.'

'That's not true.'

'Really? Then you didn't rant on about too many criminals escaping justice and tell her that there are people in this village who should be in prison?'

Keegan shook his head. 'I don't believe I'm hearing this. We talked about what had happened to Charlie Jenkins and we were both shocked and angry. And yes, I did say something like that but Lorna agreed with me. And she asked me to go because she needed to do some school work, not because I was getting on her nerves. I don't care what her son says.'

'So, who in the village do you think should be behind bars?' James asked.

Keegan clawed a hand through his hair. 'I was thinking mainly of Daniel Curtis when I said it. But there are others, including the louts who vandalise the church on a regular basis and the pricks who claim benefits they're not entitled to.'

'And what about Lorna Manning?' James said. 'Do you believe that she should have been behind bars for what she did?'

Keegan's brow knitted up. 'I don't understand. What is she supposed to have done?'

'Are you saying you didn't know she was involved in a hit-and-run accident ten years ago?' James said. 'She killed a young female pedestrian and drove on without reporting it.'

Keegan seemed genuinely shocked. 'Are you sure about that?'

James nodded. 'She left a written confession.'

'Jesus. Well, I had no idea. Honestly. But that might be why she was so troubled. And why she refused to tell anyone what was wrong.'

He sat back in his chair and rubbed the back of his hand across his brow, which was glazed with sweat. Then he issued an audible sigh through pursed lips.

'Look, I now appreciate why you're here and why you had to ask those questions,' he said. 'But I promise you, I am not your man. When each of the murders took place, I was here, in bed. It's unfortunate for me that there's no one to corroborate it, but it's the truth and trust me, you won't be able to prove otherwise. And please don't get the idea that I'm some embittered former police officer who has embarked on a mad mission to rid the village of a bunch of undesirables. I'm just an old bloke wanting to live out his days in relative peace and quiet.

'Now feel free to search the house, take me in for formal questioning, or even arrange for me to have a lie detector test. Just do everyone a favour and get it done quickly. I want this killer caught as much as you do and time spent with me is valuable time wasted.'

CHAPTER SIXTY-FOUR

While they were in Keegan's house the weather had taken a sudden turn for the worse. The snow was thicker now, heavier, and the wind drove it into their faces as they dashed towards DC Abbott's car.

After starting the engine, she had to flick on the wipers so they could see through the windscreen.

'Where to now, guv?' she said.

'Back to the crime scene. We need to see what's going on there and find out when the chopper is due to arrive. But drive carefully and slowly.'

She pulled away from Keegan's house, and said, 'So what do you think? Did he convince you that he's not a serial killer?'

'If he is it's hard to see how we'll be able to prove it. That's why I don't think there's any point going through the motions with him now.'

'He invited us to search his house, though. We could have done that.'

'You're forgetting that Keegan used to be one of us. He knows the ropes. There's no way he would have left anything in there for us to find.'

'So who was this person who witnessed him and Daniel arguing in the village square?'

'That was Annie, my wife. His account of the encounter tallies with hers.'

'Well it certainly threw him. And so did what Lorna's son told us.'

'I agree, but having spoken to both him and Patel I don't feel that we've moved forward. There still aren't any dots for us to connect.'

'What we need are more suspects,' Abbott said.

'You're right. And there are plenty of them in this village. We just have to sniff them out.'

The snow had driven the gawpers away from the crime scene, meaning they missed the flying visit of the police helicopter.

It touched down in the field opposite the garden centre minutes after the two detectives got there. On board were a couple of SOCOs and a member of staff from the mortuary. The SOCOs had been planning to examine the area around the body but the weather put paid to that.

'We need to beat the blizzard back to base,' one of the SOCOs said to James. 'The pilot reckons we'll be stuck here if we don't go straight away. Our instructions are to treat the return of the victim as the priority.'

Daniel Curtis was put into a body bag and carried on a stretcher to the chopper. It was all done in less than ten minutes and then the helicopter took off again.

The crime scene tape was removed and four marker cones were placed on the spot where the body had lain.

James told the officers that they would return to clear the snow and search for evidence once the weather had improved.

But that did not seem likely in the immediate future. The snow was still chucking it down, frantic flurries of white swirling through the village.

The windscreen wipers on the Fiat swooshed back and forth as the detectives made the short journey back to the village hall.

James wanted to update the team as well as check up on Bill's whereabouts. While there, they would also grab something to eat and drink.

He was feeling more downbeat now, and was hoping that a hot cup of coffee would help him to focus. He needed his mind to be on full throttle if he was going to breach the brick wall that was hindering their progress – and frustrating the hell out of him.

At the village hall, the first thing James did was to pour himself a coffee. He sipped at it while he updated DCI Tanner over the phone.

Once again, the boss expressed his displeasure before informing James that for the time being, he would have to make do with the team he had with him in Kirkby Abbey.

'The bad news is piling up and the weather is getting progressively worse,' Tanner said. 'More roads are now blocked and in addition to the murder here in Kendal, and the M6 pile-up, we now have another major case on our hands. Two twelve-year-old boys have gone missing in Ambleside. They went out to a local park early this morning and didn't return home when they were supposed to. The parents are frantic. You'll just have to do the best you can until we can provide more support. I suggest you arrange accommodation for the officers you've got with you.'

'I'll get onto it right away,' James said.

'I also think it's time to advise villagers to stay in their homes. I'm concerned that this weather will make it much easier for the killer to move around without being spotted.'

'It's a sure way to scare everyone even more than they are already,' James said. 'But it'll hopefully keep people off the streets.'

'Then I'll issue the advice at the presser this afternoon. And I suggest you spread the word there. Get the officers to go around with a megaphone. We want as many people as possible to get the message.'

CHAPTER SIXTY-FIVE

Annie almost didn't hear the doorbell ring. The sound of it had to jostle for attention with the TV and the wind outside. And it didn't help that her thinking had been fogged up since James had come home to tell her about Daniel Curtis.

When she opened the door, it was her uncle who was standing there. He was shivering in his bulky coat, his rheumy eyes narrowed to slits and his lips purple.

'Bloody hell, what are you doing walking around in this weather?' she said, then stood aside to let him in.

He didn't say anything until she'd helped him off with his coat.

'I heard what happened to Daniel,' he said. 'I assume you've been told.'

'Of course. James let me know. Where have you been? I rang you earlier but got no answer.'

'I went to the garage to check on my car, but it was closed so I headed back to the pub. That's when Martha told me about Daniel. I was going to call you, but as usual I couldn't find my bloody phone so I just came straight here.'

'Come into the kitchen and I'll make you a hot drink. You look half frozen.'

She made him tea and put some biscuits on a saucer, placing it in front of him at the table. He warmed his hands on the mug, and said, 'So what about Daniel, Annie? I hope you're not going to lose any sleep over it. The man was a monster and he made your parents suffer so much.'

Annie felt tears pressing again her eyes and she had to blink to keep them back.

'It's just come as such a tremendous shock,' she said. 'I can't get my head around it.'

'I don't imagine many people will be grieving for the bastard, Annie. So you shouldn't.'

She knew that Bill was trying to be helpful, to console her, but she really wanted to be by herself. The news had filled her with conflicting emotions and she wasn't yet ready to talk about them.

'They're saying it happened down by the garden centre, close to his dad's bungalow,' Bill said. 'And that he was stabbed just like Charlie Jenkins and Lorna Manning.'

Annie nodded. 'It's the same killer all right. And that makes it even more unsettling.'

'Well, it's about time that husband of yours found out who it is, Annie. I don't understand why that's proving so difficult in a village as small as this.'

Annie sat back and ground her teeth. She would have told him that he was being unfair if it wasn't for the fact that she agreed with him.

The killer was making it seem so easy, and at the same

time he was making the police – and James – appear incompetent.

'I actually saw Daniel last night,' Bill said. 'He was drinking in The King's Head.'

'Did you speak to him?'

'No, I steered clear. If he'd tried to talk to me, I would have told him to shove off.'

'So he must have been killed soon after he left there,' Annie said.

'I suppose so. I saw him walk out after Martha rang the closing time bell.'

'And what did you do?'

'Finished my drink and went up to the room.' He grinned suddenly, showing tobacco-stained teeth. 'Don't worry, Annie. I didn't go after him, if that's what you're thinking.'

'Don't be daft, Bill. That would never enter my head.'

His grin grew wider and Annie felt a shiver grab hold of her spine.

'Now that's a fib, Annie, and we both know it. You and James got it into your heads that I might be the murderer. James made it obvious last night over dinner with all his questions. I cottoned on to what he was doing pretty early on, but it didn't bother me then and it doesn't now. I know that I've been acting weird and that inevitably makes people suspicious.'

Annie felt a surge of guilt and her breath locked in her throat.

'Please don't bother to deny it, Annie,' he said. 'And there's no need to apologise. In fact, it's me who should apologise to you. That's actually why I'm here.'

'What are you on about?' Annie said.

Her uncle inhaled sharply and at the same time his hands balled into fists on the table.

'I've been keeping something from you, Annie, and I'm really sorry. I realise now that it was a mistake, and it's time you knew the truth about me.'

CHAPTER SIXTY-SIX

James had stayed in the village hall to watch the televised press conference. DCI Tanner began by talking about the hunt for the two missing boys in Ambleside. He appealed for information and photos of the two lads were shown.

He then referred to the murder of the man in Kendal. He'd been identified as a local mechanic who was twenty-five and single. No one had yet been arrested in connection with the killing.

All that was straightforward and there were no difficult questions. But when it came to the Kirkby Abbey killings it was a different matter.

After Tanner had provided details about the latest murder, he was asked some bruising questions about why the police hadn't revealed the existence of the Christmas cards containing the threatening messages. And the press also wanted to know how it was that the killer was able to strike for a third time when officers were supposed to be on the streets.

The questions came thick and fast, and Tanner struggled to provide coherent answers.

'Can you now give an assurance that the villagers are safe?'

'You knew early on that this was the work of a serial killer so why didn't you alert the public?'

'We've heard that the village has been virtually cut off by the snow. Does that mean they're trapped with a murderer stalking the streets?'

Tanner repeated that a team of police officers was on duty in the village and that it had been necessary to hold back some information to avoid a panic. He then went on to advise villagers to stay in their homes tonight.

Speaking directly into the camera, he said, 'It will make the job of protecting you much easier.'

It was painful to watch and James was glad when it was over.

The rest of the afternoon was alarmingly unproductive. A patrol car toured the streets telling people through a megaphone to stay indoors, arrangements were made to accommodate team members overnight in B&Bs, and officers did their best to try to find anyone who had seen Daniel walking from The King's Head to his father's house last night.

More work was done over phones and on laptops, but the lack of leads and the severe weather meant that little was achieved.

When it got dark, a shift pattern was worked out, but it meant that only three officers would be on the streets and manning the village hall during the night. Everyone else remained on call.

The last thing James and Abbott did before they called it a day was to visit Ron Curtis. James was pleased to see that

Janet Dyer had stayed with him all day and she'd been helping him come to terms with what had happened. She'd even promised him she'd return first thing in the morning. They informed Ron that his son's body had been transported to the mortuary and that there was no need to provide a formal identification. However, if he wanted to see Daniel, they would arrange transport as soon as they could.

They then gave Janet a lift home so she wouldn't have to walk, and when they dropped her off, James said, 'Make sure you lock your door tonight and I suggest you don't open it for anyone.'

James felt guilty about going home having achieved so little. But he had to accept that as the evening closed in, he really had no choice.

The wind continued to batter the village, piling up snow in small drifts between the buildings. He dreaded to think how bad it would be by the morning.

He'd hoped that Tanner had got it wrong when he'd said at the press conference that Kirkby Abbey had been virtually cut off. But a quick call to control before leaving the hall confirmed that it was. The only road through the village was blocked to the east and the west by large drifts.

As he walked through his front door, he was limp with worry and tiredness, and hoping for a warm welcome from Annie to lift his spirits.

Instead she greeted him in the hall with a sombre expression on her face.

'Bill's here,' she said. 'I asked him to have dinner with us because there's something we need to talk about.'

'That sounds serious,' James said.

'For him, it is.'

'What is it?'

'I think he should tell you himself.'

Bill was waiting for him in the living room.

'So what's all this about?' James asked him, without preamble.

Bill forced a smile. 'There's something I have to tell you, James. It's not good, but hopefully it will help you understand why I've been behaving so strangely.'

'I'm all ears,' James said.

Bill gave a little cough. Then said, 'Unfortunately I've been diagnosed with dementia, dear boy. I'm slowly losing my mind and my memory. I came here to spend time with Annie before it gets to the point where I won't remember who she is.'

James was stunned. 'Jesus, Bill. I am so very sorry.'

'It's not your fault, lad. But I find it increasingly difficult to carry out a lot of everyday tasks properly. Driving is one of them, and I was advised to give it up. I was planning to, after coming here, and then I lost control at the wheel the other day and was lucky not to have ended up dead.'

Annie chipped in at this point and explained that it was the dementia that was causing him to be so forgetful.

'It was why he didn't come to dinner on Saturday,' she said. 'He forgot he'd made plans with me and called his mate Sid and agreed to meet him instead. And it also slipped his mind that we agreed to meet in the square for the carol service.'

'I remember most things,' Bill said. 'But it's when I'm away from home that my mind really plays up. On Friday evening, for instance, I went into the village to post some Christmas cards through doors but then forgot where my old pals lived.'

The conversation got no easier when they moved into the dining room and Annie served up the dinner. It was particularly hard for her because she was upset and struggling to put on a brave face.

James was glad when dinner was over. It had been difficult and emotional, and Annie was understandably distraught because she knew that her uncle's life was about to go from bad to worse and there was nothing she could do about it.

She insisted on walking with him back to The King's Head afterwards. It wasn't far, but James didn't want her walking back by herself so he went with them.

A biting wind was howling through the village and the streets were empty and forlorn.

James felt his stomach contract as he watched Annie hug her uncle at the entrance to the pub and tell him once again to be strong.

When they got back home, James shoved the dinner things in the dishwasher and joined Annie on the sofa where she was stretched out with her feet on the coffee table, staring at the television.

'The end of a perfect day,' she said sarcastically as he took her hand and squeezed it. 'And there was me thinking this was going to be such a great Christmas.'

'I'm so sorry about Bill,' James said. 'But at least we're not far from Penrith. You can go and see him as often as you like. And you can make sure he's properly looked after as his condition progresses.'

They sat like that for about half an hour before Annie decided to go to bed and James went to his study.

He checked with the office in Kendal and with central control. He learned that dozens of people living in Kirkby

Abbey had phoned the police to say that they were terrified and wanted to see more officers in the village.

Mass hysteria had taken hold, as James had known it would once all the details were made public. And the fact that the village was effectively cut off from the outside made a bad situation much, much worse.

He typed up a report of what had happened today and emailed it to Tanner. He then went over all his notes to try to decide where to take the investigation tomorrow.

Finally, he turned his attention to Lorna Manning's diaries, which were still sitting on his desk. But he decided that it was too late, and he was too tired, to go through them. He wasn't even sure it was worth it now that there had been a third murder.

CHAPTER SIXTY-SEVEN

Thursday December 22nd

It should have been a day of joy and anticipation for the people of Kirkby Abbey.

Only three nights until the big day arrived. The decorations were up all over the village and a white Christmas was guaranteed.

But, of course, only the very young children were looking forward to it because they had no understanding of what was going on. Everyone else was living in fear, and the last thing they were bothered about was celebrating the birth of Christ.

James was not a religious man, but for the first time in years he had prayed during the night to a God he didn't believe in. That was how desperate he was to bring an end to the nightmare. If he couldn't do it himself then maybe he could count on some divine intervention.

He woke early to the news that the storm paralysing the north of England was being classified as one of the worst in years. Red warnings were in place across the region and in Cumbria another eight inches of snow had fallen overnight.

TV news footage showed council workers desperately trying to clear blocked roads with ploughs and blowers, and people digging their homes out from beneath giant snow drifts that, in some cases, reached as high as the roofs.

A brutal wind was still blowing through the streets of Kirkby Abbey when James was ready to step outside just before seven. The snow wasn't so heavy now, but there was plenty more of it to come, as evidenced by the thick, dark clouds that filled the sky.

Annie had stayed in bed and before he left the house, James took her up a cup of tea.

'Be careful,' she told him. 'And please don't take any risks.'

He wrapped himself in his coat and scarf and put on a woollen hat and a face muffler. In the hall mirror he saw he looked like an Arctic explorer.

The short walk to the village hall was hard going and the cold air chilled his lungs. But he got there in one piece and found that DC Abbott had arrived before him.

'I woke up at five and couldn't get back to sleep so I thought I might as well come in,' she said.

The officers who had been on duty through the night were told to go to their digs and get some rest.

James was told that no incidents had been recorded overnight and that the villagers seemed to have heeded the advice not to venture out. Of course, they couldn't be sure that there wasn't a body lying in the snow waiting to be discovered.

Before holding a briefing, James got an update from Kendal. He spoke to DS Stevens as DCI Tanner wasn't in yet.

'There's still no chance of getting reinforcements to you,' Stevens said. 'We're being stretched to breaking point as it is. On top of all that, we're also getting call outs every few minutes from people involved in accidents. And at the last count five villages had been cut off, in addition to Kirkby Abbey.'

The situation was indeed grim.

Stevens went on to say that the post-mortem on Daniel Curtis would not take place today because the pathologist and several members of her team were stuck in their homes.

'Meanwhile, we've been to Daniel's flat in Keswick,' he added. 'Nothing untoward was found and everything that was taken away, including laptop and documents, is being examined as we speak. We've also been going through the electoral roll for Kirkby Abbey and checking names against the criminal records database. I can send you a list of three men in the village who have form, one of them for grievous bodily harm against a woman four years ago. It'll be up to you to find out if any of them had a score to settle with our victims.'

They got as much done as they could even though it was far from easy. Between eight and ten, James and DC Abbott visited the three men on the list that Stevens had sent over, but none of them stood out as likely suspects and they all had alibis for the nights on which the three murders were carried out.

They dropped in on Ron Curtis to see how he was, and found Janet Dyer was already at the bungalow. She had made him breakfast and was keeping him company.

After that, the two detectives met up again with Lorna Manning's son, Chris Drake. His grief was being compounded by the fact that he hadn't yet seen his mother's body. He was also anxious to get back to his family in Southend.

James couldn't offer him much comfort so he simply asked him to be patient. He also had to admit that they still didn't know who had murdered his mother.

After another sandwich lunch James had to speak to a small delegation of villagers who had turned up at the hall to voice their concerns about the lack of progress with the investigation and the fact that they were all scared witless.

Gordon Carver was among them. The reporter recorded the exchange on his mobile and asked some questions himself, the first of which was, 'Can you be absolutely sure that a fourth murder was not committed last night, Detective Walker?'

To which James replied, 'We've had no reports of another body or of anyone missing. And despite the bad weather, my officers were on the streets throughout the night.'

He tried his best to reassure the crowd that the team were working flat out, but he was forced to concede that the storm had seriously impacted the investigation.

James ignored the few snippets of abuse that were hurled at him and he was glad when the villagers finally returned to their homes.

The afternoon was not much better for James and the team. Conditions did not improve and it became more difficult to get around.

It would have been true to say that the investigation had stalled, but James didn't want to admit that, even to himself.

He had a couple more phone conversations with DC Stevens and DCI Tanner and he wrote up yet another report.

It got to the stage around five o'clock when he reluctantly accepted that there was no point just sitting in the village hall.

When the night shift crew reported for duty, he and DC Abbott took it as their cue to leave. James felt sorry for Abbott being cooped up by herself in the B&B so he invited her to join him and Annie for dinner. But she declined, saying that she was so tired she wouldn't be good company and needed to climb into her bed as soon as possible.

James wasn't that put out though, because he really didn't feel like socialising.

Annie had spent the entire day indoors so she was pleased to see James when he arrived home. She told him that Bill had popped in during the afternoon and they had watched a film together on Netflix.

'He's still determined to spend Christmas with us, even if his car is repaired before then,' she said. 'And I made it clear to him that we won't let him leave unless we know it's perfectly safe to do so.'

Annie had prepared lasagne for dinner and they took their time eating it. But neither of them found it possible to relax. James's mind kept drifting to the investigation and Annie was too restless and edgy to concentrate on anything he said.

When he told her that he was sure they would find the killer soon, she suddenly turned on him.

'Don't take me for a bloody fool,' she snapped. 'I know that's not true and I don't appreciate being lied to by you.'

Her eyes challenged him for a moment, and then tears sprang up in them and she broke down.

To James, it wasn't entirely unexpected. He had noticed how she'd been struggling to deal with the pressure and the constant flow of appalling news.

He got up and went to her and he held her in his arms until she stopped crying. She then apologised for snapping at him but he told her that he perfectly understood.

'We're all feeling the strain of this,' he said. 'You more than most, Annie, because you had a connection with all three victims.'

Annie was in no mood for conversation after that so she went up to bed by herself again. It was still too early for James to go with her so he poured himself a large whiskey and took it into the study.

Once again, he pored over all his notes, along with the forensic findings. He studied the photos of the crime scenes and reports filed by the other officers who had interviewed neighbours and friends of the victims.

He then decided it was time to do what he'd said he'd do, which was to go through Lorna Manning's diaries.

He worked backwards from the current year, but it wasn't until he got to the one dated two years ago that he came across something that triggered a snap of electricity in his brain.

It was an entry during the month of September, and Lorna had noted down that she'd told someone about the hit-and-run secret that had tainted her life.

That in itself didn't come as a great surprise to James. What did cause his heart to jump was the name of the person she'd told. Father Thomas Silver.

CHAPTER SIXTY-EIGHT

Finally summoned up the courage to go to confession and tell Father Silver what I did to that poor girl and to explain why I didn't go to the police. I received the priest's absolution, but forgiveness is not enough to make me feel better.

The entry in Lorna Manning's diary contradicted what Father Silver had told James. The priest had insisted he knew of no reason why Lorna had often appeared depressed. James could even recall some of his exact words: '*I tried a number of times to get her to open up, but she wouldn't.*'

James was well aware that one of the cornerstones of the Catholic faith is that nothing said in confession can ever be disclosed. Priests are not allowed to break the Seal of the Confessional even after the penitent has died or has confessed to a serious crime, including murder. Priests who do so face excommunication from the Catholic Church.

Father Silver had therefore chosen not to break the Seal in respect of Lorna Manning's confession. But it struck James as odd that he had said he'd tried to get Lorna to open up. He'd volunteered that piece of information and it hadn't been necessary. So why had he felt compelled to say it?

However, that was only one of the many questions that had sprung up in James's mind. He was now wondering if it was actually possible that the killer had also been to confession at St John's Church, and that Father Silver knew far more about what was happening than he was letting on.

James was aware that he was clutching at straws here, but his sixth sense was telling him that this was something worth pursuing. And the more he thought about it, the faster his heart pounded in his chest.

He didn't know Father Silver very well, but he had always come across as an honest and open man, a man who had been a pillar of the community for years. But now he had terminal cancer and would soon depart this world. Was he therefore intent on taking a terrible secret to his grave rather than break the Seal of the Confessional?

James decided he would pay him a visit first thing in the morning. He'd confront him with the entry in Lorna's diary and ask him outright why he'd said that he had tried to get Lorna to open up. He would also ask him if he was keeping any other secrets that were relevant to the investigation.

It would be up to the priest to convince him that he wasn't. But if James sensed that he was lying, he would do whatever it took to break down the older man's resolve. It wouldn't be easy, of course, but it was necessary.

He wrote down some notes and while doing so he checked the time. It had only just turned 10 p.m.

Why wait until morning? He suddenly asked himself. *I won't be able to sleep anyway, with this playing on my mind.*

Without giving it any further thought, he went upstairs to see if Annie was still awake, but she wasn't. And he saw no need to disturb her.

Back downstairs, he put on his coat and boots, and picked up his keys, his phone and Lorna's diary.

Then he let himself out of the house and headed for the rectory in the hope that Father Silver was still up and would be willing to answer some questions.

The evening was dark and oppressive. It was still blowing a gale, but the snow was less heavy.

James huffed out clouds of breath as he trudged through the village. There was no one else on the streets and he was disappointed not to spot a uniformed officer or patrol car.

It took him ten minutes to reach the rectory and when he got there he saw that there were no lights on inside. He thought briefly about turning back, but then decided not to and rang the doorbell. Once, twice, three times.

Nobody answered and he recalled what Father Silver had said about being a heavy sleeper. Or perhaps he was afraid to come to the door so late in the evening. James looked up at the windows, but none of the curtains moved.

He turned around to retrace his steps along the path and that was when he noticed that his weren't the only footprints in the snow. There was another set leading away from the front door and out onto the road. The fact that they hadn't already been covered by the snow surely meant that they hadn't been there very long.

James saw that the prints crossed the road in the direction of the church. Did they belong to the priest? he asked himself. Or had someone else left the rectory shortly before James arrived?

Panic seized his chest suddenly as he realised that he might well be following the tracks of the killer. Had the priest become victim number four? Was he now lying dead in his own home as the killer made off into the night?

It was a startling possibility and one that James decided he could not ignore. He broke into a run and followed the footprints, which led him along the pavement and through the gate into the churchyard. From there, they went all the way up to the church entrance.

James's stomach was pitching and rolling as he hurried along the path and into the front porch, where the footprints ended. He pushed at the heavy door and to his surprise it opened.

He stepped inside the church and felt the darkness close in around him. But there was a glimmer of light at the far end, to the right of the altar. James recalled that that was where Father Silver's office was situated.

As he walked slowly between the pews, somewhere inside a voice berated him for going it alone. He should have called on one of the officers in the village to come in here with him. But it was too late now. He had already reached the office and he could see that the door was ajar and the light he'd glimpsed was coming from inside.

He held his breath and eased it open, ready to defend himself if he came under attack.

But he didn't. The room wasn't empty, though. A man wearing a black polo sweater and loose grey trousers was standing in front of the desk with his back to the door. James was about to say something when the man spun around. At once, relief flooded through James when he saw that it was Father Silver.

The priest almost jumped out of his skin, and his mouth gaped open.

'I'm so sorry, Father,' James said, stepping farther into the room. 'I didn't mean to scare you.'

It took the priest a couple of beats to recover.

'Why are you here?' he said, his voice shaky.

'I went to the rectory to have a word with you. When there was no answer, I was about to leave but then saw footprints in the snow and I feared – thankfully wrongly, as it turns out – that the killer might have paid you a visit. So, I followed the footprints and they led me here. I can't tell you how relieved I am.'

The priest appeared lost for words as he stood there staring at James whilst hauling in ragged gasps of air.

'Are you okay, Father?' James said.

The priest swallowed. 'I am now. You just gave me a shock. So why is it you felt the need to come and see me so late in the day?'

James took Lorna Manning's diary from his pocket and held it up.

'You told me that you had no idea why Lorna Manning was always showing signs of depression. You said you'd tried to get her to open up.'

'That's true.'

'But this is her diary and just eighteen months ago she wrote that she went to you and confessed to killing that young woman with her car. Which means that you did know what was ailing her.'

'I am not at liberty to disclose what someone reveals to me in a confessional booth. You should know that, Detective.'

James moved towards him to hand him the diary. But as

he did so the priest's eyes shifted sharply to the left. James instinctively followed their line of sight and saw an overcoat resting on one of the chairs. Lying on top was what looked like a large ornamental dagger.

'What the hell is that?' James blurted, pointing to it.

The priest cleared his throat. 'That, sir, is a genuine Knights Templar dagger. The Templars, as you may know, were once a powerful Catholic military order. Their relics are much sought after by collectors.'

The sight of the dagger unsettled James. It seemed out of place in the office. A frown tugged his eyebrows together and the air suddenly felt heavy around him.

He turned back to the priest and said, 'So why are you here, Father? Shouldn't you be in bed?'

'There was something I needed to finish.'

The priest licked his lips nervously and started blinking fast. James knew then that something wasn't right and a jolt of adrenaline spiked through him.

The priest then moved his body abruptly to one side, as though in an attempt to conceal something on the desk. It was so obvious that James couldn't let it pass.

'If I may say so, you're acting very suspiciously, Father. Is something the matter?'

The priest shook his head. 'Of course not. I'm just busy and I need to get on with what I was doing.'

James decided it was time to stop arsing around. He needed to find out why Father Silver was acting like this. He took another step forward and gently pushed the man out of the way with his elbow.

And he saw straight away what the priest was trying to hide. On top of the desk was a pack of cards with the

Twelve Days of Christmas design. And next to them was a black marker.

James felt his lungs empty as it dawned on him what was going on. And he couldn't fucking believe it.

But as he turned, he glimpsed the priest's right arm swinging towards him, an object clasped in the hand. He had no time to react as it smashed into his left temple and sent him sprawling onto the floor.

Before the lights in his head went out, the priest stood over him and said, 'You are not one of the sinners, Detective Walker, so I won't kill you because you don't deserve to die. But because of what you now know, I must bring my mission to an end. After tonight, I will bow out gracefully.'

CHAPTER SIXTY-NINE

In the dream Annie is holding a baby in her arms. Her and James's baby.

His name is Lucas and he's only three weeks old. But already he's the centre of their universe. Everything revolves around their little bundle of joy.

They have to feed him, wind him, change him, rock him to sleep. And they're both loving every minute of it because they never thought it would happen. But it did, and Annie can't believe that she's at last been blessed.

Eventually they'll try for another because she's always wanted two kids – the perfect sized family – and she doesn't care if it's a girl or another boy, as long as it's healthy.

She can see the smile on her own face, the pride in her eyes, the sheer contentment coming off her in waves.

So when the image suddenly fades, as it always does, she hears herself cry out.

That's when she realises that it wasn't real. It was all in her head. Again. A version of the same dream she's had many times before. As always, it woke her up and now she could feel her body shaking and the tears stinging her eyes.

She turned on her side to seek comfort from the warmth of James's body – only to find that he wasn't in bed with her. She figured he was still in his study trying to work out how to find the killer terrorising the village.

A sob swelled up inside her and she swallowed it down. She knew she wouldn't be able to go back to sleep. Best she got up, had a drink of something and popped a pill.

She threw back the duvet and hauled herself out of bed. She put on her dressing gown and slippers in the dark and stepped out of the room.

The light from the living room reached up the stairs so she didn't bother to turn any more on. Once downstairs, she went first to the kitchen to put the kettle on and then to the study to see if James wanted a tea or coffee.

But he wasn't at his desk, which put a frown on her face. She checked the downstairs loo and then the hallway, but there was no sign of him. While in the hallway she noticed that his coat wasn't hanging up and his boots weren't on the floor next to the cupboard. She assumed he'd been called out and hadn't wanted to wake her up. It was something he'd done before so it didn't worry her.

She returned to the kitchen, poured herself some tea and took a sleeping pill.

Back in the living room she sat on the sofa to drink it. She was still there ten minutes later when she heard the front door open and close.

'No need to sneak around, James,' she called out. 'I'm down here and wide awake.'

A moment later the living room door was pushed open.

Annie stood and prepared to greet her husband with a big welcoming smile and a hug.

But it wasn't James who entered the room. It was Father Silver. And in his right hand he was holding a large knife.

The smile vanished from Annie's face and a cold fear hardened in the centre of her stomach.

CHAPTER SEVENTY

When James regained consciousness the pain in his head made him wince. It felt like his brain had exploded and hadn't yet been put back together.

It took a few seconds for him to remember where he was and what had happened. As he struggled to his feet, he almost passed out again and had to lean against the priest's desk to stop himself keeling over.

That was when he spotted the Christmas cards and the black marker. He turned instinctively towards the chair on which had rested the overcoat and knife. But they were both gone.

The priest's words rang in his ears.

After tonight, I will bow out.

'Shit,' James said aloud as the magnitude of the situation hit him.

Father Silver had been playing them all along. He was the killer, the monster who had taken the lives of three people in the village.

But what the hell was he planning to do tonight?

James reached into his inside pocket for his phone, but it wasn't there. When he checked his other pockets, he made another terrifying discovery. The keys to his house were also missing.

It was obvious to James that the bastard had taken them. But did that mean he was now heading for the house? And Annie?

Panicked, he hurried across the room and grabbed the door handle. But the door wouldn't open. It was locked from the outside.

James looked at the window behind the desk and reckoned it would be easier to smash that than break down the door. As he searched for something to use, his boot collided with an object on the floor. It was a glass paperweight in the shape of a heart. When James picked it up, he saw that it was smeared with blood. His blood. It was the weapon the priest had used to knock him out.

He threw it at the window and the glass shattered, but he had to use a small statue of Christ on the cross to make an opening big enough for him to climb through.

Once outside, he started running for home whilst praying that he would reach Annie before she came to any harm.

CHAPTER SEVENTY-ONE

Annie was unable to move. She was so stricken with terror that she couldn't even scream as Father Silver stepped across the room towards her.

'The others didn't see me coming, Annie,' he said. 'So, in that sense, you're lucky. You'll know why you have to die.'

Annie's eyes shifted back to the knife in his hand. It was long and shiny and looked like a weapon from a bygone era.

'If it's any consolation, I've let your husband live,' the priest said. 'You see, I can't be sure that he's a sinner. Unlike you.'

Annie wanted to believe that she was still in bed and that her dream had turned into a vivid nightmare. But she knew she was awake and that it was really happening.

He stopped moving and there was a long, unearthly pause. He'd got himself into a position where he was standing between the doors to the hallway and kitchen. Annie had her back to the wall with the TV and it meant that to flee the room she would have to get past him.

She tried to speak, to ask him if he had lost his mind. But

it felt like a hand had grabbed her heart and pulled it up into her throat.

'Your crime, my dear, was to murder your own baby,' he said. 'You should not have done what your father told you to do. You both knew that the Catholic Church forbids abortion, and yet you went ahead with it.'

Annie found her voice. 'How did you know about that?'

'Your father came to confession to ask for forgiveness. But by then the damage was done.'

'But you killed the others, too,' Annie said. 'What did they do wrong?'

'Like you, they carried out the work of the devil.'

Annie's eyes searched the room for something she could use as a weapon to defend herself. At the same time the priest made his move and started coming towards her, the knife held out in front of him.

Annie screamed, but that didn't stop him, so out of sheer desperation she threw herself to the left and rushed towards the door leading to the hallway.

But in her blind panic her leg struck the edge of the coffee table and she tumbled face down onto the carpet. As she rolled onto her back, she realised she'd lost her only chance to escape.

The priest was standing over her now and she knew she was going to die.

CHAPTER SEVENTY-TWO

The priest didn't hear James enter the house because of Annie's screams.

She was lying on the floor of the living room, at the maniac's feet, and he was mouthing what sounded like a prayer as he raised the dagger above her. James called out, which prompted him to hesitate and turn.

Shock registered on his face, and he didn't notice Annie roll across the carpet away from him.

Once James saw that Annie was a safe distance away and getting to her feet, he moved closer to the priest and said, 'The game's up, Father. Don't make things worse for yourself.'

Father Silver looked down and realised that Annie had moved and that to reach her, he would have to get past her husband.

He turned back to James and a slow smile formed on his face.

'I underestimated you, Detective,' he said. 'And that was a mistake.'

'Just put the dagger down, Father. It's over.'

The priest nodded. 'I realise that. Ever since I embarked on my mission, I knew this moment would come. The moment when I would end my own life and offer myself to God.'

'But isn't suicide a mortal sin in the eyes of the Catholic Church?'

He shook his head. 'Not if the act is committed with God's blessing, Detective.'

He then held the dagger's grip in both hands and pointed the tip of the blade at his throat.

'This is crazy,' James yelled at him. 'God hasn't given His blessing. And do you honestly believe that you're in God's good books after killing three people?'

His smile widened. 'You don't understand. None of you do. You see, I was carrying out the will of God. When I was diagnosed with a terminal cancer, I told Him how disillu-sioned I'd become. I used this village as an example of how the devil seemed to be winning the war. Most of the villagers have turned their backs on God, and some of them openly condemn what the church stands for. St John's is to close because the congregation has fallen to just a handful of people. It's the same everywhere. Society is becoming more secular and more tolerant of sinners. Take those vile vandals who desecrate the graves in our churchyard. They're allowed to get away with it. The police know who they are but they're not arrested or punished.

'So, I told our Lord that it was time for a different approach. That when it came to punishing the wrongdoers and heathens, He needed to involve His true followers. And I asked him what deed I could perform on his behalf. I wanted to make my mark, to make a difference, to show the world that evil will not prevail. I wanted Him to know that I was prepared to do battle with the devil no matter what the cost. It was to be my final contribution to the greater good.

'And His message to me was clear. He told me to do what I believed in my heart to be the right thing, regardless of the consequences. And so I set out to punish some of those who are doing the devil's bidding.'

The priest flicked his head towards Annie, who was now standing behind James. 'Your own wife is one of them. A child killer. A woman who doesn't deserve to live. Charlie Jenkins was an adulterer. Daniel Curtis was a child molester. And Lorna Manning was a murderer. None of them deserved to live.'

James felt a dark fury well up inside him. 'You're insane, Father. And what you're saying makes no fucking sense.'

'Maybe not to you, Detective. But the people I've killed were the devil's disciples. And so too were the other nine sinners on my list who will now go on living because I failed to complete my task.'

'Who were they?'

'It doesn't matter now. I only wish I had crossed one more name off my list. One of them was going to die tonight, before you turned up at the church and ruined everything.'

'And who was that?'

'Janet Dyer. The village slut. I knew about her affair with Charlie Jenkins because several months ago I saw them together. He used to go to her house when her children were at school. She's been very lucky. Twice. I was actually on my way to end her life when I saw Daniel on that deserted street. It was pure coincidence. He was fifth on my list but presented an opportunity that was too good to pass up. And the same happened tonight. I was preparing to visit Janet again but you showed up. I realised that Annie would be here alone and when I found the keys in your pocket, I decided to move her up from ninth place on the list.'

'It still doesn't make any sense to me,' James said. 'What was the point of the Christmas cards?'

The priest smiled again. 'It took me several weeks to decide who should die. I finally reached the figure of twelve. It so happened that on that very day I'd purchased some cards in the store – those with the Twelve Days of Christmas design on them. It struck me that it would be a good way to ensure that my mission would have maximum impact and grab the attention of sinners all over the world. Twelve days. Twelve murders. I also knew it would cause confusion and that delivering a card to myself at the church would make it less likely that I would become a suspect.'

'And the dead partridge?'

'An excellent touch, don't you think? The bird was a regular visitor to the churchyard and, as I said in the note, I thought it would be a good way to seize your attention. So it became a sacrifice. But you chose not to tell the public about the cards, which was why I had to send one to the reporter.'

'And what about the framed photo of Lorna Manning that you put on Nadia Patel's grave? Why did you do that?'

'Two reasons. I wanted to draw attention to the fact that a woman who didn't deserve to die is buried there. And I knew it would be a good way to bring you and I together again so that I could find out where you were with the investigation. It worked perfectly.'

The priest's hands were shaking now and James tried to work out if there was any way he could stop the guy from topping himself.

'I've got nothing left to say,' the priest said. 'But I would ask you to make it known what I've told you. Sinners of the world need to be aware that things are changing. God is striking back against the devil and there will be more people like me who will carry out the work on his behalf.'

He closed his eyes then and started mumbling a prayer. James reacted by stepping towards him, but before he could get close, the priest plunged the dagger into his own throat.

CHAPTER SEVENTY-THREE

Friday December 23rd

The priest was dead but the nightmare wasn't over. James and Annie had to wait twelve hours for the body to be moved from the house. That was how long it took for another helicopter to arrive in the village with a small team of SOCOs and a pathologist.

The village GP had already officially pronounced Father Silver dead; he'd died within minutes of stabbing himself. James had tried to revive him, but had quickly realised it was a lost cause.

James had found his phone in the priest's pocket and had alerted the other officers in the village. They'd arrived on the scene in minutes, along with DC Abbott.

He was now in the village hall with the rest of the team, having moved Annie into a room at The King's Head.

DCI Tanner had been briefed and his relief that the murderer had been found was coupled with shock.

'I'm thankful that you and your wife are safe,' he'd said. 'I have to admit this is not how I thought it would end.'

'He's not the first madman to claim that God instructed him to kill,' James said. 'And he joins an ever-growing list of Catholic priests who chose to ignore the Ten Commandments. I just wish I'd spotted the signs sooner. I should have given more thought to why he received the cards. And, with hindsight, I realise I should have asked myself what sort of person would harp on about only killing those who "deserved" to die. It now seems pretty obvious that it's something a mentally disturbed member of the clergy might say, especially one who hasn't got long to live and so has nothing to lose.'

'Hindsight is a wonderful thing, James,' Tanner said. 'That man fooled us all. But thanks to you he didn't succeed in fulfilling his objective of killing twelve people.'

The rectory and the church were now being searched by officers who had already found the priest's kill list. It was handwritten, and next to the names were one or two words describing their 'sins.'

Lorna Manning – murderer

Daniel Curtis – sex abuser

Annie Walker – child killer

Those on the list who were still alive would be informed in due course, if that was what the powers-that-be decided was appropriate.

As the day progressed the weather improved and it stopped snowing. Then, for the first time in days, the sun burst through the clouds.

There was, naturally, disbelief among the villagers that

Father Silver, their friendly priest, turned out to be the killer, and shock turned to confusion when they learned that he'd claimed that he had acted with God's blessing.

James took it upon himself to break the news to the victims' loved ones and those he had interviewed during the investigation – to varied responses. Sonia Jenkins swore she would never set foot in a church again and Ron Curtis claimed that if the police had done their jobs properly his son Daniel would still be alive. Janet Dyer reacted by saying, 'I always thought there was something dodgy about the priest. I could see it in his eyes.'

And Keith Patel made it known that he would seek to have his mother's body removed from the graveyard and cremated, so that he could leave the village and start a new life elsewhere.

EPILOGUE

Saturday December 24th

Christmas Eve rolled around, and James and Annie were having a late evening drink in the bar of The King's Head. Bill had been with them until a few minutes ago, when he'd decided to turn in.

By now a degree of normality was returning to Kirkby Abbey. People were going out and socialising, but there was only one topic of conversation.

James had sent all the necessary paperwork regarding what had happened to head office, but even though the village was no longer cut off it had been agreed that he should stay put, at least until Boxing Day.

The killer priest still dominated the news headlines, but two other stories were also given extensive coverage.

The two boys who'd been missing in Ambleside had at last been found safe and well. It turned out they'd been exploring a derelict house and had become trapped in the basement. And a man had been charged with the murder of the young mechanic in Kendal. He'd already appeared in court where he was remanded into custody.

James and Annie had decided to stay in the pub for the holiday. Their living room carpet was covered in the priest's blood and needed to be replaced but the earliest that could be done was Boxing Day.

Still, they had a comfortable room and Uncle Bill would be right there with them for Christmas.

It was coming up to ten and they'd got through a bottle of the house wine between them. James asked Annie if she wanted another drink. She thought about it for a moment and then grinned.

'I'd rather go upstairs to bed,' she said with a coy smile. 'It's been ages since we tried to make a baby.'

James laughed. 'And wouldn't it be something if we managed to do it on Christmas Eve?'

THE END

ACKNOWLEDGEMENT

A big thank you to Molly Walker-Sharp, my editor at Avon/ HarperCollins. This book was a true collaboration and without her help and input it would not have been written.

If you've enjoyed *The Christmas Killer*, then we think you'll love the DCI Anna Tate series!

Nine missing children.
The hunt is on.
But has time run out?

IN SAFE
HANDS

A DCI ANNA TATE THRILLER

J. P. CARTER

A gripping crime thriller that will have you on the edge of your seat.